MORNING STAR

MORNING STAR

Marian Wells

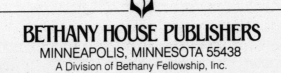

BETHANY HOUSE PUBLISHERS
MINNEAPOLIS, MINNESOTA 55438
A Division of Bethany Fellowship, Inc.

Published by Bethany House Publishers
A Division of Bethany Fellowship, Inc.
6820 Auto Club Road, Minneapolis, Minnesota 55438

Printed in the United States of America

Library of Congress Cataloging-in-Publication Data

Wells, Marian, 1931-
Morning star.

(The Starlight trilogy ; bk. 3)
Sequel to: Star light, star bright.
I. Title. II. Series: Wells, Marian, 1931- .
Starlight trilogy ; bk. 3.
PS3573.E4927M67 1986 813'.54 86-14781
ISBN 0-87123-651-6 (pbk.)

MARIAN WELLS was born in the state of Utah, and attended Northwest Nazarene College. Though the *Starlight Trilogy* books are fictional, the author has thoroughly researched and documented the historical events surrounding the stories. Two of her other books, *The Wedding Dress* and its sequel, *With This Ring*, are written in a similar style.

Introduction

Jenny Timmons' story begins in the first book of this trilogy, *The Wishing Star.* As an eleven-year-old child from a poor family, living on the fringes of South Bainbridge, New York, Jenny becomes acquainted with Joseph Smith. Jenny's brother, Tom, introduces the mysterious youth who is engaged in searching for money with his peep stone while working for Josiah Stowell.

Life for a poor child living in a small New York town in 1825 could have been insipid were it not for Joseph Smith, the curious stone, the money diggings, and the strange, shivery feeling of excitement it all gave Jenny. There was Pa's green book, too.

That first year Joseph's money digging nets him trouble and the town of South Bainbridge, excitement. After it is all over, Joseph moves on, but Jenny doesn't forget him.

The next summer Jenny's father starts his westward trek, and the first leg of the journey lands the family in Manchester, New York. The following year the Timmons family—except for Tom and Jenny—move farther west. The brother and sister gain employment with Martin Harris—Tom at the livery stable, and Jenny as a hired girl in the Harris home.

Lucy Harris is good to Jenny and she learns to *do* for Mrs. Harris, developing skills she had not learned at home. Jenny also attends school and becomes friends of Joseph Smith's family. Again the paths of their lives cross.

Honoring a promise to Jenny's mother, Mrs. Harris sees to Jenny's religious education. Jenny joins the Presbyterian church, but at the same time delves into the mysteries of the green book that she has stolen from her father.

Also, during this period Joseph Smith marries and comes to live in the Palmyra-Manchester area just long enough to find the gold Bible.

Martin Harris, one of the first three witnesses to the *Book of Mormon*, soon becomes deeply involved in the gold Bible work. This new interest quickly pulls life down around Jenny's head. As the Harris home is broken apart by his new interests, Jenny and Tom are forced to move on.

Mark Cartwright, a youth both Jenny and Tom knew from the South Bainbridge days, steps into their life with an offer which takes them to eastern New York State.

Jenny's maturing years are spent away from Tom while she works and finishes school. During this time the whole focus of her life is wrapped in a twisted desire to have life on her own terms. This desire is fed through her friendship with Clara and the secret green book.

Meanwhile, Tom, who has never lost interest in Joseph Smith, follows the fledgling prophet to Kirtland, Ohio. When Jenny visits Tom, all the old fascination is reborn, and Jenny moves to Ohio to become a member of Joseph's church.

It isn't long until Jenny discovers that to be a follower of Joseph Smith demands total obedience. When he instructs her to marry, and tells her whom to marry, she proposes to Mark Cartwright.

The second book of the trilogy, *Star Light, Star Bright*, begins with hope and promise as Jenny and Mark celebrate their marriage and start their life together in Kirtland, Ohio.

There is the promise, and by rights it should be fulfilled. It is the promise of young love, the "true" church, and a life together which is to extend throughout eternity.

But promises require obedience. Soon Mark is tapped for the first major missionary endeavor to England. Jenny is left behind. The letters dwindle, but that was the result of problems surfacing in the young couple's life.

Problems are surfacing in the young church, too. With every quarrel and painful misunderstanding seen between the young couple, the counterpart is mirrored in the uneasy marriage of church and people. But for both, life struggles on. Problems are resolved and an uneasy peace effected.

That next spring Mark returns from his missionary journey with news so shocking that Jenny nearly surrenders her marriage. Mark has become a Christian and he makes certain that Jenny knows this is something world-shattering and totally different than the message Joseph has given to his followers.

It is Mark who surrenders and follows Jenny as she joins the exodus to Zion. He surrenders, not because of Jenny's strengths, but because of her weakness and fear.

Even before Joseph's church was established, the young prophet had received revelations commanding the people to set up an earthly Zion, to be founded in the state of Missouri. Immediately after the church was organized, a group of converts migrated to the state and settled in Jackson County. Unfortunately, the Missourians didn't accept the command of the Lord given through Joseph. From the beginning there were serious problems.

Long before the expedient removal of the Kirtland Saints to the state of Missouri, the difficulties in Missouri between the Saints and the Gentiles had forced the governor of the state to step into the affair. The Saints were subsequently ordered to leave Jackson County and move farther north to Caldwell County.

But shortly after Joseph's move to Caldwell County from Ohio, life became just as difficult in this new area. Once again the prophet stepped over the boundary set for his people.

It is no wonder that Jenny, fearful and sensing the greater dangers lying ahead, turned from her new religion back into the ancient religion of nature. No wonder, that is, since she was certain *her* understanding of God was right and Mark's was wrong.

Before long the troubled issue resulted in bloodshed, and finally the Mormons were forced to leave Missouri. Once again they were driven out, penniless and homeless, while their prophet, Joseph Smith, remained behind in jail.

CHAPTER 1

Jenny thrashed her head on the pillow and moaned. The movement sent pain stabbing through her head. Eyes closed, she groped for the pillow beside her. She felt an empty expanse of smooth linen, and her eyes flew open. Sunshine flooded the room and shot arrows of pain into her eyes. Covering her face, she moaned and rolled over.

It was at least ten o'clock; the sun glared into her bedroom. The white curtains hanging over the open window were motionless.

Mark must have left hours ago, moving quietly to allow her to sleep. Her lips twisted in a perverse grin. Strange that a man as intelligent as Mark should so readily accept her excuses, even giving credence to her midnight tryst by his gentle trust and unquestioning acceptance.

Especially strange, since he claimed a special place with God. He called it being born again, redeemed. Her claim to religious devotion was as genuine as his. But never would she try to explain that the rituals and traditions she practiced with a select group of women were rooted in the ancient worship to the true god of nature. She was still wondering about Mark when she fell asleep again.

When Jenny awakened later, the sun had shifted off Mark's pillow, and the white curtains moved just enough to allow the summer scents of the garden to invade her rest.

As she slowly bathed in tepid water and dressed, she felt the last traces of her headache leave. By the time she left the bedroom she was hungry, and life began to press in with its demands.

Jenny paused at the head of the stairs and admired her home. This Springfield, Illinois, home contrasted sharply with the little log hut in Missouri—and even with the stone house in Kirtland, Ohio. She kissed the tips of her fingers and flung kisses about the house.

"Beautiful one!" she cried. "Good morning to you, fair walls and shiny floors. Polished furniture and gleaming windows, how silently you keep your distance until I'm ready to be your mistress again!" As she walked down the stairs, she continued to admire the ivy-sprigged wallpaper, the plush furniture in the newest shade of plum. She cocked her head for just a moment. Were the green and plum really suited to the deep rose of the new carpet?

Jenny crossed the hall and went through the shaded dining room with its dark mahogany, feeling again the urge to shake the room into life. But the room seemed alien no matter how she polished the furniture and shifted the china. Perhaps it was the china.

She frowned at the rose pattern, a duplicate of the dishes Mark had purchased for their first home. They did make her think of the possessions destroyed in the fire in Missouri. She looked at the grandfather clock just as it began to boom out the hours in its authoritative bass. Noon?

With a sigh Jenny hurried toward the kitchen, still rubbing her arms, conscious of the chill of the room. If the spirits were active, they weren't friendly ones. Why would the room goad her into an unwilling memory of those terror-filled months in Missouri?

In the kitchen the cold remains of Mark's lonely breakfast sat on the table. She chewed her lip, reading the message of the room. Mark usually tidied up after himself. Today a smear of cold beans crusted the single plate. A crumbled slice of bread lay beside an untouched glass of milk.

Guilt touched her. She saw in the scene symbols of her neglect as well as a touch of uncharacteristic absentmindedness in Mark.

As she cleared the table and began to heat water, her thoughts were busy tossing the guilt back and forth. *But the coven called, and they can't be denied*, she defended herself. As she ate bread and drank milk, she was thinking of the group of witches. Was it luck, or was it spirit need that had sent petite, dark-eyed Crystal into her life?

Soon after arriving here, just when Mark's associates had undertaken the task of introducing them to Springfield society, Jenny had met Crystal Matison, wife of a newly appointed state representative, Haddon Matison.

As Jenny cleared the table and poured hot water over the dishes, she pondered the events that had drawn her into the coven over which Crystal had charge. What joy, what sisterhood after the barren years with only occasional contact with Adela!

Chuckling, Jenny recalled Crystal's daring move. Very shortly after becoming acquainted, Crystal had casually dropped a talisman at Jenny's feet.

Jenny sighed, straightened her shoulders, and looked around the kitchen. Only a practicing witch would recognize the signs: the wisp of rosemary, the crossed twigs, the hint of lavender. Now she frowned and moved her shoulders uneasily.

It had been a year since she and Mark had moved to Springfield—a year of being back into the craft on a practicing basis—and still she felt the familiar void in her life. The powerlessness, the lack of growth and direction in her life filled her with frustration.

Just last night, after the coven had held their solstice ritual, Jenny had confided to Crystal her disappointment. After listening, Crystal had shrugged and wiped at the perspiration on her face, saying abruptly, "I've no sympathy. You've been advised to go to sabbat. You knew when you started meeting with us that we were no more than white witches. If you want more, you know what must be done."

In frustration Jenny had cried, "And you—why will you be content to be a powerless white witch?"

The woman had looked at her with a stony face. "I might wonder what you have in mind. I enjoy the craft, but I intend to be master of my own fate. You might say I'm frightened enough to accept my own limitations. I have all the power I need. I enjoy our coven and the ritual of worship. *I am*, and that is all I need."

Jenny slowly dried the dishes and returned them to the cupboard. She was frowning, puzzling over Crystal's statement and the strange icy blast her words had left.

Restlessly, Jenny took up her trowel and walked slowly out the back door and down the garden path. It was past noon. The herb garden was shadowed and cool. Perhaps digging through the soil would straighten out her muddled thoughts.

As Jenny ducked under the chestnut tree, her hair tangled in the branches. Impatiently she shook the branch and picked at the pins in her hair. When the coil of her hair slipped down her back, she was freed. But the action immediately plunged her into being more than Jenny.

Kneeling in the soil, breathing deeply of the mingled odor of pungent herbs and moist earth, Jenny thought again of those words. *I am*. Jenny sensed a hidden meaning, and knew only that she was left curious and vaguely uneasy.

Jenny pulled weeds from her herb garden and dug into the loam with her fingers. The crumbled soil smelled faintly of last autumn's leaves. As she lifted her hand to sniff at it, her mind immediately filled with scenes of their life in Missouri.

Though the events had happened eighteen months ago, the damp earth scent bridged the gap as if it were yesterday she and little Tamara had walked the woodland paths as serene and happy as woodland nymphs. But the serenity was an illusion.

She winced, remembering the ugliness and death at Haun's Mill. Closing her eyes she saw the tortured faces of the Saints. Homes, family, even faith were stripped from them.

Settling back on her heels, she stared up at the sun-dappled trees and wondered about the people. Were they happy now? How easy it had been to drop the faith as soon as she left Missouri! But what about them? If their new life was not better than hers, they were in a desperate situation.

And what about Joseph? He had escaped from his Missouri prison, and his flock had settled across the river in Illinois. What a commotion that had caused! She grinned. Good old Joseph had landed on his feet just as she expected. The newspapers had been full of the stories. Illinois had welcomed the Saints with open arms.

A twig snapped behind Jenny. Without raising her head she murmured, "Is that you, my husband?"

"Is that a disappointment?" Mark's voice was heavy, bitter. Jenny got to her feet and turned. He looked at her soiled hands and the tumble of hair spilling down her back, and she saw the frown and his tightened lips.

"You're angry because I went last night," she whispered, widening her eyes to allow him to see the pain. It worked; the cold expression softened a bit and he bent to press a kiss against her forehead. But he turned away, and she knew the matter wasn't resolved.

She had tried to tell him the truth about her nature worship, about God, but that had failed. He didn't understand, and discussing it only fortified this stony wall between them.

She tried the dimpled grin, and that won out. As she carefully held her soiled hands away from his dark suit and lifted her face, he murmured, "At least my rival is a bunch of women, dotty with their strange ideas. It could be worse."

He stepped back and pulled a black lace scarf from his pocket. "Letty Harrison asked her husband to pass this on to you. So now Letty is a member of your group! I am amazed that

Lew takes it so lightly—he's a deacon at the First Presbyterian Church."

Jenny's voice was throaty, "Everyone takes it lightly except my husband. True, most of the husbands are being indulgent, but some are seeing the value in it all."

"Value?"

Jenny ticked off the list. "How do you suppose Lew Harrison won a seat to the senate? He knows. Remember the ulcerated leg of Mather Johnson? It wasn't that addle-pated doctor who cured him. Mark, I could go on and on—the storm that broke up the rioting last month, as well as the reversed finances of William Frank that kept him from running for the House of Representatives."

"And your group is taking credit for all of this?" Mark turned away. "Come, let's see if there's anything for dinner. After these meetings of yours the Cartwright household suffers for a week."

As Mark followed Jenny to the house, he stuffed his hand in his pocket and felt the letter. He pushed it down out of sight, deciding he needed more time to think about it. The outrageous letter had initially evoked a solid *no*, but now, strange as it seemed, it was causing him to have second thoughts. Most certainly those second thoughts would never have been necessary had it not been for the scarf and those midnight meetings deep in the forest.

Mark turned away from the door and went instead to sit on the porch swing. The pleasant street reflected all the values of a prospering, growing city. Just recently the city had become the seat of state government. Springfield was attracting settlers with money and influence. In response to demands, the small city was quickly assuming a cosmopolitan atmosphere.

Up and down the wide, tree-lined street, houses similar to the Cartwright home had been built during the year since Mark and Jenny had arrived.

He contemplated Jenny's reaction if he dared propose leaving this comfortable white bungalow. With a sigh Mark shook his head.

"Mister Cartwright, sir—" A woman stood at the gate, peering up at him. "I've come from the post office. They gave me a letter to deliver to the missus." She still hesitated at the gate, glancing uneasily beyond him.

"Mrs. Callon, if I remember correctly," Mark said, going down the steps toward the elderly woman clutching her shawl about her head. "I haven't seen you for some time. I understand your husband is ailing."

" 'Tis, but I intend taking him to the doctor. I don't believe in the likes of this witchin'." She watched him stuff the letter in beside the first and glanced sharply at him. He opened his mouth to speak, but she hurriedly continued.

"Good thing you were accepted by the Supreme Court to practice law in the state of Illinois before it come out that your wife is in the witchin' business."

Mark heard Jenny's step behind him as she answered, "Why, Mrs. Callon! You talk as if it's bad. I'm a white witch. I'm not out to harm a soul. You need to investigate the craft. We witches are intent on helping people, doing good to all mankind. See, someone's in need of the power to move nature in response to our needs. If you'd like, I'll come past with some things to help your husband."

With a snort of alarm, the woman backed toward the street. " 'Tis using the devil's powers to do the devil's work and then lay claim to the powers of heaven."

Jenny watched the woman leave, then in a bemused voice she said, "Mark, your dinner is ready." Mark pulled the flap of his pocket down over the letters and followed his wife into the house.

After dinner, while Jenny was washing the dishes, Mark took out the letter Mrs. Callon had given him. "Jenny, here's a letter. Mrs. Callon brought it from the post office."

With her hands in suds, Jenny exclaimed, "Letter! Who ever could be writing to me?"

"Don't you want the surprise of discovering on your own?" he teased. "Here, I'll dry dishes for you. There are dark circles under your eyes. I know you're tired."

"And no one believes it's anything except a silly lark," Jenny brooded. He knew from the shadow in her eyes that Mrs. Callon's words had disturbed her.

When she had dried her hands, she took the thin folded sheet and carefully opened it. "Oh, it's from Sally. How did she ever know where to find us?"

"We told her before we left Missouri that we'd be going to Springfield."

"It's been so long. Why did she delay writing?"

Mark had to admit, "Likely she needed confirmation. I didn't tell you, but Joseph Smith was through Springfield last autumn. He stopped to see me at my office. I'm sure he carried the news back to Sally."

He saw the brief flare of anger in her eyes and watched as

she chewed her lip. "If Joseph was here, it was for a reason. Why didn't you tell me?"

"I didn't think it important to the welfare of the Cartwright home." He said lightly, "He was on his way to Washington and hadn't time to spare on us."

"Washington," she mused. "Whatever for?"

"He was just following up on his campaign for national notice and sympathy. You saw the newspaper articles. You know the Nauvoo newspaper, *Times and Seasons,* had published accounts of the Haun's Mill massacre as well as a complete story of the Saints' expulsion from the state."

"I also know of the nationwide interest and sympathy," she said soberly. " 'Tis only fair."

For a moment Mark was silent. He was thinking of the reply to those articles given by the editor of the *Chicago Democrat.* That editor had stated that the stories were being used to the profit of the Saints. Given more bloody marks in their history by Illinois or any other state, he predicted, the sympathy generated would insure that the Mormon religion would become firmly entrenched in the land. Mark sighed and reviewed his unwilling involvement in it all.

He looked at Jenny. "Joseph carried hundreds of affidavits and petitions to Washington seeking redress for Missouri's persecutions. Right off he bumped into what we've been hearing so much about lately—states' rights."

Jenny nodded. "I remember, but I thought it mostly dealt with slavery."

"No, it's a touchy situation. The state's constitution makes the legal entanglements far-reaching. Washington couldn't afford to get involved. There're too many out there just waiting to see how far Washington and the Constitution can be pushed."

"So they wouldn't do anything for him."

"Not only that, but seems Joseph let the cat out of the woodshed. Since he's gone home, Missouri sent a few notes of their own. Boggs furnished Washington a complete transcript of the Mormon problem in Missouri. That didn't set well, and Washington told Joseph's lawyer, Higbee, to take the case to Missouri."

"I guess that settles that," Jenny said soberly.

"If Joseph is inclined to leave it there," Mark replied. "I hope he will."

Jenny was reading her letter. "Sally mentions Joseph in Washington. That's how she knew we were here." She read silently and then said, "There's much happening. Oh, Mark, I feel so out of touch!"

He couldn't help asking, "You'd trade this for another frontier town?"

She looked around her home for a moment and with a sigh lifted the letter and began to read aloud:

"Nauvoo is a lovely place. The name means a beautiful plantation in Hebrew—the Gentiles had called it Commerce. We were here from the beginning and have watched the struggle from a plague-infested swamp with a handful of poor houses to what it is today. In just one year's time it has grown to a place to be proud of. Joseph laid it out in nice square blocks. There's a goodly lot for each home. We started out with log houses, like Missouri, but already there's brick and limestone buildings going up.

"But we'll not forget our past. Already Joseph says Nauvoo is just a stopping place until we are strong enough to claim our inheritance. Now the army is being built up. The temple will be set high on the hill. Plans are in the making, including the temple, a grist mill, and other such businesses. In another year we'll be on our feet again.

"Which comes to the purpose of my letter. Jenny, I fear for your soul. It's going on two years, and you need to be thinking of Zion. There's to be a gathering. The prophecies still hold: Joseph warns us that destruction still awaits this nation. Only the true church will be saved."

Jenny lifted her face and Mark watched her rub at the tears. "There," he chided, "there's nothing in that letter to make you cry."

"Oh, Mark, you'll never understand!" She was shivering, and now his thoughts were on the past. Jenny's fear was a reminder: at one time her brother Tom had asked if his fear of God was keeping him from following Jenny to Missouri. And when he had joined the wagon train, he had given her his whispered promise, *In sickness, in health, I pledge you my love.* Could those dark shadows in her eyes reflect a soul sickness?

With a sigh, Mark slowly pulled the other letter out of his pocket. "I've had a letter from Joseph asking me to come to Nauvoo. Seems he needs another lawyer, and he knows Illinois has granted me a license to practice law in the state."

CHAPTER 2

Mark stood at the window of his second-floor law office looking down on Springfield's busy main thoroughfare. Accustomed as he was to the brisk passage of buggies and wagons, and the cluster of women visiting on the streets while their parasols and billowing skirts forced a detour upon the male pedestrians, today's unusual activity kept him glued to the window despite the piles of paper on his desk.

When he heard the quick steps on the stairs, Mark turned to face the door. It was Aaron Turnbull, his partner.

Aaron nodded at the case of books on the floor. "You've settled your affairs to the point you must pack law books?"

"Yes." Mark said with a note of regret in his voice. "The house has been sold and Jennifer has begun to pack our belongings."

"I still can't quite convince myself you'll really do this. Certainly I can't believe it's a wise decision." His curious eyes held that wary expression Mark had come to expect since he had admitted his connection with Joseph Smith, the Mormon prophet. Mark sighed and turned toward his desk.

"By the way," Aaron said, "is there any possibility you're related to the evangelist, Peter Cartwright?"

"Yes, he's a brother of my father. Why do you ask?"

"Well, he's a part of the reason the streets are nearly impassable. He's holed up in the lobby of the Continental Hotel."

"I should pay him my respects," Mark murmured, shuffling through the papers on his desk.

"The other reason is that the esteemed prophet is in town. I understand he's the guest of Judge Adams. That makes me question his religion."

"Joseph's in town?" Mark said in surprise. "I didn't know. I'm sure he'll want to dine with us. You say he's staying with Judge Adams? That really surprises me, although I know little about the man. It's just—"

"Well, let me fill you in." Aaron said shortly.

"If it's only conjecture—"

"It isn't. You need to know if you intend to make Nauvoo your home and practice law there. Abe Lincoln has circulated a handbill. I'll try to get you a copy of it, but for now, Lincoln's charged him with being a forger and swindler."

"I wonder what the connection can be?"

"Since he's involved with the Masons, I'd guess it has something to do with that."

"That's impossible. Joseph is dead set against the Masonic Lodge, always has been. His gold book strongly teaches against secret societies."

Aaron shrugged and went to his desk. Mark closed his desk drawer and said, "Well, I'll head for the hotel and then try to find Joseph."

"That won't be difficult," Aaron replied in a muffled voice. "When I left the hotel they were having a shouting match in the lobby. If you look out the window, you'll notice their audience is streaming inside. I doubt you'll get a ringside seat."

For a moment Mark weighed speed against dignity and decided that speed was the more important. He headed for the hotel.

Aaron was correct; the lobby was full. Mark elbowed his way through the crowd. Although he hadn't seen his uncle Peter for years, he recognized the man.

Joseph was talking. Both men were seated in comfortable chairs in the lobby, but only Joseph looked the gentleman at ease and sounded—Mark winced—like the same old Joseph. His clothes were costly, elegant and rumpled. Peter Cartwright looked the part of a circuit rider—dusty, threadbare, and careworn. The man leaned forward with hands on knees and gave Joseph his undivided attention.

Joseph's eyes flicked across the crowd, lighted up when he spied Mark, and then returned to the evangelist. He was saying, "I'm convinced, sir, that of all the sects in existence today, we'd find the Methodist to be the closest to being correct." His broad palm warded off Peter's words as he said, "Now mind me, they are not correct right now, but if the sect would advance in the knowledge, they would take the world."

Peter moved impatiently and said, "Sir, you see us all wrong; we've no intention or desire to take the world. I'm not spending my life on horseback to preach the gospel of human endeavor. I'm here to preach Jesus Christ as Savior of each individual who comes to Him looking for grace to rescue him from the wrath of God. You, sir, are advertised as living a life of sin. If you would be great in God's eyes, you must repent."

Joseph's voice rose, overlapping Peter's, and Mark squirmed. When Mark realized it was Joseph's voice spewing out the curses, he began backing away, and then the voice stopped him. Joseph was on his feet, with clenched fist raised he shouted, "I proclaim that I am here to raise up a government in this country of America, these very states, which will overthrow our present form of government! I promise you, I will lift high a religion which shall overcome every form of religion in these United States!"

There was a moment of silence and Peter Cartwright lifted his shaggy head. Slowly he said, "The Bible tells us that bold and deceitful men will not live out half their days. I venture to say that the Lord will send the devil after you one of these days unless you repent."

"No," Joseph's voice overlapped Peter's again. Breathing heavily he added, "I prophesy that I shall live and prosper while you die in your sins."

In the weeks that followed, Mark often thought of the exchange between his uncle and Joseph Smith. He hadn't told Jenny of the encounter and didn't intend to. Right now, recalling that incident, Mark looked at their new home and shook his head.

Jenny and Mark stood on the tiny porch of a weatherbeaten house, nestled in the woods halfway between Warsaw and Nauvoo, Illinois. Mark looked at Jenny's dismal face and said, "It could be worse."

"You mean Missouri. I loved the little cabin."

"I'm rejoicing right now. After paying off the mortgage, the money we realized from the sale of our home in Springfield completely paid for this little patch of earth and shabby cottage. Besides, the agent promised that when—I say *if*—the railroad comes through here, they'll want to buy our land."

His toe nudged at the boxes and barrels clustered on the porch. "Frankly, given the condition of the state, it'll be years before that can happen. Right now I'm just happy to be out of debt."

"Oh yes, I remember the battle cry back home." Jenny's voice dropped to mock the well-worn refrain. " 'Thirteen hundred citizens and fifty miles of railroad.' And all we've seen are molehill piles of dirt."

"But given everything, you've had your wish. We are now

residents—or nearly so—of Nauvoo, Illinois."

"Do you suppose we've been wise to choose the country instead of waiting to build in Nauvoo?"

"Are you fond of sleeping in a tent? Few homes are finished, and they're mostly little Missouri-style log cabins. Even Joseph's house is small and cramped. Don't forget, my dear, Nauvoo has been in existence for only one year and a few months.

"Now shall we go inside and see what surprises await a couple who grab up real estate, sight unseen, just in order to have a roof over their heads?" Mark opened the door and led the way.

Jenny sighed and said, "At least it looks as if it has been occupied recently."

"By folks fleeing the Mormons. No cause, that's certain, but nevertheless—" his voice trailed away.

Jenny ignored him and marched through the rooms. "There's a good kitchen with a decent stove. The floors are clean but terrible. The walls need to be papered, the stairs are in need of repair. Oh, for a clothes press!"

"Unless our furniture arrives before nightfall, we'll be forced to spend the night on the floor."

"Bless my precious brother for volunteering to drive the wagon so we could ride the stage together." Jenny's voice was warm. "Since he left long before we did, surely he'll be finding us shortly."

"Then I'll bring in these barrels and find firewood," Mark said as he removed his coat and hung it on a nail beside the door. Jenny eyed the coat and shook her head in amusement as she rolled up her sleeves.

Nauvoo, even in late August, was hot—and much different than Jenny had anticipated. True, the mighty Mississippi did wind like a circling arm around that rearing bluff of their land, but she hadn't expected to find forest treading nearly on the toes of Nauvoo's residents.

And the riverport was a disappointment—a rattletrap wharf, a ferry, and a tumble of shabby dinghies. In her mind she had imagined a real port with steamers. In truth, the real port was in Warren, close to Warsaw.

That next week, she had a chance to view the river and town from the high point. The land already showed activity in preparation for building; Jenny looked downstream to the line that was Warsaw. "Why?" she turned on the seat of the wagon to address Mark. "With all this water, why go beyond Warsaw for a port?"

"The river rapids keep the big ships downstream. Joseph plans to build a wing dam which should take care of the problem. But Warsaw has trouble with sandbars."

Jenny shrugged and turned back to study Nauvoo. Mark said, "Homes are to be built much as Joseph planned in Zion, with large lots and wide streets. I understand some of the poorer Saints have been given land for farming on the outskirts of town. Right now Joseph's selling off parcels of land in town. I hear he's given some of the parcels to the favored ones."

"Will we be out of favor by buying through the agent instead of going to Joseph?"

Mark shrugged. "Joseph's lots are expensive. There are big interest payments on his land purchases. I've also been investigating this man, Galland, who's sold the land to the Saints. Part of his dealings has involved forged deeds. I preferred not taking any chances, and fortunately I found this little house and land just out of town."

"Gentile property," Jenny said. She sighed and continued, "This new place is a poor substitute for what we've given up. But Joseph has reminded us again and again that the Lord expects us to sacrifice for Zion. Also he's promising us something much better than we've left behind. Why does Joseph need another lawyer in Nauvoo? Is it something to do with the land problem?"

Mark shook his head. "He didn't give me any details, just offered me a good position."

He turned away and Jenny continued, "I wonder where we'll find Tom. I haven't seen him since he left the furniture."

"He isn't in town," Mark replied. "I have been doing a little asking around. I know where Andy and Sally Morgan are living. If we hurry, after we visit Joseph's store we'll have time to stop by their place." He turned the wagon and flicked the reins across the horses' backs.

Slowly they made their way down Nauvoo's main street. Mark pointed out a two-story log house with a white clapboard addition. "That's Joseph's home. I don't know who owns the other houses on this street, but there's evidence of building going on all over town. I've seen brick and limestone buildings going up. From the size of them I'd guess them to be businesses."

Jenny was still silent as Mark pointed to another building under construction. "I understand that building is to be the *Times and Seasons* office." At her questioning look he added, "Newspaper and printing office. I just heard Joseph's men made a covert trip back to Missouri to recover the press and type they'd buried in Far West. The next place is Joseph's store. Looks like he has a good-sized office upstairs."

He looked at her drooping mouth. "Cheer up, dear wife; in another year this little town will compete with the best of them. Just the sheer force of numbers will guarantee that."

"What do you mean by that?" Jenny asked slowly as she turned to face him.

"Progress. I hear the latest missionary endeavor to England has netted two hundred converts. Right now they're on the way to Nauvoo. And more Canadian converts are coming. It's whispered that the army's being reorganized. That's bound to put heart into the Saints. See that hill? It's been marked out as the spot for the new temple."

"There was a revelation that the temple in Missouri was to be commenced in 1839. I haven't forgotten that. Has Joseph?"

Mark studied her face. For just a moment he wished his answer could be yes. "Jenny, in April of last year, Brigham Young and several of the other brethren slipped across into Missouri and rolled a log into place at the temple excavations, thus starting construction on it." She grinned with delight. Mark jumped from the wagon and looped the reins over the hitching post.

As Mark turned to help Jenny from the wagon, he was caught motionless for a second, seeing sharply the contrast between this Jenny and the Jenny he had known in Springfield for the past year. Now neat in her dark calico dress with its demure white collar, serene with smiling lips and neatly coiled dark hair, she was a wife to make any man proud.

He frowned, for a moment caught up with that vivid picture of last year's Jenny. With troubled eyes and drawn face, wearing a frown that seemed to indicate she was miles away in thought, her hair tumbled and her home looking as if she'd forgotten it existed, Jenny had sent signals to Mark which filled him with despair.

Mark now took Jenny's arm and smiled down at her. Her eyes danced with anticipation, and the contentment on her face told him she knew herself at home once again. But that same contentment made Mark sigh. He need not remind himself that his experiment had failed. In Missouri he had been confident that once they moved to Springfield, all Jenny's strange ideas would disappear. Once under the teaching of a Bible-believing church, Jenny would see the truth. Since her early years he had sensed her forthrightness and intelligence, and that had led him to believe in her desire for knowledge and truth. But belief was not enough. His silent waiting for time to right the wrongs wasn't working.

As Mark mulled over the past year, he briefly wondered if moving to Nauvoo represented a decision not to wait for God to act in Jenny's life. Did the decisions he made reflect a lack of trust in his life?

When they stepped through the door of the general store, Mark and Jenny were struck by the mingled odors. "It's obviously a store carrying everything," Mark muttered. He could identify smoked ham, pickled herring, even sour pickles crowding the open barrel. The smell of leather goods, and the nose-prickling lint and dye wafted from the far corner. But the line of black books caught his attention.

As Jenny swung her basket and headed for the dry goods, Mark stopped in front of the display of books. "Them's just Bibles, we're outta the *Book of Mormon,*" the youth behind the counter advised him.

The excitement was growing in Mark, but he carefully picked up the book and slowly turned. "Jenny, you don't have a Bible, do you? No good Mormon should be without one."

As she stopped and turned, he saw the wary expression in her eyes, and for a long moment those gray-brown eyes held him as if searching out deep thought. Did her ivory cheeks pale even more? He waited. "No, Mark, I don't," she said slowly. "I've never felt the need—maybe the curiosity, but not the need."

"Curiosity should be enough," he said, reaching into his pocket for coins. "Besides, we're reforming."

Again there was that stillness as she waited. "We haven't been as faithful about attending the Sabbath services as we ought. Now I intend to take my wife to church each Sabbath," he said, looking into her eyes. "And you'll need this black book to go with your new dress."

Her dimples broke through and she laughed up at him. Coming to him, she said, "Then, my husband, it seems I need a new bonnet with a plume of ostrich feathers to make the costume complete."

With a grin he answered, "You may have two if you can find them here."

She wrinkled her nose, "I win. Not here, but I've seen them already. Down the street a home has a display with a sign advertising bonnets made to order."

The clerk was nodding his head vigorously as he accepted Mark's coins. "That's Hannah Ells; she's a dressmaker."

Jenny finished her shopping and the clerk accepted more of Mark's money, saying, "You're new, but Nauvoo's a goodly town already."

Curiously Mark questioned, "How do you know we are new? Nauvoo is growing too fast for you to know everyone."

The clerk looked surprised, then cautious. "Seems the careful thing's to make a point to know your neighbor. I must say, there's a good feeling about the state. Sir, you don't know, but when we first came from Missouri, we were a sorry lot—hungry and nearly naked. But the folks in Quincy were right good about taking us in and giving us a hand until we got on our feet. We'll not be forgetting their kindness. Makes a person take a deep sigh of relief after Missouri."

CHAPTER 3

Jenny had made her curtains, scrubbed the worn floors, and stocked the large pantry. She polished the banister on the stairs that led to the two bedrooms on the second floor, and bemoaned the lack of a clothes press.

Mark pruned apple and pear trees, cut underbrush, and pulled weeds. He also grinned mysteriously at Jenny but said nothing until the day Tom came and the two of them harnessed the team.

At her questioning frown, he responded, "It's a surprise. We'll be needing a hot apple pie. I put a basket of early pippins in the kitchen."

The pie was fresh from the oven and Jenny's cheeks still flushed with the heat when the team returned. She reached the front door in time to see Mark and Tom wrestling a blanket-shrouded bundle out of the wagon. On the porch they paused to wipe their sweating faces and unwrap the blankets.

Jenny caught her breath and reached out to touch the satiny wood. "Cherry," Mark informed her. "It was the only clothes press to be had in town, and because we're Mormons, it cost twice what it should. There're some carpets too."

Jenny was still stroking the wood, remembering for an unaccountable reason the gleam of the McBriers' furniture as it was being carried out of their home and loaded into a wagon. For a moment she wanted to gather the clothes press into her arms.

Tom snorted in disgust and Jenny looked up at him. "After what happened today, I'm guessing the Missouri stories have made their way to Illinois. The things they said!"

"Weren't overly friendly," Mark agreed mildly.

With a sinking heart, Jenny whispered, "Tom, tell me. Don't keep anything away, that's worse than not knowing, even if it's only stories."

"Oh, they started in on Joseph for what he gave out at conference time. Said if that's the case, they wouldn't be extending credit."

"Tom, what are you talking about? We weren't here in April and we've no way of knowing—"

"Joseph cancelled all the Saints' Missouri debts. He just plain outlawed them, saying it was unchristian to demand payment, anyhow."

Jenny was still staring at Tom incredulously when Mark said, "That's only one thing we heard. Right now it seems they're looking for offense, and there have been other irritations. The people of Hancock and Adams counties are fussing about the Legion, and they're also saying Ripley has been running surveys.

"The charge today in Warsaw is that Ripley has been plotting out the whole countryside for Mormon territory. Seems a Mormon community to be called Zarahemla is being plotted to take in Montrose County across the river. Most certainly Ripley and his men didn't win friends for the cause when they drew up street and property lines running right through the homes of the Gentiles living there. The townfolk took it to be a pretty good hint that they should pack up and leave." Mark was silent for a moment, then said thoughtfully, "I hadn't realized there was a move to create a new territory of this section of the state."

Tom shrugged and added, "Now they're blaming us for runnin' off their cattle, stealin' their tools and everything else. Boats get cut loose and we get blamed. A store is robbed and they look at the Mormons. Now they're a-callin' the Nauvoo Ferry the horse thieves' ferry."

Mark nodded soberly. "I'd heard back in Springfield that Nauvoo is a haven for criminals from three states. I discount that, but since we've arrived, it seems obvious there's an undue amount of traffic in stolen horses."

Mark saw Jenny's stricken face and reached for her. "Now, don't fret. Surely you didn't think we'd be free of problems, did you?" He circled her with his arms and looked at Tom. "Come on, let's go have some of that pie."

"Let's get this monster upstairs first," he grunted. "I'd enjoy my pie more knowing we've lived through the task."

The next day while Mark was dressing for his first meeting with Joseph, Jenny picked up the conversation. "In Springfield they were talking well of the Saints."

"Springfield's not neighboring with the Saints. Right here we're close; in fact, you might say we're sitting on the fence between the Mormons and the Gentiles." He paused to grin, but Jenny saw the mirth didn't reach his eyes as he added, "We might need to adjust to having them heaving rotten pumpkins back and forth over the fence."

"Things can't be that bad?"

"I don't suppose they are, but the talk won't help. The Saints'll get their back up and then there'll be trouble. Right now, Illinois is in big trouble with her finances. There's also the political side. Every fella with dollar signs or votes in front of his eyes will be currying the favor of Joseph. That won't help his cause with his neighbors.

"When Joseph first landed in Quincy in '39, a bunch of politicians were there, among them Stephen A. Douglas. Joseph lost no time in getting acquainted and extracting promises from him to get the state legislature to guarantee protection for the Saints."

Jenny was wearing a thoughtful expression when he turned from the mirror. "Look, I'll be in a meeting with Joseph all day. Put on your bonnet and come along. You can visit with Sally, and I'll join you there this afternoon."

When Mark slowly climbed the stairs to Joseph's office, he was thinking of the last time he had seen the prophet. He winced and his steps faltered. "Mark Cartwright, whatever possessed you to show that letter to Jenny?" he muttered to himself.

Surprisingly, as Mark walked into the room, Joseph stood and leaned across his desk with his hand outstretched. "Mark Cartwright! Am I ever glad to have you join our staff! I'll need all the legal advice I can get during the next few years. As you can see, the Lord has important plans for the people. Granted, when we were in Missouri, everything looked hopeless. Little did I dream we'd have to take the Illinois route to accomplish the Lord's designs."

His grin was disarming and his expression frankly curious. But Mark decided to avoid mentioning the last time he had seen Joseph.

Mark took a deep breath and said, "I must admit, it is because of Jenny that I've agreed to come."

"At least I've one loyal Saint in the family," Joseph said with a faint shrug. "You challenge me. I'll trust the Lord to make a loyal follower of you."

He turned to pick up a sheaf of papers and Mark realized the Prophet was once more in control. He winced abruptly as he realized Joseph was also his employer once again.

"You've no doubt kept informed of all that's gone on in Nauvoo. You can see the progress we're making in building up the city. Now let me tell you about what's going on behind the scenes. I trust you're aware of the conversion of Dr. John C. Bennett."

"No, but from your voice I gather I'm supposed to know something about the man."

"He's a doctor, a physician, but he's also informed about politics. We need help on that score. Right now he's working hard to get the Nauvoo Charter through the state legislature."

Mark frowned, "I'd heard the Mormons were asking for preferential status. I discounted that just as I have most of the other rumors, such as asking the Nauvoo area be designated as a separate territory."

Joseph grinned, "Rumors do fly about. That's all right—doesn't hurt people to know we have a little power."

For a moment Joseph's eyes were fastened on Mark's. A growing question loomed in those eyes, and for a moment Mark thought he should throw all the rumors out before the Prophet. But Joseph returned to the sheaf of papers.

"I'll have you meet Bennett later and go over the charter. Right now it reads just the way I want it to read, and I don't want an item changed. I just want you to check the spots which might cause problems. Don't bother to say all the goody things. I know the Lord will work out the details."

"Then why do you want me to look at it?"

He paused and straightened in his chair. "Because if there are problems, I want to be able to say, 'The esteemed Springfield attorney, Mark Cartwright, has checked the charter and approves of it.' Do you get the picture?"

"I get the impression that you are trying to buy me. What's the price?"

"Only a place in the kingdom. I promise you, Mark, your sins are forgiven. You shall inherit the kingdom along with the best of my men. Eternal kingdoms are yours."

"You mean I can skip the other steps? The surrender of property, the obeying of the laws, the—well, whatever you come up with tomorrow. You know you've done a lot of that. In the beginning I had to join the church or be damned. Now I have to do this, that, and whatever else you say, or I'll be damned."

"Mark, I can't make special concessions to you. I don't know what the Lord will demand of us tomorrow. Remember, I'm in this just like you are. He demands obedience of me and I can't buck Him on that."

Joseph jumped to his feet and paced quickly back and forth

in front of Mark. "Prison was a humbling experience to me. I grew closer to the Lord, more holy than I've ever been before. He showed me the order of things. Mark, you've no idea of all the Lord has in store. I can't reveal it all now; there just isn't time. Besides, some things must wait—the Lord hasn't given me the complete plan yet."

"Joseph, I'm not wagering for a part in your kingdom. You know how I feel about all this. I didn't hide my feelings when we were in Missouri."

"Not my kingdom—it's the Lord's kingdom. Besides, Mark, you love your wife. You wouldn't want to make decisions that would completely cut you off from her, both now and for eternity."

Mark was still pondering the last statement of Joseph's as he walked back to the Morgan home. There had been an underlying note of excitement in the man's voice, an excitement which stirred uneasiness in Mark.

The Morgans' log house was little better than their Missouri home. Sally opened the door to him and immediately turned back to Jenny. With amusement, Mark studied the sparkle on her face and realized that Sally and Jenny were scarcely conscious of his presence. Playfully Andy clapped his hands over his ears and grinned at Mark.

Sally interrupted her discourse long enough to push around Andy. "Oh, Mark, stay for dinner—we need to talk."

"With me?" he asked in surprise.

"No, Jenny and I. It's been so long."

"I hope we survive this meal," Andy said gloomily. "Let's take a walk. I want to show you a few things."

"No," Sally declared. "Dinner is ready. Here, Jenny, put the plates on."

Andy raised his voice. "Did Joseph tell you about the writ?"

"Sit down, Mark," Sally ordered. "Here's the applesauce."

"What writ?" Mark asked cautiously.

"Then he didn't, or you'd know."

"Andy, don't talk business."

After dinner they walked through Nauvoo's streets. Sally and Jenny chattered; under the cover of their talk, Andy muttered, "Joseph's been served with a writ from the new Missouri governor, Reynolds. The Missouri problems have reared their head again." He glanced at Mark. "I knew he'd got wind of it this afternoon. Must have hightailed outta there just after you left his office."

"Hightailed? You mean the sheriff didn't catch up with him?"

"That's right. I suppose it'll be a while before we see much of the Prophet." Mark looked at Andy, hardly believing the grin of amusement he was seeing.

Sally scooted back to them. As Andy lifted little Tamara, Sally leaned close to Mark. "Did Andy tell you what that place is?" She pointed to the little white frame building across the road.

Mark surveyed the building, "No, but I'd guess it's a store of some kind."

Sally leaned closer. "A brothel!" she hissed. "Some say it's Bennett's idea. I can't believe the Prophet will tolerate that once he gets wind of it."

"I can't believe Joseph would have that under his nose and *not* know about it," Jenny said slowly, looking quizzically from Sally to Andy.

Mark watched Jenny for a moment, at first feeling elation; then the questions began. They were back in Joseph's territory. With a tired sigh, he waited until the women moved ahead before he took up the conversation with Andy.

"Have you any idea what the charges were in the writ?"

"No, but you know Joseph and Hyrum escaped from prison. On Missouri's books they are fugitives. You didn't think the Legion was just for show, did you?"

"I'd heard the army was back in business," Mark answered slowly. "Frankly, I hoped it was just a result of Joseph's boyish desire for the theatrical."

"It isn't. You know he hasn't given up on Zion."

"I know that in Springfield he was expending a lot of energy cursing the Missourians, especially Boggs."

Mark took a deep breath and turned to face his friend. The passing years had changed Andy. The boyish exuberance was gone, and Andy's mouth had settled into a grim line of determination. Besides the unexpected touch of gray in his hair, Mark had noticed the shadows in his eyes.

"Andy, how's it with you? Do you still believe Joseph is a prophet?" Andy hesitated only a moment before nodding. Mark pushed, "With the keys of the kingdom, that he's the Christ for this dispensation? Do you really, Andy?"

They walked in silence. The mid-September evening was full of the clarion echoes of life. They were hearing the shouts, the ring of a horses' hooves against stone. There was a distant sound of a waterfall, the faraway toot of the ferry and, close at hand, the innocent laughter of their wives.

Mark sighed and said slowly, "Andy, I believe a man's relationship with his God is the most important part of life. Not just from man's viewpoint, but from God's, too. This makes me believe God'll do more'n we could ever hope to make himself known to man. The information is there if man will go about getting it in the right way. Part of it is believing that God's not going to strike a man down for having an honest question about what the Lord expects of him."

"Well and good," Andy said slowly, "but there's got to be a point of contact. Where does that begin? Sometimes us humans are so poor and ignorant we have to let someone else do our thinking and make contact with God for us. Surely God won't fault a man for that."

"He'll fault a man for stumbling over truth and refusing to acknowledge it is truth. There's a verse in the Bible that's been burning into me. I can't quote it, but the gist of it is that there's a way that seems right to man but it ends up leading to death."

"How can God fault a fellow for doing his best?"

He shook his head. "Only, seems to me, if the fella is ignoring the obvious . . ."

"How's that?"

"God wouldn't put out two books with completely different instructions."

"You're back on that old tack, about not believing that the Bible is translated correctly."

"No, I'm talking about the *Book of Mormon* contradicting the revelations Joseph's giving out as from the Lord."

Andy turned and grasped Mark's arm. "Who told you about the revelation? Who's been talking? This is not to be spread around right now. With the other problems, we can't afford to let it leak."

Mark knew his face gave him away. Andy dropped his hands and shoved them into his pockets. He watched Andy hunch his shoulders as he muttered. "Forget it, Mark; forget I even mentioned it. Do me a favor and pretend this conversation didn't happen, huh?"

Mark promised, but Andy's excitement made him ponder the question he had so innocently raised. Whatever the secret, the revelation must be very important.

CHAPTER 4

Monday dawned—a bright, clear September morning. Mark had just left for Nauvoo. Jenny sat on her front steps, enjoying the morning and waiting for the wash water to boil. In the kitchen the sheets and towels waited beside the stove, along with a bar of brown soap shaved into wafers to dissolve quickly in the boiling water.

Jenny's front door faced east; to the south, beyond the pasture, the forest pressed close. To the west, the trees and the craggy slope of their land dipped down into the deep river gorge. When the night silence held the land, Jenny could hear the water crashing over the rocks upstream, and she could imagine it gentling, moving into the shallow basin at the bottom of the gorge before taking up its rapid trip down the Mississippi River.

The gorge was a separator—only a minor gouge in the terrain of the land and water, but a deep chasm between neighbors. She knew Gentiles owned the land on the bluff across the basin. Beyond them was the Gentile town of Warsaw, and already Jenny was learning they best be shunned.

Turning her face to the south, feeling the sun and hearing the peaceful morning song of the birds, Jenny brooded. Was Nauvoo to be only another Missouri? But nature said *no*, and she tried to take heart from the message.

The water was beginning to simmer. Jenny went to stir in the soap and push her sheets and towels into the tub.

When she came back to the porch, the mood of her thoughts had broken. The steps needed to be swept, and the apple tree had released a shower of fruit to the prying fingers of last night's wind.

For a brief moment, she was caught and separated from the familiar pattern of her thoughts and the demanding spirit-tug which so often held her captive for days at a time. She thought of yesterday; the Sabbath-day worship had broken the tide of spirit control. But it was more than that.

On the Saturday before, the day she and Mark had shopped in Nauvoo before visiting Andy and Sally, she had felt the nudge.

The linens were threatening to boil themselves out of the tub. Jenny pushed herself off the step and hurried into the kitchen.

When the last of the clothes were pinned to the line, Jenny returned to the step, realizing now her need to do some serious thinking. What about the contrast between Springfield and Nauvoo, between those women who had been her friends and Sally?

She frowned and bit her finger. "Same old thing," she muttered. "It's Sally. From Kirtland time, even when I've not been seeking the craft, I've always had Sally to remind me of all I'm not. She's holy. Doesn't take much to realize that. She's living her religion, and I can't even call the power down."

With a snort of exasperation, Jenny got up and went into the house. The talisman was still pinned to her Sunday frock. She smiled at the memory as she released the medal and slipped it into the pocket of her apron. "All spiffy I was," she said with a chuckle. "Me in my best calico with the talisman and the Bible and the *Book of Mormon* going to meeting with my apostate husband."

She paused to sigh over Mark and her thoughts fled back to Springfield—how fruitless that time had turned out to be! In the beginning there had been such promise of winning Mark to the true gospel.

"I can't be held totally responsible," she murmured, moving about the living room. She assembled the pile of charms and opened the green book to a new and untried way of calling down the spirits. Dutifully they had gone to church, not the one true church but one which Mark had selected.

He would never know the churning inside, the nerve-tearing anguish of hearing those words read when she knew they were all wrong. *After Joseph teaching us the Bible wasn't translated by men gifted to handle the job,* she thought, *how nigh I was to pushing my hands over my ears; trying to keep from hearing the words contradicting everything Joseph's been teaching!*

Jenny paused to clear the table between the two chairs. Her lips twisted. Mark had it all planned. The pretty new table with the lamp centered there and the Bibles on each side, his and hers. She stacked the Bibles on his chair and opened the green book.

For the next hour Jenny murmured the words and mixed

the charms; when she finally stood to her feet, her heart was pounding. Already she was sensing the swirling forces moving nearer and she slipped easily into the trance, chanting with determination, then feeling her body slipping into the disjointed, released world of the spirits. The room about her receded and grew dim.

Coming back to her world was a shock. She knew it first in a moment of disappointment and nausea as she stood trembling and blinking in the noontime sun. She was outside, but she couldn't recall getting there. Her frock was soaked with perspiration and her hair streamed down her back.

A sense of awe gripped Jenny as she walked slowly into the house. The mood she had wrapped about herself with the chants and charms had become the most intense experience she had ever felt. As she moved slowly across the room, she caught the reflected image in the mirror and turned to study herself. But could that image be Jenny?

The room seemed dark. She stepped close and leaned toward the mirror. A smoky floating cloud surrounded the image she was seeing. She blinked and pressed closer. The image twisted, her own familiar features distorting, warping. In horror she saw the familiar becoming strange and repelling. The dark cloud was tearing at her hair, poking her eyes until they were only black pits. The scene before her became the forest. Tree branches grew into torturing hands and dug into her face, her body, wound in her hair and held her suspended, helpless.

Jenny's heart was pounding—a drum of thumping, compelling anxiety. Suspended, perspiring, at the mercy of nature, she swung. Life returned. Not seeping, trickling back, but life rushing, demanding. The distorted face remained, but in the background, beyond the trees, a dot of red was growing, moving.

"No!" On tiptoe, Jenny surged forward, her fists pounding, shredding the image into slivers of meaningless light that for one moment glowed deeply purple.

The heavy frame with its fragments of glass crashing against the floor broke the spell. Jenny was flung back into life. In awe she looked at the floor and then at her bleeding fists. Blood. Trembling, horrified, for one clear moment Jenny saw herself at the mercy of the unknown.

When Mark returned home, a serene wife was moving about the kitchen. The pile of fresh laundry wafted woodland perfume from its wicker basket. Mark kissed the freshly washed and coiled mass of dark hair, nuzzled the pale cheek and noticed the bandaged hands.

"Now what have you butchered or broken?"

"Oh, Mark, the mirror! I'm so sorry. It just happened."

Mark captured her hands and she saw him pale. "My dear, you could have been badly hurt!" He studied her face and pushed her into the chair. She allowed him to fuss about the kitchen and later wash the dishes.

The next day Jenny made her decision. Again Mark had gone to Joseph, and she was left alone. She sat on the steps and studied her bandaged hands. "It could have been worse." She shuddered. Blood. That was bad.

She was still shivering, now at the memory of that shadowy image in the mirror. She dared not say it aloud lest the spirits hear, but the words trembled through her being—*I am done with them, forever.* She knew the emotion she felt was fear, but it was also acceptance of defeat.

Jenny closed her eyes and leaned against the porch railing. The warm breeze ruffled her hair while the river crashed and the birds sang in the trees. It was a lonesome feeling to be the only human in this place. Even the birds seemed confident and at peace in their world.

"If only I could tell Mark," she whispered. But she visualized the horror on his face and shivered. Never would Mark understand, even if she were to explain that the power was really for his sake.

Then she felt a nudge inside, and she returned to the contemplation of the Sabbath meeting, held at the place called the temple grove. Sally had pointed out the hill, telling her it would be the site of the new temple. But for now, the grassy plot circled with trees would be the temple and meetinghouse.

Joseph's unexpected appearance had made the meeting special. Over the cheering and shouting, the tears and clinging hands, Joseph had stood before his people.

"Governor Reynolds of Missouri—" he began, then paused to grin while the boos and cat-calls filled the arena, "has issued a writ for my arrest. I needn't be reminded that I'm a fugitive from the wrath of Missouri, so I went for a little walk by myself while the sheriff's posse visited our friendly city." He paused, waiting for the laughter to end.

"Seems he didn't like the general atmosphere of the city and therefore gave up and went home. Brethren, hopefully that will be the last of them. I think he may have been motivated by fear of the Legion and the goodly number of people who are a great deal more friendly to me than they are to him."

Jenny had lost ears for the rest of the sermon. The movement of people and the tide of emotion had her attention. She was overwhelmed by the contrasts—the careworn and the excited, the old and the young. But all alike were reflecting back to Jenny a mood much different from what she had felt in Missouri.

Once again she saw Joseph's people as proud, confident, and very holy. She knew herself scrubby, poor, and unholy in comparison. Her gaze had fastened on Sally standing in front of her. Her blonde hair had been captured under a smoky-gray bonnet which shaded her face and shadowed her wide blue eyes into a mysteriously regal expression.

The wind rose, but Jenny remained huddled on the steps, powerless to move. The air was filled with autumn's treasure of brilliant leaves. They swirled, lifted on the wings of the wind. When one brown missile was flung against her cheek, Jenny lifted her face. The air was full of the brilliance of the leaves. Wind-borne, they circled high.

Abruptly the sun broke through the clouds, lighting the fire of scarlet leaves, and Jenny saw the scene again: red, grasping branches, smoky clouds. Jenny's heart began to pound. Scrambling to her feet she fled into the house and stood pressed against the closed door, knowing again the horror of the mirrored vision.

The room was darkening, but Jenny was conscious only of the alien wind and the amplified horror of the mirror. The wind buffeted the door as she pushed against it. Did she hear her name thrown into the wind? As she strained to hear, there was an anguished groan and crash. Now the door strained against her.

"Jenny, it's me, Mark. Let me in."

She stepped backward and pressed trembling hands at her tumbling hair. Biting her lips, she fought for calmness, knowing it wasn't working. His eyes widened and his hands were moving over her. "Are you hurt? Jenny, what is it? Answer me."

She gulped, but her voice came out a thin whisper. "Whatever is wrong? I'm not hurt; why do you ask?"

He held her close and then looked into her eyes. She saw his jaw tighten. "It was a mistake, wasn't it? I should never have brought you this far away."

"From Springfield? Nonsense, Mark. I wanted to come." Now she knew her voice sounded threadbare, without substance. He led her to the kitchen and poured hot water over the tea leaves. His face was still pale and lined, but the expression he turned on her was level, demanding.

"Jenny, why don't you tell me what is happening to you? From the time we decided to move to Nauvoo, you became a different person. You came back to life—the old Jenny. But for the past six weeks you've been wandering around in a cloud."

Her voice was deliberate, flat even to her own ears: "You are saying this because I've become a slothful housewife. But I've been bored by it all. Mark, if only we had a child. If only—"

For a moment his face relaxed, "If that's all, I'd—" In his silence he paced the kitchen floor. "Jenny, I'm going on instinct. I know you are deeply troubled—perhaps it is our childlessness. I'm willing to abide by that for now. But why do I feel as if I can no longer touch the real Jenny? I was certain that bringing you to the shelter of the church—to Joseph's Nauvoo—would be the answer to your problems."

He fell silent, and Jenny sensed the hesitancy in his statement. Painfully she gripped her wounded hands and pressed them against her. The temptation to pour it all out was nearly more than she could bear. But looking up at her husband, she saw not concern and questions, but instead horror, shrinking away, even outrage if she were to tell him the truth.

She studied his face, saw his attempt to smile as he said, "I suppose you miss those silly games you and the senator's wife were playing with the scarves and herbs. Jenny, I must insist—"

She was breathless. "What?"

"You're going to be ill unless you break this tide. As soon as it is possible, we are going to move into town. But until we can, I insist you make every effort to get acquainted with the women of Nauvoo. There's Sarah Pratt, Sally, Eliza Snow. Miss Snow teaches school; perhaps you could help her with the children."

Jenny jumped to her feet, "Mark! I don't want—"

"All right, I won't tell you what must be done. You decide for yourself—just don't stay out here alone day after day. I heard that group of women inviting you to be part of their sewing circle. I also heard your answer. You sounded haughty; no wonder they haven't asked again." He moved away, saying as he turned, "I intend to buy you a light buggy as soon as I can find one. Jenny, I am worried about you and I intend to act on your best interests. Even if that means returning to Springfield."

CHAPTER 5

Jenny snuggled her face into the warm folds of her shawl and flicked the reins across the mare's back. It was only Mark's insistence that had her out of the house today. The January sky was slowly releasing snowflakes, nearly as reluctantly as Jenny was to receive them.

The mare's pace quickened. As many times as she had taken this trip in the past two months, she need not be urged toward the livery stable.

Tom was there to take the reins from her. He frowned and studied her face. "Still a mite peaked. Mark's worried; thinks you're fretting yourself sick."

"Mark's bothering himself for no reason," she answered smartly. She took Tom's hand and stepped down. "He can't stand for a body to think or feel a bit different than he does."

Tom's brow unfurled itself and he grinned. "He's pokin' you about religion again?" She gave him a level look and said nothing. "Oh, been into the book again! Tryin' to raise up a storm?"

"Tom, for the years you spent following the Prophet while he did his money digging, you are a mite sarcastic. I'd expect more sympathy. Would you like me to give you a love potion?" He reddened, and Jenny pressed on, "I intend to have the power, no matter how it must come about."

"What you want power for?" Jenny closed her eyes for a moment and tried to line up the reasons, but saw only that vision of Sally, assured and confident. "Jen," he said impatiently, "why is it you can never be satisfied with anything?"

"It goes deeper than being satisfied. I suppose I'm just tired of being a nothing."

Tom's eyes widened. "Married to one of the most important men in town outside Joseph and his twelve, and she calls it nothing."

"It's how I feel." Now the new thought came. Jenny contemplated the visions of Joseph. "Maybe," she said slowly, "I need to go talk religion with Joseph."

Tom frowned again. "Meaning?" His eyes were watchful.

"Meaning, I can't spend all my time with the sewing circle or at Sally's. Meaning, sometimes I have serious thoughts in my head."

She knew he was still watching her as she headed down the street toward Joseph's office. Her heart was heavy as she contemplated the lonely figure of her brother—silent, faithful, undemanding. She couldn't help wondering whether he ever had experienced this brooding need to split through the seams of life and discover something for himself.

Unexpectedly, her latest discovery burst into her mind and she shivered. Would autumn's terrible vision ever leave her? Again she murmured, "I'm through with the craft forever." The familiar discontent settled upon her. All the spirit-world's promises of power and knowledge had come to naught. Except for the bid for higher status offered only through the dreaded sabbat, she had tried every trick of the craft, and still she was only weak Jenny.

As Jenny approached Joseph's store, she began to wonder how she would win an audience with the Prophet alone. Surely Mark—or at least some of the twelve—would be with him.

She hesitated at the bottom of the long flight of stairs stretching up the exterior brick wall of the store. She was self-conscious, aware that every eye on the street would take stock of Jenny Cartwright going to Joseph's office. "And every Saint in town will be chewing over Jenny, wondering what problem has sent her running to the Prophet for advice." Jenny abruptly decided she needed a bit of cloth to stitch.

Joseph was inside, in his shirt sleeves, stocking shelves as casually as a junior clerk. When he noticed her he said, "Mark's gone to Carthage for me. Business. You could buy a ham or a nice new plow while you are here."

After greeting him she lowered her voice. "Joseph, it's you I must see."

His hands slowed among the boxes and rolls of twine. She nearly squirmed under the questions in his eyes, the faint smile. "I need advice. Joseph, it's important. There's no other place to go."

"Have you seen Dr. Bennett? Surely he can help you out."

"What? Joseph, not medical. I want to talk about the craft and—religion."

He frowned, then his face cleared in a smile. "Then wait by

the stove." He jerked his head toward the women in the store. "They'll soon be gone."

When the store was empty, he came back to her. Sitting down on the bench beside her, he clasped his hands and leaned forward. "Jenny, my dear, what seems to be the problem?"

She backed away, too conscious of the small space between them and the warmth of him reaching through her chill. Caught by the significance, she frowned in annoyance. For a moment she studied his face, wondering again at the magnetism of this man. His smile was encouraging.

"Joseph," she groped for a beginning. "Do you still have the talisman?"

"Yes, but I'm wise this time; I'll not take it out for you to see."

"I'd forgotten that," she said, and his grin flashed, underscoring the lie while she blushed. "Joseph, I didn't forget. I just didn't want you getting the best of me right off."

"Right off?"

She ignored the thrust. "I need to know. Do you remember in Missouri at Captain Patten's funeral you said that you had the power to give to those who wanted it? I want that power."

He was silent for a long time. In the dim building, the fire snapped in the stove and the red light of it shone through the open door, reminding Jenny of the mirror and the spirit world she had seen. She shivered, and he lifted his head. Now shadows from the threatening storm were hiding Joseph's eyes.

"Jenny," he said slowly, while she peered at him. "I believe you are serious; but let me ask you some questions. You mentioned the talisman. I've told you I'd renounced the craft. No longer do I get my power from this source. It is through the church and the promise given to the priesthood that I now know power. Are you unaware that the promise of the priesthood is only for men and, through them, their wives?"

"I don't understand the priesthood, I've heard little about it. Seems no one knows enough to talk about it now."

"That's good. Most of the details haven't yet been revealed. It shall be soon. I'm waiting for my people to purify themselves through the ordinances; then the Lord has promised the fullness of the gospel will be given."

"But, power!" Her voice broke. "Joseph, the need is destroying me. How long can a person take the promise without the fulfillment? I tremble with fear of my inadequacy. Please—"

"Don't push. There's nothing I can do unless you meet the requirements of the gospel. Have you prepared yourself by reading the Scriptures? Are you paying your tithing, doing your part to build up the Saints?"

"I . . . I don't know. There's much I don't know right now."

"I suggest you become a learner. I've plans to have some of the older women teach the younger all the ordinances of the faith. Until we can do this, just do your work at home."

"What do you mean?"

Joseph took a deep breath and reached for her hand. "Jenny, your husband is as nearly apostate as I can tolerate. He's always given me a difficult time. Without disclosing the details of our talk, my instruction to you is that you win him to the church by your saintly life. This is very important. Without a husband to take you to the highest degree of heaven, you'll never receive the power on this earth, never be more than a slave in the hereafter."

It was snowing hard when Jenny left the store, but she was so deep in thought that she was unconscious of the wet, cold flakes against her face. She was also unaware of Mark dismounting and walking toward the store just as she hurried away.

Looking after her retreating back, he frowned and faced Joseph. "That was Jenny. Why was she here?"

"Mark, remember, I'm Jenny's spiritual advisor. Why else would she be here? I've told her to pull up tight the reins around home and in time she will inherit all the blessings of the Lord, which she so desperately longs for."

For a moment he frowned at Mark and then he clapped him on the shoulder. "Come in and tell me what you've been able to come up with in Carthage."

Mark reached the livery stable just as Jenny stepped back in her buggy. Tom was beside her, and Mark handed the reins of his mount to him. "Old Nell's had enough for the day. Put her up for the night. I'll drive Jenny home."

Jenny slid over and Mark said, "Your nose is like a cherry already, and we've nearly five miles to go. Why did you venture out in such a storm?"

"There were only a few flakes when I left—besides, I was taking your advice. I was sick of my own company."

"Did Joseph give you some good *advice*?" He stressed the word slightly and Jenny glanced up at him. She frowned, and Mark was instantly sorry. He settled into his overcoat and reached for the lap robe.

He was still berating himself for allowing his jealousy to

show as he tucked the robe around Jenny. "Now, let's see how fast this rig will move," he said lightly.

He flicked the reins across the back of the mare and headed through Nauvoo. Glancing at Jenny he saw the faint smile on her lips and felt that twinge again. Was it related to the angry scene he had interrupted in Joseph's office this morning?

Jenny turned her head toward him and asked, "Did you have a good trip to Carthage?"

He shook his head. "So Joseph told you. Actually, I could see no reason to have gone. The fellow I was to contact has been out of the state for a month. His business partner looked at me as if I were slightly deranged when I asked after him." He was silent, thinking again about the confrontation between the two men that morning. Those words had capped all the ugly rumors he had been hearing. He knew a confrontation with Joseph was fast approaching.

Mark shot another glance at Jenny. The faint smile was still on her lips. "You look pleased," he stated. "That must mean *your* meeting went well."

She turned to him with a puzzled look. "It was the snow I was smiling about. It's pleasant now that I needn't ride home alone. I don't know what to think about my meeting with Joseph. I'm feeling more was left unsaid than was said."

"How's that?" he asked cautiously.

"There are so many gaps in my religion. So much I don't understand, and so much more I need. Joseph put me off by saying there's new revelations to be made to the church in the future. He didn't give me any help except to tell me to go home and read the Scriptures."

Mark straightened and turned to study Jenny's face intently. She was busy flicking snow off her shawl and drawing it more tightly around her head, and she didn't see his excitement. Carefully he settled back and compared this with the information rolling around in his mind. *So Jenny isn't happy with her religion!* he mused.

He felt his grin disappearing. New revelations. That seemed to fit in with the scene he had interrupted between Joseph and his brother, Don Carlos.

This morning he had arrived early at the office over the grocery store. Obviously neither man had anticipated an audience to their angry scene. He had heard Don Carlos as he walked in. The man's flushed, angry face had emphasized his words, and his wrath had delivered the rest of them. Turning to Joseph, he shouted, "I don't care if you are my brother and the Prophet of the living God. Sure as I stand here, you'll go to hell if you preach the spiritual wife doctrine. Hyrum feels the same. He told me last night that he's confident it will break up the church."

The angry red left Don Carlos' face, and he paused on his way to the door. Mark saw the anguish in his eyes. "Hyrum said it could cost your life. I don't know what he meant by that unless—" Suddenly he noticed Mark. He ducked his head and hurried out the door.

Mark became aware that Jenny was throwing worried glances at his frowns, and he snatched up the conversation again. "Jen, tell me where your church has failed you." He saw the startled expression and watched her shrug.

In the morning, Jenny was still wondering how to answer Mark. As she broke eggs into the sizzling fat, Mark came into the kitchen. "One thing I did find out yesterday," he said, as he turned the bread toasting on the stove, "Joseph has had communication from Dr. Bennett."

"Isn't he in Springfield?"

"Yes. He wrote that the Nauvoo Charter passed the house without being read."

Jenny dropped the knife she held. "You mean after all the fearing you and Joseph went through over that charter, they didn't even read it?"

"That's right." She studied his frown and waited. "Seems like careless legislation. I have a hard time reconciling that with my friend, Lincoln. But those are the facts. The state has granted the little Mormon municipality a charter that, if it goes unchallenged, virtually makes us a state within a state."

"Well, tell me what the charter is all about."

"I can give you a copy to read, but for now here are the facts: Besides the expected items such as incorporating the city, even providing for a university, there's the clause calling for a militia to be called the Nauvoo Legion.

"The charter will give the city council power to make and execute ordinances not repugnant to the state or United States constitution." He paused, adding, "Note this, my dear, it is an ambiguous statement wide open to all kinds of interpretation.

"Among other items, the mayor of the city will be chief justice of the municipal court, empowered to issue writs of habeas corpus, with the power to try those issued from other courts, including trying the original actions in the case. In effect, the court has the power to cast out everything that goes against the desires of—you guessed it—Joseph. I don't think he'll have to worry about Missouri as long as the charter is in effect."

"This is the first big step toward getting approval to be designated a territory." Jenny's eyes were wide, and Mark winced. "That's not good?"

"It will be impossible. I just wish he would give up on his foolish dream. Jen, if I'd any idea Joseph hadn't learned his lesson in Missouri, I would never have accepted his job offer."

"The people here have been so good to us, except for those in Warsaw, Warren and—"

"And anyone else close enough to be touched by the Saints." He followed Jenny to the table. He had only taken two bites of his breakfast when he said, "Lincoln made a statement concerning the law that goes something like this: municipal law, that is, local law, is a standard for conduct approved by the state governing bodies, and it's for the purpose of fostering right and correcting wrong."

"But you're talking about law—not about a community set up to live under God's holy Prophet and kingdom rules."

"Jenny, my dear, you sound too Mormon."

"What do you mean by that?"

"I can practically quote chapter and verse. You don't really believe that. Why don't you think it through? Why don't you read and question, even argue just as you have done in the past?"

"I suppose because I am an adult now. I should have the questions settled. It isn't mature to go through life fussing over everything."

"It isn't mature *not* to, if you know a question deep down inside."

She was slowly lowering the dishes into the dishpan when he came back into the kitchen. He was wearing his coat and drawing on the mittens she had knit for him. "Jenny, what's wrong? Why don't you bring your questions to me instead of to Joseph? I saw how torn you were in Springfield when you were practicing what you called your nature religion, worshiping in the forest by the light of the moon. That didn't satisfy you—as a matter of fact, it was destroying you. Now I'm seeing the same dissatisfaction. Will you let me help you?"

"Mark, you are apostate."

"Perhaps. Yet Joseph values my judgment enough to offer this position."

CHAPTER 6

Events concerning the Mormons seemed to move just as rapidly as spring was moving upon the country. Jenny stood on her front porch watching the birds flitting back and forth across the pasture, carrying twigs to the large oak tree beside the barn. Some of the events taking place in Nauvoo were puzzling to her.

The town was growing rapidly. Just this month ten thousand had gathered at the temple for the ceremony of laying the cornerstone. Nearly every Sabbath, the meeting in the temple clearing produced a larger crowd and new faces. She thought of last week's sermon and winced. Even Mark didn't know the reason behind Brigham Young's sermon. His face had been very sober as he had watched the stranger turn and slip out of the crowd just as Brigham Young had put his pistol back inside his coat.

Now Jenny shook her head. "Brigham, I don't know you very well, but I'd always credited you with more intelligence than that," she murmured to herself. "In the past Joseph's always made the wild statements, but you nearly capped them all when you said what you did."

Shivering, Jenny whispered the words Brigham had roared at the crowd: " 'The earth is the Lord's and therefore it belongs to the Saints!' But Brig, you shouldn't have waved that pistol and said this is the way we intend to take it."

Walking back to the house, she stopped at the pasture to look at the lambs. The chickens were nesting, and there was another new lamb in the pasture. Mark predicted the cow would be freshening soon. Even the women of Nauvoo seemed to be blossoming with expected life.

Everyone except Jenny. It was becoming increasingly painful to go to the weekly sewing circle—except that it was a good place to pick up the latest gossip. She chuckled, shaking her head.

"Jenny." Mark came down the stairs two at a time. He paused to finish tucking his tie under his collar and then said, "There's a parade and speeches in town today; want to ride in with me?"

"Oh, I suppose so. I've nothing much else to do."

"It isn't that bad, is it? It's spring and the world is blossoming out all over, even in our pasture."

"Everywhere except in me," she sighed, turning away.

He nuzzled the back of her neck. "Don't give up yet," he murmured.

"Do you suppose I should see Dr. Bennett?" she turned.

Mark's head snapped, his answer explosive. "No!"

"What is the problem? Mark, he's the only real doctor in town and you should see the way people—"

"People, or only women?"

"Well, the women at the sewing circle. I must say I can't understand them. Just mention his name and there are all kinds of funny reactions. Still, it seems safer to go to a qualified doctor instead of that fellow who just hands out herbs."

He looked at her quizzically, "A couple of years ago you were handing out the herbs."

"True." She paused, frowning over the things she had heard. "There're whispers of Dr. Bennett misbehaving with some questionable women—those fancy ladies living down by the wharf. I heard he's responsible for that brothel. Remember? Sally pointed it out to us."

"And you want to see *him*? Why don't you just talk to Patty Session? I've a feeling she'll just tell you to stop worrying."

"Mark! We've been married nearly five years. I would think—"

She turned away, and he came to put his arms around her. "Hey, tears won't help. Come on now, you need Nauvoo today."

The parade had begun by the time Mark and Jenny arrived in Nauvoo. In silence they sat in their buggy and listened to the brass band and the shouts of the people. When the first line of men appeared after the band had passed, Mark whispered,"The Legion. See, there's Joseph standing in the wagon waving to the people."

"What an elegant uniform!" Jenny exclaimed. "Look at the men dressed in white. Why there's John D. Lee."

"That's Joseph's special contingent of body guards," Mark muttered, and she wondered at the note of irony in his voice.

With a glance at him she asked, "What is the significance of the white?"

"I think it's supposed to project the idea of protecting angels."

Jenny snickered. "I don't think Porter Rockwell looks like an angel."

Mark turned the buggy in behind the parade and followed it to the clearing beside the temple grove. By the time Mark had found a place for the buggy and they made their way to the clearing, the band was playing again. But this wasn't marching music.

"Dancing!" Jenny gasped when they stepped into the clearing. "In Kirtland it was expressly forbidden."

The young man in front of Jenny turned with a cheerful grin. "Ma'am, this isn't Ohio. Be glad the Prophet's relaxing a bit."

"Are there going to be speeches?" Mark asked.

"Seems." The young man moved impatiently. "Mostly it's a rallying cry to get started building the Nauvoo House."

"Oh," Jenny said. "That's to be the boarding house the Lord ordered built, isn't it? Is that all?"

"No, they're saying he's going to lay the polygamy rumor to rest again, and he's going to give instruction about baptism for the dead. Already Brigham Young's declaring it is a great and mighty work we are to be doing for the Lord." The fellow's face wore a pensive grin for a moment and then he aroused himself, "Personally, I'd rather be dancing and—" He looked at Jenny and, with a teasing salute, walked away.

"Why, Phelps!" Jenny looked up at Mark's exclamation. Mark was holding up his hand, and his glad surprise seemed to embarrass the man. "You've rejoined Zion's camp?"

With a wry grin, Phelps nodded. "Only I'm hearing the Zion part has been put on hold."

"Then you've been informed about the revelation that Joseph received from the Lord in January?" Jenny asked, nodding at the woman beside him. "My, you missed something; that revelation was chockful of direction for the Saints."

"I've heard a little about warning the kings and rulers of their prophesied end, and about how Zion must wait until the proper time." He shook his head sadly. "I'd already started for Nauvoo when I learned Joseph had to drop his plans to begin building up an army to march on Missouri immediately."

Mrs. Phelps stepped forward, eyeing Jenny curiously. "We heard there are converts streaming in from Canada and England, also that there's a temple to be built here. My, there's excitement in store for the people of God!"

"I don't understand about baptisms for the dead," Jenny said, "but I hear they've already started. Someone said they heard one fellow got baptized for George Washington."

"There's going to be great days ahead," Phelps said.

"But there's much to be done," Mark warned. "Right now we're having financial problems. Seems the real estate sold to Saints in Iowa was based on fraudulent deeds. A large number of poor Saints are even poorer now. I hear Joseph intends to give some of them work in construction of the temple."

"Have you heard rumors about the new bankruptcy law?"

"It hasn't passed the house yet," Mark said shortly.

"Well," Phelps said lamely, "seems it's an answer to the claims Missouri's been making against us."

"Oh," Jenny said brightly, "then you haven't heard that Joseph dismissed those debts a year ago."

"Jenny," Mark interrupted, "I must go to the office. I'll take you to Sally's home first." As they turned to go, Jenny saw the expression on Phelps' face—an incomprehensible question. Phelps didn't trust Mark.

The year 1841 snowballed with one event after another, and through it all the new Mormon community grew at a rate that left Jenny giddy. From a village with two hundred and fifty homes, a straggle of shops and a temple lot gouged enough for a cornerstone, Nauvoo was now spreading into a modest-sized city. From generous lots in town to the farms clustering like timid chicks around their mother hen, Nauvoo was making her presence known in Illinois.

During that first year Mark and Jenny lived in Nauvoo, they watched with trepidation as the bold prophet continued to lay claim to more territory.

While Jenny had held her breath because of the daring of the Nauvoo Charter, Mark cringed at the political machinery of the Saints released upon the state. The influence of the Saints' solid voting bloc caused Illinois to tremble.

In 1840 when the Saints voted as a man, their unified action helped place the Whigs in power. Again in 1841, Joseph Smith boldly declared the Mormon vote would shine most brightly on the party willing to extend favors.

It would have been a daring move for any group of people; but for the Prophet it seemed the ordinary, logical result of seeking the will of the Lord.

Nearly as soon as the Nauvoo Charter passed the House, Saints and Gentiles became increasingly aware of the role John C. Bennett was playing in Nauvoo—and not only in politics.

Rigdon, ill since the Missouri days, was replaced with Dr. Bennett as Joseph's right-hand man. Mark carried home the news to Jenny.

"Mark," she said slowly, studying the frown on his face, "this should be good news—after all, Rigdon was a drag on the heels of everything happening in Nauvoo. Why are you so troubled?"

As he hung up his coat, he responded, "I distrust that man's ambition. Joseph seems entirely blind to a personality that is causing most of his friends to shudder."

He took a deep breath and paced the floor of their kitchen. "There are letters. From the beginning Bennett has had some of us puzzled and worried. He's just too smooth. Now Joseph's had letters saying he's held in disrepute back east. The letters state he's abandoned a family, and the Masonic Lodge expelled him. I have no idea what the charges are." Mark paced the floor and then turned to Jenny. "All of this mess is enough to make me want to quit, to get out of Nauvoo while I still have my sanity."

"Oh, Mark, you wouldn't, surely!"

He looked at her pleading face close to his shoulder and tried to grin. "No, my sweet, I wouldn't." He watched her brow smooth and tried to guess her secret desires.

Mark still carried the churning need to help others understand the mystery of Jesus Christ. The compulsion pressed against his heart each time he saw the confusion on Tom's face. And what about Jenny? He turned away with a sigh. How true it was that the most difficult burden was the one nearest a person's heart!

CHAPTER 7

May had arrived, and in the temple grove the air was warm and heavy. Brigham's voice droned on. Some of the other women moved restlessly, no doubt thinking—as Jenny was—of the basket dinner. Jenny wondered whether she had remembered to pack butter.

When Mark moved impatiently and yanked at his collar, Jenny realized her mind had been wandering. She glanced at him as he began chewing at the corner of his mouth. Brigham Young's voice carried clearly over the crowd; she tried to listen as her gaze skimmed the crowd pressing as close as possible to the speaker.

Nancy Rigdon turned her head and flashed a dimpled smile at Jenny. She was standing close to Sarah Pratt, and it was Sarah's turn to glance at Jenny.

As Jenny smiled toward the women, she was thinking of the sewing circle. In the past months, since spring had offered more diversions, the crowd had dwindled. Recalling with amusement the fun she had shared with Sarah and Nancy, Jenny couldn't regret the change.

What a strange pair the two were! Nancy, the youngest daughter of Sidney Rigdon, was all spice and froth. Much younger than Sarah, she obviously adored the graceful, attractive woman. Sarah was married to Orson Pratt, one of the twelve. Jenny knew they had one small child.

Mark stirred again, now frowning. Jenny tried to fasten her wandering mind on the sermon. Brigham's monologue poured out more words and Jenny sifted through them, looking for the ones irritating Mark. She heard, "Our religion is founded upon the priesthood of the Son of God."

Jenny was still puzzling over Mark's reaction when she heard more: "The Son of God labors to build up, exalt, create, purify all things on the earth, bringing it to His standard of glory, perfection, and greatness. I want you to know, my friends, that we are to be helping Him. When the fullness of time has come, we will have been partakers in the task of bringing the kingdom to perfection. Those who buck this perfection will just have to go. Also, I want you to understand that Jesus Christ can't return to this earth until we have the kingdom prepared for Him."

It was midafternoon before Jenny and Mark left Nauvoo. Jenny was thinking about Nancy's new frock when she recalled Mark's reaction to the sermon. She studied his face, saw that he was miles away in thought, and said, "Who was the man standing beside you? He's as big as Joseph and looks nearly as important."

"He's a Canadian; William Law is his name. Was converted to the church in Canada and has just arrived this spring. Seems to be an enthusiastic person, full of ideas. More than willing to do his share around here."

She waited a moment and then asked, "Why were you so irritated by Brigham Young's sermon?"

Mark looked surprised. "I'm displeased because what he had to say doesn't line up with what the Bible teaches. I'm hearing more of this all the time, particularly slanted toward an idea that's being whispered about."

"What's that?"

He moved restlessly and glanced at her. "A kingdom of God that is going to take over—and I'm quoting current whispers—'Illinois, Missouri, Iowa, and finally all the states and then the world.' Now you are frowning—why?"

"I'm wondering how you've come to know so much about what the Bible teaches."

"Jenny, I've been reading. It's right there just as plain as it can be for anyone who cares to read.

"Joseph told me to read the Scriptures. I think he meant both the Bible and the *Book of Mormon*. But then the sermons tell me so much, it seems foolish to waste time reading."

"You read to check it out—to make certain what you're hearing lines up with God's Word. Matter of fact, if you *don't* compare the revelations and the *Book of Mormon* with the Bible, how do you know you aren't being—" He stopped and both of them looked up as they heard the horse rapidly approaching.

"It's Tom!" Jenny exclaimed. "Is he coming from our house?"

"Well, he wasn't in Nauvoo this morning."

When Tom wheeled his horse around, Jenny noticed the lines of strain around his mouth. "I'd given up waiting for you and decided to head for Nauvoo."

"Sabbath meeting," Mark said tersely, then waited.

"Joe's in big trouble. I've been sticking with him, fearin' to leave him for a minute until today. Thank goodness he finally was able to get a writ of habeas corpus."

"What's happened?"

"Joseph had a meeting with Governor Carlin. On the way back to Nauvoo, a sheriff from Missouri with his posse appeared on the scene. 'Twas so well-timed I'm thinkin' it was planned higher up."

"So Joseph's wild prophecy has reached the ears of Missouri, particularly Boggs."

"You mean the prophecy he gave out a couple of months ago, sayin' that within a year Boggs would die? Mark, that was from the Lord. Did you expect Joseph would fail to give the warning? Of course he wanted Missouri to hear." Tom shrugged. "They nabbed Joe, and I just tagged along, tryin' to figure out what to do."

"And?" Mark prodded.

"They hauled him clear to Quincy before there was a chance to take a breath. That's gettin' mighty close to Missouri. We tried several places to get a writ and not a soul would issue one. Don't think they'd a done it in Quincy but for the fact his old friend Stephen A. Douglas was in town hearing a case."

"Douglas is on the Supreme Court," Mark said thoughtfully. "That should mean something."

"You're tooting right. Word barely leaked about Douglas stickin' his neck out for Joe when a couple of Whig lawyers scooted for Quincy to offer *their* services. Douglas being Democrat and political himself done the trick. We're about ready to have a caucus over there."

"For once Joe's politics is standing him in good stead," Mark remarked dryly.

"Yes, but he needs all the help he can get. He told me to fetch you."

Mark sighed and glanced at Jenny. "I don't like leaving Jen alone; also there's a pile of paper work at the office."

"Can't be as important as this."

"It could be more important. There's going to be a real storm if we don't get Joseph's financial affairs in order before the next meeting of the district court."

Tom's horse pawed impatiently. "Head back for Quincy," Mark said. "I'll ride over, but if things are under control, I won't stay."

"I'm to alert the men."

Mark winced. "The Danites. That's the worst order Joe could have given."

"Not the Danites," Tom stressed the words, "nor even the Legion. His *bodyguard*." He wheeled away without waiting for a reply.

Jenny couldn't restrain her dismal words. "It's like Missouri all over again."

Mark took a deep breath and said, "We can leave any time you give the word."

Jenny considered and shuddered, remembering that shadowy image. Only to herself did she dare admit the alternative was unthinkable. She said, "You'll be away tonight."

"Do you want me to take you to Sally?"

"It's so far, and you need to hurry. Is there a chance you'll be back tonight?"

She felt him studying her face. Slowly he said, "I'm of a mind to make certain I'll be back."

"Oh, Mark," she whispered, "thank you." She blinked tears out of her eyes as she smiled at him.

She saw the concern. Always it was there, but sometimes it nearly forced the words she didn't know how to say. "Jenny," he began, then gave a feeble grin. "Lock the doors and read your Bible. That'll keep the spooks away. I promise I'll be back before midnight."

He helped her from the buggy and went to saddle up. She was still staring after him, wondering whether the light words carried a hidden message. What a strange way to tease!

When Mark disappeared down the road, Jenny went into the house. She dropped the latch into place on both doors and pulled the curtains over the windows. Although the late spring afternoon was warm, she stirred up the coals in the stove and added wood, still thinking about Mark's statement.

Since the afternoon she had broken the mirror with her bare fists, Jenny had not made another attempt to use the charms and book. At times she trembled with a fearful urgency to be back into the craft. But the memory of those contorted images was stronger.

When the water was boiling, Jenny brewed tea for herself and settled down in the rocking chair. As she sipped her tea, she studied the smooth leather cover of the Bible Mark had given her. "Like a talisman," she mused, "he wants me to read it to keep away the spirits. Only read, not rub it like I would the medal."

Suddenly she began to giggle. "How silly!" The picture was

strong in front of her—Jenny briskly buffing the black cover and chanting the prayer to Luna the moon goddess. Now a new thought took over. Was it any sillier than stroking the medal and burning the herbs?"

She shivered. "I may not be seeing the power I hope for," she murmured. "But certain as I sit here, there's something out there, and I'm finding it very frightening."

Jenny silently explored all the reaches of her thoughts, knowing with certainty that a question was being forced upon her. "It was the green book in the beginning that opened it all up, but then Clara taught me more. And Joseph."

She closed her eyes and relived the excitement of South Bainbridge. With the digging and witching that went on that year, with the sure thread of strange excitement moving through them all, there could be no doubt. An idea presented itself, and she must consider it. Would she go back to it all? It was strangely attractive, drawing with an appeal that was more real than the chair under her.

But even as she was slipping into a floating sense of ease, being drawn gently in, Jenny abruptly faced reality. She remembered that day with the mirror—her own face, twisting into ugliness. And the sabbat awaited her—a threat which would never leave as long as she poked into the spirits' territory.

She jumped to her feet and reached for the black Book. Holding it tightly against herself, she waited for her wildly beating heart to slow. But she couldn't stop the forbidden thought and the wish. "I wish I could see Adela; she was so beautiful! She could tell me what has gone wrong." Once verbalized, the wish was an uneasy cold spot against her heart.

The afternoon light was becoming dim; ahead lay all those dark hours before Mark would come. Jenny picked up the Bible and her empty teacup.

Back in the kitchen she lighted the lamp, stirred up the fire and cooked an egg, which she didn't eat. The Book lay on the table in front of her.

"Funny," she mused. "Since I could say the alphabet I've wanted to read everything in sight. Now I have this Book, and no desire for it."

Outside the wind was rising. Jenny could hear the moaning in the trees and she tried to force her mind away from the curious question: Was it wind? She reached for the Book and held it tightly.

The wind continued. Abruptly she envisioned Mark fighting the wind. Darkness was total now, and it was too early for the fragment of moonlight. Jenny peered through the curtains and hoped the chickens were safe, and the lambs. There had been wolves sighted. Were there Indians? But no matter—at least Indians were flesh and blood.

With a shiver she went back to her chair and opened the black Book to the middle.

"The Lord is my shepherd," she read slowly, then paused. The picture that came before her eyes was not the same kind of picture she saw when Joseph preached about the Lord commanding the Saints to avenge Him of His enemies.

Jenny flipped the pages, looking for the messages Joseph had been preaching. Words caught her eyes and she lifted the Book to study the pages. "*I am.*" Jenny thought back to Springfield and the woman who had said those words. Why did they still make her shiver? She moved her finger down the page and read, "Stand now with thine enchantments and with the multitude of thy sorceries, wherein thou hast laboured from thy youth. . . . Now let the astrologers, the stargazers, the monthly prognosticators, stand up, and save thee from these things that shall come upon thee. . . . They shall not deliver themselves from the power of the flame: . . . None shall save thee." She shivered and flipped more pages.

Another word caught her eye: *blood.* She went back. "But your iniquities have separated between you and your God, and your sins have hid his face from you, that he will not hear. For your hands are defiled with blood. . . ."

She remembered that dream after the day at Haun's Mill. "But I didn't shed blood!" she cried, and then was caught by more words: "Your lips have spoken lies, your tongue hath muttered perverseness. None calleth for justice, nor any pleadeth for truth: . . ." Could other things be as bad as shedding blood when God looked at the sins?

Carefully Jenny folded the page so that the words were hidden.

She was still sitting beside the stove when Mark came. Jenny had returned the Book to the parlor table. She had combed her hair and washed her hands, but the words were still there.

CHAPTER 8

Mark noticed Jenny standing at the parlor window as he rode out of the yard, past the puddles in the road. The rain had flattened March's dandelions, and the road was a mirror reflecting sky and clouds.

As soon as the horse had cantered beyond Jenny's vision, Mark tightened the mare's reins. "Hold it, girl, there's no sense getting to Nauvoo a minute sooner than necessary."

He slumped in the saddle, grateful for his lonely ride into town. For the past two months his face ached continually from the cheerful grin he forced himself to wear.

This morning bone-weariness, his constant companion, helped him discount the misery of the moisture hanging in the air. Once again, as he rode, he found himself reviewing all the facts and considering the two options open to him: stay and endure, or leave Nauvoo.

It had been a year since Joseph Smith had first laid all his cards on the table. In the beginning, Mark had been grateful. It had signaled a change in their relationship and indicated a chance to help Joseph.

From the beginning, Mark had been uncomfortable with Joseph's role. This feeling, coupled with the tension created by the man's "prophet" image, had grated against his nerves. The image was supported by all those around Joseph, reminding Mark that *he* was the sore thumb in Nauvoo.

Mark had become tired of tiptoeing around in deference to Joseph and yearned for the relationship they had shared in Missouri. Open warfare seemed preferable to some of the pussyfooting he was seeing. Mark thought of Clayton, the man who had recently begun serving as Joseph's recording secretary. He wanted to tell the fellow it was all right to sneeze once in a while.

Mark winced. Open warfare? That left no alternatives—it was an all-or-nothing situation. But he couldn't help feeling that either all or nothing merited the same results.

With a sigh Mark acknowledged a showdown in the offing. But could he explain this to Jenny? There was too much forbidden territory in their marriage.

She wouldn't tolerate talk about Jesus Christ and all the Bible had to say about a personal relationship with the Lord. But was her dabbling in the occult a constant statement of her need for God? She evidently found no satisfaction in Joseph's church.

As Mark rode, he reminded himself that he should be rejoicing in this fact. But for some reason he couldn't identify, knowing only this much left him shaking with fear for Jenny, and this unknown made him fearful of leaving Nauvoo.

With a sigh, he murmured, "Oh, Lord, I know I'm to be leaving this in Your hands, but I must admit, I'm shaking in my boots. There's just too much going on that I know nothing about."

Mark went back to mulling over Joseph's problems. From the Kirtland and Missouri years, Mark had known of the chaotic state of Joseph's financial affairs. He also knew the step Brigham Young had taken just after returning from his mission to England.

Mark had heard of Brigham's despair back in 1840 when he saw the condition of the church finances. Young had immediately set himself to the task of convincing Joseph he must turn over the financial affairs of the church to the twelve apostles.

Brigham's success had encouraged Mark when he received Joseph's offer of a position in Nauvoo as his attorney. But a complicating situation had now surfaced.

During the summer of 1841, Congress had passed a personal bankruptcy law; then just two months ago, Joseph threw all his financial problems before Mark.

As Mark shuffled through the pile of debts with a sinking heart, Joseph's countenance had become more cheerful. Quickly Mark realized that Joseph was depending on the new statute to work a miracle in his finances.

Last week the situation had climaxed in a heated argument between Mark and Joseph. Unfortunately, it had served only to remove the last polite hedge between them.

On that morning, Joseph had dumped the pile of paper on Mark's desk and declared, "See here, this is what I intend to do. I'll declare total bankruptcy. I'm insolvent."

"No, you are not!" Mark had snapped back. "Let me show you. See this and this?" His finger flicked through all the items.

"To begin with, you've taken upon yourself the position as sole trustee of the church, which you know is illegal. In the State of Illinois the church act requires a board of five trustees. Besides that detail, which is bound to be questioned, you've set yourself up to handle all the real estate dealings in the community. According to the books, you've made yourself a bundle."

Joseph had opened his mouth to protest when Mark interrupted. "Your words are working against you. More than one man in the state can point to the statement you made recently, remember?"

"Yes, I shot my big mouth off, saying I own a million dollars worth of property hereabouts."

"Joseph, I've seen the books. I happen to know that you've acquired city lots for a few dollars and are selling them for a thousand. And you expect *me* to be party to this fraud?"

"I'll transfer the titles. My young'uns will inherit it all anyway—might as well do it now."

"Joseph, need I remind you that the bankruptcy law will allow no transfer of goods to take advantage of this law? You can't transfer the property to the church either. The state law allows a church to own only five acres of land."

Shaking his head as he recalled that interview, Mark straightened in the saddle and took a deep breath. Jenny was right—he was prone to carry everyone's load on his own shoulders. He tried to shove away the oppressive feeling that he must do something—and quickly.

The rain clouds had moved on. Looking around, noting the signs of spring, he dug his heels into the mare's ribs and tightened his grip on the reins.

This road between Warsaw and Nauvoo had been a lonesome road just last year, but now with the influx of the English settlers as well as the addition of more Canadians, the countryside was becoming dotted with farms. Neat fences bordered the road. Trees had been cleared and the plow had been set to the virgin acres.

As Mark studied the landscape, he thought of his Gentile neighbors. At times when Mark listened to the grumbles and studied the hostile stares of the Gentiles living around the area, he wondered where the discontent would lead. What he saw and heard made him uneasy.

Back in 1839, that first traumatic year of the exodus, the people of Illinois, living close to the old town of Commerce, had welcomed the Saints with compassion and tolerance.

But the feeling was fast disappearing, for several reasons.

One was the disappearance of prime farm land from the market. Nearly all the prairie land had been purchased. And the fact that the deeds were in Joseph's hand, waiting for new converts to claim them, didn't help.

But Joseph chose to see only the pleasant side of life right now. Mark writhed under the Prophet's arrogant confidence, even though he realized he should have expected it. How could he have forgotten even for one minute Joseph's reaction to the hordes of visitors streaming into Nauvoo?

The rapt audience of strangers listening to him, and the admiring throng of people there to watch the Nauvoo Legion parade through the streets, worked like blinders on Joseph. Finally, with a sigh, Mark tried to dismiss Joseph from his thoughts.

The early morning sun slanted light across the plowed acres. Mark watched it tunneling under the cluster of clouds capping the forest. Birds pecked at the fresh-turned soil, while across the meadow a thin spire of smoke marked a cabin. The trees showed fresh color, splashing yellow-green, pink, and white against the dark pine.

Mark's appreciation was forming into a prayer when he heard the creaking wagon wheels behind him. Pulling the mare aside, he turned as the wagon reached him.

"Mornin'," said Daniels, the Gentile who lived across the ravine. The old man pointed his whip toward the sky. "Right pretty with the clouds and sunshine. God's in His heaven, all's right down below."

"I hope that is so," Mark said soberly. "If it isn't, I expect we've been responsible." The man considered, nodded his head, and passed on.

At the next break in the fence, another rider met Mark—Orson Pratt. He pulled his mount even with Mark and turned a worried frown on him. "What do you think about this getting the Lodge in Nauvoo?"

Mark studied the apostle for a moment before replying, "Seems a bad time to be taking a poll. The installation is to be next week. Pratt, you know my feelings, and I haven't backed down. I expressed my view last fall when things first started rolling that direction. I'm against the secret societies in general. However, I'm not the best informed about masonry because I've never considered it.

"The *Book of Mormon* talks enough about the Lord being against secret—is it called murderous combinations? Can't believe Joseph would go against the gold book."

Pratt's frown deepened. "That's what bothers me. Seems I can't reconcile Joseph allowing it, either." He shot Mark a quick look, and for a moment Mark felt as if he were being measured by some unseen rule.

Jenny had returned to her kitchen and was washing the dishes when the tap came on her window. Tom was grinning at her and she went to unlatch the door. "Am I in time for breakfast?"

She gave him a quick hug and pulled him into the room. "I'll have some ready immediately. Eggs?"

He nodded. "Mark left?"

She sighed. "Yes, 'twas awfully early, but he acted as if he couldn't wait to get out of the house. Tom, there's something troubling him. I wish he'd feel free to talk it out."

She turned from the stove and saw the curious expression on Tom's face. "Now you look a dark brown study yourself. Tom, what's going on? No one's said a thing to me—won't, in fact, though I've tried to find out. Seems I've no friend to trust me with a lick of gossip."

He snorted. "With Joseph starting up that Relief Society meeting this month, there's bound to be lots of loose gossip floatin' around."

"Well, there isn't," Jenny sniffed. "However, I'm put out at him. In the first place, we women would like to do the organizing. Most of us were well content with having a small sewing group so we could share a little refreshment and the latest stitching patterns. But no, Joseph's pushing every woman in town to be a part of it."

"Aw, that's it. He found out you ladies were sipping tea and breakin' the word of wisdom, so he's had to sic Emma on you."

"Mind your tongue," Jenny said with real irritation. "Emma's nice enough if a body doesn't cross her. It's just the bossiness of it all."

"Now, Jenny, you know a female isn't goin' to make it to heaven at all without a man to take her there. No sense in buckin' the word of the Lord. We've got the priesthood, and there's no sense in wanting the old ways."

"Tom, did you just come to fuss? Besides, when are you going to do your part and get married?"

She watched the play of expression on his face—fear, puzzlement, then embarrassment. He ignored the question. "Not to fuss. Wanted to ride in with Mark." He was silent for a moment. Turning, she was surprised to see the scowl again. "I've been over Warsaw way, listening to more of the rumbles. Sure's discontent when they talk about things."

"Like what?"

"Oh, to start, the Nauvoo Charter. Seems they're thinkin' we Mormons are uppity. The rumbles over the charter makes me believe Missouri's tossing out information. I heard talk about wantin' to see Joe go back for trial. Also there's the prophecy he gave out last year, about Boggs and Carlin both dying."

"Well, I guess they can take that with a grain of salt unless it comes true."

"Jen, the way you said that surprises me." Tom paused for a moment to scratch his head. Slowly he said, "Seems in the past you shivered over all the prophecies; now it's 'wait and see.' Are you not believing anymore?"

"In Joseph? Of course. I have to believe; there's nothing else. It's just . . ." Her voice trailed away and she chewed at her lip for a moment. "It's just that I've been counting up in my mind all Joseph's said that hasn't come to pass."

"What possessed you to do that?"

Slowly she said, "I've been reading the Bible." His eyebrows went up. "Joseph's been urging me to read the Scriptures, so I do. One day it's the *Book of Mormon* and the next it's the Holy Bible. Just yesterday I read about God telling how to distinguish a true prophet. The Bible says if a fellow is a prophet from the Lord, then all his prophecies come to pass, and if they don't, well, then he's a false prophet and he's to be taken out and killed."

"Jen, that's the Old Testament."

"But everything else we believe comes from there, doesn't it? The law and the sacrifices? Joseph himself said that the sacrifices of animals is to start up again soon as the temple is finished. I know for a fact that they did some sacrifices in Kirtland temple."

"Well, 'tis so, the law and sacrifices." Tom paused to scratch his head. "But there's Jesus Christ. He's New Testament."

"So far I can't understand where He fits in. Mark talks about Jesus being the only important part. The Atonement, he calls it."

After Tom left, Jenny sat in the rocker beside the window and watched the robins building their nest. Her dishwater was cooling, but she couldn't move away from the thoughts. She sighed. Her reading was bringing up questions, some of them as irritating as pebbles in her shoe.

When Jenny finally returned to her tasks, she was thinking

about the melodious words she had read; they sang through her, and she wondered why she'd never discovered the beauty in the Bible before. At the very back of the book, she had found the words, "And he that overcometh, and keepeth my works unto the end, to him will I give power over the nations: . . . And I will give him the morning star."

As she went to dust the table holding the Bibles, she whispered, "The morning star. I've seen it—bright, promising, I—" She stopped and cocked her head. "That section talks about power over the nations, but I like the part about the morning star."

She was sweeping the porch when she began to ponder the rest of the verse. Leaning on the broom, she murmured, "I wonder if that's where Joseph got his power. I'd like to ask him what works it's talking about."

CHAPTER 9

The warmth of the April sunshine made the clearing in front of the temple uncomfortably hot. Jenny loosened the shawl from her shoulders and shifted her feet.

She nudged Mark with her elbow. "There's Dr. Bennett. With all the fuss he's generated, I'm surprised to see him."

He frowned. "Are you referring to the newspaper articles?"

Jenny tilted her head to see his face. "Then there's something else?" The muscle in his jaw tightened, and she recalled the gossip, most of it unsavory, that had started at Relief Society. "There are whispers at Society about the way he takes advantage of women," she murmured.

"Jenny, let's talk later," he whispered, looking uncomfortable.

William Law stopped beside him. Jenny looked up into his stern face as he touched his hat, "Ma'am." Then addressing Mark, he asked, "Have you succeeded with Joseph?"

Mark started to reply just as the line of dark-coated men walked toward the crowd. He paused and said, "Law, why don't you stop by this afternoon? Seems best, considering."

He nodded and moved away as Heber C. Kimball began to address the crowd. Jenny's attention wandered away. She watched as William Law returned to his place beside his wife. Jane Law gave Jenny a quick glance and nod.

Jenny's gaze shifted across the crowd, nodding to the other restless ones, and then she studied the pile of limestone which would be the temple.

She thought of the promises Joseph had made about the temple—the promises and the warning. Baptism for the dead. Although she'd heard often enough about the rite from Brigham Young, she still felt uneasy.

Heber C. Kimball's words caught her attention. "Brethren, sisters, in the Lord. We are all concerned with how we get right with our God. But don't let this uneasiness possess your soul. I will tell you—it is knowledge. We must all increase in wisdom in order to gain salvation. The very act of believing on another man's testimony helps us increase in knowledge. Thereby we gain wisdom and the power of God. As for your leaders, my advice is simply this: Whatever you are told to do—do it. If our advice leads you astray, the burden will be upon our shoulders, not yours."

Joseph Smith stepped forward and Jenny felt the tension and excitement grow. Unexpectedly Jenny found herself responding, leaning forward to catch his words.

More soft-spoken today, Joseph repeated words they had all heard before, but even Jenny acknowledged the need to hear them again. "My people, I must remind you that the ordinances you have received, and more, will be multiplied and increased for your good in the days which lie before you. But these are not new. In the beginning, the ordinances of the priesthood were passed on to Adam. This sacred trust was given to him at the creation, even before the world was formed. Remember that Adam is Michael, the archangel. Do not forget that Noah himself is Gabriel. When Daniel speaks of the Ancient of Days, he is referring to the oldest man who lives, our Father Adam. I will not keep you long this Sabbath day. I want only to remind you again that Father Adam presides over the spirits of mankind. He is our God."

The crowd was breaking apart, drifting homeward, when Sally and Andy hurried toward them. Sally threw her invitation across the people. "Come home with us?"

Mark shook his head and Jenny called, "You come with us; there's chicken in the oven."

When the Laws arrived, Sally and Jenny had just finished the dishes. As they came into the house, Jenny stood awkwardly in the doorway, suddenly shy and inadequate. She spoke tentatively, "Shall I prepare tea?" Jane Law glanced at her husband as she slowly drew off her gloves.

William frowned, but Mark said, "Some of us will enjoy a cup."

As Jenny turned into the kitchen, she was very conscious of Sally's trill of excited laughter. "*Kitchen maid,*" she muttered to herself, cringing as she reached for the teacups. She had heard that Jane and William Law were wealthy. She peeked through the doorway. The Canadians' British accent was nearly as intimidating as their fine clothes. Jenny eyed the fluffy gray fur edging Jane's brocade cape before she turned to load her tray.

Graciously Jane accepted the cup of tea. "Lovely china," she murmured with a smile. "My favorite pattern."

Tamara cuddled close to her mother, and her solemn blue eyes watched every move Jane made.

The conversation between the men cut through Jenny's thoughts. As she brought Mark tea, she lingered beside his chair. William was saying, "I'm fearful of what will happen if Bennett's excesses aren't curbed. I've tried talking to the man."

"Bennett?" Sally's laughter interrupted and the men turned, "But the council took care of him when they pushed his brothel into the gully last autumn!"

"Unfortunately that isn't the scope of his endeavors." William rumbled on. "Women aside, his biggest threat right now is the image he's projecting of the Saints."

"You're referring to the articles?" Mark asked. Jenny knew he was talking about the series the *Times and Seasons* had published.

Jenny couldn't hold back the words, "I wondered why the Saints' newspaper printed them."

William scrutinized Jenny before he said, "I wondered too—certainly there was nothing good to be accomplished."

"What were they about?" Sally asked.

"Well," Jane replied, "most certainly he informed the world at large that Joseph is a power to be reckoned with, that he now has at his disposal the power to avenge the wrongs inflicted upon his people in Missouri. He has demanded satisfaction for wrongs, and hinted Missouri land must be restored to the Saints."

William added, "We weren't in the States when this all happened and, to be certain, the information we've had is limited, but nevertheless we saw it as a war cry."

Heavily Mark said, "I'm afraid it was intended to be. I tried to get Joseph to stay Bennett's hand, but . . ."

Andy continued, "He's too powerful. He had Joseph eating out of his hand. Now it's too late to curb the man. Our only hope is that he will tire of the game and go home."

William frowned. "You seem convinced the man is insincere. Is there a possibility he's warping the mind of the Prophet?"

"A man of God being warped by a mere mortal?" Mark snorted, and Jenny, studying his face, saw how ludicrous the idea was. A secret question which had its birth in the articles slipped away and she sighed with relief. Obviously Joseph didn't support the articles. She caught Mark's sharp glance;

then William began speaking again, his voice rumbling slowly and thoughtfully.

"Mark, it's a different problem that plagues me today. You know Foster and I are engaged in trying to put up homes in Nauvoo as quickly as possible. Some of these poor people spent the winter in wagons and shanties. That ought not be so. You also know Joseph is determined the temple and his precious Nauvoo House will be built first. There's a real tug-of-war taking place. I'm here to ask your intervention."

Mark replied bitterly, "What makes you think I have any more influence with Joseph Smith than you?"

The man sighed, "I'd hoped." When he spoke again his voice was thoughtful. "He threatened to excommunicate any man who bought land without consulting him. I don't like some of his financial ventures, such as publishing his revised Bible. I honestly feel he's misusing the money he has collected to build the temple and the Nauvoo House."

Mark's shoulders straightened. "Law," he said sharply, "that's a serious charge."

"I know. Right now I wouldn't make it in court, but there're indications he's invested the funds in real estate and then sold at a profit."

"Is that all that's bothering you?" Mark asked.

"No. I'm deeply disturbed because of the workers on the temple site. They're living on parched corn. There's no income for the work, and they're practically starving."

Andy added, "These are the men who bought land on the Iowa side and then lost everything when the deeds proved to be fraudulent."

"Foster and I are fighting to get the materials to erect houses before winter. Now Joseph is saying the Nauvoo House must be built, that our salvation depends upon this happening." For a time, William sat with his head bowed to his chest. When he finally sighed and straightened, he looked around the room and muttered, "I tried to remonstrate with him about some other things. I can't tell you all, but I was sorely tried when he informed me in a lighthearted manner that if the results were as I feared, we could both go to hell, and that hell is by no means the bad place it's been pictured. To the contrary, Joseph thought it was a pretty agreeable place."

Jenny felt the shock of the statement, but Mark's eyes holding hers made her shiver even more. The question in their depths could not be avoided: he was challenging her commitment to Joseph. She turned away from them all with a tired sigh, but even then she knew the questions couldn't be avoided any longer.

That Monday when Mark guided his mare out to the main road, he had put William Law's conversation behind him. As he faced the sunshine cresting the rolling hills of Nauvoo, he thought of the blank page of the week stretching out before him. He knew of the items that needed to be placed on the page, he also knew of the problems that were pressing him, demanding their rightful place. His lips twisted in a rueful smile as he thought of the Prophet. With his usual pleasant smile, he would sweep Mark's page clean and dump another load upon it.

When Mark reached the office, Joseph was there. He was sitting behind his desk, and Mark immediately recognized that this was the day for confrontation. Joseph's suit for bankruptcy had been pushed aside for the last time.

After the polite words had passed between them, Mark took a deep breath and said, "The answer is *no*. Morally, for you to declare bankruptcy is wrong. If you insist on this line of action, you'll need to find another attorney to represent you."

Joseph's level gaze was unwavering. Mark was conscious of all the implications of his decision. What about Jenny's spiritual groping? Would her wavering spirit be crushed by leaving Nauvoo with her questions still unanswered?

Even as Mark realized he must push the hard questions at Joseph, he was aware of the risk he was taking. *Excommunication*. "Joseph, I feel I must warn you that there's a great risk to be taken in following this course of declaring bankruptcy. Are you prepared to subject your personal life to legal scrutiny?"

Joseph leaned back and grinned. "I see you've been listening to gossip."

"Is it gossip? I thought it common knowledge that you've begun teaching something the brethren are calling the spiritual wife doctrine. I—"

Joseph's chair thumped to the floor and with a scowl, he leaned toward Mark. "I've inquired of the Lord. Of course I knew the gossip. The Lord assures me that I *have not* committed adultery. Mark, judge not. If you are to remain in the good graces of the church, sooner or later you must receive this doctrine. The spirit tells me you are not sufficiently righteous to receive it now. Until that time, I suggest you join the Lodge and take up your religion."

"What are you referring to?"

"I've been advised you display no interest in becoming acquainted with the endowments and, specifically, baptism for the dead."

"You know I don't believe that way."

For a moment Mark was pierced by Joseph's questioning look. Then the Prophet said, "Mark, I'm considering sending out another group of missionaries. It's being made clear to me that I'm to gather money from all the people before the Nauvoo House can be completed."

Mark jumped to his feet, anger surging through him. Joseph's message was very clear. As Mark opened his mouth, there came the clear picture of Jenny's ravaged face and terror-filled eyes. Slowly he turned to pace the room.

On his second trip back across the room, there was a tap on the door as it was shoved open. William Smith stood there, wearing a wide, lazy grin. "Gentleman wantin' to see my esteemed brother, the Prophet. Better not keep him waiting; he looks important."

Joseph hurried out of the room and Mark slowly extended his hand. "Hello, William. I don't believe I've had a chance to talk to you since Missouri days. Is your family well?"

William nodded. There was a question in his eyes as he turned to survey the room. "I hear you're Joseph's lawyer. Didn't know you were here. Sorry for exploding in." A low grin moved across his face. "Keep hoping I'll catch him teaching some lovelies the secrets of the kingdom."

Mark ignored the remark and said, "I understand you've been involved in mission work. What do you think about the climate out there? Are people being attracted to Joseph, or is it the promise of land and freedom?"

William shrugged, still wearing his gleeful grin, and pushed on. "What do you think about the new doctrine?"

Mark replied, "I know absolutely nothing about it."

For a moment he looked disappointed and the glee disappeared, leaving his face surprisingly thoughtful. "Hyrum was terribly against it in the beginning. Don Carlos told me before he died that Joseph had prophesied to Hyrum there would be a witness given to him about the rightness of the doctrine. Well, sure enough, he got it." He paused to scratch his shaggy thatch of hair and pace the room.

His face was now very sober, nearly frighteningly so, Mark saw with surprise. Fastening Mark with a steely gaze he said, " 'Tis upsetting to say the least, but the *Book of Mormon*—"

Joseph stepped through the door. He eyed William as the unfinished sentence hung in the silence. Glancing sharply from

William to Mark, he said, with his voice cold and level, "And just what about the *Book of Mormon*, my dearly beloved brother? Just what had you in mind to say to Attorney Cartwright?"

Astonished, Mark looked at William and saw the sober expression replaced with wicked glee. His lips were twisted in derision. Abruptly he laughed and turned toward the door.

With a quick movement, Joseph was there. "Not so fast." His hand grasped William's shirt and twisted, pulling the big man closer. "William, you are not keeping your part of the bargain. I suggest you snug up your religion good and tight. You may need it more than you think you do." With a thrust he propelled his brother out the door and slammed it behind him.

Joseph was still trembling with anger as he turned around. Mark watched him take a careful breath, settle his collar, and move behind the desk. After another breath he said, "Just a little problem with Judge Adams. Mark, I'm afraid I'll be involved the rest of the day."

Mark could see that Joseph was in control now. He also saw the curiosity in his eyes, a deeper expression Mark didn't understand. Joseph spoke slowly, "I hope you didn't get the wrong idea. I wasn't thinking of sending you on a mission. I'm certain of your loyalty and I know you'd be willing, but I need you here."

Mark was on the street before he could identify that look in Joseph's eyes. It was fear. As he walked toward the stable he muttered, "Just maybe there's something to those rumors about William having something on Joseph. More than maybe, I'd say. Seems the words *Book of Mormon* has something to do with it."

Mark's thoughts were full of the scripture he had read that morning. It had excited him with a mysterious promise. When he had read it aloud to Jenny, she had just looked puzzled. Now Mark murmured the words. "So they shall make their own tongue to fall upon themselves."

CHAPTER 10

The spring morning was lovely enough of itself, Jenny thought, but another joy wound itself around her heart this late April day. She flicked the reins along the mare's back and smiled to herself. It was Mark. For the past two weeks he had acted like a man who'd dropped his sack of potatoes.

"God's in his heaven, and it's all right in the world," Jenny happily misquoted to the blue sky and wild plum trees.

A creaking, groaning wagon was approaching and she looked over her shoulder. "Morning, ma'am." The white-haired farmer yanked on the reins as they drew abreast. The apple-cheeked woman beside him nodded brightly. "You be Mark Cartwright's wife?"

Jenny nodded. "Saints?"

"No." For just a moment the smile dimmed and then she added, "We met your husband a-goin' into town when we're on our way with the milk. Nice, friendly fella." With another smile they were on their way, and Jenny realized they hadn't introduced themselves.

Snapping the reins across the horse's back Jenny said, "Must be our Gentile neighbors across the ravine, the Daniels." She rode on.

The Pratt farm was just ahead. Jenny studied the log house tucked back in the curve of trees and felt her curiosity welling up again. Sarah Pratt had become the object of gossip for the past two Relief Society meetings. Strange things those women could find to pick over—talking about her and Dr. Bennett. Thinking of Sarah's winsome face, her honest smile, Jenny shook her head and her curiosity grew.

The lane leading to the Pratt home was coming up. Jenny compared the story of Sarah's unhappy husband to her own cheerful Mark. They said he nearly committed suicide when he came back from his mission and heard the gossip.

Abruptly giving way to impulse, Jenny tugged the reins and

wheeled the buggy into Pratts' lane. She had only a few troubled minutes to sort the things she might say to Sarah, and then she was at the house.

Sarah was standing in the doorway and Jenny called. "Just passing this way. I wonder, would you like to go into Nauvoo for the Relief Society meeting with me?"

Slowly Sarah came down to the buggy and lifted her face. Jenny saw the frown, the questions in the clear gray eyes and waited. "I heard there's a bit of talk. Would it help or hinder if I were to go? I understand Emma's a mite sharp."

Jenny frowned. For a moment she was caught up in wondering why Emma was involved in the gossip. "Sharp? At times she seems so," Jenny said slowly. "I was thinking not of the gossip, but of your husband. I know he's better now, but remembering how unhappy my Mark has been, I wanted to encourage you."

Sarah's eyebrows arched in surprise. "I'm sure it isn't for the same reason."

"Reason?" Jenny frowned, beginning now to regret her hasty decision. She slanted a glance at the woman and saw her unexpected smile.

"Yes, I would like to be out this day. I've felt house-bound. If you could come in while I dress the tyke and smooth my hair—"

Jenny hopped from the buggy. "Wonderful!"

Sarah's little boy, Aaron, was nearly the same age as Sally's Tamara. He carried his boots to Jenny as Sarah went to change her frock. Over the little fellow's chatter, Jenny heard her horse nicker and Sarah said, "There's someone. Please—while I finish dressing."

Jenny opened the door and with surprise said, "Why, Dr. Bennett!"

He bent over her hand in a way that warmed Jenny's cheeks, saying, "We've not been introduced, but I'm certain you are Mark Cartwright's wife."

"And I know you only through—" she hesitated, and he grinned.

Sarah came into the room, looking startled as she saw the visitor. "Why, Dr. Bennett, what brings you this way?"

"I've a task out this way and I decided to check on my friend." He turned to lift the child. Over little Aaron's head he asked, "I haven't seen Orson. Is it well with him?"

Sarah paused only briefly. "Aye. But there's so much inquiry this morning, I'm beginning to worry. Is there a new story afloat?"

Dr. Bennett glanced at Jenny with surprise. "Oh, no," Jenny said hastily; she took a deep breath and felt she had much to explain. "See, Mark's been so . . ." They waited. "Well, not himself. Remembering what they said about Orson, I just felt . . ." The two faces were changing. Jenny saw Sarah's stony expression and saw the lines crinkling across Dr. Bennett's. He was amused!

"I assure you, my dear," he chuckled, taking Jenny's hand, "Sarah is just as virtuous as she claims to be. If you have a problem, let's just sit down and discuss it. You won't be able to shock me. Is it Joseph?"

Sarah interrupted, "Dr. Bennett, I do believe—"

He glanced at her and Jenny watched his face change. When he faced Jenny again, he said, "I'm on my way to do another task." Again he paused and studied Jenny's face. "I can assure you, my dear. At any stage in the problem, I can take care of the situation. There will be no danger to the mother and this will not prevent future increases, if she so desires."

"What—where?"

Sarah interrupted, "He has a kind of—hospital. Surely you've noticed the little building out on the flats. It's only about a mile and a half from town. But I can't believe that you've—"

Jenny was shaking her head furiously. "You're talking about taking a baby out, aren't you?"

"Abortion." Sarah's voice was flat. " 'Tis a common task in town." Her voice was bitter. "And a very common need."

"I can't believe that," Jenny said dully, thinking of her own great need. Now she lifted her head, realizing the unstated questions. "Dr. Bennett, I wanted to come to you for advice on *how* I could—And you think it's just the contrary situation!"

Sarah put her arms around Jenny. Now the hard lines were gone and she smiled. "Oh, Jenny, I'm so sorry. Seems we all think the worst of each other around here."

After Dr. Bennett left, Sarah seated Jenny at the table and made tea. "I do not condone all that's going on in the name of religion," she said as she sat beside Jenny. "The reason Dr. Bennett and I are friends is because he has been a friend to me in my need." Jenny watched her compress her lips as she picked at the lint on her sleeve.

When she lifted her head she smiled. "I don't want to hurt people or hurt the Saints' cause, but I have been misunderstood by people—" Again she paused and then took a deep breath.

"Just this one thing. I was hungry and nearly destitute while my husband was on a mission. Dr. Bennett befriended me. Contrary to the gossip, he was never my lover. Even if it weren't for my husband, whom I love dearly, John Bennett and I are too close friends for that."

Jenny, recovering from the shock she had felt, was beginning to understand the dark looks, the hinted questions of the women at Relief Society. "Sarah," she whispered, "I would like very much to be your friend. Perhaps in time, if you'll go with me, the others will forget the terrible stories and we'll all be friends."

She hesitated a moment and then continued, "But will you please tell me about Dr. Bennett? I know nearly nothing about the man except mentioning him makes the women giggle."

"Well, there are a few things I don't know. I haven't questioned him about his morals, and I don't know much about his past. He is a doctor. In the beginning he contacted Joseph. Some call him an opportunist, and it could look that way when you consider the way he eagerly walked into the church and started taking control of everything.

"But then, I have a feeling Joseph really needed him. There is a flair, a sophistication about the man. But he's also capable of being a sincere friend.

"He was secretary of the Illinois Medical Association at the time he came to Nauvoo. I don't condone the abortions he's doing, if you are wondering about that.

"Bennett wrote the Nauvoo city charter, and with his influence was responsible for getting it through the state legislature. He became mayor of Nauvoo, assistant to Joseph in the church, chancellor of the university, brigadier-general of the Legion and even had a revelation addressed to him, calling him blessed. You know about his brothel and how it was shoved over the hill. Dr. Bennett is also quartermaster general for the state militia; that influence enabled him to win concessions for Joseph's Legion, including cannon.

"His newspaper articles make me uneasy. I feel there's more to Dr. Bennett's aspirations than we know about. But then, I'm not a man and needn't worry myself on that score.

"I do believe that he and Joseph aren't nearly as much in agreement as they have been in the past," she finished thoughtfully as she gathered up little Aaron and smiled at Jenny. "I'm ready to go."

Mark was nearly to Carthage when he realized he'd forgotten to pick up the papers from Joseph's office over the store. Disgusted with himself, he wheeled his mount and headed back to Nauvoo. As he rode he realized it would be too late to return to the land title office in Carthage that afternoon, but he pressed on, muttering, "I'll get the papers and head for home. Tomorrow I'll take the shortcut and save an hour. Don't know why Joseph couldn't have held off until the end of the week when Clayton makes his usual trip. It would save my going."

He was still feeling like a disgruntled errand boy when he reached the store and took the back stairs two at a time.

The door at the top of the stairs was opening as Mark reached for the knob. He nearly collided with the scarlet-cheeked woman rushing past.

"Beg your pardon, ma'am!" he exclaimed, stepping back.

She paused and turned to him. "*I* should apologize," she insisted, attempting a smile.

Mark saw the compressed lips, the shadowed eyes. With dismay he said, "I've offended you; I'm terribly sorry."

"No, sir." Her reply was sharp and her hand descended on his arm. "But, if you will be so kind, please escort me."

Mark accompanied the young lady to her front porch. He was frowning as he started down the path to the office. "Miss Martha Brotherton," he muttered to himself. "You've been seeking counsel from Brother Joseph, and I don't think he's helped you at all. It's been a long time since I've escorted a young woman who galloped down the street in such a huff. I can't believe a grizzly bear would have failed to take to the bushes under that threat."

Within a week, Mark's questions about the encounter were explained, but all Nauvoo seemed to know before the information reached Mark. As he rode homeward, hashing over the story, he mused, "Of all the gossip that's circulating around about Nauvoo concerning Joseph and the twelve misbehaving, I suppose I've come as close as possible to having the evidence squashed in my face by an irate victim."

He paused, then reflected aloud, "So this is the little English lady who dared refuse the Prophet and Brigham, and even published their indecent proposals! The world knows now that there's one woman in Zion who didn't like the idea of being married to Brigham Young in this world or the next, especially since she wasn't the first one he'd approached with the same proposal."

He continued on his way home, pondering the advisability of telling Jenny the story. She had a nebulous feeling of change about her. He considered again and then regretfully shook his head with a wry grin. “Hands off,” he muttered. “Much as I want to do it my way, I’ll keep my mouth shut. Just as I was tenderly instructed by love, so Jenny must be.”

CHAPTER 11

On the day that news about the Boggs' shooting reached Jenny, she was with Sally.

After completing her shopping, Jenny had walked to Sally's home. For an hour she followed Sally around the kitchen as she worked, and it was nearly time for Andy to be home for his noon meal.

Jenny's chatter initially kept her from noticing how quiet her friend was. Finally, when Sally paused with hands on hips, Jenny asked, "What is it?"

Sally looked startled. "I was thinking—all this food, and only the two of us. Why don't you go after Mark?"

"Well, I suppose I could. He's carried a snack with him, but—" She paused, contemplating. "That's nice, Sally. I'll be back with him shortly." Jenny swung out the door. With a sigh of relief, Sally followed her to the door.

Jane Law was just coming up the path and Sally saw her hold out the packet of papers. Jenny shook her head, pointing to Sally. Jane walked up the steps. "Jenny said to give these papers to you. She'll return with Mark."

"Oh." Sally looked from the papers to Jane, searching the face of the older woman. She took a deep breath. "Have you heard the latest?" She was surprised at the waver in her voice.

Jane glanced at her sharply. "No," she said slowly. "Seems it's something you need to say."

"Could be it's nothing more than gossip, but there's a letter."

Jane's head came up. "From whom?"

Slowly Sally said, "Joseph. To Nancy Rigdon."

Now Jane's curiosity surfaced. "What's in it?"

"Well, first, Ann Eliza told me she'd seen it herself."

"They are friends," Jane said slowly as she carried her tea to the table.

"Right off, Nancy Rigdon told her that Dr. Bennett warned her that Joseph was going to approach her with a proposal to become his spiritual wife." Sally glanced sharply at Jane. She could see by the older woman's nod that she was familiar with the doctrine.

She took up her story. "Ann Eliza said when Joseph came to Mrs. Hyde's place—you know, the printing office where she and Dr. Richards live—"

"Together?" Jane was surprised. Sally took time to nod, and she began to wonder how much she should tell this woman. Right now she decided, eyeing her, it wouldn't be wise to tell her deepest secrets.

"Well, Nancy came to the printing office, but Joseph was busy. He had Richards tell her to come to the store later. But one of the men there leveled with her, told her what was going on and suggested she go ahead and find out.

"I'm guessing she didn't believe the fella at the time. Poor girl. Had confidence in him—Joseph."

"What do you mean?"

"According to Ann Eliza, Joseph took Nancy into the office and locked the door. That kinda scared her. She told Ann Eliza she was glad Mrs. Hyde had gone with her. He started in about how the Lord had given Nancy to him, and so on. There sat Nancy, crying and fussing. He tried to kiss her and she told him to stop or she'd scream and get the whole town there. Seems to have done the trick, 'cause he unlocked the door for her.

"Ann Eliza told me confidential-like that if it weren't for the letter, she wouldn't have believed such an outlandish story. Have you ever heard the like?"

Jane shook her head. "What about the letter?"

"Well, first off, Nancy told her pa and he confronted Joseph. Then Ann Eliza said Joseph kept denying everything until they waved the letter in front of him.

"First, the letter said that happiness was the object of existence, and that the path to happiness is virtue, faithfulness and holiness, and so on, including keeping all the commandments of God—which led him to explain *the* commandment. He also said a thing which was wrong under one circumstance was right under another. Ann Eliza said he was meaning you-know-what. So then he said everything God requires is right, no matter what it is. And that God is more liberal than we are ready to believe.

"Nancy told Ann Eliza this was all explaining what he'd told her in the office, about how she was to be his wife, because God had given her to him." Sally stopped and looked at Jane who was staring into her teacup.

After a long moment Jane lifted her head. "I don't know what to say; it's just so unbelievable." As Jane stood to leave, Sally saw again the dark question in her eyes.

Leaning against the doorjamb, waiting for Jenny and the men, Sally whispered. "She doesn't believe me!" But as she turned back to the kitchen, the ache around Sally's heart was easier. She wondered, if in time, she also would come to disbelieve the story.

Jenny was through the door first, "Oh, Sally, you just can't imagine! The prophecy has come to pass!"

Sally turned with the tureen of soup in her hands. Carefully placing it on the table she asked, "What?"

"Boggs has been shot. Already they're blaming Joseph."

Andy came through the door as Sally cried, "Oh, is he in trouble?"

The men were both shaking their heads and Andy said, "Joseph's preparing a statement for the newspaper. He'll admit to the prophecy—after all, he's a prophet. His statement will show his belief that Boggs was a victim of a political opponent, backing it up with the declaration that his hands are free from the stain of murder."

As they ate the soup, Mark said, "There are rumbles that Porter Rockwell is missing. If he's innocent of Boggs' blood, he'll save a lot of trouble for the Prophet if he just stays missing."

Later, Mark and Andy headed back to town together. They walked over the hill and through the temple grove, pausing to inspect the work at the site. Andy had recently been appointed as superintendent of the temple construction. Mark turned to Andy and said, "I know that Law's working independently, on houses and such. Is there a conflict between you?"

"Naw, my tasks keep me close to the office." Slowly Andy said, "I often wonder how long Joseph will tolerate a man of Law's stature. He's closer to being real competition than any other man around, even Brig."

As the men walked around the excavation, Mark remarked, "Since you and Law were at the house, you've been appointed to supervise the temple work. How do the complaints Law made that day affect you?"

"That's a strange question. You know I dare not let them if I am to work in peace and harmony with the Prophet."

"Does that disturb you?"

"No. I value my standing. Also, Joseph is ultimately responsible both to God and the people for any wrongdoing."

"That's small comfort when a man's hungry and can't provide for his children."

"Seems Joseph's doing the best he can."

"Seems—if you don't look at his resources and the comfort of his own life."

"Mark, he said, for all to hear, that if a man's hungry he can come to the Mansion House for dinner."

The two turned away from the temple and started down the hill. Mark was lost in thought when Andy said, "The temple reminds me that I need to say something to you.

"Mark, when do you intend to follow through? You realize, being as close to Joseph as you are, that everybody's watching your life. It doesn't speak well for a man's success when his attorney doesn't go along with the teaching."

"You're saying?"

"Every man in town who amounts to a hill of beans has joined the Lodge. Except for you."

Mark moved his shoulders uneasily. "Andy, I know. I'll admit I don't know too much about the Masons, but the Holy Spirit is warning me that something's wrong. I know it's a secret organization, but if you're my friend and you're serious about my joining, I need to know what I'm getting into."

"Well, it can't be bad," Andy's voice was rueful. "The ritual closely parallels the temple endowments."

Mark frowned. "That seems strange, particularly since the endowments came soon after the Lodge was started. Are you saying there's real religious influence in Masonry?"

"Of course, in a kind of oblique way. It's about God. It's religion without being a religion. It focuses on an individual helping himself, not keeping churchy rules."

Mark studied Andy's face for another moment. There was that second unanswered question. He plunged. "Andy, tell me about the Council of Fifty."

His lips twisted, "John D. Lee refers to it as the council of gods. Mark, it's all related to the kingdom." He paused and studied Mark's face intently before saying, "You know Joseph's received the revelation about setting up the kingdom. Nothing official's been done. There's a need to wait. Right now the time isn't ripe to reveal it.

"You'd have been in on it all, just like I've been, except you've bucked authority. It's common knowledge that Joseph's favorite attorney's saying things that makes it hard to talk to him. In a place like Nauvoo, particularly after the troubles the Saints have gone through, the disagreements are hard to take."

Mark sighed, "Andy, going back to the Masonic Lodge, I don't know the teachings. I only buck it because the *Book of Mormon* is against secret societies. Seems there's an awful lot of secrets suddenly cropping up in Joseph's church. If what Joseph claims about the *Book of Mormon* is true, then how dare he teach something that goes against God's word to him?"

"But there are other things that stick in the man's craw about you."

"Name a few."

"For one, why does it trouble you that Joseph wants to be called *General Smith* instead of *president*? The men were calling him *squire* while we were in Missouri. And why buck the Nauvoo Charter? Seems if Joseph's going to push the kingdom in another year or so, we might as well have the legal advantage to begin with."

Mark knew his face was reflecting surprise, and Andy studied him thoughtfully for a moment. "You know I'm talking when I have no business doing so."

Nodding, Mark said, "I don't ask you to betray confidence. But all this muttering and rumbling I hear in the background makes me uneasy. From a legal point of view, the charter's passing is nearly ludicrous. I can't believe the state legislators did that."

The two men finished the walk in silence and parted at the store. Mark slowly climbed the stairs. Joseph lifted his head as Mark walked into the room. "Must have been a heavy meal you had. Sounded like you weighed a ton walking up those stairs."

Abruptly Mark said, "Tell me about the Lodge. Why did you apply for a lodge in Nauvoo? I'm aware of the *Book of Mormon* stance against secret societies. What advantage is there to your going against it?"

Joseph leaned back in his chair and tented his fingers together while he gazed out the window. He was silent for so long, Mark thought he had forgotten him. When he finally glanced up, he wore a brisk, friendly grin.

"Mark, you're nearly apostate, you've bucked me so much. Do you realize what would happen to your family if I were to follow through according to what you deserve?"

Frowning Mark said, "I don't believe I understand you."

"You've questioned my judgment for years, even during the times I've functioned as a prophet. You won't go along with council to join the Lodge like the rest of the men. Your walking behind light is crippling your chance to gain the power of the priesthood."

"I am aware you are initiating some of the men into the higher teachings of the priesthood," Mark responded, "but Joseph, I haven't asked for that concession. In truth, just like Masonry, I'd question it deeply before I'd consent to being a part of it. It goes against the grain to say yes and then find out I don't like what I bargained for."

Joseph said heavily, "That isn't faith—either in the Lord or in me as prophet. If all of my members were like you, where would the church be?"

"If all the church members had the freedom to question and even make an ecclesiastical error without endangering their salvation," Mark countered, "perhaps you'd have an exhibit of more love and less fear."

Joseph thought for a minute and then settled back. The dreamy expression was back on his face. "All right, I'll tell you. I've felt for some time that the Lord was leading me to investigate Masonry. You saw me in Springfield. I was talking with Grand Master Jonas. I've discovered more than I'd guessed."

Again he was silent. When he looked up his face was radiant and for a moment Mark was caught, understanding for a clear moment the compelling charm of the man.

Joseph leaned forward and his voice was soft as he said, "Mark, my friend, for one thing I've discovered that just as God's Word has been distorted and filled with errors by the hand of those transcribers who had not the gift and calling from God, so Masonry has suffered.

"You know that I have preached of Adam receiving the priesthood back in the beginning days of creation. Now I will tell you something which is not common knowledge—Masonry is degenerate from the priesthood."

"Then how can you allow the Lodge in Nauvoo?"

"Oh, the first principles are trustworthy. Masonry is a steppingstone for something more."

"What are you referring to?"

Joseph glanced at Mark. "First, the principles. By the time I finish, you'll be wanting to join. We are beings lost to perfection. It is the business of living to make us into perfection, completeness. This is done through seeking the elder brother, first off. Now in Masonry, this isn't church—in fact, the belief is that there are many paths upward. Nowadays we have the understanding that there's only one true church, containing the keys to the kingdom. But it is still our cognizance to build upon these principles."

"What special knowledge do you have?" Mark asked slowly.

"That intelligence will save; that knowledge will lead to the eternities. When a man takes and builds upon what the Lord has given him, he begins to grow into communion with God—verily, even into a god himself.

"Granted, Mark, I see in your face the disbelief, but even Masonry supports the idea that it is by striving and working at the task of controlling our humanity and all the passions which must be perfected that we arrive at this state."

"I hear you say Masonry has taught you to become a god?"

"That and more. There's a certain center to it that allows a man to learn all there is to know, to understand and think like god. There is a light and knowledge hidden in this universe which we are obligated to obtain. I warn you, Mark, there's a very real danger for you to try to obtain these mysteries of knowledge apart from the true church.

"I also warn you that moral suicide awaits the man who tastes of the things the Lord offers through the church, particularly the priesthood, and then turns aside. You've gotten enough that you are in danger of this. I admonish you, enter the secret center where truth abides forever."

Mark got to his feet. "Joseph, I can't say I'm convinced. I've never had a desire to be a god. I don't even consider myself a good follower of the Lord Jesus Christ." He turned to go, but Joseph's words stopped him.

"Mark, you're near to being an apostate. I suggest you pull the reins up tight within these next few weeks. The Lord himself has led me to understand that for an apostate spouse there is nothing.

"If you leave Nauvoo, Jenny will stay behind. I know she's trying with all her heart to be a good Saint. If you leave—" he paused, and his eyes were curiously light, "your marriage contract will be null and void."

CHAPTER 12

It was raining—not the usual summer rain, but instead a cold drizzle that chilled the bones. Mark had left for Nauvoo looking as dismal as Jenny felt. She pushed more wood into the kitchen stove and went to the window.

"Here it's June, and I should be weeding the garden and gathering peas," she advised herself, rubbing her chilled arms. "Instead, I shiver and look for something to do."

She was caught with remembering, muttering, "If Clara were here, she could help me drive the clouds away. Or Adela." The thoughts threw open the door she had firmly closed that dismal day of the broken mirror.

Restlessly Jenny paced the floor, troubled but unable to stop the probing questions surfacing in her mind. After thinking she had moved beyond the book and charms, why did she still feel the pull?

"I've lived my religion," she whispered into the silent room. "Why is there no contentment? The others seem to be happy with their lot in life. I still feel like the young'un with my nose against the window of the candy store."

Jenny slowly pulled the broom across the floor, looking for a stray particle of dust. Reasons for feeling this way began to surface. "Power," she muttered. "I need to know what's out there. I want to do something that will make me feel a part of the whole universe. I liked the mystery, the charms. I enjoyed Adela's company. Now there's nothing."

She had taken her broom into the parlor. Pausing to lean on it, she looked at the table centered between the two chairs. Carefully arranged on opposite sides of the china lamp were the Bibles, hers and Mark's. Jenny's rested on top of another black book—the *Book of Mormon*.

Jenny went after the dustcloth. As she moved it over the table and around the pink roses on the lamp, she noticed the differences in the books. Mark's Bible was scuffed, and the pages curled invitingly outward. *It's almost as if the words were trying to escape,* Jenny thought with amusement as she looked at the smooth leather of her own Bible, still shiny with newness.

Joseph Smith told me to study the Scriptures, she thought. She had started, but somewhere along the way too many days had passed between the readings.

"I know why," she said thoughtfully. "I was just plain tired of reading about Nephi, and the books in the Old Testament were either listing a bunch of men I didn't know or saying things I didn't like. The wrath of God. The people getting swallowed up for doing a little stealing. If the Lord were around hereabouts, there'd be a mighty big hole in the ground. Leastwise, Joseph preaches a lot about thieving."

Her dustcloth slowed. What would happen if she were to read the New Testament first? She looked at Mark's Bible and couldn't keep from wondering why it looked as it did.

She put away the broom and dustcloth, washed her hands and settled into the rocking chair.

Jenny looked up when she heard the horse. She recognized Tom's shout and saw him riding to the barn. By the time he reached the back door, Jenny had pulled the teakettle over the fire.

Tom hung his coat on the hook behind the door and carefully tilted his hat against the stove to dry.

"What brings you out today?" Jenny asked, reaching for the skillet.

"Carried a message to Mrs. Pratt for the Prophet and thought I'd come this way before headin' back to town."

"Is her husband away?"

"Yes, but he's due back shortly. I think that was the information in the letter." He shook his shaggy head. "Don't like being mistrusted."

"How's that?"

"Joseph. He sealed the letter, like he wanted to make sure I wouldn't read it."

"That's strange." Jenny began placing dishes upon the table.

Tom picked up the open Bible she had placed there and looked at the page. "How's come you put all these lines under the words?"

"I didn't. That's Mark's Bible. I've been reading it."

"Don't you have one of your own?"

"Yes. I'd only intended seeing why the pages bulge. He has

pieces of paper inside and all these marks around verses. I had to discover why."

"Could ask."

"No." She took a deep breath and faced Tom. "Seems when we get off on religion, Mark and I disagree something terrible. I think he knows now how I feel about his picking at me. Every once in a while I see that look in his eyes, telling me he's all ready to give it all out and then suddenly he just closes his mouth and goes off."

"Guess if that's what you want—"

"I do and I don't. Tom, I don't want him shoving his ideas at me. Besides, they're scary."

"Why do you feel that? I've listened to him. Sure it's different, what he has to say; but somehow the strange things are almost believable when Mark says them. I'd expect him to back them up." Tom fell silent as he picked up his fork and stabbed at the potatoes and bacon. "I've been feelin' a mite disappointed in my religion lately."

Jenny studied him for a moment before saying, "Kinda like it isn't satisfying?"

Tom nodded. "I expect I'd not feel that way if it weren't for listenin' to Mark talk about his, and seein' he feels so different." He nodded toward the Book. "What did you read today?"

"Oh, lots. I got bored with Chronicles, so I started in with the New Testament. Just opened it to John. It was like a cow swallowing a pile of hay in one gulp. Now I find I'm back to chewing my cud. Some things stick, and I need to think about them for a time."

"Like what?" He reached for the bread.

"I read quite a bit in the first chapter before I discovered the *He* the fellow was talking about was Jesus. I get the feeling this all doesn't line up with Joseph's teachings. Guess I need to ask him. Tom," she continued slowly, "there's some things I really like about this man—Jesus. He seems so loving, but then He can be hard."

She fell silent, watching Tom eat. Then unable to hold back the words, she rushed on. "Mark had things written down on pieces of paper. Some I couldn't understand. On one piece he'd written references. I looked them up, and the thoughts all strung together were strange. According to them, God calls us into fellowship with His Son, and with love. God adopted us as sons through Jesus.

"Today I read in the first part of John that we have power to become the sons of God if we believe in Jesus. I wonder what that means, because I believe He's God's Son and I don't feel any power. Right now I'd settle for enough power to get rid of the rain."

Tom's brow furrowed in a frown. "Somehow I get the feelin' that isn't the kind of power the Book is talkin' about. Better go ask Joseph."

Jenny had forgotten the Legion was parading on the day she rode into Nauvoo to see Joseph. After she left the horse and buggy at the livery stable, she joined the throng of Saints lining the streets.

It was a clear, bright day, the beginning of summer. Despite the upheaval of construction the city was beginning to wear the homey look of grass, flowers, and garden patches. Neat picket fences and young fruit trees gave Nauvoo a look of permanence which had never existed in Far West.

As Jenny nodded to the Saints she recognized, smiled at the strangers, and studied it all, she was aware of more in the Saints' favor. The beginning of prosperity was evident in round cheeks blooming with health. Jenny also noticed bright parasols and bonnets with lace and plumes. More men wore black frock coats and tall dark hats.

The band was coming into view. The children surrounding Jenny were jumping up and down with excitement. Their dancing steps mimicked the prancing steps of the band and the smart steps of the Nauvoo Legion. She watched one youngster toot his imaginary trumpet while another swished a sword made of two crossed boards.

Jenny shouted across the blaring trumpets, "Your sons will make good soldiers."

"Aye!" their proud mother exclaimed, "both are members of the youth military corps. Joseph will have a fine army. 'Tis between four and six hundred young'uns right now."

The woman beside the mother said, "Did you hear how they nearly captured Nauvoo?" Mystified, Jenny shook her head. "Well, Joseph's oldest boy dreamed it up."

The mother took up the story. "The Prophet got wind of their intentions and routed the Legion to play at their own game."

"But unbeknown to the Prophet," her friend chimed in, "the boys were armed with every pot and pan in Nauvoo. When they came out of the woods, the Legion rushed them. The little fellas set up such a clatter with their ma's pots and big spoons that all the horses spooked except for old Charlie, and he daren't with the Prophet on his back."

She paused and cried, "And look, there comes the Prophet now!"

Jenny turned as the prancing black stallion moved into view. She was hearing the excitement sweeping the crowd, watching the people waving and shouting as he drew abreast. Jenny blinked at the glory of his uniform of blue and buff, decorated with gold braid and punctuated with the flashing sword and brace of pistols.

The shouting dwindled to a murmur as the Legion marched down the street. Beside Jenny the dark stranger moved and muttered, "I've never in my life seen anything like this."

"You know nothing of armies?"

He looked at her. "Madam, I am an officer in the United States Artillery. I simply mean there's no troops on the state level that could meet their match." Jenny couldn't control her pride, and his shrewd eyes saw it.

"Why this strict discipline, the ardor? Do they intend to conquer the world? I've not seen such enthusiasm even in our ranks." He turned to stare down the street, murmuring, "General Smith, the Prophet, huh? At this rate, in a few years they'll be thirty or fifty thousand—and that's a formidable foe, capable of instigating a religious crusade. I hope they don't intend to subvert the Constitution of the United States while we sit back and look on." He took one last glance at Jenny. "The fortifications Bennett's planning for this little monarchy are impressive. But I understand the Prophet is trying to oust him. Too bad for Joseph. Bennett seems to be an intelligent man with a great deal of courage. He'll be hard to replace. So Joseph's talking about an earthly kingdom of God, huh?" Without waiting for an answer, the man turned and strode down the street.

CHAPTER 13

"Who is this Jesus?" Jenny whispered into her pan of soapy dishwater. Her hands were moving slowly through the dishes, washing and lifting the china cups adorned with pink roses.

Her hands rested in the water as she questioned herself, "Matter-of-fact, Jenny, why are you so caught up with all of this wondering?" Her nagging curiosity had, during the past weeks, led her to complete neglect of the *Book of Mormon*.

What would Joseph say to that? Or Mark? His notes had aroused her curiosity. What would he think of his wife running to his Bible every morning as soon as she was alone, searching out the newly scribbled references and the intriguing words he had inserted?

"Mystery, mystery of Christ," Jenny murmured, acknowledging the tingle of excitement and wonder the words caused. Quickly she reached for the skillet, eager to finish her work and take up Mark's Bible again.

But she had other thoughts as well, ones she had discovered on her own. "Who *is* this Jesus? Joseph says He's a son of God just like we are; that Lucifer is His brother. The only unique thing about Him is that when He and Lucifer volunteered to go save the world because of original sin, He was chosen instead. Because of that, He had a special body, which God was responsible for when He came down to sleep with Mary."

Jenny gave a troubled sigh. She poured hot water over the cups and reached for the towel. "The only thing is, when I heard *that*, it didn't give me a turn at all. But now every time I pick up the Bible and read about Jesus living on this earth, healing people and telling them stories, even giving out strict sermons, I just get more curious."

Jenny held a teacup up to the sunshine and admired the way light rays put rainbows of pastel color through the milky china. "Hold it up to the light, you see more," she mused, rubbing her thumb across the cup.

She turned away to stack the clean dishes in the cupboard, but her hands were slow. In her reading, the word *believe* was causing the problem. *Seems I keep falling over it,* she thought.

As she picked up the broom and headed for the parlor, she addressed the empty room. "I find myself wishing more for Tom. I have a better time trying out my questions on him 'cause he knows enough about me that I can't get scared out of questioning. It's been a long time since he reminded me it's a sin to ask questions, or to doubt. Could be he's having some questions too."

By the time Jenny finished sweeping and dusting, she had decided to seek Joseph's advice. The decision left her satisfied, and she carried the Bibles to the kitchen table.

Yesterday she had found the paper marked "mystery of Christ," but after being caught up with all the *believe* verses in the book of St. John, she had put it back in Mark's Bible, carefully, lest he guess she was looking through his notes.

As Jenny thumbed through her Bible, she mused over her need for secrecy. "Mark shoves so much at me I can't accept. I'd rather find out for myself. I'm fearing he's been led astray. Like atonement."

Moving carefully through the Book, discovering she could now more easily find the references, Jenny followed Mark's notes leading her to Ephesians. She read, and then leaned back in her chair, slowly putting her thoughts into words. "This Paul is talking about having a knowledge of the mystery of Christ. Seems from his words, the mystery is that the Gentiles can have the same promises the children of Israel have—through Christ."

Now her eyes caught two things on the page in front of her, the first was a drift of words across the page—the *unsearchable riches of Christ.* The second was a scripture notation—Mark had written in: *Romans 9:30–32; 10:2–4.*

Jenny didn't know about Romans, and it took her a long time to find the passage; when she did, she read and then puzzled over it. The implications filled her with dismay. "It says the Gentiles who aren't even related to the children of Israel found righteousness by faith, but that the children of Israel didn't have righteousness because instead of using faith, they were using works of law," she murmured.

"Why, Joseph says we're the children of Israel by baptism, whereby the Holy Spirit changes our blood into children of Israel blood, and he teaches we're righteous by keeping the law and by doing the works of the church."

She was thoughtful for a moment before returning to Romans. Then she read: " 'For Christ *is* the end of the law for righteousness to every one that believeth.' " She closed the Book, saying, "There's that *believe* again. I wonder what it means?" All the other verses stacked up in her mind, like a towering pile of library books.

With a sigh she went back to the final verse Mark had listed, 1 Corinthians 2:7. "More mystery," she muttered. "Now it's talking about the wisdom of God being a mystery, and that if it weren't, the princes of this world wouldn't have crucified the Lord of glory." For a long time she struggled with the words *princes of this world* and *the Lord of glory.*

When she finally closed the Bible, it was with an impatient snap and a sigh of frustration. The verses she read told her that God was calling her into fellowship with His Son Jesus Christ. And all those other verses said the same. But they didn't tell her *how.*

Jenny replaced the Bibles, straight, just the way Mark had placed them. She cocked her head, looking at them, then decided. "I'm going to have to visit Joseph, even if I must chase him clear to Carthage.

"I don't understand all those verses, and some of them he's not been reading himself. I wonder if my saying carries enough weight to change the church. *By faith.*"

She grinned at the foolish picture of Joseph leading Jenny to the front and dramatically acknowledging the new revelation.

"Silly. Joseph thinks women are to be seen, not heard; and besides, it isn't a new revelation; it's been there all along."

On Relief Society day, Jenny decided again to approach Joseph with her questions. The meeting itself had spurred on the idea.

Since the day Jenny first urged Sarah Pratt to accompany her, the two had been riding together. Jenny was beginning to enjoy Sarah's company, but since that first time together, Jenny sensed there were many deep and hidden places in the woman's life.

Not daring to probe with questions which might raise the specter of gossip again, Jenny listened and learned. She guessed there were deep hurts, but she also saw Sarah's loyalty.

Sarah's references to her husband were guarded. Jenny knew he had been cut off from his apostleship. Soon she realized that part of the gossip was correct. Orson's quarrel with the

Prophet had been responsible, but surely it wasn't because of the rumor of Sarah's adultery.

This fine June day, Sarah loaded Aaron into Jenny's buggy, saying, "I'll not be riding back with you. Orson has a meeting with Joseph this morning and he will take me home from the meeting."

Her face was radiant with pride and Jenny said, "That's good, isn't it?"

Sarah looked astonished, paused, and then said, "Seems you don't know that we've both been rebaptized. Joseph has accepted us back into full fellowship."

"I wonder why he had to rebaptize you?" Jenny saw the embarrassment on Sarah's face and hurried on. "I was baptized in the Presbyterian church years ago. At that time I learned that just one baptism was necessary. When I joined this church I went along with the Prophet since he told me my former baptism was to be nullified by being baptized into the Latter-day Saints Church. Apparently the first was not any good to begin with."

Abruptly the symbols of sacrament and baptism surfaced in Jenny's mind. She was again seeing the sun-shot window with its glorious brilliance, and a finger of purple light beamed at the chalice of wine. Just as abruptly, overlapping the picture, came the same chalice—now dark and shadowed, bearing the horror of blood.

Jenny shivered and Sarah looked at her in concern. "Are you coming down with the ague? I'd thought we'd put that behind us."

"No," Jenny shook her head, "I was just thinking about baptisms and such. It's scary—this not being sure of things, only doing the best you can, and then wondering."

"You're talking about the church?" Sarah frowned and slowly said, "I know what you mean. The troubles of the past year have left me wondering. Might of been, if Orson hadn't needed so badly to be restored to fellowship, I'd have been gone forever."

Jenny studied her, remembering the talk she'd heard in Kirtland. "Then you don't really think Joseph is the Christ of this dispensation?"

Sarah thought and then sighed. "I've got to—there's nothing else to lean on, seeing the Bible's polluted and the true Christian church has been gone for fourteen hundred years. I felt the witness confirming it all, or I'd never have joined in the first place."

She looked curiously at Jenny and then asked. "Looking at your face, I'm thinking you need to be asking, too. Mostly you look like you've more questions than a person should be asked to handle."

"Are you talking about the burning in the bosom like Tom talks about?"

She nodded. "Have you been into the museum since it was finished? The mummies are on display." She paused and added, "You know, if you aren't interested in the burning of the bosom, there's the writings.

"You know the translation of the text they found with the mummies turned out to be the writings of Abraham. Did you know Joseph has finished the book and it's being printed now?"

They had reached Nauvoo; the horses slowed in the press of traffic. Sarah said, "There's Joseph's Nauvoo Mansion. Just looks like a nice home to me. Wish he could be satisfied for a time. This building a hotel seems a little too grand right now when we're still so poor."

"Mark says there's many visitors coming to the city." Jenny turned to look at the neat home, adding, "Sure, it's bigger than most of us will ever have. I suppose his needs are greater."

"I hear Emma's expecting again." Sarah sighed. "Poor woman, I'm really sorry for her with feeling so badly and then having to contend—" She glanced sharply at Jenny, looking embarrassed. "I—where are we going for meeting today?"

"Rooms over the printshop. Good thing there's places like that. Our need for meeting places is getting bigger."

"Soon as they get Joseph and the twelve moved into their offices in the temple things will open up for us. Meanwhile, the men come first."

"It will be soon?"

"Before the winter's out, at the rate the building's going on."

Jenny left the buggy at the livery stable and the pair walked the short distance to the printing office.

As soon as they entered the meeting hall over the pressroom, Jenny realized Emma was in one of her unpleasant moods. With a sigh she whispered to Sarah, "Looks like no sewing today. Shall we wager the subject she has on her mind?"

"I just object to her personal questions. For the past month she's been after information. Everyone is squirming."

"Why? Certainly there's nothing to worry about." Astonishment was in Sarah's eyes, "You haven't heard—" but before she could finish, Sally approached.

"I hope you've been keeping a tight ship," she cautioned Sarah and Jenny. "Emma's got everyone on the carpet today.

"You've heard all the outrageous things Dr. Bennett's been saying—that horrible confession Joseph insisted he make before the brethren in the Masonic Hall. Andy says the men were ready to take him apart, limb by limb when Joseph started pleading for him. So much for that confession. That man's going to be—" she gulped as Emma Smith approached.

"Sally, my dear, must we have gossip? Are you really criticizing the Prophet for moving with compassion and interest in the salvation of one soul? Joseph will be here in just a few minutes. Will you women please be seated?"

She turned away. Before Jenny had time to react to Sarah's raised eyebrows, Joseph came into the room. Jenny felt the excitement sweep through the room. She felt it touch herself even as she studied the faces of the women around her. Sarah Pratt was the only woman not viewing the Prophet with eyes filled with adoration. That troubled Jenny as she settled herself to listen to Joseph.

Wearing a slight frown, Joseph was terse, to the point. "All of you women have heard of the confessions of Dr. Bennett. I consider you representative of the city's virtuous women. I've come to beg your help. The disclosures Dr. Bennett has made are a reflection upon his character, but they will be damaging to the virtue of this city and to the Saints who are living their religion and seeking to please God.

"Remember, a little tale will travel many miles, and it can set the world on fire, particularly our world. I urge you, my dear Saints, please listen to me. At the present time a truth involving the guilty must not be aired. We are attempting to hold our influence with the world, and spare ourselves extermination. The brethren wish me to caution you to be prudent, wise, virtuous. If there is a need to repent, then reform, and do so in a way which will not destroy those about you." With a quick wave of his hand, the Prophet was gone and the room was silent.

Jenny was aware only of Emma's stern gaze. Although the woman was studying every person in the room, Jenny felt as if she were on trial. All too clearly she was remembering Emma's interruption the evening Jenny approached Joseph in his office while Mark was in England. Today Emma was wearing that same expression.

Sarah and Jenny walked down to the street together. When Orson arrived Jenny watched him bundle his wife and son into the buggy before she made up her mind. She turned back to the printing office, saying, "I'll just pick up a copy of the *Book of Abraham* while I'm here."

Jenny could hear the press running as she stepped through the doorway. The door leading into the pressroom was open and Jenny walked toward it.

Willard Richards and Mrs. Hyde were facing the press. Just as Jenny stepped forward, Mrs. Hyde slipped her arms around the man's shoulders and lifted her face. Jenny watched the kiss and all the implications burned through her. She started to turn and bumped against the table.

Nancy Hyde dropped her arms and turned with a smile. "Oh, sorry, I didn't hear you." The smile faded and she studied Jenny with a quizzical look. "You've been listening to Joseph's talk?"

"Yes," Jenny said slowly. "About—I thought it was all gossip."

"Remember what he said," Nancy replied sharply. "The Prophet's interested in keeping things nice and smooth around Nauvoo. Now, what do you want?"

Jenny blinked and through stiff lips murmured, "Oh, Sarah Pratt mentioned the *Book of Abraham* is finished. I thought I'd just pick up a copy."

"Joseph's just taken the entire batch. You'll have to see him for a copy." With a flounce she moved away and because Jenny couldn't think of anything to say, she turned and left the office.

On the street she realized her mind was a jumble of confusion. Bible verses were flying around in her head, along with the sure decision that she must tell Joseph about the ones he hadn't read. And she thought of Nancy Marinda Hyde kissing Willard Richards right under Joseph's feet as he talked. Jenny's forehead pricked into a troubled frown.

Slowly she whispered, "I'd thought all the gossip was just a way to pass the time of day. Now I wonder. How do I tell Joseph without getting Nancy into trouble?"

CHAPTER 14

Jenny still hesitated on the street, her mind a jumble of confusion. But as the beauty of the summer day intruded, she took a deep breath and looked around, delighting in what she was seeing. The buildings revealed the mix of brick and lumber, the smell of old and new; on the streets she saw the contrast of growing greenery and busy people.

Nauvoo was becoming a respectable city. Respectable? She cringed. The new brewery was being built under the sanction of Joseph Smith, while in the background the temple was being erected as quickly as possible.

At Relief Society, when Emma wasn't within hearing distance, there had been a great deal of criticism of the brewery. Mrs. Ingersoll had summed up the discussion by saying, " 'Tis either right or wrong. According to the word of wisdom, 'tis wrong. We'll have to throw out the brewery or the temple."

Jenny looked at the lorries and buggies moving briskly down the street and tried to forget the problem of the brewery. The lumber and kegs of hardware the lorries carried spelled prosperity, as did the buggies loaded with gaily dressed women and serious men.

On the bluff overlooking the river the Nauvoo House was rising. Very soon the hotel would be ready for the first occupants—the Prophet and his family.

At the other end of town, on the hill overlooking the city, the new temple was being built. The limestone gleamed in the noon brilliance, making Jenny blink.

As she shaded her eyes and turned away, Joseph Smith came out of the store and started up the stairs to his office. She hurried after him. Hearing her steps, he turned to wait. "I've sent Mark to Carthage to register land sales."

"It's you I've come to see." Jenny was surprised when his face brightened.

In his office, she was suddenly caught by memories. Silently she studied the room, thinking of the poor cubbyhole of an office in Kirtland. This office was spacious, and there were other rooms on this floor—probably offices for Mark and Mr. Clayton.

Jenny turned to meet Joseph's quizzical expression and blurted out, "It's been a long time, hasn't it—that we've known each other. Since Bainbridge days."

"Yes, Jenny it has. You were such a scrawny thing, bony legs and arms and big eyes." He looked around his office with satisfaction. "We've both come a long way. I'm here with more of this world's goods than I ever expected to have and you—" He studied her until she felt her face warm.

"Little Jenny has become a beautiful woman, a very beautiful one, who, I imagine, could have anything she wanted. What do you want, Jenny?"

"The *Book of Abraham.*"

For a moment he looked astonished and then began to laugh. "How in character, and how much I've forgotten! Are you still the serious little girl inside?"

Jenny considered and finally admitted, "I suppose I am. Somehow there's never been that much to laugh and frolic over." She thought for another moment and the jumble of her mind began straightening itself. "I guess I'm too much caught up with the things happening under the surface of life."

"What do you mean?"

"The wondering about all that makes life move on—God, and what He's about. More than anything, what I can do about it all. Power. You used to be like this; don't you ever think this way anymore?"

He settled lower in his chair and seemed to forget her presence. "Yes, but the whole situation is changing for me. The power is there; now my problem is learning how to harness it up like an old team and plow my own field just the way I want it. Jenny, I have power in abundance."

"Do you still want to give it out to people?"

"It isn't so much giving it out; it's teaching people how to lay hold of it for themselves." He shot her a quick look.

"You said once that knowledge leads to salvation. I think that was what you were referring to when you told me to read the Scriptures. But power—" She stopped abruptly.

Joseph sat up and leaned forward. "What is it, Jenny?"

"I'm saying all the things I *didn't* want to say. I came here to talk about the Scriptures and all that's going on in Nauvoo, not about power."

"Have you been reading? Tell me what's troubling you."

"The Bible, Joseph. It says that having Christ doesn't do us any good if we're justified by law; it only means we've fallen from grace. Then I found something about the mystery of Christ which I don't quite understand. The Bible talks about the Israelites trying to establish their own righteousness by law instead of by faith. The same section says the Gentiles have reached righteousness through faith in Jesus Christ. Joseph, it's so confusing! It all seems just the opposite of what we are learning."

"Then it's obvious, my dear, if it's confusing you, it's wrong. I've told you the Bible hasn't been correctly translated. Why don't you just follow the teachings of the *Book of Mormon* and forget about the confusion?"

"But you said to read the Scriptures, and that's what the Bible is. There's even parts of it in the *Book of Mormon* and the church accepts it. And something else. The Bible talks about our being adopted by God. That doesn't sound like we're children of God to begin with. Then it talks about how the law can't clear the conscience, that the law isn't reality; it's only a shadow of reality. Joseph, sometimes I feel so confused and frightened."

"Seems you need some help understanding."

"I suppose."

"Maybe for right now you'd better stop the reading."

"But the strange part is," Jenny said slowly, "that as confusing as it is, it is also very appealing. I *want* to read it. If you could just answer my questions."

"Which ones?"

"Well, these. But I want to bring more. I want to read the new book and then talk about it."

Jenny got to her feet and moved restlessly around the room. "Joseph, I must admit, I just don't fit in around here. I've tried to belong. But the rest of the women, well, they seem so serene and happy in their religion. All my religion does for me is send me looking for more. I guess besides power I want to be content like these women, feeling like they do, like the queens of heaven."

"Jenny, be patient! The Lord has given us much in the priesthood that will help you reach the contentment you desire." For a moment he studied her with a frown and abruptly Jenny was aware of her impudence. This was the Prophet Joseph Smith and she was treating him like the young'un in South Bainbridge.

She moved to apologize, but he continued, "What you are

referring to will in these last days be realized, but not in an abstract way." He leaned forward and placed his hand on hers. "Jenny, it isn't a vision or a promise on paper. Our kingdom and the manifestation of it will be real. You talked about the law being a shadow of reality. Well, very soon the reality of the unseen next world will be revealed to you.

"Jenny, God will make me to be God to you in His stead. Now, will that suffice? I will take you to heaven with me if you will keep all the ordinances of the gospel. I will be your salvation and you shall be queen of heaven."

He got to his feet and paced around the room. "Jenny, I am certain that the Lord is preparing you to accept the teaching; the evidence of that is indicated by your restless spirit. Remember, the Lord wants to show you the way to feel like a queen of heaven. Let this suffice for now."

When Jenny left Joseph's office, she carried a copy of the *Book of Abraham* under her arm. Her head was still full of all Joseph had said, particularly the exciting story the new book carried.

She had nearly reached home before she realized that all Joseph had told her had completely chased the puzzling scriptures from her mind.

It was midafternoon when Mark returned to Nauvoo. He carried the receipts directly to Joseph's office. Walking into the room, he found the Prophet pacing his office. With a nod, he said, "Come in, Mark, give me some advice."

After Mark settled in the chair, Joseph said, "I've been going over this Bennett situation. The tide of feeling is arising against the Saints in an alarming fashion."

"Like Missouri?" Mark asked, watching the man's face. Today Joseph was dressed in a manner befitting his prophet role. Mark noticed that his stiff white collar pointed to the beginnings of a fleshy second chin. He also decided that Joseph's sensuous lips and smooth hands were more noticeable when his face was relaxed and his usual dominant nature bent to another voice.

Joseph didn't answer Mark's question. As he continued to pace the room, he picked up a newspaper and said, "I've been so caught up reading the good articles about myself that I've nearly been caught short."

"What do you mean?"

He struck the newspaper. "Since Bennett was ousted, he's gone to fighting through the papers. I fear that vile tongue. All lies, but we can't afford the luxury of letting them poison the minds of the public. We've too much at stake."

"You're speaking of the upcoming state election?"

"Yes, that and more. Perhaps I was too hasty back in January when I let it drop that we'd vote Whig this election. There's much to risk." He paused to look at Mark and added, "If only you were part of the Lodge and the planning committee, I'd feel free to confide in you."

With amusement, Mark said, "I thought attorneys enjoyed a higher level of confidentiality."

He was shaking his head, "Not when matters of the Lord are at hand."

Mark decided to level. "You know, Joseph, it's that very thing which seems so wrong to me—perhaps the biggest reason why I can't go along with this. A church should be the last institution on earth to be restricted or secret."

"That isn't the only problem." He tossed the newspaper to Mark. "See this? Seems we had a military officer witness the drilling of the Legion. He questions our excellence as if it were monstrous, asking if we intend to take over the States. He goes on to prophesy that we'll be a fearful host with the intent of subverting the Constitution of the United States, implying we'll roll over them all. He's calling us religious fanatics, intent on shaking the country to its center."

Joseph reached for more papers, and Mark said, "You've been saving these?"

"Of course. Now, listen to this one. This is a January 1842 paper from Springfield. I won't read it all, but the important criticisms are against the Army of Israel with the warning that I should let someone else lead the army, and stick to church business. Here's the quote: 'His situation in Illinois is . . . more dangerous than ever it was in Missouri. . . .' " He lowered the paper. "Mark that's a threat. Do you see? I have a job for you.

"Now here's another. The *Alton Telegraph* is complaining about my issuing a proclamation. They're saying: 'commanding his followers to vote . . . bold stride against despotism.' " The expression he turned on Mark for just a moment was one of bewilderment. In that brief flash, Mark was astonished. Joseph didn't see in himself any of the attributes of a despot.

With a sigh, Mark said, "I suppose you've decided I should write rebuttals to all these articles."

"No," Joseph folded the papers and tucked them in a drawer. When he stood up, he looked at Mark and said, "I want you to go on a goodwill tour for me. There're a few things I have on my mind that need to be presented to Washington before next session. You might as well deliver these papers in person. Stop in Springfield and anywhere else you think this is necessary. Just let it be known you are the attorney of General Joseph Smith and then let them do the talking and the questioning. A goodwill trip like this will be more valuable to me right now than a million dollars." Mark was still staring at him, not believing what he was hearing. Joseph continued, "Go talk to John D. Lee; he might have some suggestions for you."

Mark's voice was flat and even as he said, "You command me to go on a goodwill trip for you, to dig up all the information I can about how people are seeing the Mormon movement. You expect *that* when you know what my views are? Joseph, I suppose you expect me to defend you and build up your cause in Washington and Springfield and every hamlet in between."

"I expect it," Joseph said calmly.

"Then you listen to me first. Laying aside all the stories about the visions and the gold plates and the revelations, you haven't a leg to stand on in front of God. Yet you want me to build up the church in the eyes of those fellows out there."

Curiously Joseph looked at Mark, "Why do you say I haven't a leg to stand on?"

Mark reached across Joseph's desk and picked up the Prophet's Bible. "Listen to what God's Word says and then compare it to what you are saying God says." He took a deep breath and turned the pages of the Bible.

"For a starter, Matthew 5:44 says: 'Love your enemies, bless them that curse you, do good to them that hate you . . . that ye may be the children of your Father which is in heaven.' And then the words of Jesus in 7:17, 'Every good tree bringeth forth good fruit; but a corrupt tree bringeth forth evil fruit.' A few verses on He says the corrupt tree will be burned.

"Joseph, I could stand here all night reading until my voice gives out. This Book is full of verses saying that Jesus Christ is God in the flesh, come to this earth to die for our sins. Jesus also tells us that 'God is spirit: and they that worship him must worship him in spirit and in truth.' "

Mark closed the Book and replaced it on Joseph's desk. Then he faced the Prophet. "There's another section, found in Romans 9 and 10. Paul is talking to the Gentiles about his countrymen, the Israelites, and the words show his heart is nearly breaking as he says Israel has pursued a law of righteousness, but it isn't working for them because they are doing it by works instead of faith. With their own proud hands they think they're working their way up to God. Paul admits the children of Israel are zealous for God, but their zeal isn't based on knowledge. Somehow they missed the point. We don't *make* righteousness; we *submit* to God's righteousness. Paul is practically shouting out the words on paper, 'Christ is the end of the law so that there may be righteousness for everyone who believes.' "

Leaning forward Mark continued, "Prophet, the Bible clearly says Christ delivers us from the law, yet you not only want the law, but you even want the sacrifice. What a kick in the face to the God who came to die on the cross!

"While we were in Missouri, Joseph, I began to understand that Jesus Christ wanted me to stick around the Mormon camp and say to everyone who would listen that Jesus Christ is Lord, the Lord bearing salvation to all who will *believe*. I'll go, Joseph, but I'll talk on my own terms, saying what I want to say. I'm just as curious as you to know what the people think."

CHAPTER 15

It was late when Mark rode home. The long rays of the afternoon sun cut through the outcropping of trees bordering the bluff. The light laid bars of yellow across the pasture green, pointing to the cattle grazing there.

Still stunned by Joseph's order, he could think only of the unimportant. Who would plow the garden patch for Jenny when the last of the pumpkin was harvested? What would she do with the extra milk? What about her night fears?

And in the end, just before he reached his own lane, Mark knew his responsibility to Jenny demanded that the hard things, the unspoken, must be said before he could leave.

Jenny was reading when he walked in, so deeply absorbed she scarcely lifted her head. He saw the table set and the supper pot simmering on the back of the stove.

Taking a deep breath, Mark asked, "What are you reading?" He carried the kettle to the table as she lifted her face. He bent to kiss the bemused expression away.

She finally eluded his lips and said, "Oh, Mark, it's so fascinating! See, here's a drawing from the parchment. And right here's a list telling all about the meanings of the illustration."

She pulled him over to the rocking chair, placed herself on his lap and began to point out the pictures and tell about them. Mark nuzzled her neck and tried to push aside the numbness in his mind.

"See?" Jenny pointed. "Did you know this star Kolob is a *governing* star? I didn't know there was such a thing. It's nearest to the place where God lives. Oh, Mark, think of that! It makes me feel high and lifted up, almost there beside God. Isn't that what people really want deep down inside? Joseph didn't say as much today, but I'm sure that's what he's feeling. Not just the need to know about God, but the need to be right there close to Him."

Mark rested his head against the back of the rocker and

watched Jenny's animated face. It was full of the sweep of mystery he had seen so often, but today there was a brightness, even hope, in the depths of her eyes. For a moment he felt his spirit move with uneasiness and then she pressed her cheek against his.

Holding her close, thinking of all that needed to be said, he mused aloud. "There's a section in Jeremiah that's running in my mind. God tells the people a man isn't to boast about riches or any such thing, but instead to boast that we know and understand God."

Her curious eyes questioned, examining his face, and then she returned to the subject, saying, "There's more: I saw illustrations about Shinehah, the sun; Kokob, a star; Olea, the moon; the Kokaubeam, which stands for stars. Think of that! Not the stars so much, but that God and Abraham talked together, just like a couple of men. In fact, Abraham said he talked face-to-face with God. I guess that's one more instance where man saw God."

"One more?" he asked puzzled.

"Well, Joseph saw God and His Son, Jesus Christ."

"In several places in the Bible, it says no man has seen God; in fact, no man can see God *and live*. Jenny, doesn't it bother you that Joseph teaches so much that is in contradiction to the Book which he claims to accept as God's Word?"

"But he believes only insofar as it is correctly translated."

"Jenny, we've gone over that before. Joseph is saying that the *Book of Mormon* is the most correct book on earth. It contains much from the Bible. Isn't he contradicting himself? It seems strange to think a God of power unable to keep His word safe for mankind. Seems particularly strange when that Book says His word will never pass away. I find myself having to accept either Joseph's word or God's word; I can't have both because they disagree."

Jenny moved restlessly and he knew he was crossing the unseen line which they both knew existed. "Jenny, my dearest wife—" He paused to cup her chin in his hand and force her to meet his gaze. "I must tell you that Jesus Christ is God. He is God come to this earth for the purpose of reconciling men to himself. He did it by paying the blood sacrifice required for sin. Jenny, do you see? Sin is terrible—it isn't something we recover from, or overcome, it is something from which we must be rescued. God must swoop down like an eagle and snatch us up to himself."

Jenny got off Mark's lap and walked to the stove. "Mark, I

don't want to hear your ideas. You are throwing me into complete confusion. I've got to believe that God has put the right way within me and all I need to do is follow. Joseph has been helping me understand. I must admit, I've been miserably aware of my need for God. It started as a realization that I didn't have the power to control my life at all. Most certainly, I'll admit I've gone a curious route searching for God and the happiness which is my due. But in all my groping, I know I've found the right way now."

He looked at her curiously, "What has convinced you it's right?"

"Because my spirit and his spirit are in harmony. There's none of this turmoil inside when he speaks."

"Is it possible your spirits really are the same spirit? It sounds that way. If so, it's probable Joseph is just as unhappy and miserable on the inside as you are. Jenny, I've lived with you long enough to see the agony of your life. I've held back my words because you've rejected everything I've said to you, but now I must point out something you'll have to consider."

Getting out of the rocking chair and going into the parlor, Mark picked up his Bible and returned to the kitchen. He murmured, "That's strange. I had a piece of paper here; it must have fallen out. No matter, I know the section well enough." He thumbed through the pages, and read aloud. "It's in 2 Corinthians 11:4, 'For if he that cometh preacheth another Jesus, whom we have not received, or *if* ye receive another spirit, which ye have not received, or another gospel, which ye have not accepted, ye might well bear with *him*.' Then Paul goes on in verse 13 to say, 'For such are false apostles, deceitful workers, transforming themselves into the apostles of Christ.' The next verse says that Satan himself is transformed into an angel of light." He closed his Bible and looked up.

Jenny was trembling, tears running down her cheeks, but her hands were clenched into fists. "Mark, you are trying to destroy every bit of soul peace I have. I will not allow you to tear me apart in this way."

"Jenny!" He came and caught her hands. "I'm not forcing you. I have only this tremendous desire to say to you these words. You do with them as you see fit. God himself will not insist you take the right way, worship the right Christ. He gives you the freedom to choose, and I can do no less."

Her eyes were moving, studying his face, seeking a confirmation, and he gave it. "Jenny, I love you, and I'll always stick by you, no matter what."

"But why are you saying these things now, while our dinner is getting cold?"

"Jenny, Joseph has given me a job to do which will take me out of Nauvoo for a time."

She was silent for a while, searching his face. "Will I be able to go with you?"

"No. I'll probably be gone for months. There are still two weeks of July left, and he wants me to leave immediately. He mentioned my being back by December."

He watched a cloud of dread move over her face. "We could go back to Springfield," he said gently.

She was shaking her head, managing a smile. "No, Mark, it's best. Without Joseph's help and counsel, I am fearful I'll miss the way. Soon they'll have the baptismal font open at the temple. You know how they feel about this ordinance. I must be here to participate. Besides I—" Her chin trembled and she flew into his arms. "Mark, oh, Mark, please—"

She could say no more, and Mark folded her close. The time was so short.

Within the week Mark had settled his affairs at the office. He turned over detail work to Clayton, Joseph's secretary. The legal affairs went to Higbee, who would handle Joseph's petition for bankruptcy.

Tom volunteered to move in with Jenny. Still heart-sore, Mark saw the arrangement satisfactory to the point where he wondered whether he would be missed.

Finally at the stage stop, Jenny's white face and trembling hands made him turn to Tom with genuine warmth. "I don't know what I'd do without you."

Tom grumped around the farm for the first few days, and Jenny was grateful for his sympathy as she listened to his discourse on the subject. " 'Church widows,' they call them," he said. "Seems like every man in the church gets the tap sooner or later. Take John Lee. He'd only been back in the area a couple of months. Didn't even have time to complete his house before the presidency was tapping him on the shoulder ready to send him out. He went, too."

"I'm surprised they haven't sent you out."

"I'm too dumb to talk and convince."

"That group waiting for the stage didn't impress me as being overly educated. Seems all it takes is a *Book of Mormon* under the arm." Jenny sighed and turned away, but she was grateful for Tom's presence.

Mark had been gone only a week when Jenny took the horse

and buggy into Nauvoo. She was scheduled for another meeting with Joseph Smith in his office. As she set out, she glanced at her satchel to make certain it held the list of questions, the *Book of Mormon* and the new *Book of Abraham.*

Continuing on her way, she mulled over the questions. *What was Jesus referring to when He said He'd come so that we might have life more abundantly?* Jenny sighed and addressed the horse's back. "There I go again, asking questions about the Bible when I should be remembering he said—"

As Jenny went up the stairs to Joseph's office, she tried to put a pleasant smile on her face, tried to feel anticipation. Her thoughts were wrapped around Mark, wondering where he was and what he was doing. She swallowed the miserable lump in her throat.

She tapped on Joseph's door and heard a feminine voice call, "Come." Jenny stepped into the room. There was a tiny woman in Joseph's chair.

She grinned impishly at Jenny, saying, "Surprise! The Prophet had to be out of town today, seeing it's time for his petition for bankruptcy to be filed. Since he said I could do the job as well as he could, well, here I am."

"Oh," Jenny said, disappointed. "We were to be studying the doctrine of the church and the books. I could come later."

She shook her head, saying, "I'm Patty Sessions, midwife and mother in Israel."

"What does that mean?"

Taking a deep breath, Patty said, "Well, the job's a new one, but Joseph's expecting those of us who have the teaching to start instruction with the young women of the church who will be learning the doctrine of the priesthood."

"I thought that was for the men only."

"Well, the priesthood is, but some of the ordinances involve the women."

Jenny placed her satchel on the floor and sat down. "I've been hearing from Sarah and some of the others that the men are being initiated into the endowments right now. Seems it's not fair, when the women want the privileges, too."

"Won't be much longer before the women are included. One of the rites is what I want to talk to you about today."

She came around the desk and Jenny studied her, remembering that she had seen her at the Relief Society meetings. Patty was a tiny, slender woman; with her quick movements and bright eyes, she reminded Jenny of a sparrow.

She smoothed her graying hair and then folded her delicate

hands over her gray calico dress. "Much of what I'll teach today has already been said from the pulpit and discussed at Society meeting. Jenny, there are three degrees of heaven. You know that in order for a man to enter into the highest degree and thereby be granted the privilege of having his own kingdom, he must enter the new and everlasting covenant of marriage. If he does not, there will be no possibility of having a kingdom and he shall have no increase."

"What of those who won't live up to their religion?" Jenny asked softly, thinking of Mark.

Patty shrugged. "There's no possibility. If it's your spouse and there's no chance of winning him to the church, you best be looking farther afield; otherwise you'll be left out, too."

"You're suggesting I leave my husband?"

"Yes. It's been revealed to the Prophet that since these marriages weren't preached over by an elder having the priesthood, meaning the ordination from God, then they are invalid anyway."

"But not under the Constitution of the United states," Jenny protested.

Patty shrugged. "Jenny, the kingdom of God will be around long after the United States ceases to exist."

For a moment Jenny closed her eyes. She saw the white lace and the yellow roses, and heard her vows echo through her mind: *I will cleave to no other as long as we both shall live.*

Patty was speaking again, but her words held no meaning. Jenny stored them in her mind without giving them further thought.

When the meeting with Patty finished and Jenny turned to leave, Patty reminded her, "Next week at the same time; the Prophet promised he'd be back by then. Don't worry, he'll have some good advice for you."

Later, on her way home, Jenny impatiently flicked the reins across the horse's back and the words crowded to the surface of her mind. Patty called it the spiritual wife doctrine. Funny, she'd heard the term, but it had always been mentioned with snickers.

So a woman couldn't go to heaven without her husband taking her there! Several women referred to their husbands as their saviors. Curiously Jenny considered the thoughts Patty had planted. She hadn't snickered when she spoke the words. Her earnest eyes had sparkled with a zeal Jenny couldn't doubt. The unbelievable became real. Some of the men in the community really had been selected by God. Jenny shivered at the memory, just as Patty shivered, saying, " 'Tis a privilege a man can't take lightly, and a woman daren't refuse."

Jenny thought of Mark and sighed. She spoke her troubled words into the afternoon air. "Mark says he loves me, but he never will consent to this." She trembled, remembering Patty's advice.

CHAPTER 16

When Jenny drove her rig into the yard, she saw Tom's horse in the pasture. Surprised, she glanced at the sun. It was only midafternoon. She stepped out of the buggy just as Tom appeared.

"I'll handle it," he muttered. He started to lead the horse into the barn.

"Tom, it's so early. Is something wrong?"

"Tell you in a minute," he growled. She watched him unharness the horse and lead it to pasture. When he returned he took her arm.

The unusual gesture alerted Jenny. Wheeling around, she grasped his sleeve, saying, "Mark? Is something wrong with him?"

"Naw," he growled. "Joseph stopped by the stable on his way to his bankruptcy meeting and told me I was picked for a mission."

"Tom, when?"

"There's a bunch leaving in less than a week and I'm to be going with them. He's calling it a training session—intends to make me into a missionary. Says I'll only be gone for a month, but that isn't the point. I'm no more missionary material than a hog is."

"What'll I do?" Jenny whispered, looking around the barn, seeing the half-completed pig sty and the hay that needed to be stacked. But deep inside she was thinking of the dark night hours.

"That's what I said. But Joseph, seein' he's responsible, said he'll send a boy to take care of the chores until I get back."

Later that evening when they were seated at the table, Tom said, "I feel you fear being alone more than the work."

"I do. Oh, Tom, it's so far to the nearest neighbor! At night I hear the coyotes howl. Even the screech-owls in the forest make me nervous."

"Aw, you're a big girl," he chided with a grin, but she saw the worried frown and nearly confided in him her dark night visions and the strange laughter. "Dreams," he would say. Dreams they might be, but dreams didn't walk through the house. She shivered as she fingered the talisman tucked in her pocket.

And that next week when she went to her meeting with Joseph, he looked at her and frowned. "You're all alone out there. I see you're troubled. If being alone is that bad, I think I'd best take you home with me."

He turned and she followed him up the stairs to his office. "Just a minute; I've an order to write," he murmured.

As she waited, Jenny moved quietly around his office, looking at the display of arrowheads and bones, the fragments of pottery marked with strange figures. She studied the line of books and pulled one down to read.

The windows were open to the summer breezes. She watched the curtains move and listened to the clop of horses, the shouts of playing children. With the sudden shock of awareness, Jenny turned to look at Joseph.

Now it seemed the sounds of life beyond the room marked their isolation while the intimacy of their surroundings pressed in upon her.

She watched him write. He had discarded his coat, and his heavy shoulders strained at the light linen of his shirt. His hair curled across the back of his neck, and she felt her throat tighten.

Abruptly he lifted his head and grinned. As their eyes met she saw the grin disappear. She turned away, disturbed and ashamed of her response to him. Sitting down, she fingered the book and wondered if she dared beg off today's meeting. Would a headache do?

"I'm sorry I've kept you waiting." His voice was brisk and businesslike. Jenny turned as he pulled a chair close to the desk. "Patty Sessions told me that you had a good meeting last week, but that you've questions you want to ask. Well, I've a little instructing to do; then I need to step out for a time. Do you wish to ask your questions first?" She shook her head, realizing she couldn't remember them.

Joseph continued after a sharp glance at her. "Patty said she began by instructing you in the covenant of marriage, given to the priesthood. You understand that the covenant of marriage is eternal, unchanging, don't you? The Lord has asked me to unfold the covenant to the people a small portion at a time.

In due time, all of the church will be involved, but for now only a favored few. Also, I must instruct you, that the specific privileges are assigned by the Lord."

"But Mark won't follow the church!" Jenny burst out in torment. "That means I'll never have a chance to fulfill my calling. Talking about my being a queen of heaven is as bitter as gall. I've no chance. Why are you instructing me in the way when Mark is the one who must be convinced?"

Joseph was very sober as he shook his head and sighed. "Jenny, I've tried. One of the most important reasons I offered him the position as my attorney was in order to bring him back into the fold and allow him the privilege of the priesthood. Just before he left for Washington I had a most unpleasant interview with him. There is no doubt in my mind that Mark is apostate at heart."

Jenny bit her lip and tried desperately to control her tears. Joseph put his hand on her arm, "I know, my dear, it is a difficult situation. We can only pray the Lord will give him opportunity to see the error of his ways. Meanwhile, there's you to think about."

Getting to his feet, Joseph went to his bookcase and removed a large leatherbound book. He put it on the desk and opened the cover. Jenny attempted to put aside her own personal unhappiness. Trying to show interest, she leaned forward to watch.

Inside the book was a collection of heavy paper packets, folded and sealed with wax. She tried to see the imprint on the seal as Joseph thumbed through the sections. When he reached the packet labeled *Armyeo*, he stopped and sat down.

Folding his hands across the open book he began to speak again. "Jenny, I want you to know that the presidency and the council have met together to pray over these most solemn matters. The Lord's blessing must rest upon each decision, but there's more to it than that. We have His personal instructions as to His will. Now what I am going to say will seem to you to be lacking, but in the press of time and circumstances—" He paused and a flicker of amusement touched his face. "I must say, the Lord is much more abrupt and to the point than we humans are." He turned back to the book.

"Before me is this document, containing His special blessings for a number of women in the community who have been selected to be initiated into the covenant of eternal marriage. Jenny, your name, the secret name given by the Lord himself, is on the front of this packet. What is inside is to be revealed to you by the Lord's instructions. When you are ready to obey the Lord and accept your responsibility in this ordinance, I will allow you to break this seal."

"What will I have to do?" Jenny whispered.

"You will be taken to the Masonic Hall, where you will be united with me for eternity. This ceremony will provide for a spiritual, eternal marriage relationship between the two of us. Do you understand this? It is God's will. He has given me the responsibility of assuring your place in glory." He paused until she nodded and then continued, "The conclusion of the matter is this: For you this means a union complete, with worlds and kingdoms and powers forever. Amen."

For a long time, Jenny stared at the packet on the desk. She was only vaguely aware of Joseph leaving the room.

The curtains moved and Jenny looked at the curious seal and the name, *Armyeo*. For some undefined reason, the strange name stirred a mysterious response in her. As she concentrated on it, her thoughts winged backward in time.

There was that scrawny little girl proclaiming to the world that she intended to marry Joseph Smith. And then there was the talisman and the wax.

Abruptly Jenny threw back her head and laughed. "Through the powers given I nearly settled for an earthly marriage. Now he's offering to marry me for all eternity. I'll have the best of heaven and earth. Here my darling Mark and there—" Again she was laughing, trying to strangle her giggles in her hands.

When Joseph came into the room, Jenny was composed, sitting rigidly upright, with her hands folded. At his question she said, "Of course, Joseph. I'll be proud to be your queen. What must I do?"

Together they walked down the street and climbed the stairs to the Masonic Hall, located in the second floor of Brigham Young's store.

The large chamber was dim and gloomy, with strange emblems and symbols decorating the walls and the long table spread across the front of the room. A solemn line of dark-coated men stood at the end of the room with hands clasped before them.

As Jenny took her place in front of them, their quietness made them seem unreal, nearly unearthly, until she saw the quizzical gleam in Brigham Young's eyes.

It was a strange ceremony. The book holding her name linked to Joseph Smith's was spread between them. With her hand resting lightly on his, they listened to Brigham Young's sonorous voice lifting to the ceiling. "Brethren, and sister Jenny, we are gathered here in the sight of God to join in eternal union Joseph Smith and Jenny Cartwright. This marriage, decreed by heaven, was commanded of the Prophet by an angel bearing an unsheathed sword. Dare mortal man fight heaven's command? Let no mere human challenge the edicts of the eternal. What God has joined in this ceremony is to remain throughout eternity; the consequences of shattering this union will result in eternal damnation. Amen."

As soon as the ceremony ended, Jenny collected her horse and buggy from the livery stable and started for home. She did not need Joseph's warning of secrecy. That strange ceremony scarcely penetrated her mind with reality.

Even if she were so inclined to talk, who could be expected to believe it had truly happened? She murmured, "Neither token or script to indicate the transaction. Seems I can only whisper my confidences to Luna."

In the days that immediately followed, the heat of July blasted into August. The first day of August in Jenny's hot little house she was miserably aware of the deficiencies in her life. First, there had been no letter from Mark, and Jenny was consumed with fear for him. Joseph's promised boy hadn't come to milk the cows and cart the product away. The profusion of the garden begged for attention. And there was only Jenny to face the task.

Standing on her back steps, wiping a weary hand across her brow, Jenny irritably tugged at her sticky cotton dress and wondered why she couldn't button the bodice.

She heard the crunch of feet on the path paved with river pebbles and turned. It was Joseph Smith, smiling, immaculate, and confident.

She met his happy greeting with crossness. "Where is that fellow who's to do the chores? I milked three cows and poured it all as slop for the pigs. Milk in this hot weather is nauseous."

His grin disappeared, "Jenny! I'd forgotten! I promise you, there'll be someone here tomorrow." He came up the steps, saying, "You'll have a sunstroke out here. Come inside."

"I should be saying that, Joseph!" she snapped. He looked startled and immediately she apologized. "I'm sorry. Nothing is going right today." He stared at her gaping bodice and she yanked at it.

He was following her into the house as she said, "I was ready to wrestle with the pail at the well. The rope's frayed. There's not even water to offer." Without a word, he picked up the pail and went out the door.

Jenny was smoothing her hands over her hair as he came in with the water. She splashed water against her hot cheeks. "Thank you, Joseph."

Puzzled, she watched him over the top of the towel as he set the pail on the bench. Taking a deep breath, she said, "What brings you out this way so early this morning?"

"You." She blinked, and he continued. "I haven't been able to get away. With the press of things right now, it seems we'll have to snatch our moments when we can. Fortunately, both Mark and Tom will be gone for some time."

She hung the towel and faced him. Rubbing at the frown she felt forming, she said, "What on earth are you talking about, Joseph? I didn't call for you. If it's just to discuss Scripture, I'll gladly forego that pleasure until cool weather."

"You are uppity today, my dear. Unfortunately I haven't all day to tease you back into good humor. Come now."

He reached for her hand and she backed away, slowly saying, "Joseph, you're talking like a husband of twenty years, reminding a willful wife of her duty. Do I hear you correctly?"

He looked astonished. "That's one way of looking at the situation. Unfortunately my station leaves neither the time nor energy for the niceties of life." She was still backing away, too shocked to think. He studied her face closely and, turning, went to sit in the rocking chair. "We'll have it your way. Come here."

Jenny focused on the rocking chair and she saw herself and Mark there. For a moment, as she smiled over the memory, her heart was twisted with loneliness.

Joseph was reaching for her hand, and reason returned. She stepped backward and said, "Joseph, you have no right to come into my house in this manner."

"But I do. Have you forgotten that day just one week ago?"

Suddenly she saw the total picture. All the fragments of gossip and innuendo began to have meaning. But surely not! She looked at him. Seeing the guileless smile, she could not doubt him.

"Joseph, our marriage is a spiritual marriage, one for eternity only. That's right, isn't it?"

"No, Jenny. That is only part of it; there is a very real earthly marriage too, and I want you as my wife, now."

She closed her eyes briefly and he said, "I know what you are thinking. It isn't adultery. The Lord has told me so. It is all right for us to have our fun as long as we don't tell anyone about it."

As she pressed her hands against her eyes, she felt his hand upon her arm. She put her fingers against the pulse in her throat and tried to sort through the jumble of thought and emotion. Abruptly a word filled her mind—*talisman.*

Blinking, Jenny looked around, "Did you say—"

"I said, come here."

Thrusting her hand into her pocket she felt the medal burning against her skin. Slowly she began backing toward the door. The knowledge of what she must do was there—not accepted or questioned, just there. She must rid herself of the talisman if she were ever to be free of Joseph's power over her.

The rocking chair creaked. She looked at Joseph, just beginning to push himself up out of the chair.

Jenny had just put her hand on the doorjamb when she saw the chair slip backward on her polished floor, flying out from under the surprised prophet. One second she hesitated; then she ran.

She threw herself over the pasture fence, sobbing as she streaked across the pasture toward the trees. Only one thought filled her mind. *The talisman—get rid of the talisman!* From where had that thought appeared?

The dark trees edging the bluff were coming close. She ran into them, feeling their branches snatch at her hair as their roots tripped. Jenny flew on, only guessing Joseph would be behind her.

Nearly fainting now, Jenny reached the edge of the bluff and felt the wind tear at her as she gasped for breath. Far below was the surging water of the inlet. For a moment, as dizziness swept over her, Jenny braced herself against a tree, groping in her pocket with trembling fingers. The talisman. She felt the hot, burning link and knew what she must do.

Taking a quick step to the tall bank, Jenny raised her arm to throw the talisman. "Jenny!" She knew his call. She hesitated. Again his voice echoed off the trees, coming nearer. Quickly she spun, and immediately the earth gave way.

She felt the swoop of air. Trees spiraled past; grass, water, and then sunshot sky. The cold shock of water took her, swirling her downward.

She was engulfed in a flood of purple. As the water broke over her, she saw the chalice, tipping, throwing purple wine over her body.

CHAPTER 17

Jenny heard his voice before she opened her eyes, saying, "Like a shooting star she came over the bluff, whirling with that black hair streaming out. How she ever managed to hit the one deep spot in the river, I'll never know. Could have been the rocks."

A woman's voice answered him, and Jenny opened her eyes. There was a giant's wet boots and britches planted beside her and a white-haired woman kneeling over her. The woman said, "Why, you're Mark Cartwright's wife."

Jenny tried to speak and choked. The whole of the giant emerged. He knelt and rolled her over. "Get that water out." When he helped her into a sitting position, she met his worried blue eyes and saw a question in their depths.

"A miracle!" he added. "There's rocks along the river. A miracle Pa and I were fishing." Now she saw the old gentleman hovering in the background—Mr. Daniels.

He stepped forward and she saw the same troubled question. She was still wondering about their expression when Mrs. Daniels said, "Lands, child, you're shivering!"

"And this morning is hotter 'n blazes." Jenny could only nod at the giant as he lifted her to her feet. "Ken ya walk or shall I pack ya?"

"Walk," she managed; taking a deep, choking breath, she set her feet to follow Mrs. Daniels. In the cabin, beside the remnants of the breakfast fire, Jenny dried herself. She donned the cotton dress belonging to the little woman moving around the kitchen, and then Jenny sat down to watch her.

Shaking her head, Mrs. Daniels was stirring up the fire and caring for Jenny's clothing as she talked. " 'Twere a miracle. I heard the splash and the menfolk yelling." She paused to cast that questioning look at Jenny.

With a sigh Jenny started her explanation. "I was running, in this heat, dizzy. I had something in my hand and I was trying to throw it in the river. I slipped," she finished lamely.

Mrs. Daniels had been reheating the breakfast coffee and she carried a cup to Jenny. With the first sip, Jenny's stomach went into immediate revolt. She jumped to her feet and fled to the door.

When she returned, dizzy and trembling, Mrs. Daniels led her to the bedroom. "You caught?" she asked as she wiped Jenny's face.

Jenny puzzled over the strange statement and finally pushed herself upright. Mrs. Daniels was saying, "Could be because you're not used to coffee."

"Could be," Jenny murmured, remembering the smell; then she asked, "What do you mean, *caught*?"

"With a young'un," Mrs. Daniels said, sounding as surprised as Jenny was feeling.

"A baby! after all these years!" She grasped Mrs. Daniels' arm. "Could it be? We've been married six years and we've given up hoping. Could it?"

Mrs. Daniels' face relaxed and she was smiling back at Jenny. "Could be cause for being dizzy, too. Now you just lie back and rest a time. The menfolk had to take the milk into town, but I suspect they'll be looking for your husband without being told."

Jenny's excitement withered. Dully she said, "He's gone." Then she rallied. "But if it's so, then I'm not really alone. Oh, I can hardly believe it! If only he'd come soon," she added wistfully.

Late that afternoon the young giant took her home. For a minute, considering the events leading up to that plunge over the bluff, Jenny longingly considered the invitation to stay. But there was only the loft where the giant, Alson, slept, and the tiny bedroom where she had rested.

As the wagon rumbled down her own lane, Jenny found herself glad for the long afternoon shadows. Joseph would be at home with his family.

When Alson lifted her from the wagon and said, "Ma'am, those cows and pigs are needing attention. I'd be happy to oblige you."

"Oh, would you? I am still shaky. And if you'd care for the job, I'll hire you to do the chores until Tom returns."

He nodded with a pleased grin. "I'm obliged."

When Jenny entered the kitchen, she immediately noticed the rocker upside-down. For a moment she hesitated in the doorway while the words and the emotions of the morning tumbled through her. Guilt surged over her as she recalled her strange, unwilling response to Joseph.

Frowning now, she righted the chair and sat down. *Why the guilt, if this is God's will for me?*

No answer came, and it was late when Jenny left the rocking chair and went to lock the doors and close the curtains against the night.

During the past lonesome nights, Jenny had formed the habit of murmuring a chant against evil as she went about the evening ritual of preparing for bed. Tonight the words began to slip easily from her lips. "God of light, protector of the hearth, spread circles of power—"

Abruptly she stopped. She was in the parlor, looking down at the table where her Bible lay. Would there be more power if she were to find words from it to recite each evening? The scenes from the morning flashed across her memory. With a shiver she picked up the Book and carried it into the kitchen.

She placed the lighted lamp on the table and bent over the Book. Her fingers were hesitant, unsure as they turned pages, first one way and then the other.

One word caught her attention and her fingers found the beginning. Isaiah 8. She read slowly, " 'And when they shall say unto you, Seek unto them that have familiar spirits, . . . should not a people seek unto their God? . . . To the law and to the testimony: if they speak not according to this word, *it is* because *there is* no light in them.' " And farther down, the phrase, " '. . . and *they* shall be driven to darkness.' "

"Familiar spirits," she murmured slowly, remembering there was talk of such in the green book—spirits sent to help those seeking power. For a moment another thought pricked her mind and then was gone. "Light, darkness," she puzzled as she went up the stairs to bed.

The words were with her in the morning. Now she could look at the previous day and marvel.

The heat was still upon the Mississippi lowlands. Jenny saw it in the mists rising from the river to cloud the forest. Alson Daniels came; she heard the clank of his bucket.

When he left, she went out to gather from her garden; sharply conscious that busy barnyard sounds contrasted with her silent house. She washed the vegetables at the well and sat in the shade to eat them. Her stomach was in revolt again, but today she welcomed the sign. She also welcomed the tight frock and hugged herself with excitement.

"If only Mark would write!" she sighed. "I want so badly to

tell him." She stood bemused, drawing a memory picture of his face and painting it with delight. Suppose there were a letter at the post office right now? She nearly gave in to her impulse to go to town, then quickly changed her mind at the thought of a chance meeting with Joseph.

A plaintive cry came from the pasture, and Jenny went to lean across the fence. "Oh, you scamp," she said with a sigh. The tiniest lamb had crawled through the pasture fence. Now he was bawling his fear from the dark forest side of the fence. "You baby," she called, crawling over the fence and heading across the pasture. The remainder of the flock contentedly chewed their cud in the shade of the apple tree.

Jenny paused before jumping the creek. She was hearing the murmur of water washing over smooth stones. It was peaceful, all of it. Again she heaved a contented sigh and started after the lamb.

"Come, little scamp," she called, stretching beseeching fingers through the fence. The pink mouth wailed his protest while his spindly legs wobbled. With a sigh of exasperation, Jenny went over the fence.

The woods were dim and cool. After pushing the lamb through the fence, she followed the creek into the trees.

The rock she selected was flat and inviting. Bracing her shoulders against a tree, Jenny settled back to listen to the brook and the birds. A tiny warm breeze touched her face; she closed her eyes against the flickering pattern of leaves, and the sounds grew faint.

When Jenny opened her eyes it seemed darker. Getting to her feet she stretched, surprised at the sense of well-being that enveloped her. Her dream had been filled with yesterday's kaleidoscope of purple and silver.

Until the dream, she had forgotten the images of yesterday. Only now the memory surfaced, stamped upon her mind. Never would she forget that spiraling downward while purple light and flashing silver surrounded her.

Now settling back on the rock, she allowed the memory to flow through her, wondering at the meaning. "Purple—the church window. At the time I was baptized there was that window and the chalice and the wine."

Suddenly, as if yesterday's water swept over her, she intoned, "I baptize thee—" Jenny frowned. The words wouldn't come. But there, as if caught in a balance scale, she recalled the baptism in Joseph's church compared with that first baptism. There were no purple-shot images, no hint of a hovering just beyond her touch. She recalled only mud and river slime, and meaningless words.

Jenny got to her feet, still trying to remember that word and tie it to the fleeting impressions. She finally shrugged and turned away from the creek. As she bent to pick the graceful frond of fern at her feet, she heard, "Jenny." It was the lilt of the wind. "Jenny."

She turned and searched the dark shadows shifting with wind-born light. "Jenny!" The call was louder, insistent, and she looked beyond. A flash of red shone through the trees. Dropping the ferns, Jenny ran, not thinking, merely triggered by her deep need.

The shadows grew darker and Jenny slowed, picking her way through bushes and rocks. The figure in red was waiting on the next rise. "Adela!" Jenny called, and when she repeated the name, it was a scream of frenzy.

"Oh, how I've longed to see you!" Jenny stopped. Now pressing fingers against her forehead, she tried to remember why she must see Adela.

The woman moved, her smile familiar and warm. The same red chiffon floated softly about her figure, lifting with the breeze. Jenny took a step and hesitated.

Her words were stilted as she said, "You look so familiar in that old red dress, why—"

The lost words were before her. "That's it. The name of Jesus. In the name of Jesus I was baptized." She raised her delighted smile to Adela. "I was—" The red figure seemed to be retreating, dimming.

Jenny hurried forward, across the rocks, up the slope. Now sunlight slanted through the trees and she stopped. The light clearly outlined the scene before her. The red chiffon still swirled, the woman still smiled. Jenny blinked and passed her hands across her eyes.

The dress was the same, but those perfect features were sagging, twisting. Before her eyes, Adela became a wizened figure, fading, disappearing. Stunned, Jenny whispered, "Jesus."

Then she was brought back to herself by a clap of thunder. In terror she listened to it growing, exploding, then rumbling away. While the air was still filled with the sharp odor of sulphur, the rain burst upon Jenny, and she ran.

In the days that followed, Jenny doubted the vision her memory periodically cast before her, but she didn't forget running into the house, panting and crying. She also recalled groping through the storm-dimmed room until she found her Bible. And in the days that followed, she didn't forget the comfort she felt simply from holding the Book.

CHAPTER 18

Over the dishpan Jenny murmured, " 'Jesus saith unto him, I am the way, the truth, and the life: no man cometh unto the Father, but by me.' " She lifted the cups and watched the soap bubbles burst and disappear. "Adela said there were many ways to worship God. Why did she disappear like these bubbles?" The truth was clear, and Jenny could only whisper in awe, "Jesus."

Very sober as she continued to wash dishes, Jenny pieced together in her mind all that she had refused to consider before. Did it matter that Adela was a familiar spirit? With a sigh Jenny said, "Yes, it does matter. I thought she was a friend. She was everything I admired—beautiful and strong."

Jenny's mind nudged her with another fact. Adela had power, and if she were a spirit instead of a real person, this meant the promise of power for herself was a lie—or was it? Could there be something she didn't understand?

Jenny moved uneasily and stared out the window. Was power to order life beyond the scope of human beings? Immediately Jenny remembered the pressure Adela had used to get her to take the vows at sabbat. That oath, the blood in the chalice—even now they made her shiver. But there was another thought. Jenny whispered it to herself, her voice filled with awe. "I simply said the name of Jesus. I wasn't even thinking of Adela—my head was full of baptism and purple light. I said 'Jesus,' and Adela disappeared." Abruptly Jenny was trembling.

As soon as the kitchen was tidied, Jenny fled to the only comforting presence in the house, her Bible.

She read the Gospels, feeling as if she were looking over Jesus' shoulder. With awe she watched and listened, as thirsty as the woman at the well.

Daily Jenny flew about her work and then settled to read, conscious only of her desperate need. But the reading was not without pain. There were hard words which caused days of uneasiness and questioning: *sin, the wrath of God, judgment; believe, trust, the blood of Jesus.*

In her silent house she brooded in isolation and then fled, desperate for companionship. One hot August day she took her light buggy to Sarah Pratt's home.

As she let the mare amble down Sarah's shady lane, Jenny was thinking the trees looked as limp as she felt. But then she had a reason. She grinned and flicked the reins.

Instead of taking the mare to the house, Jenny stopped the buggy in the shade of a tree and left the horse to graze. Just as Jenny reached the front door, she heard Sarah's voice coming from the shady side yard and circled around the house.

Hearing a strange voice, she hesitated momentarily. Then, with a shrug she stepped forward just as the woman laughed and said, "Sarah, such outrage! Why do you make a fuss about a little gossip. Even if it isn't true, people will speculate. Besides, you should consider it an honor. Why, I've been his mistress for four years now."

Jenny gasped and as the women turned, said, "Oh, I . . . I'm sorry. I didn't mean to sneak up on you."

The stranger threw back her head and laughed. "Don't look so appalled. I'm not."

Looking surprisingly relieved, Sarah hurried toward Jenny. Taking Jenny's hand she said, "Do come sit in the shade. This is Lucinda Harris."

While Jenny frowned, wondering why the face was familiar, Lucinda drawled, "Yes, I was in Far West while you were there. Seems we didn't have time to get acquainted. I suppose I knew most everyone because we were part of the early settlement. Your husband is the attorney. Didn't I hear that Joseph sent him to Washington to present another bill?" She turned to Sarah. "Do you suppose that's where Joseph's gone?"

Sarah shrugged and addressed Jenny. "I suppose you've heard the latest news, though it's been so long since I've seen you."

Jenny muttered, "I haven't heard any news for ages. I've not even had a letter from Mark."

"Oh," Sarah added quickly. "Then you don't know that Joseph's disappeared. Don't look so alarmed! It's that Boggs affair."

"If only he'd kept his mouth shut," Lucinda said. "Coming out with his prophecy about Boggs being shot and then broadcasting his views hither and yonder when it did happen."

"I'd heard about that," Jenny replied.

"Well," Sarah continued, "as you know, Boggs didn't die. Now Governor Carlin's issued a writ for Joseph's and Porter Rockwell's arrest."

Lucinda's smooth voice cut in. "The Nauvoo Charter came to the rescue again. They were released under a writ of habeas corpus and the city council stepped in and issued a new ordinance which required Nauvoo court to inquire into the validity of the writ."

Sarah said, "Well, I know the charter was designed to help Joseph's cause, that's obvious, considering the trouble in Missouri. Somehow it doesn't seem quite right. But by the time the sheriffs returned from seeing Carlin a second time, Joseph and Porter were both gone."

Jenny lost the thread of conversation; her mind was busy with the implications. She breathed a deep sigh of relief. Perhaps by the time the legal problems simmered down, Joseph would have forgotten all about that piece of paper in his office.

Jenny soon found an excuse to leave Sarah and her friend. She turned her rig onto the road and headed for Nauvoo, still hoping for a letter from Mark.

The afternoon Tom rode his horse back into Nauvoo, he was conscious only of being tired with the bone-weariness of discouragement and physical fatigue. He was so busy planning his speech to Joseph that he scarcely noticed the first hint of autumn this September day.

He was still mulling over his dilemma when he reached Joseph's Mansion House. Although it was still early afternoon, a peculiar crystal stillness held the deserted streets. The thread of smoke rising from the mansion's chimney was slender and wick-straight.

Now he noticed the horse hitched to Joseph's fence post. Slowly Tom dismounted and looped his reins around the post nearest a succulent patch of grass.

Pausing to scratch his head and flex his shoulders, Tom took time to notice the clear blue of the sky. A white cloud puffed across his vision like a ship under full sail.

Tom turned toward Joseph's front door just as it burst open. He recognized the Prophet's heavy voice as the two figures came through the door.

To Tom's astonishment, the first figure was hurrying and the second figure was kicking. Tom scratched his head while he waited until the rotund figure picked himself up out of the street, dusted off his suit, straightened his tie, and mounted his horse.

Joseph's face was flushed and he was still breathing heavily as he stepped close to Tom. He jerked his head at the departing figure. "Justin Butterfield, United States Attorney for Illinois. Came in here accusing me of misbehaving."

"How's that?"

"Bankruptcy petition. Says I transferred property illegally. Guess he won't do that again." Joseph was at ease as he led the way into the house. "State's in a hole financially, so they're going to take every advantage of a fellow they can to save a cent. What's on your mind? What are you doing back in Nauvoo?"

Tom gulped and cringed. That scene was too sharply etched on his mind. Feeling like a ten-year-old, he started his explanation. "Joseph, I'm just not cut out to be a missionary. Figured I was doin' more harm than good so I settled for comin' home. I was dragging the rest of the fellas down, honest." He braced himself and, surprisingly, Joseph only shook his head.

"I guess I wasn't much of a judge of character, Tom," he said. "You can do everything else, including putting out the best shoeing job in the state. Go back to the stable. I guess I might as well admit, we've been missing you sore.

"So's my horse. Take a look at him first thing in the morning, will you? It's the right front shoe."

Tom sighed with relief and started to get up. Joseph's hand stopped him. Tom settled back and was surprised to see the dark frown back on his face.

"Tom, I don't know how to tell you this. But Mark's gone and you're closest of kin. There's some talk that Jenny's been pretty unhappy. Alson Daniels and his pa fished her outta the river a couple of weeks back. When Alson came into town with the milk, he told me about it. Says she jumped off the bluff, clearly intent on ending it all."

Tom stared at Joseph, trying to put meaning into the words. "My sister? Jen's not the kind a person to do herself in."

Joseph shook his head and leaned forward. "Unfortunately, I've not had time to visit with her. It turned out that Porter and I had to take a little trip to avoid Missouri sheriffs with writs for our arrest. I didn't want the task of trying Nauvoo's charters in court right now, especially since I was being laid on the line."

Joseph settled back in his chair and studied his fists. When he spoke again, Tom thought it was as if the words were pulled from him. "Tom, from what I've heard, I'm really worried about your sister's mind. Sometimes women get all kinds of funny ideas. The suicide try indicates that to me.

"I realize you don't know much about females, being you're not married, but watch out for her. Let me know if there's anything I can do to help. I'll try to see her as soon as the pressure is off my neck."

Tom had started for the door when Joseph said, "One thing more, Tom. Since you're not hankering to be a missionary, I'll put the touch on you for the priesthood."

Tom was nearly to the farm before he was able to shake his mood. He straightened in the saddle and looked around. The Pratt farm was off to his left, and he could see Orson herding his cows into the barn. The apple trees were beginning to show color. He noticed that Orson had propped up the heaviest branches.

By the time he started down Jenny's lane, Tom was whistling. He saw Jenny turn and set her pail down. When he swung her up in his arms, he saw the tears on her face. "Jen, it's just your old brother."

"I'm just so glad to see you; it's been so lonely!"

He hugged her again and said, "Hey, you're treating yourself well—gettin' chunky, aren't ya?"

She leaned back grinning at him. "I'm going to have a baby."

"Well, I'll be switched," he said slowly, studying her face. Even as he spoke, he was putting facts together, "I'd about given up on hopin' you'd ever get around to that. What does Mark think about all this?"

He saw the cloud on her face. "He doesn't know. Tom, I haven't had one letter from him since he's left. Can he possibly be that busy? Why must he be gone so long?"

"I don't know," Tom said, troubled by what he was seeing. He was thinking of the way he had sloped out of a disagreeable job as he said, "I'm kinda wonderin' why Mark doesn't jump ship like I did."

"Does Joseph know you're back?"

"Yeah." Tom remembered the conversation as he searched Jenny's face. She looked pale and tired, but there was that happy smile. Surely, if circumstances were as he was thinking, she wouldn't be so happy about it.

Tom sighed and took up his conversation again. "He's lettin' me off easy. I expected to get sent to China, but he's sending me back to the stable. Might be he's had a report on my preachin'."

The next morning at breakfast Tom said, "One thing Joseph

did do which surprised me; he's earmarked me for the high priesthood."

Jenny nearly dropped the skillet. Astonishment flooded her face as she turned to him. "That's nice, but it sure surprises me too. Seems such a limited group from what I'm hearing; guess I just didn't realize how special you were to Joseph." She hesitated and frowned. "Tom, there's lots of funny talk going on. Don't get yourself into something you'll regret."

"How's that?" he asked, chewing slowly.

She sighed and frowned, saying, "There's talk of building up the Legion more. Is it true Joseph's not given up on Missouri yet?" After a pause she turned to him and shrugged, shaking her head, "Oh, I just don't know; this Legion business worries me. I know there's rumbles around about it. I heard a fellow on the street. A stranger. He seemed uneasy. Just things floating around making us wonder. At Relief Society we talk."

"Gossip session?"

"I—I just don't know. One minute I get the feeling the women are all the best of friends; then next meeting I see the tides moving, telling me there's something going on underneath all the nice smiles. There's an undercurrent in Nauvoo I don't like."

CHAPTER 19

Jenny was pulling the curtains across the windows when Tom came into the house carrying the pail of milk. " 'Tis a mite nippy out there tonight; reminds me this nice October is about to bid us good-bye."

With a shiver, Jenny went to the stove and pushed the simmering pot to one side. "I keep worrying about Mark. Since that one letter I've heard no more, and I can't help wondering if it is well with him. It bothers me that there are letters I didn't receive."

"Mail service isn't the best out here," Tom reminded mildly. But Jenny was brooding over the note of alarm in Mark's letter. Was he doubting her love because he didn't receive a letter from her? She moved her shoulders irritably and saw Tom's glance.

"It's terrible to not know where to send a letter," she explained. "And he doesn't even know about this," she patted her stomach. "Tom, just think, his baby is poking at my ribs, and Mark doesn't even know about him."

Tom sat down at the table and grinned at Jenny as she pressed her hands across her thickening waist. "Might be it'll be a girl. Think he'll trade it off?"

"I doubt. After waiting this long, we'll take anything we get. Just, please God, let it be healthy."

She felt his quick look and knew he wondered about the prayer. Strange how it seemed the words came without thinking.

Jenny went to strain the milk and slice the bread. "You want milk with your stew?"

He nodded. "I 'spect I'd better. I'd rather have hot tea, but tonight's priesthood meeting. There's a little talk that Joseph'll be there. I'm not thinkin' it'll be likely though, since they're still lookin' for him."

"How do you know?"

He hesitated and looked sharply at her. "Remember those

fellows we saw last time we went to shop?"

She frowned, "You're meaning the bunch sitting around in front of the store whittling with those terrible knives?"

Nodding, he added, "Those are Joseph's men. They make it a point to know what's going on. You needn't worry. There ain't no surprises around here."

Silently Jenny ladled the stew into a bowl and carried it to the table. When Tom reached for his third slice of bread, he added, "Bennett started all this with his running to Missouri. Seems all's fair—"

"How Joseph could have taken that fellow in, befriending him and making him the mayor of Nauvoo as well as being in charge of the Legion, well, it seems strange." Jenny slowly picked up her fork, thinking of the man she had met at Sarah Pratt's home. Thoughtfully she added, "Bennett seems nice enough. Mark hesitated over him though. Well, he's gone. Beyond making so much trouble for the Prophet now, I suppose we'll never know what's in the heart of the man. But no matter; I'm against the letters he's written to the press."

Jenny had just hung her dish towel to dry when they heard the tap at the door. Tom opened it and exclaimed, "Brother Joseph! Is there trouble?"

Joseph Smith came into the room, nodded briefly at Jenny and turned to Tom, saying, "Only that I need to get a message to Mark. He's to be in Springfield this week, but I don't trust a letter to reach him."

"Problems?" Tom took the packet of papers the Prophet offered and studied Joseph's face.

"I'm just covering every detail I can. Thomas Ford will be inaugurated as governor of the state come the first week in December. That's not much more'n a month away. I need to remind him of his promise to test the Missouri writ in court. Mark can fill him in on the details. He's got papers with him. But he mustn't come back here without seeing Ford and wringing a promise out of him. I can't spend the rest of the winter dodging the sheriff and posse from Missouri."

He paced the floor and added. "Tom, tonight is as good a time to start as tomorrow. So pack a grip and be off."

Tom threw a quick glance at Jenny. "Brother Joseph, think about my sister. I'm not of a mind to walk out on her right now."

"I'll have John Lee take her back to the Mansion House. Just be about your business; she'll be okay." Going to the door he said, "Lee's minding the horses. I'll speak to him and then be here to get you off."

Tom looked at Jenny. She swallowed hard and said, "Best do it, Tom. I'll be better in town than by myself. Could you stop past the Daniels' and have Alson do the milking? Tom, please tell Mark how miserably lonesome I am for him, tell him—please hurry home."

Jenny carried her valise downstairs just as she heard Tom close the door behind himself. Joseph was sprawled comfortably in Mark's chair. "The fire feels good tonight," he said, gesturing toward the fireplace. "Now come sit; I've a few things to say to you."

"Joseph," she warned; "this is my home."

"And you are my wife."

"I can't believe you are still talking in this manner," her voice was low, but she challenged him with her eyes. "When this took place, you indicated it was a marriage for eternity."

"And you thought that was all I meant? Jennifer, I didn't see that in your response. I see you are laboring under a lack of understanding. Seems Patty Sessions didn't do a thorough job of teaching."

He pointed to the chair. "I've some things to say to you. First, I must remind you of the very idea brought forth in the Bible. This is the idea that things change. Some things are wrong under one circumstance—and I remind you of the instances involving murder. The Bible says 'Thou shalt not murder' in one place, and in another advocates killing off the enemy. The same applies here."

"Are you referring to adultery?"

He continued, "You call it adultery? When I came for my rights, you named it thus. God doesn't. What might very well be adultery in one circumstance is commanded of God in another. Jenny, when God instructed me to take you as wife, the angel told me, with a sword in his hand, that I was to fulfill the command or die. I dare not disobey."

Jenny's heart sank. Feeling as if the weight of the universe rested upon her, she slowly got to her feet. She faced him and groped for words, murmuring the only word that was there, "Jesus."

He raised his head, "What did you say?"

She stepped forward and clasped her hands across the precious swelling. "Joseph, I regret that ceremony more than I can say. I sense there's no backing out of it unless I forfeit my eternal salvation. But this is earthly life. I can't understand mixing the two. Besides, I'm carrying Mark's child. To let you—"

She paused and took a shaky breath, weaving now through

the maze of contradictory thoughts. "I don't have anything to go on. I don't know enough about God or even His Holy Bible—but I'm reading and trying very hard to learn. It's just—Joseph, it *feels* so wrong. There's Mark. I love him and I've always been taught you don't let another man touch you."

He looked up at Jenny, slowly shaking his head. "My dear, how twisted this has all become in your mind! I will pray for you.

"For now I'll just have to trust the Lord to protect you from the evil attack and spare your life until you have your eyes open to truth. But, Jenny, my dear, you must devote yourself to praying about this matter. God will give you a sure knowledge of the rightness of the message. Just as I have seen Him, you'll see Him filling your room with such a brightness of His presence you'll never doubt again. Meanwhile, I must urge you to not speak of this to anyone. Keep it to yourself and pray lest you be tempted and lose the blessing to another."

With a sigh, Joseph got to his feet and went to the door. "Lee," he called and then turned back. "I'm running for my life. John will take you to the Mansion House. It's crowded, but Emma will make room for you. I'll try to get back into town soon."

It was very late when John D. Lee aroused Emma Smith and delivered the Prophet's message. He carried in Jenny's bag and took the buggy to the livery stable.

Jenny faced the woman swathed in a robe which didn't conceal her pregnancy. She studied Emma's weary, lined face and said, "I'm so sorry to disturb you. I wanted to wait until morning, but they said no."

With a terse nod, Emma led the way up the stairs and opened the door. "We're packed to the rafters. You'll have to push Julie over. Could be tomorrow I'll be able to settle you in a room."

It was late that next morning before Jenny went downstairs. She had been aroused early when the adopted daughter of Joseph and Emma slipped out of the room. Lying in bed, Jenny considered the twist of circumstances in her life—first, Joseph's visit the previous evening. Now, she considered with dismay the necessity of facing Emma as well as Joseph's children.

As she left the bedroom, Jenny looked about the house curiously. There was still that raw, unsettled air about the house, but the rooms seemed large and bright. In the upstairs hall she noticed the rooms opening off the hall had doors bearing numbered brass plaques.

When she reached the foot of the stairs, Jenny paused, confused. She peered through the first open door and saw the large room. It looked more like a lobby than a parlor. At one end there was an attractive fireplace and comfortable chairs.

Then she looked to the other end and frowned. It looked as if cabinets were being removed. As she considered the long bar, she nodded with understanding, remembering the stories she had heard. That was the bar Joseph had installed while Emma was away from home.

Jenny felt a spark of admiration for the woman as she chuckled over the story. Joseph had installed his bar and set up Porter Rockwell, pigtail and all, as bartender. Emma, so the story went, had taken one look and condemned the addition. Joseph, Porter, and all the liquor had speedily departed when Emma threatened to take the children and move back to the old cabin.

The next door Jenny tried led back to the kitchen. Hearing voices, she went in. Emma and her children, as well as several women, sat at the table.

As she sat down, Emma pointed out the children. "This is Julie, our daughter; she's twelve now and a big help. There's Joseph our firstborn, Frederick, and Alexander. This is Eliza Snow. Miss Snow is a schoolteacher by profession. And Emily Partridge. Emily is living with us and earning her keep."

Jenny looked at the comely girl as she bobbed her head and went to the stove. "Mrs. Smith says you'll be staying for a time. There's little room right now. But two gentlemen just passin' through will doubtless be leaving in a day or so."

Jenny glanced at the shy Julie, and with a smile said, "I do appreciate the hospitality, but I'm imposing. I don't know why I didn't just stay at the farm. Surely Tom will be back soon." There were questions in the eyes of the women, but Jenny dismissed them as she accepted the bowl of porridge from Emily.

Emma was looking out the window, watching the procession of wagons and buggies on the street. Slowly she said, "I'll be happy just to have life back to normal again. Joseph's promised to be back for the birthin' in December. But it will take more'n that. There's this coming and going of all the strangers. There's the fear and unrest. These men they're calling the Whittling Deacons bother me. Seems holiness shouldn't have to worry people on either side of the fence."

Eliza Snow had pushed aside her breakfast dishes. With her arms propped on the table she folded her hands under her chin and dreamily addressed the ceiling. "There's little of holiness going on right now. It isn't the Prophet's fault. 'Tis the responsibility of the people to be holy in order to free the powers of God."

She paused to smile slowly at Emma. "You remember yourself all the promises. All the miracles expected at Kirtland had to be postponed until we had a temple in Missouri. That blessed event still hasn't happened. Therefore we wait until the people purify themselves and accept all the commandments of the Lord; then He will make our enemies live at peace with us."

Emma moved impatiently and said, "I suppose I'm too practical for Zion talk. I worry about the present, about the children and their future. They need their father at home. We all need to know we can depend on a surety."

Eliza was shaking her head. "Emma, dear woman, of all of us, I expected you to have settled in. From the beginning, Joseph has taught us all that we know by the spirit, not by sight. You know that Joseph knows all things that will come to pass right up to the end of the world. Granted, he isn't allowed to reveal them yet."

Emma got to her feet and shooed the children out the door. "Now get your books and be off," she admonished them, then turned impatiently to Eliza.

With a quick cry she said, "I don't like the uncertain; I want to touch and see."

Jenny watched Eliza, the dreamy expression on her face and the slight smile as she raised her head. "I know, 'tis womanlike to want it so, but Emma, my dear friend, I must admit there's such a mysterious power when he speaks. It makes me willing to forego the material and draws me on to the spiritual."

For a moment Emma was caught. Jenny saw the wistful expression on her face and then she turned impatiently, " 'Tis not the spiritual that'll feed me and the young'uns."

When Emma had left the room, Eliza turned to Jenny with a gentle smile. "Emma needs to have the experience of being carried away by the spirit. She's too earthly-minded. 'Twill get us into trouble, I fear."

Jenny spent another uncomfortable night on the narrow cot with Julie, and then Sally came.

Eliza and Jenny were beside the fire, poking at needlework for Emma and probing, just as tentatively, each other's thoughts when Sally sailed into the room, crying, "Jenny, why didn't you come to me? I shall be angry if you don't pack and come now."

Jenny packed and came, but she did so wondering why, after

months of neglect, Sally had appeared in such a rush of compassion.

The answer came out as Sally settled Jenny in the spare bedroom and confided, "Andy saw Tom just last week. We've learned of your good fortune. A baby." For a fleeting moment Jenny saw the question in her eyes before she added, "My, Mark will be surprised. Tom said he didn't know yet. All these years . . ." her voice trailed away.

Jenny turned from hanging her frock and said, "Is that too unusual? After all, there's only Tamara in your family."

In the silence Jenny turned and caught Sally twisting her hands together. She looked up and smiled. "I haven't told Andy yet, but there's to be another one. Not until next summer, though."

"Oh, Sally, that's wonderful! Now we can share this together. Do you want another little girl or a boy for Andy?"

There was a white line around Sally's mouth as she smiled and said, "A boy, of course. But please don't mention it to Andy just yet."

As they started down the stairs together, Sally impulsively hugged Jenny. "I'm glad you've come."

"I am, too," Jenny admitted. "For more than just the joy of being with you. After two days of Eliza I was starting to feel like a grubby child."

"Why?" Sally asked in surprise.

"Well, she talks so much. About her poetry and how she's complimented on it. She says things like 'the spirit told me,' and then she talks about how the spirit ministers to her. On and on.

"I think even Emma's annoyed by it all. Julie loves it. She hangs on to every word. But then Eliza's good with the boys, too. Seems to have time for cookies and things, even games with them."

CHAPTER 20

In the days that followed, Jenny settled in with Sally. The bond between the two had always made their friendship easy. Even after long separations, and despite their differences, Jenny and Sally quickly moved into an intimate relationship. Sally called it a sisterhood.

Now Sally was having morning sickness and Jenny asked, "You still haven't told Andy? Why?" A shadow crossed Sally's eyes, and she shrugged.

As Jenny resolved to mend her meddling ways, Sally said, "I suppose I'm fearin' and not believin' it true. But I will. I just don't like Andy fussing."

Jenny grinned, "But telling him means you don't have to sneak your sewing away when he comes." Jenny looked at Tamara playing beside the fire. The child was six now. "She needs to know just as much as Andy."

Sally's eyes were thoughtful as she frowned at Tamara. The child's angelic fairness had darkened until she now resembled her father. Smiling, Jenny watched her play with her dolls. To Sally she said, "At times I'm tempted to pinch myself just to make certain it's real. I can hardly wait."

There was a cynical twist to Sally's smile. "Let's hope Mark will feel the same. Seems it's always the woman who wants it the most."

"Mark isn't that way." She paused. "Sally, what's wrong? I don't understand, but there's something. Our friendship has just about slipped away this past year, we've seen each other so seldom. I don't like it at all. If you've got troubles, say them."

Sally looked surprised and then embarrassed. "I'm sorry, Jenny. It's just Andy. You know how jealous he's always been. I'm afraid with all the talk buzzing around that telling him I'm pregnant will just make matters worse."

"Oh, Sally, how could it?"

Sally didn't answer, but she got up from her chair and went

to the desk. Picking up the newspapers there, she came to sit beside Jenny. "I suppose you've read the pamphlet put out by Udney Hay Jacobs called *The Peace Maker*?"

Jenny shook her head, "I haven't heard of it. Don't forget, I've scarcely been into town except for Relief Society meeting." Sally went back to the desk and opened a drawer. She carried the booklet to Jenny and dropped it in her lap. When Jenny picked it up, she noticed the front cover bore the name, *Joseph Smith, Printer.*

Jenny read quietly for a time, then she gasped and looked at Sally. "Have you read this? How terrible! It makes women sound like monsters."

Sally nodded and said, "I see you don't like being told you've enslaved your husband."

"Or that marriage has made him effeminate. I shall be afraid to ask a thing of him for fear—"

"He'll think he's in bondage to the law of the woman." Sally snorted. The dark shadows came back into her eyes. "What I can't understand is the purpose behind the thing. Do you suppose we'll risk having our husbands leave just because we ask them to take out the trash?"

"Oh, that's silly," Jenny protested and then studied the booklet. "Somehow I don't think that's the purpose," Jenny said slowly. "It seems to me it's coming down hard on women for being even a mite snippy. What woman hasn't had a headache?"

Sally was shivering and Jenny looked at her in concern. "You're chilling. Could you be catching something? Come to the fireside."

Settling in the rocker beside the fire, Sally said, "What did you get out of it—The meaning behind it all?"

Jenny picked up the paper and picked out sentences. "Says here that if a wife doesn't love her husband sufficiently and gets a young'un by him, the child's apt to be deficient. And that such a fact means the wife's committing fornication against her husband. He identifies fornication as lack of love and respect on the wife's part."

"Do I understand there's something about people like that not making it?"

"Well, it says the children of such don't make it into the congregation of the Lord. I suppose that means heaven." Jenny studied the paper again and then said slowly, "Sally, seems to me there's a lot of stuff in here just rolling around in circles, trying to hide the real message."

"What's the real message?"

"That in order for the women to keep from sinning and for the children to make it into eternity, it's best for a man to have more'n one wife. Mostly, I guess, laying up against those times when his wife's got a headache."

"Makes me so angry to hear them say a woman's a man's property, just like an old cow," Sally muttered.

"Seems this is egging a man on to have more'n one wife; here it's saying, oblique-like, to not do so just proves he's under the law of his wife."

"I'd like to get a hold on that Jacobs," Sally continued. "Like to shake some sense into him."

"And there you'd just be proving his point," Jenny added. "According to him, you're wrong if you're anything but a sweet little wife." Jenny returned to the pamphlet. She read more. He says that to outlaw polygamy shows the stupidity of modern Christianity. He's calling for us to restore the law of God, that's plural wives. I guess that's different from spiritual wives, isn't it?"

Sally began to have a coughing spell, and Jenny hurried to get water for her. "I believe you're coming down with the croup. Do go to bed for a rest."

She watched Sally go up the stairs and went to put away the pamphlet. As she folded the paper, she noticed the final line and stopped. "I should be grieved to see you slain before him," she read. *Strange*, she thought, *that phrase reminds me of what Joseph said. Could there be a connection between this and the spiritual wives doctrine?*

As Jenny went to the desk with the pamphlet, she saw the newspaper lying there and picked it up to read. It was an old one. The pages had been turned back and the article on top was by Joseph Smith. Words caught her attention.

"In response to the protest over the Jacobs work, I must advise my innocence . . . Had I known, the paper would never have been printed. . . . It is nothing except a sensational piece of trash, designed to excite the minds of the uneducated."

Jenny was thoughtful as she replaced the paper. When she went into the kitchen to prepare dinner she was still thinking about Joseph's article, and only momentarily did she pause to wonder why Sally had kept the old paper.

That evening, at dinner, Andy told Sally and Jenny of his plans to go to St. Louis on Joseph's steamboat, *The Maid of Iowa*. "There's material to be ordered for the temple. It will be to my advantage to see to it personally," he added. With a smile he looked at Jenny and said, "You two can keep each other company. I'm glad to have you here, Jenny. Sally's been looking puny these last weeks."

Jenny looked quickly at Sally and said, "I'm thinking she's trying to catch the croup. She keeps this up, I'll be going back to doctorin' yet."

The first morning after Andy left, Sally came into the kitchen still wearing her nightgown and swathed in a shawl. Her voice was muffled as she said, "I don't care for breakfast. I've taken some medicine and will sleep. Why don't you take Tamara over to the Whitneys'? She's been wanting to play with Amy."

It was nearly noon when Jenny left the Whitney home, with the promise to return for Tamara before evening. As she started the short distance to Sally's home, Jenny stopped at Joseph's store for more flannel.

Back on the street, she began thinking about Sally. With a sigh she shook her head. Sally's strange silence was beginning to trouble her. Now she began to wonder about the medicine Sally had taken.

As soon as Jenny stepped into the house, she heard the moans, the weak call. When she rushed into the bedroom, Sally was on her knees beside the bed. "Oh, Sally, the blood! Is it the baby?"

That day and night was a nightmare. Patty Sessions came, and then the doctor. At the week's end, Andy returned.

His face was nearly as pale as Sally's, and Jenny was filled with guilt. She felt a pin-prick of knowledge, and had ignored the responsibility.

After the first bad days were past, Jenny showed the empty bottle to Sally and asked the question. Sally wore a guilty expression, and Jenny had to ask her, *Why?* She couldn't forget Sally's failure to answer.

During Sally's time of recuperation, Tom returned and went back to the farm, while Jenny lingered on with Andy and Sally.

On the day that Sally could face the dishes and broom again, Jenny said, "I need to go home. Soon Mark will be here." She hugged the joy to herself even as she felt the guilt Sally's pale face aroused.

Sally noticed and said, "Go. We can make it now. But today there's a storm a brewin'. If you go today, you'll travel in snow. Linger 'til tomorrow."

"My Mark will travel in snow, too, if he doesn't hurry." Jenny shook her head, packed her valise, and said, "First to the store for more—" she stopped.

Sally said, "You needn't fuss. I'm fine. You can't quit talking babies because of what happened." She hugged Jenny and sent her on her way.

Jenny did her shopping and then went on to the Mansion House to deliver the packet of candies she had bought for the children.

Emma was touched, and Jenny forgot her shyness as Emma pulled her into the kitchen and poured tea, saying, "Joseph doesn't keep the word of wisdom with his wine; neither will I withhold the tea on a blustery day."

She looked at Jenny. "So Sally Morgan has lost her baby. That's too bad. Is she well now?"

Jenny looked at Emma's drawn face and bulging figure and nodded. "Your time will be upon you soon. Will you need help?"

"Only my husband. I won't lack." She sighed and in a low voice said, "I've been poorly, I just hope—" For a moment Jenny saw her tortured eyes before she bent to pour the tea.

"I—I hope you'll be delivered of a fine, strong baby," she said.

The front door flew open and Joseph, Emma's eldest child, raced into the kitchen. "Snow!" he shouted. "By morning there'll be enough for a snowman."

"Oh," Jenny started up in dismay. "I must leave now."

"No, you shall not start out in this. You've no need to be at home this evening. Pray stay."

Emma went to look out the window. "Joseph came last night. He's been working at the office today, but he'll stay, too. Luckily the Missourians aren't prone to come this way in a snowstorm. We'll have a lovely dinner, all of us together. I'm guessing from the past, there'll be more guests before the evening is over."

The dinner was lovely and the crowd grew, just as Emma said it would. It was late when the last lamp was snuffed at the Mansion House. Jenny knew, as she tumbled into bed, that she would oversleep. Thinking of all she needed to do at home, she yawned and snuggled into the quilts.

When she awakened, Jenny guessed by the pale wash of light at the window that it was early. As she lay still, reluctant to face the day, she heard a whisper of sound outside her door, then the creak of floor boards. Thinking it was Emma, Jenny slipped from bed and went to open the door.

There was no one at the door and Jenny poked her head into the hall. Light from the window at the end of the corridor outlined the two figures as they met and merged. Jenny recognized Joseph and Eliza Snow, but surprise held her motionless.

Now the door across the hall flew open. Jenny saw Emma's face turned toward that scene at the end of the hall.

Jenny was still standing dumbfounded as Emma quietly turned, and snatched up the broom leaning against the wall. Moving swiftly despite her bulky body, Emma charged down the hall with broom flying.

Joseph stepped back, and Jenny saw the astonishment on his face. But Joseph was not the object of her wrath. Onward she ran, flailing the broom at the fleeing woman.

With a gasp, Jenny ran through the hall just as Emma's broom drove Eliza down the stairs. Jenny moaned and clasped her hands over her mouth as she heard the thump on the stairs.

Behind Jenny another door banged. "Mother, Mother, don't hurt Auntie Eliza." Pushing past her, young Joseph screamed and ran toward the stairs.

It was afternoon before Jenny collected her buggy and mare and headed for home. Still numb from the events, her mind held only the sights and sounds of horror.

The contorted faces were stamped on her mind—Emma's, Eliza's, and little Joseph's. The significance of all she had seen still eluded her, even though she had been there to hover in the hallway as the doctor came to attend Eliza.

Jenny pulled the buffalo robe about herself and flicked the reins across the mare's back.

CHAPTER 21

Mark reached the outskirts of Nauvoo on an early December afternoon. As he rode rapidly through the streets, his mind was clicking off the changes five months had made in the town. *City*, he reminded himself. The shops and sidewalks teemed with bustling people on this snowy afternoon. Lorries and carriages filled the streets. From factory, to shop, to the *Times and Seasons* newspaper office, the place was filled with activity.

Mark was noticing the strange faces, but he was also hailing friends. As he lifted his arm to salute Andy Morgan, he saw Phelps, William Law, and his brother Wilson.

To all he called, "Not now! I'm going home. I'll visit later."

Turning in at the livery stable he found Tom shoeing a horse. "I'm back," he clapped his brother-in-law on the shoulder. "I'm heading home as fast as I can go. Soon as you finish that horse, will you take this packet of papers to Joseph? Tell him I'll see him on Monday."

Tom recovered from his surprise and slowly said, "Can't ya take a bit to talk?"

Mark was backing out the door. "No. That's why I'm letting you deliver the papers. See ya later."

He met Orson Pratt at the door. The shock on his face had Mark apologizing. "Didn't mean to run you down."

" 'Tweren't that. Just surprised." He hesitated and studied Mark's face. "From the grin I'm guessing you're heading home. Give a half hour and I'll ride with you."

"Man, *give* me a break—I haven't been home for five months!" Pratt hesitated; Mark, sensing the unsaid, studied his face and waited, but Pratt shrugged and turned away.

Mark cut away from the main street of town. He followed the ravine down to the wharf and then cut south along the river road. The road was coarse and uneven from heavy wagons, but it was quick.

He touched his tired horse lightly with his heels and pondered again the futility of his mission. He was also mulling over the effect of the separation on Jenny. "Not one letter," he muttered, feeling a familiar sinking sensation which had dogged his life during the past months.

Again he reminded himself, "If I'd known what I know now, I'd never have gone. At times I think Joseph invents these missions just to prove his power."

When Mark cantered up his lane he saw the lonely figure. His Jenny, swathed in a shawl, was dragging a pail toward the barn. His throat tightened and it was a minute before he could shout her name.

He was off the horse and running toward her before she could move. When he finally released her, he said, "Give me a minute to pull the saddle off the mare, then let's get in the house. The tears are freezing on your face. I'll feed the pigs later."

Inside she pushed him into the rocking chair and knelt to pull off his boots. She could only smile and mop at the tears. When he lifted her, he asked, "Has it been that bad?"

"Oh, Mark, if only I could put it in words! But, yes. Please don't leave me again, ever—I'll die!"

"Jen." He held her close and pressed his cold face against her warm neck. "I won't. I can't take another separation either—no letters, nothing except that worthless time."

The afternoon light was a pale gleam when he stood, saying, "I've got to take care of the stock."

When he set her on her feet, she smiled and spread her arms. "Mark, look!"

It took a moment to understand the difference he had been feeling. "I'm pregnant. Oh, Mark, we're going to have a baby."

"Baby?" He knew his voice was stunned.

The smile faded and she whispered, "Aren't you glad? After all these years—"

"That's what I was thinking," he said slowly. "After all these years. Jen, it'll take me a spell to get used to the idea." Abruptly it sunk in. "We're going to have a child, a baby. My little boy!"

She was laughing. "That's the way I felt. I should have guessed before you left. But for Mrs. Daniels' guessing I don't think I could have believed even then." She was quiet for a moment and he watched the strange shadow momentarily mingle with the joy on her face.

Then she lifted her face and smiled as Mark said, "Be back in a few minutes." He went out to care for his horse and feed the pigs.

When Tom came, Mark was still in the barn, bemused, and lost in thought. Tom pulled down hay for the horses and said, "Well, what do you think about being a papa?"

Mark faced him and grinned, but he saw the expression on Tom's face as he avoided his eyes. "What's the problem? You don't look like you're crazy about being an uncle." Tom turned away, and Mark didn't press the question.

During the night Mark felt Jenny turning restlessly and he reached to pull her close. "Mark, I worry. It's such a responsibility."

"And you think about that now?"

She pressed his hand across her stomach. "But feel him; he's so tiny and alive!" Abruptly she asked, "Mark, who is Jesus?"

"God."

"Like Joseph says?" Her voice was flat.

"No." He raised to one elbow and tried to see her face in the dim moonlight. He was guessing a difference and wondering if it was the pregnancy. He felt his heart lift as he carefully answered, "Not the brother of Lucifer, not the child of Mary and Adam. Not the spirit brother of all good Mormons. Jenny, I've told you before that the Bible teaches there is only one God and that there will never be another God.

"If that is so, biblically there's only one answer. If Jesus is God, as the Bible says, then He is *the God*. Just as the Bible teaches. He is God come to earth to take upon himself a human body, to live among men and to be their atonement for sin."

Later when Mark recalled that nighttime conversation, he held it as an extra blessing, crowning his first night home. But too soon it was forgotten.

By Monday evening, after his first day back in the office, Mark had garnered enough of covert glances and questioning eyes to become alarmed over Joseph's unusual arrogance. The uneasy questions began to grow in his mind.

When Tom reached home, Mark met him at the barn.

Tom started the conversation when he turned from his task of forking down hay to the cattle. Looking over his shoulder at Mark, he said, "Mark, there's been a heap of strange happenings since you've been gone. And some not so strange."

"That's what I came to ask you about. Joseph hinted at a couple. I tried to avoid showing my ignorance."

"Well, you know about the Boggs shooting, and how the Prophet's prediction about it nearly did him in." Mark was nodding and Tom went on. "Seems all that leaked back to Missouri. Unfortunately, Boggs didn't die.

"Just after you left a sheriff and posse from Missouri appeared with a writ for Joseph and Porter Rockwell's arrest. The Nauvoo court shoved it back to Governor Carlin. By the time they had satisfaction from Carlin and came back for him, he'd skipped."

"Where did he go?"

"Not far. Porter Rockwell headed for Pennsylvania, but Joseph's been layin' low. Couple of times the posse got pretty close. One time he was at home, havin' a nice dinner with friends when this knock came. Joseph ducked into his hidden room, went up to the roof and shinnied down the trees, all unbeknownst to the fellas at the door." Tom paused to chuckle, "Joseph sure had the gift of prophecy when he had that hidden staircase built to the roof."

Tom bent to pick up the pails of milk. "Don't think he's ever been farther than across the river. Plenty of friends around to hide him out. I saw him a couple of times."

"Today Joe mentioned he'd surrendered and is to stand trial in Springfield after the first of the year."

Tom nodded. "Kicking Bennett outta the church and all his positions sure turned him sour. Seems his contrite spirit didn't last long. I hear he's out stirrin' up things in Missouri. Guess you saw all the newspaper articles he's put out."

Mark nodded and Tom said, "Well, Carlin's out of office as of the first of the month and Ford's governor of Illinois. Joe has a lot of confidence in him. Says he isn't political. I think he means he won't be hard on the Saints."

Tom paused and looked at Mark as he asked, "What else has happened since I've been gone?"

"Just after you left, Orson Pratt had a bad time. Seems all the gossip about Sarah got to him."

"About the situation while Orson was in England?"

"Yes, there was a lot of rot. Gossip sproutin' both ways. First off, Bennett was sayin' Joseph was trying to starve her into submission to him, after promising her husband he'd see she had enough to eat and such. I did hear before you and Jenny moved to Nauvoo that she was in a bad way, not havin' enough to eat or fuel to keep warm. Finally heard she'd took to sewin' in order to have a livelihood.

"About the time Orson came back, the gossip surfaced that she'd been carryin' on with Dr. Bennett. Well, that kept gnawing on Orson. Some say he nearly did himself in. Took a bunch a fellas a while to talk him back to normal. I never heard him myself, but I understand he was walking the streets for a time, tellin' ever'body he met that Sarah was innocent."

"What else?"

Tom paused and hedged, scratching his head. "Well, I've been gone too. Joseph had me out on a couple of assignments. Weren't gone long. The Daniels young'un took care of the stock." His voice trailed off and he looked at Mark.

"That isn't what I'm referring to."

"Aw, who's been talkin'?"

"Not a soul. It's the looks, and the way Pratt and Andy Morgan are dodging around avoiding me. It's a pile of impressions, and I think you can tell me about it. Does it have something to do with the baby?"

Tom winced. He lifted his head and Mark saw the dark questions. "Mark, I don't know. I just don't know what to make of the whole affair. Jen seems so happy now. When I got back in town after the first trip, Joseph came to give me the sad news that Jen had tried to do herself in.

"Says Daniels told him all about it. How she jumped in the river and they pulled her out. Joseph said he was right worried about her mind. Seemed to indicate she might not be remembering and able to hang life all together. I've not had that impression, but I've sure been watchin'."

Tom had been silent for some time before Mark realized it. Lifting his head out of his hands, he said, "Sorry, Tom. What did you say?" Tom shook his head, his expression bleak.

Silently they sat together. When Mark began shivering, he realized the last of the afternoon light was gone. With a sigh he said, "Well, guess I'd better be getting in the house."

That evening, while they were eating, Tom said, "Well, I can't see that you two need me around here, and I'm right anxious to get back to my cozy hole over the livery stable before the blizzards begin. I'll be movin' out tomorrow."

In the morning, as Mark prepared to leave, he kissed Jenny's cheek. He was still reflecting on all Tom had said. Last evening, he had tried to give Jenny every opportunity possible to talk about her fall in the river, but she had said nothing.

Mark was still brooding as he headed for Nauvoo. Orson Pratt rode down his lane; just as Mark passed, he hailed him.

Bringing his horse even with Mark's mare he said, "I suppose you're glad to be free of traveling for a time. Sarah says there's to be a little one at your house come spring."

Mark noticed the man's nervousness and recalled Tom's remarks as he acknowledged the news. "Yes, we're pretty proud."

In the silence he added, "I'm hoping to settle into that pile on my desk today. Whatever the Prophet's activities, he's managed to stack up enough work to keep me busy until spring."

"He tapped you for the council yet?"

"Priesthood?" Mark waited for Pratt's shrug before he shook his head. "I don't intend to be part of it."

"Mark," Pratt warned and then paused to take a deep breath. "Sarah's been talking about how deeply involved Jenny is in the church. I know you've had some trouble with the beliefs in the past, but if I can counsel you to accept Joseph's direction, I'd be glad to."

Orson continued, "I've been in disfavor because of my attitude. The Prophet's forgiven me, and there's not much I wouldn't do to help his cause right now. Without revealing any of the hidden doctrines, I must advise you that things are moving forward at a rapid pace. There's much to learn yet of the kingdom business. To deny Joseph endangers your soul. To refuse to progress means trouble for you with your wife."

"What do you mean by that?"

"You know Joseph is teaching now that an apostate spouse voids the marriage contract." Mark didn't reply, but he saw Pratt's troubled expression. In a moment Pratt continued with another line—at least Mark thought so as he listened to the gossip.

"They're saying Emma Smith sent Eliza Snow tumbling down the stairs after catching her with the Prophet. I know for a fact that Doc had a time with her. Seems she won't be having increase very soon." Again there was a pause, and Orson said, "In these latter days we're being called upon to pick up all the old ways of the church. It's our holiness and our salvation to do so."

While they were talking, the two had reached the main street in Nauvoo. They overtook a figure hunched nearly double on his horse. He straightened and turned. "Hello, Taylor," Pratt said, pulling on the reins. "I was just advising Mark he's about to be tapped on the shoulder."

Taylor nodded soberly and peered at Mark. "Joseph's declared that the church is at the crossroads. Unless these higher teachings are embraced wholeheartedly, there will be no further progression for the church. We must work to that end.

"Just last meeting Joseph was telling us that as soon as the temple is completed, there's instructions to be given out which are of the utmost importance. He says, for example, the keys of the kingdom are signs and words whereby false spirits and persons can be detected." His piercing gaze held Mark's for a moment before he bid them farewell.

Later Mark had reason to be grateful for the strange conversation with the two men.

By the time the Prophet had arrived at the office, Mark had pieced together all the facts and the ramifications of the invitation Joseph would extend to him.

Sitting at his desk he muttered, "Number one, my wife will forfeit our marriage before she will surrender her only hope of salvation. Number two, if I don't cooperate, I'll be forced to leave. My marriage vows still mean more to me than anything else in life. Joe's teachings aren't biblical. I can give in to the anger and frustration I feel, or I leave, standing no chance of being an influence for Jenny's salvation. Number three, the baby." He winced and tried to push out of his mind the dark thoughts that surfaced every time he saw the questions in the eyes of the brethren. He sighed and added, "Number four, even though I don't count with Jenny in these new circumstances, I love her more than—life."

When Joseph walked in Mark got to his feet. He looked at the smooth, smiling face of the Prophet, and found that the distance of five months allowed him to be objective.

Narrowing his eyes, he saw Joseph as a stranger would. In the rush of the Prophet's words, Mark tried to steel himself against the charm, against the bid to like the man.

In the back of his mind a picture was forming, compiled of the bits and pieces of six years' worth of scenes and words. While he stared at Joseph, he found himself wondering how he could know the man as intimately as he did, how he could add the new knowledge he was accumulating, without hating Joseph hopelessly.

Mark composed himself to listen to Joseph's smooth recital. He was seeing the words punctuated with the ethereal look on Joseph's face as he rehashed the events Tom had told him the night before.

Later Mark nodded his head, agreeing to become part of Joseph's inner kingdom workings, with the task of preparing to offer up to the world the lately revealed secrets; Mark did it with Jenny's heart-shaped face and shadowed eyes firmly before him.

CHAPTER 22

On Christmas Eve Tom came into the house, sniffing, bringing a cradle he had made. Jenny had been baking pies, and the savory odor of dressing for the goose mingled with the apple and mince and pumpkin.

"Oh, Tom, it is absolutely beautiful!" she cried, bending over the cradle. She fingered the carving and nudged it into rocking. "Mark, come see!"

There was a sigh of exasperation from the parlor, and Mark emerged from the depths of the teetering fir tree.

Tom eyed the tree sagging against the wall and said, "I see I have my work cut out for me. Mark, how come you still can't put a stand on straight?" Addressing Jenny he said, "Besides me, who's going to eat all those pies?"

"The Morgans are coming. Andy's sister is visiting them; she'll be here too."

"I suppose she's young and fat with buck teeth."

"You're going to have to start someplace," Mark said darkly.

Tom saw Jenny's sharp glance, but her voice was smooth as she said, "She's a nice girl. I met her at Relief Society meeting last week." As Jenny continued to talk up the virtues of Helene Morgan, Tom saw the shadows in Jenny's eyes.

When she paused for breath, he asked, "You ailin'?"

She threw him a startled glance and then the brooding expression shifted to Mark struggling with the tree. "No. It's just that—I guess I'm tired."

Mark was standing in the doorway. "Jen, let's put on candles for decoration, but don't light them. Can't see any sense in getting the house on fire. The red will look nice with the string of white popcorn."

She nodded without looking up. Addressing Tom she said, "I understand the Prophet's having a big party at the Mansion House. We were invited, but Mark didn't want to go." She sighed wistfully, "I would have loved to see their tree. And there's to be music."

Mark's voice was sharp as he said, "You shouldn't be traveling that far in the snow in a buggy." To Tom he added, "I've ordered a sleigh; unfortunately it hasn't been delivered yet. It's just too risky for her to be out in a buggy now. Sam Wright's family was stranded in a drift while he had to go for help."

Abruptly Mark turned back to the parlor. Tom was silent, struck by Mark's cold voice and impatient manner. He watched as his brother-in-law began struggling with the tree, then he went to help.

Late that evening, after a quick supper of bacon and corn chowder, more gifts were presented. Tom was still admiring his new muffler as he watched Jenny open the big box.

When the color slowly drained from her face, Tom looked at Mark and saw his frown. Jenny's face was strained as she lifted the brilliant red robe from the box. Tom saw the question in her eyes as she held the wool against her face.

Frowning, Mark said, "You don't like the color? I bought the heaviest one I could find. It's a boudoir gown. I thought with the baby—"

"Oh," she whispered, and Tom wondered at the relief in her voice and then he began to chuckle as she explained, "it's beautiful. I just wondered for a moment if I were to wear it to church." Mark began to laugh, but Tom saw she still wore the strange expression.

"With the size you are getting to be and the color," Tom shook his head, "you'd be a sensation!"

Mark was grinning as he went to kiss Jenny, saying, "Merry Christmas, my dear wife. I'm sorry the sleigh isn't here. I just can't risk you now."

"Young'uns don't grow on trees," Tom said dryly, feeling a relief he couldn't identify when Jenny lifted a radiant smile to Mark.

That relief stretched through the following day, and Tom discovered that Helene wasn't all that bad.

When Tom returned to Nauvoo Christmas night, he shook his head over the doings at the Mansion House.

Sitting horseback outside the house, looking at the line of carriages, and listening to the roar of masculine voices rising above the fiddles, he slowly said, "One thing, with the twirling and dipping going on, and the eating and drinking, I'd say the Lord's up to changing the emphasis again. Back in Kirtland days"—now he was addressing the white uniformed men standing guard at the gate—"back then there was no unholy frolic. 'Twas good business to be sober and holy. Times have changed."

Shaking his head, he rode toward the livery stable. But inside, Tom looked at the cold forge and with a troubled frown he said, "Leaves a body wondering. Will this church end up as cold and lifeless as all the others? I feel the high tide of excitement giving way to secret whispers which bode no good."

He went upstairs to his lonely room. With a sense of relief, he stoked the little sheet metal stove into cherry-red comfort.

He looked around his barren chamber and addressed the festoon of cobwebs. "Not likely I'll get married unless forced into it. Me and the dirt are comfortable. Even the smell of horses I don't object to. Besides, I can't afford a wife—or two or three." He glumly surveyed the *Book of Mormon* resting on the wooden crate beside his bed.

He was thinking of the barroom whispers the men were passing around along with the drinks. "Is having more'n one wife the way to beat the doldrums the church is having? Or is there a bigger reason for it?" He shook his head and wondered at the dismay in his own heart. There were shadows in Jenny's eyes, too. Could Mark have been touched for the teaching? With a regretful sigh Tom admitted to himself that he could very likely be next.

As he pulled the kettle of water over the heat, Tom was thinking of his initiation into Masonry last spring and now into this new council.

When he finally moved and sighed again, he said, "One thing's sure. Mark's joined up in Joseph's high priesthood, and they're teaching the way to earn salvation is through having more'n one wife. Right now he's not the most gladsome individual alive, and seems his confidence has slipped, but I guess I can trust him." He frowned. But what about Jenny's wan cheeks and her shadowy eyes?

Tom tried to imagine how his sister would feel about sharing her home with another woman. It was impossible, but he guessed her expression told him something. "Makes a body wish there were a different way to get into God's good graces." He shook his head and sighed. It was John Taylor himself who said the teaching would last forever because a revelation, once given, wouldn't ever be taken back.

The twenty-seventh of December dawned crystal clear, full of sunshine. As Mark rode into Nauvoo he considered the week before him. He knew Joseph would be leaving for the Springfield trial immediately.

The church had engaged the District Attorney for the state of Illinois to handle the case; when Mark found out, he breathed a sigh of relief. He now could easily decline Joseph's invitation to be part of the group traveling to the city.

Later in the day, Mark stood in the doorway of the office and watched the men set out for Springfield. Just as they had earlier escorted the Prophet to the office, now John Taylor and Orson Hyde, on either side of Joseph Smith, supported him as he cautiously stepped down the stairs. Obviously the Prophet still suffered from his exuberant celebration of Christmas.

As the trio left, Mark found himself shaking his head over the picture. The subdued Prophet, with dark circles under his eyes, hung on Taylor's arm, walking as if each step jarred clear through his frame.

Mark walked back into his office, chuckling and shaking his head. Patty Sessions was waiting, and noting his humor, she released her sharp tongue. "Why are you rejoicing over his misery? Seems a body can always pick out a man who thinks he's abused by the Prophet. A body who loves him sure won't be gleeful over his misery."

"What makes you think I feel mistreated?" Mark asked, astonished. Without answering, she pressed her lips together. Mark began wondering why his bruised spirit was so evident to others. He thought it carefully hidden.

Jenny's new sleigh was delivered just after the first of the year, the day before Joseph and his men returned to Nauvoo.

Mark had been standing at his office window when he became aware of the surge of excited people, and the sound of drums and bugles.

Within hours all of Nauvoo knew of the victory, and the city reverberated with the sounds of celebration. The people continued to crowd the streets to welcome their Prophet, and Mark went down to join them.

Later Mark carried home an invitation to dinner at the Mansion House, explaining to Jenny that all the city notables and church leaders had been invited to a gala dinner the following evening.

When Mark gave his news, he couldn't help grinning at Jenny's bright-eyed joy. "Yes, my dear wife, we'll go. My neck was saved by the sleigh, wasn't it?"

"Did you join the parade? I suppose the Legion was out in all their glory. Will Sally and Andy be there? What about Emma? 'Tis so sad that her baby died." Now she was sober, and for a moment Mark responded to her secret fear.

For the first time in weeks, Mark scooped Jenny up to sit in the rocking chair with him. "Your questions? Yes, yes, and I don't know." He was forcing the grin, trying to seem lighthearted over the sudden awareness of the blue-veined fragility of her face, and weight of the child moving against him.

He resisted the desire to crush her to him and unburden himself of all the hidden fears. Lightly he said, "My dear, you need to rest if you intend being out half the night."

"Rest!" she wailed, "I *must* find something to wear that will fit around me. Oh, Mark, do I look awful?"

"You are beautiful," he said. With a sharp pang he added, "I don't want to risk you unnecessarily."

She leaned back and he saw the questions. "Is that why you—you are always busy?"

He pressed his lips to her forehead, "Am I too busy?" She was nodding and he felt the moisture against his face. "What shall I do for you?"

"Oh, Mark—talk." She leaned back to look into his face, but even as she lifted her hand to touch his lips, he remembered the shrinking away, the shadows. Because he feared those shadows as much as she, he held her close, hiding his face in her hair.

The next evening was crisp and the snow sang beneath the runners of the new sleigh. "Oh, Mark, it's wonderful!" Jenny cried from the depths of the buffalo robe. "It rides as smooth as ice skating. See even Tupper loves it." She pointed at the mare swishing her tail.

Jenny's cheeks were pink and her eyes were sparkling, reminding him of a time long ago. "You remember ice skating."

She only nodded, but he could see her eyes were soft with gentle memories. He found himself wishing to hold the moment, but wishing even more desperately, to wing back through the years. "The beautiful young Jenny," he murmured. With a pang of regret, he saw his words brought back the shadows.

The Mansion House glowed with lamps in every window. There was music and the sound of laughter and clink of dishes. As Mark and Jenny stepped through the door, Jenny looked toward the stairwell.

The sweep of polished stairs was empty of all except memories. Jenny stared at that spot and remembered the horror of Eliza tumbling and screaming. She shivered under her shawl as she followed the crowd into the parlor.

A pale-faced Emma, isolated in her chair by the hearth, her figure swathed in black, was the only somber note in the room.

For several minutes, Jenny stood near the back of the crowded room and wrapped her shawl tightly around herself as she listened to Joseph. She wondered if her condition were making him seem a braggart. He was giving every detail of his trip to Springfield and the trial while his audience hung on every word. She found herself watching his face, but his words slipped passed her.

In a few minutes, Jenny moved slowly through the visitors to that dark-clad figure by the fire. As she walked, her attention was caught by the expressions of those around her.

Sarah Pratt blocked Jenny's path. She lifted her face, saw Jenny's figure, and smiled broadly. But Jenny was struck by that first expression.

Only Sarah's face, of all those in the room, reflected complete boredom. Their eyes met again and Sarah murmured, "Jenny, you are looking well." Then she turned abruptly, and Jenny went on.

Emma pointed to the chair beside her. "Oh, Emma," Jenny whispered under the cover of the excited outburst around them, "I'm so sorry you've lost your baby."

"Was it punishment? No." Her lips twisted, knowing that only she and Jenny shared the memory of that last time together. "I've had eight babies and only three survive. Jenny, I am getting to be an old woman. Where does it all end?" Jenny saw her fear and bowed her head. When she next looked, the small polite smile was back, and Emma was extending a limp, powerless hand to the gentleman beside her.

After dinner, when the group had reshifted and settled into new comfortable segments, Jenny found herself shuffled toward the end of the room. Wedging into a chair beside the door, she loosened the concealing shawl and picked up a book to use as a fan.

She heard a murmur of voices behind her, coming from the kitchen. Recognizing Mark's voice, she went into the hallway.

Joseph and Mark, with their backs to her, were in the kitchen talking to another man. As Jenny hesitated, Joseph reached out to take the paper extended toward him. The men shifted and Jenny saw Orson Pratt.

Before she could make her presence known, he was saying, "He considered me a dissenter. He's accused me of having designs of my own." The light flooded the expression on his face. Distaste filled Jenny at the overweening manner of the man as he continued, "Little did he dream I would use the letter to advantage."

Joseph was reading and murmuring, "Written at Springfield. Wonder if he was at the trial? It wouldn't surprise me at all. Addressed to you and Rigdon, huh? Well, let's see . . ."

In a moment he said thoughtfully, "Thank you, Pratt, you've done me a great favor. Mark, says here that Bennett's had contact with Missouri authorities. Now in the making is an attempt to revive the old charges. He's mentioning murder, arson, theft, larceny, and stealing. Well, well, my dear Dr. Bennett, seems we're one up on you."

Jenny was beside Mark when Joseph raised his head to study Pratt's face. "You've done me a favor, Pratt—is it more than just a bid for recognition? You've been rebaptized into the church, you and your wife. Is there something else you want?"

The man's voice was low, "Just my old position. I want to be back in the Quorum of Twelve. Might even be a good example, encouragement to others, seeing me back where I belong."

Joseph clapped him on the shoulder, "Wanting to be our gauge of philosophy again, eh, professor? Well, we need you nearly as much as you need us."

Jenny and Mark were silent as they rode homeward. Once Jenny roused herself to comment on the dinner. But she faced Mark's dark scowl and dared not reveal her own churning emotions.

CHAPTER 23

"Mark. You'll be at the meeting tonight?"

Mark lifted his head and saw Joseph lounging in the doorway of the office. "Huh? Yes, Joseph, I'll be there. Sorry. I was in the middle of this and didn't hear you." He gestured toward the book he had been reading and got to his feet. Unexpectedly his eyes met those of William Clayton.

The hang-dog expression in the eyes of Joseph's secretary caught his attention. He hesitated, but Joseph jerked his head toward his own office and turned away. Mark sighed in frustration. Sharing office space with Clayton created problems; but, he had to admit as he shuffled the papers on his desk, the problems seemed related to Joseph's desire for secrecy.

Slowly Mark picked up the brief and started to follow the Prophet, but Clayton's expression nagged at his attention. Why was the man constantly in a state of tension?

Joseph was at his desk with his feet up, placed in the middle of the papers, and his hands clasped behind his head. "What's Clayton finding to complain about?"

"Why, I don't think he was." Mark frowned with the effort to remember the man's words. "Honestly, I wasn't paying him much attention. He does ramble at times. Oh, seems he was talking about your sermon. Joseph, you can't be checking on everything that's happening," he said in exasperation.

Then he continued, "Jenny and I didn't get out this last Sabbath. It was too cold, and her time is getting close." For a moment Mark saw interest flare in the Prophet's eyes. Anger surged through Mark, but holding his voice even he continued, "Clayton mentioned you'd talked about the kingdom of God, and I asked him to define *kingdom*. He said where the oracles of God are given, there is the kingdom. I guess my attention drifted after that."

"Do you agree?"

"Jesus Christ said His kingdom isn't of this world. *Oracles* is an Old Testament word I'm not very familiar with. Right now the only scripture I can think of dealing with oracle is where the prophets are warned against declaring their own words as oracles of the Lord."

Joseph paused for a moment and then nodded. " 'Tis a fearful thing to take upon one's self the burden of claiming the Lord's word when it isn't."

He leaned forward. "About this priesthood meeting. I know you've bucked counsel, but I believe I can rescue you from apostasy. The Lord has shown me great and wonderful things which are to be unfolded before the Saints in the coming months and years."

Mark shifted restlessly. "You'll insist even when you know how I believe?"

"To your soul's salvation." As he continued speaking, Mark was caught in a moment of seeing Joseph through the eyes of a stranger. There was something very compelling about the man. His pale eyes gleamed with the new idea, while the expression lighting his face momentarily touched Mark with a tingle of excitement.

"Mark, there's lots about the priesthood meetings which is old hat. Business and the mundane of kingdom planning. But believe me, if you'll handle counsel, I promise you there'll be no regrets." Again Mark saw the flare of excitement. After a moment's hesitation Joseph said, "Might as well let a little of this slip. If I can't trust you to keep it quiet until the appointed time, then who—"

Mark watched Joseph flexing the steel letter opener until Mark expected to see it fly from his hands. It still held his fascinated gaze as Joseph continued, "The Lord's told me now's the time to begin the organization of the kingdom.

"There's been just a few of us in meeting, planning and discussing in preparation. It's all great and far-reaching; I must start by recruiting every man of intelligence and integrity in the church."

Mark was lining up all he had heard: the facts, the whispers, even the expressions of doubt and fear. He was readying his refusal when words thrown into air dropped into his mind with understanding: *rule the world, king, President of the United States*.

But Joseph wasn't waiting for his answer. He moved on to a new subject. "Mark, I know you started bucking this all when you heard about the Lodge coming to town. Man, I tell you, if you haven't vision and faith to grasp all this on your own, at least for your soul's welfare, be willing to accept on the faith of the others."

Joseph paused and leaned forward, searching Mark's face with those penetrating eyes. He whispered, "This is from God. Mark, I was utterly compelled to embrace the teaching. Would it help if I were to tell you God revealed to me new information about the order of Masons? He told me this is the ancient wisdom. The same priesthood was given to the first father, Adam. Later it was passed on to the great fathers, Noah and such. By the time it reached Solomon, it had become corrupted. What has happened now is that God has restored it to us in all its pristine beauty and holiness. It is to be part of the deep inner workings of the kingdom."

"Including the secret rituals?" Mark added. "This is the type of thing the *Book of Mormon* speaks against." He paused and then added, "Why is it the church is departing from the original revelations?"

"It isn't."

"I ran into David Whitmer and William McLellin in Springfield last November. We had quite a talk. They had a lot of questions about the church and Nauvoo."

"Yeah?" Joseph's face brightened. "They coming back?"

"I doubt it. They brought up some pretty hard questions, and I couldn't find an answer that would satisfy you."

"What questions?"

"Well, for a starter, *they* answered a question I'd had since I heard about it, related to the big to-do when the Kirtland temple was dedicated. I knew you'd promised there would be a tremendous endowment for the men, particularly those who'd been part of the army sent to rescue the Saints in Jackson, Missouri. A few had told me the endowment was a great success. Both Whitmer and McLellin said it was a trumped-up farce. Not only a failed revelation but a sham of the lowest kind perpetuated by suggestion and wine."

"Anything else?" Joseph asked.

"Have you made the statement that the revelations are the recorded words of the Lord Jesus Christ?"

"That is so. You've heard me say that more than once in those words, more or less."

"McLellin told me he'd been closely connected with you at the time they were being prepared for publication. He mentioned that the revelations, just before printing, had been altered so much they scarcely resembled the original.

"Joseph, isn't it presumptuous—no, more than that—isn't

it blasphemous to change the Lord's words?"

Before Joseph could answer, Mark added, "David Whitmer was troubled by the idea of even considering that God might change His mind. I feel the same way. If I can't depend upon God to say something and stick by His words, then what can I depend upon?"

Jenny draped the black cloth over the mirror while the herbs curled and crisped in the pan on the stove. They were beginning to smolder when she put on the red robe.

It had been the similarity between the robe and Adela's red dress that seized her attention at Christmastime. Had it been the spirits' urge to enable her to search once again for more power? Jenny knew how desperately she needed power for the months ahead.

Shaking off the strange foreboding that she knew signalled the gathering of the spirits, Jenny began walking about her house, holding high the pan of smoldering herbs. The chant she muttered rose and fell in the prescribed rhythm, corresponding to the dipping of the pan. She was in the bedroom when the pounding began.

She froze in horror, staring at the smoking pan in her trembling hands. Immediately her thoughts flew to that forest scene, seeing the twisting apparition and hearing the thunder.

Immediately the resolution born of that time flew into her face to confront her. The pounding came again, and she cried, "Oh, God! It is *wrong*!"

Just then she heard a voice, "Jen! Are you in there?"

It was Tom—not spirits, but a very human Tom. Trembling with relief, she placed the pan on the floor and stumbled down the stairs. "Tom, I'm coming!" she called.

Wrenching the back door open, she gasped, "Give a body time! I don't move as fast as before."

Tom came grinning into the room. He was carrying a small parcel which he handed to Jenny. "From Sally. Came into the livery stable with it, she did; said hurry, you might need it before she could get out."

"Oh." Jenny collapsed into the rocking chair and opened the package. It was a soft knitted shawl.

"That's as blue as the Prophet's eyes," Tom said admiringly.

Jenny dropped the shawl and stared at him, whispering, "Tom, whatever made you say that?"

"Why," he stammered, "I don't know. Jest seemed to be the same color."

She looked at it and said, "I may hate it because—"

Tom was sniffing. "What's that strange smell? It's nearly like burnt wood."

"Oh!" She was out of the chair, moving faster than she thought possible. When she reached the bedroom, Tom was right behind her.

He stared down at her kneeling on the floor as she gingerly lifted the pan. "Ugh. It's stuck to the floor, took some of the paint off. What'll Mark say?"

"I don't know. Is he that bad a fusser?"

"Seems lately—" her voice was faint as she scuffed at the spot with her fingernails.

"What were you trying to do?" Tom was holding up the pan and peering at the contents. "It couldn't be dinner. The whole house is full of the stink."

With a sigh, Jenny pulled herself to her feet and started wearily for the stairs. Suddenly the ritual seemed utterly foolish.

Tom was behind her and as they passed through the parlor, he paused. "You break this mirror, too?"

She turned and snatched at the scrap of cloth draped across the new mirror. The tears were starting down her face, and she tried to dab at them as she hurried back into the kitchen.

Tom took her shoulder and pulled her around. "Hey, give a little. What's got you so upset? So you were trying to cook supper in the bedroom and you burned the floor. Can't you jest level with your old brother?"

Jenny flew into his arms, crying and denying the need. "It's just being pregnant, I guess. I feel so ugly and everything."

He eased her into the rocking chair and said, "I thought females were supposed to feel just like they look—Hey, I didn't mean that! Girls, women! Ah, Jenny, hush!"

She tried, and he added gloomily. "My first impressions are right. I'm not cut out to be a husband, and all this other. Regardless of what Joseph says, I just can't."

Abruptly Jenny was laughing through the tears. "Oh, Tom. I didn't mean to upset you. It's just that—"

Just as abruptly he said, "Okay, now level. What were you doing? Why the rag over the mirror?"

She stopped mopping her eyes and looked at his frown. The years had taught her evasion was impossible. "I've been using the charms and herbs."

"Mind telling me why?"

"Suddenly you nearly make it seem silly to believe—but

Tom, I had to have something. Nothing works. I've tried to be a good Mormon, even reading the Bible like Mark does. The only thing I regret is throwing the talisman away."

"Talisman? What are you talking about?"

"I've had a talisman, like Joseph's. I bought it from Clara years ago. Well, in a tight spot I was thinking the power was working against me and I took it out and threw it in the river. Now I'd give anything to have it back."

The tears were starting up again and with a sigh of exasperation, Tom said, "Aw, Jen, I can't understand through the bawlin'. Lay off. Tell me why you want it back."

She was shaking her head and dabbing at her eyes. "No, Tom, you don't believe, and you'd just make fun of me."

He settled back on his heels beside the chair and said, "Got anyone else you can tell it to?" She shook her head and he continued, "Well, it seems to me you're going to spend the rest of your life a bawlin' unless you tell someone." Jenny was crying again. Tom waited. "Okay, let's hear it."

"Tom, I didn't realize it or I'd never have pitched the talisman. See, I had the talisman when Mark and I got married. I just didn't realize it was the power that was making him love me. Now that I've pitched it, there's nothing. He looks at me like he doesn't even see me. We used to talk so much—even when we were disagreeing there was something there. Now it's nothing. Tom, I'm so miserable I could die."

Tom was silent, chewing his lip thoughtfully. "I can't believe a little old medal could have that much power."

"I do. There's no doubt about it. Even I feel different about—" She paused and gulped, adding, "well, things."

"Could be he's just taking the responsibilities of bein' a pa pretty serious. I know he's kinda worried about you. Thinks you're looking puny. Would you want me to talk to him?"

"No! Tom, of course not. I told you only because you pushed at me. Please, don't say anything about this. Now I've got to get the smoke out of the house before he comes home."

"I'd pull a rug over that burned spot fer now." Tom headed for the door and then turned. "The mirror?"

"Oh." Jenny stared at her hands.

A strange expression filled his eyes, nearly like fear. "Something to do with the charms, huh? I've heard of spirits manifesting through mirrors. Jen, are you bitin' off more'n you can handle? Seems religion's safer."

Jenny was still sitting at the table long after Tom left. The afternoon was nearly over and soon Mark would be coming home. For a moment she felt her heart leap and then she contemplated the emotion. Perhaps it did help to talk to Tom.

She pushed herself out of the chair and went to find potatoes and carrots and onions. The pan was still full of the charred herbs and she began to scrub it clean. She shook her head and shuddered, "Land, what a start Tom gave me!"

Soberly she thought of those words, "Seems I said what I was denying all along. I have to admit, those words I was reading in the Bible just yesterday were speaking to me." She paused to consider, wondering why it took fear to strip away everything except the real need. Would she be able to follow after what was necessary?

Washing her hands, she went into the parlor and picked up the Bible. She sat in the rocking chair and turned to Isaiah, saying, "Seems I have to deal with the verses catching my attention first. This Isaiah 8:19 is talking about people seeking familiar spirits. That's me. I finally realized it when Adela just disappeared. What about her saying we could worship any way we pleased, 'cause there's only one god. Seems God doesn't like it, because He's saying in seeking God, if they don't speak according to God's Word, then there's no light in them." Silently she reread the words and had to admit that the truth was there.

Finding the other section in Isaiah 47:12, she read aloud, " 'Stand now with thine enchantments, and with the multitude of thy sorceries, wherein thou hast laboured from thy youth; if so be thou shalt be able to profit, if so be thou mayest prevail. . . . Let now the astrologers, the stargazers, the monthly prognosticators, stand up, and save thee from these things that shall come upon thee."

Slowly she closed the Book. "Jenny, it's saying right here, first, God doesn't like people seeking out the spirits." She was shivering now as she whispered, "I must admit, the spirits never helped a mite. I can't stand with them. Never has the green book led me to anything good. When this baby comes, the charms and herbs'll do me no good."

For a time she sat in silence while her thoughts drifted, searching for a sureness to believe in. "Funny how the words just popped out of me," she mused, recalling the day in the forest. "All those years, I never realized once that Adela was a familiar spirit." She shivered with awe. "I just said 'in the name of Jesus.' Adela couldn't stand against the Name, and she just disappeared like smoke."

Slowly Jenny closed her Bible and stood up. She needed to do something. Thinking a moment, she clasped the Bible to her bosom and looked up. “I renounce the way of the spirits. Because I'm fearing them—no, God, I fear what You'll do to me if I don't. I'm going to read my Bible and become a good Christian like Mark and Joseph Smith.”

CHAPTER 24

Mark stared out the window of the municipal building, watching the water drip off the roof. Carriages sloshed down the main street of Nauvoo, flinging arcs of dirty slush into the air.

It was late February and the afternoon sun streamed through the windows of the city council chamber. As attorney, Mark had been asked to sit in on the council meeting which would begin just as soon as Joseph arrived.

Mark moved his shoulders restlessly and stretched his shirt collar. Pratt was watching him with amusement.

Joseph hurried into the room with a sharp salute and Hyde called, "General Smith!" With a friendly smile, Joseph bowed. Still impatient with waiting, Mark scowled. He could see only Joseph's arrogance and the lateness of the hour. He met the Prophet's smile with a frown.

Without ceremony, Joseph plunged into his prepared speech. "These are great days, my brethren. I feel the power of God upon me. The purposes of the Almighty shall prevail. I intend to see they happen. I am a man empowered by the great Jehovah, and this influence is not to be taken lightly. With the children of God the power does more with a handful than a million men could do without the power."

"Hear ye, hear ye!" shouted Kimball. Mark was gloomy as he listened to the upbeat tenor of the laughter greeting Kimball.

Jospeh was into the heart of his message. "Do you see Nauvoo correctly? We are a state within a state. Soon we shall petition Congress for that recognition. The Nauvoo Charter, which passed the Illinois Legislature unanimously, signifies our relationship. We are to the union the same as a state."

He paused and leaned forward, saying in deliberately paced words, "You brethren know as well as I do that the laws of the state of Illinois are unconstitutional. We would be a pack of fools to keep such laws as our own."

"Prophet, General," came a voice from the back of the room. "I would like to remind the brethren that the charter provides that should any man come into the city with a writ for your arrest, we shall arrest him and try him. If he's found guilty of pushing the old Missouri offenses, he can be sentenced to life imprisonment."

Amid the uproar, Clayton added, "And he can be pardoned by the governor of the state only under the consent of the mayor of Nauvoo himself, which is the prophet Joseph."

Mark was back in his office when Joseph came in. With effort, Mark attempted to control himself as the Prophet entered the room. As he looked at Joseph he was still thinking of Clayton's statement and wondering how many of the men of Nauvoo agreed with him.

"What's on your mind?" Joseph asked, flopping into Mark's chair.

"I was thinking of your slave Abel."

"He isn't a slave; he's a free man."

"Free when he dumps his money in your lap and is happy with shining your shoes and being your valet?"

"That was his idea. Any suggestions?"

"It isn't just Abel," Mark admitted. "Nearly every man close to you has this same shoe-licking air about him. I come near boiling every time I see their blind adoration. Joseph, it isn't normal."

"You speak like a man who's never had a friend to love him. I'm able to accept the love."

"Accept? The smiles and pats, yes—but what about those who disagree with you? Why can't you allow criticism without labeling them dissenters and chasing them out?"

"Have anyone in mind?"

"Last week, during the priesthood meeting I was listening to you lay on us all the new teachings. Joseph, you know as well as I those teachings are completely contrary to the Holy Bible, contrary to all we've been taught through our growing-up years. Yet those men sat there and took it. I was thinking, too, of David Whitmer.

"You remember I mentioned having a talk with him in Springfield. One of the things that struck me so forcefully was his statement that some of the men are so blinded to reason that they believe anything you say. I'm beginning to think that's right."

"Mark, I'm called of God. I have the keys to the kingdom.

Need I keep reminding you of the fact?"

"And the fact that the revelations you've given are the very words of Jesus Christ? Whitmer says you made changes in the *Book of Commandments* which ended up supporting you as a seer in the church. The same changes also to support the idea of the priesthood in the church. He charged you with departing from the teachings of Jesus Christ revealed in the *Book of Mormon* when you made these changes. If the Book is from God and is Scripture, how do you respond to his claim?"

Joseph got to his feet. "The reason I came in here, Mark, is because I don't like your arrogance. I came near to flogging you in city council meeting just to wipe the sneer off your face. I think the spirit of Satan is in your heart, and you'd better be getting it out. There're not many around here who can take such an attitude."

Joseph continued. "Funny you should be talking about men who displayed the same spirit. Better learn from them. They're out. They and their families have lost their estate in the hereafter. Mark, take the warning to heart."

Mark was still seething when he left the office and went to the livery stable to get his horse. It hadn't helped to have Clayton's counsel after Joseph left the room.

Joseph's secretary said, "I tremble with fear for you, Mark. You know Joseph has the keys of the kingdom. There's not a one of us who will make it in the hereafter without the Prophet meeting us and taking us in to be with him for eternity. If he says the word, there's damnation waiting for us."

As Mark prepared to mount his horse, Tom's staying hand gripped the bridle. "Something the matter?"

"Just irritated at Joseph."

"I rode out to see Jen. Mark, you know she's a bit teary right now."

Mark frowned. "Seems natural in her condition."

"I'm not an authority, but I'm guessing she's feeling as big as she looked in that red outfit. Might be just a hug or pat would let her know you still love her." Tom turned away.

Mark's black thoughts kept him company until he had nearly reached home. The first timid hints of spring were becoming evident. The snow had melted from the roadway and the water gurgled through ditches. Spikes of green tipped the branches of trees and bushes. He heard the burst of song from the robins, saw crocuses in the snow.

On the last stretch of road, he reined in the mare and let

her browse as he tried to collect his thoughts and shake his dismal mood.

He regarded his commitment and scowled. What high hopes he had felt, what tide of need he had seen that day in Far West when he'd whispered, "Yes, Lord." He recalled thinking brave thoughts of bringing all the Mormons to an understanding of truth and a joyful acceptance of the way of Jesus Christ.

Now he slumped in his saddle. What had the dedication merited? Nothing except—Mark winced and as the pain grew inside of him, he began to face the fact he had been ignoring since December. The teaching at last week's priesthood meeting had linked together the gossip and innuendos. Could he admit it and carry on?

The mare grazed her way down the road and turned into the lane. When she stopped beside the barn, Mark was able to admit he had a problem. He pulled the saddle from the horse and carried it into the barn. "How do you say 'yes, Lord' when it means giving up your wife to Joseph's embraces and raising his son as your own?"

Mark was still sitting on the edge of the manger when the last of the sunlight touched the apple tree and disappeared. When he shivered with cold, he realized nothing had been resolved.

With a sigh, he headed for the house, muttering to himself, "One thing's certain. My lousy attitude has got to go. Didn't realize Jen was suffering the backwash." He winced and pressed his lips together. "Never will I deny her anything she wishes, even if it's that monster."

Jenny, wrapped in the red flannel robe, was huddled in the rocking chair beside the kitchen stove. She lifted her face as Mark walked in the door, "Oh," she whispered, "I didn't know you were home."

He saw her swollen face, the pile of newspapers and books on her lap as she attempted to get to her feet. "Jenny, is there something wrong?" The dread nearly held him motionless.

"No," she sighed. "Just lazy, I guess. I was trying to read and dropped off." Her brooding eyes watched as he took the books from her and carried them to the shelf.

As she removed the robe and folded it, he said, "I wondered if you were going to wear it. Is it warm?" She nodded. He forced the words, just then realizing how seldom he had mentioned the baby. "You'll be needing it soon. I understand new mothers spend lots of nights walking the floor with their babies." He saw the corners of her mouth lift as she went to the stove.

Thinking of the picture Tom had created with his accusation, Mark watched Jenny. Seeing the delicate curl on her neck, the soft curve of her chin, he felt as if his heart would explode.

She turned and met his eyes. "Mark, what is it?"

In the shadowy kitchen it was impossible to keep back the words. "Jenny, I can't get along without you."

She rushed at him and crowded close. "Oh, Mark, it isn't that bad. Not very many women—Mark, it'll soon be over, and then we'll be happy again, won't we?"

The words were almost worse than the silence, he decided as he held her. She had brought up a fear he hadn't even considered. "Jenny, hadn't you ought to have someone here? It's so far to town. What if you need me in a hurry?"

Serenity swept across her face. "Mark, first babies take forever to get here. Besides, I'm trusting the Lord to take care of it all. See, I've been reading the Bible, the *Book of Mormon* and the *Doctrine and Covenants*. I am obeying the ordinances; what can happen?"

For a dismayed moment he considered the things he might say and said instead, "Shall I take you in to Sally?"

"For a whole month? Mark, it might be nice, but let's wait."

That night when he awakened he saw her outlined against the moonlit window. "Jenny, come to bed; it's too cold for you to sit there."

When she turned he saw the pale oval of her face. "Mark, what was your father's name?"

"John."

"John Mark was a Bible name. Could we call him that?" The constant pain stabbed him afresh. He was silent as he considered it, wondering if having the baby here would diminish the hurt. "Maybe you'd better pick a girl's name as well."

She was beside him in the bed and her hands were on his face. "Mark, what is it?" He could only shake his head as she curled against him.

When she was breathing gently, again he thought of the revelation Hyrum Smith had given them in priesthood meeting—the revelation on everlasting marriage. Several of the men had winced when Hyrum revealed the section dealing with the righteousness of having more than one wife.

He delivered his final statement to all the members of the High Council. Mark had dared not look into the faces of those men as Hyrum said, *Now you have been delivered the revelation concerning the celestial marriage. You who accept and obey will be saved; those who reject the teaching shall be damned.*

CHAPTER 25

"Oh, Mark!" Jenny called as Mark ran down the stairs. "Come look—there's a new lamb."

She was standing at the kitchen window, the red robe not quite covering the bulge of her pregnancy. Mark looked at her pale face and shining eyes, "My dear, tomorrow you go to Sally. I've talked with her and she urged me to insist you come soon."

Her eyes were still shining as she turned. Now he saw the shine was tears as she whispered, "Just last spring I was pounding on heaven's gates because the sheep were having babies, while I was barren. Oh, Mark, it is too good to be true, isn't it?"

"Yes." His voice was flat, and he turned away.

The excitement was gone from her voice as she passed him, saying, "Your breakfast is ready. Are you staying for priesthood meeting tonight?"

"Yes, but Joseph's promised the important part will be brief, and then I will leave." He carried the coffeepot to the table. "Will you get your things together today? I'd like to leave early in the morning. There's a meeting I can't afford to miss."

"And the baby's." Her voice was smug.

"What? Oh." He stared at her. A baby would be coming back with them.

"Mark," her voice was timid and he looked up, "I've been reading—I have so many questions. How do we know we'll go to heaven when we die?"

"I've told you, Jenny. By trusting in Jesus' atonement."

"The books say so, too, but then there's more, and I get so confused. Seems everytime I turn around there's something else I must do." She sighed and rubbed her hand across her face.

Mark was caught by that gesture. It said more than her words, more than ever before.

Mark's day was busy—full of paperwork and Joseph's talk. Until later, during the High Council meeting, there hadn't been time to think about Jenny again.

But at the meeting, as Mark watched the man standing before Hyrum Smith and listened to the accusation, he recalled Jenny's question and the way her trembling hands had pressed her face. When the realization struck him, he could scarcely wait for the session to be over.

Jenny's questions were not idle curiosity. A fervent prayer welled up in him; it was the first hopeful prayer in weeks.

But now Hyrum was speaking again. "Brother Hoyt, we have heard testimony. Please face the council for instruction." The man moved, and Hyrum added, "You are ordered to cease using the divining rod. In addition, you will refrain from calling certain individuals witches or wizards, and in conjunction with this, no more are you to indulge in the burning of boards to heal or deliver those so-called witches from their bewitchment."

Old man Walker sitting in front of Mark muttered, "Some teaching. It's different than from the beginning of the church. Back in those days Cowdery got mentioned in a revelation, telling him he had the gift of using the divining rod."

When Mark left the meeting, Lewis Wilson, who had been sitting beside him, moved up to touch Walker on the elbow. Mark nearly collided with the two. Lewis was saying, "You ought not to talk against the Prophet. It isn't safe."

"Walls have ears?"

He shrugged and his voice dropped. "Joseph called me in and told me every word I said to Kimball last week when we were talking—" He glanced at Mark and nodded, drawing him close. "Joseph said the spirit told him ever'thing I said. So both of you, be watching what you say."

When Mark reached home, Jenny was back in the rocking chair. Her Bible and the *Book of Mormon* were in her lap, and folded on top was a newspaper.

He pulled a chair forward and sat down facing her. Today she seemed relaxed, her faint smile delivered as if from a great distance. "Jenny, you asked me what you were to believe. The Holy Bible says that Jesus is God, come to this earth for the purpose of redeeming us, reconciling us to God. He did it through dying on the cross as atonement for our sins. It is grace, Jenny. That's all.

"Jenny, believing, having faith in order to receive this glorious gift from God is simply taking God at His word. Just believe, just accept the gift, and you'll never again have to wonder what you must do to please God."

She lifted her dreamy eyes to him and said, "Nothing, only believe? Mark, that doesn't seem right. Nothing? That's impossible. I must *do* something for God. I can't accept the *only believe* idea. Seems Joseph's more nearly right when he gives out the commandments, the rules and regulations."

She was quiet for a moment and then she added, "I don't believe there's a person in town who wouldn't rather do something to work for his salvation. That's love."

She picked up the paper. "Sometimes I do get a little confused, though."

"How's that?"

The glance she slanted at him was quick, and just as quickly it slid away, but not until he saw the wise-owl expression. "There's this article in the *Millennial Star*. It's an old one."

He leaned back. "Well, tell me about it."

"The writer says there are tales circulating saying that we Mormons have the practice of polygamy. But the writer is in a fuss about it. He is stating emphatically that no such practice exists among the people, nor will it ever be so, since our books are very strict about talking against it. Mark, did you know the *Book of Mormon* forbids polygamy, calling it adultery?"

Slowly he asked his question, dreading the answer. "Does that bother you?"

"Yes," she said slowly as she rolled the corner of the newspaper between her fingers. "It bothers me because there's something going on that makes the statement a lie." Now her eyes were questioning, looking directly at him. "Mark, you've joined the priesthood. Is there talk?"

"A little." He was considering the question and planning his answer when she spoke.

"I am fearful," she said with a troubled sigh. Glancing up at him, she added, "More'n I can say, the church means so much to me. I can't ever leave it—I'm fearful to do so. But—" Mark found himself holding his breath. Jenny sighed again and finally said, "I believe there are hard times ahead for the church."

Mark got to his feet, nearly stumbling in his haste. "I've got to milk the cows. Stay in the chair. I'll find something for us to eat when I bring the milk in."

Grabbing the milk buckets, he headed for the barn. Mark flung hay and corn until the effort sent perspiration pouring down his back. When he finished the milking and gathered the eggs, he still lingered on.

Finally he sighed and lifted his face. "God, I hear you. I can't. Somehow forgiving her when we had such love—somehow it's impossible."

He gave most of the milk to the pigs. Eyeing the remainder

in the bottom of the pail, he was filled with heaviness as he considered the days ahead.

Jenny was asleep when Mark slipped out of bed the next morning. Moving quietly, he dressed and left to milk the cows and prepare breakfast.

He was still staring at the skillet and thinking of last night's conversation when Jenny came into the kitchen.

Dully, without looking up, he asked, "Got your things together?"

When there wasn't an answer he turned. Jenny was leaning against the doorjamb. Even her lips were colorless as she slowly bent against the pain.

Mark took a deep breath and shoved his hands into his pockets. "If you don't need breakfast, let's just get going."

"Mark," her breath ended in a gasp. "It's too late."

"Jenny," he implored, "we've got to go!" She was shaking her head. "Shall I go for Sarah, Mrs. Daniels?"

"Mark, don't leave. Hot water." She straightened and tried to smile. "I've delivered babies before, I—oh!"

He lifted her in his arms, wondering how his shaking legs would get him up the stairs.

Mark boiled the water, found the baby clothes, and watched the circle of sunlight move from the patchwork quilt to the middle of the rag rug. And when it was over, Jenny was in command.

Mark held the squalling, squirming boy and Jenny sponged him clean, wrapped the blanket around the child, and held him to her breast. She took a deep breath and leaned back against the pillows.

"It's done, it's happened. Mark, this is your little boy. John Mark." She looked at him and the smile disappeared from her face. "I think you'd better lie down, too."

The sun hid behind the clouds, and in the afternoon, Mark managed a meal and brought the diapers. He pulled the cradle close to the bed, and when Jenny's arms released the bundle, he lifted the child, feeling him stir. He watched the little fists uncurl and the eyelids flutter, and he felt the lump growing in his throat.

When he escaped to the barn, the tears had him stumbling, groping until the hay was under him. It was much later, nearly dark, when Mark dragged himself out of the hay and went to feed the stock. He tried to whistle and the sobs came again. "Jesus, Lord. I don't deserve your forgiveness, even if I do forgive her. I don't care whose baby it is—I'll love him and raise him like my own. And I'll love Jenny more than ever before."

CHAPTER 26

"How's the little tyke?" Tom asked as Mark came into the stable.

Mark grinned. "For only being a month old, fine. I don't think he'll be playing ball with you before summer, but he has a good appetite and doesn't complain about sleeping most nights. Can I expect more?" As he led the mare out he added, "Tom, Joseph wants you at his office as soon as possible."

Tom watched Mark head down the street and slowly wiped his hands. "Seems fine now, even proud of the young'un. My brother-in-law just might have had the pre-baby grouch. Leastwise, he seems pretty happy." Tom frowned as he reached for his hat and headed for Joseph's store. There were enough rumors running around Nauvoo to scare any husband.

The Prophet was in the barroom at the back of the store. When he saw Tom he shoved the glass back and walked to the door. "Upstairs, Tom." He led the way.

They passed Clayton's office and the man lifted his head long enough to nod at Tom before he picked up his pen.

"Catching up," Joseph murmured as he opened the door for Tom. "Wish all my men were as eager to do their work."

Joseph dropped into the chair behind his desk and pointed to the chair opposite him. "John D. Lee's outta town. Will be for up to a month. Family problems. Something about his wife's sister; the whole family's headed to Vandalia.

"That's why I wanted to see you. You haven't been much involved in the Danites since Missouri, and I felt it best to start pulling up the reins tight. Never know when it's important to have trustworthy men close to you."

"Problems?" Tom asked.

"Nothing new. The Missourians keep me a little edgy. I hear Bennett's over that way trying to stir up trouble. It's just wise to prevent trouble before it happens. Lee's been serving as bodyguard since '41, all the time except when he's on mission work.

Right now I need you to hang out around the Mansion House evenings. When I go out I need someone with me; that's where you'll fit in."

As Tom got up to leave, Joseph added, "By the way, Clayton had a conversation with Kimball. Seems he found out about a plot to trap members of the secret priesthood. Keep your ears open. Could be advisable to send the Whittling Deacons out that way. Don't know who's involved or what the motive. I've a hunch Bennett might be in back of the deal."

Tom left Joseph, wondering how he could manage working at the stable days and the Mansion House nights.

As he walked back to work, Tom mused on the changes in Nauvoo. As the weather warmed, hordes of strangers were making their way to the city. It was easy to spot the visitors, Tom thought as he stepped past the group on the sidewalk. The women seemed to all have that wide-eyed expression, while the men wore a curious, half-envious one.

By now Tom had adjusted to answering questions and to seeing a trail of people moving in and out of the museum, the unfinished Nauvoo House, and the temple. He was also accustomed to seeing Joseph on the street, discoursing with gusto on any topic.

He winced, recalling the last curbside speech Joseph had made. "Seems a mite hot-winded," Tom muttered, "comparing himself so high up, sayin' 'Is there not one greater than Solomon here? He built his temple with his father David's money, and I've had to do my building by myself.' Joe's not countin' the hours we donated to building and the money the Saints have dished out." He brooded for a moment and added, "Seems it's more *our* temple."

Just before Tom entered the stable, he raised his head to look at the temple rising on the highest city hill. "Sure going to look good with all that gold leaf on the dome, isn't it?" Tom turned to greet Andy Morgan.

"And you've done a great job on it," Tom complimented.

"We're moving as fast as possible. Joseph says we're not going to progress very fast until we get the temple done so we'll be able to move on with the endowments."

"He's also said our salvation depends on gettin' the Nauvoo House built," Tom added.

Andy sighed and shook his head. After a pause he added, "Saw you coming out of the store and wondered if you'd like a ride out to see the new baby. Sally and I will be leaving shortly."

Tom was already shaking his head. "Sorry, taking on a new

job. Prophet's asked me to do guard duty at the Mansion House. Lee's outta town, maybe for a month."

"Is that so?" Andy studied Tom's face. "The job could be interesting."

"What do you mean by that?"

"Oh, nothing," Andy replied hastily. "Maybe we'll get together later."

Jenny had just started dinner when Mark arrived. She reached for his kisses and said, "Oh, I'm sorry. The baby's been fussy and I haven't started the potatoes yet." She paused, then asked, "Would you please hold him?" Mark nodded and bent over the cradle.

"Sarah was here. She came to bring some of Aaron's clothing and some little blankets. I'd expect her to be keeping them for the next one. Strange."

"What's strange?"

She looked startled, "Oh, it's not what she said. She just looked kinda sad when I asked if she'd like them back."

In a moment she added, "Sarah said the temple offices are nearly complete and that Joseph and the twelve will be moving in shortly. She's been in the Nauvoo House and says it's going to be beautiful when it's finished." Jenny paused and added, "A little bitter she was about it all."

"Sounds like Sarah's unhappy; do you know why?" Mark asked as he carefully shifted the fussing baby on his shoulder. "There, did you hear that? No wonder John was unhappy. Takes pa to get the bubbles out, huh?"

"Nauvoo House. Because it is so luxurious. Sarah's that way. Worried about the poor emigrants coming in."

"It's a valid worry. But Joseph seems to think giving a good image of the Saints to the world is important."

"Sarah told me something else. Did you hear anything about a fellow named Wiley who lives at Kinderhook digging up some ancient plates?"

Mark looked up. "News travels fast. Clayton told me a week or so ago."

"And you didn't tell me?" Jenny wailed. "Sarah even had a newspaper clipping to show me. It says the plates prove the *Book of Mormon* is true."

Hastily Mark said, "Honestly, I didn't have much confidence in the tale."

"Sarah says Joseph has started to translate them."

Mark sat down in the rocking chair and watched John chew his fist. Finally he looked up and said, "Clayton was telling me about them last week. When Joseph walked into the office he verified the finding, saying there were six of them. Wiley cleaned them up and brought them to him for translation."

"And he's going to translate them?"

"Of course. Joseph said he'd started, and that so far he's discovered they contain the history of the person with whom they were found. Seems this fellow was a direct descendant of Ham through Pharaoh. He also said the man received his kingdom from the ruler of heaven and earth."

Jenny glanced sharply at Mark; as he grinned she said, "You aren't taking this very seriously, are you?"

"If those potatoes aren't done, I'll eat them raw."

"If Joseph could hear you, he'd run you out of town for an apostate."

"He's tried. I can't imagine why he keeps me here. Probably it's his pride."

"What do you mean?"

"He intends to humble me, make me another groveling Clayton."

"I do know from gossip that he considers you a plum," Jenny said slowly. "Even Orson knew of your reputation in Springfield. Do you suppose it's because Joseph is seeing how important it is to be on the good side of the governor?"

"That doesn't sound like a Saint," Mark said slowly, studying her. "You're starting to sound like a woman with her eyes wide open."

"Not like a good Mormon who believes God's going to drop everything in our laps, no matter what?" A thoughtful expression crossed Jenny's face, one which Mark hadn't seen for a long time. Still holding the baby, he went to kiss her.

On the Sabbath, the day sparkled like a jewel. When Mark drove the team out onto the road, he had difficulty holding Tupper back. "Frisky as a colt," he said, grinning down at Jenny. "And you look prettier than any married woman with a baby has any right to be."

"Oh, Mark, it's such a beautiful day and it's good to be out again. I can't wait to show little Mark to everyone."

"John," he said firmly.

"John Mark?" He studied her clear eyes and looked at the baby's blonde hair curling out from under his cap.

When they reached Nauvoo, Mark said, "Looks as if the service is going to be in the temple grove today. Shall I place the buggy under the trees, or do you want to sit down front on the benches?"

"Oh, on the benches. I want to see everyone. There's Tom. Sally and Tamara are over there."

Mark lifted Jenny and the baby from the buggy and settled them on a front bench. As he walked back to the buggy, the women began clustering around Jenny.

Leaving the rig and mare at the stable, Mark headed back to the grove. Although it was still early, crowds of people streamed toward the grove.

As he walked down the street, he saw Clayton and Joseph Smith on the sidewalk in front of Joseph's store. A crowd was gathering, and Mark paused to listen. Joseph was saying, "While I was praying, a voice said to me that if I live to be eighty-four, I'd see the Son of Man. Right now, I don't believe the Second Coming will be sooner."

"I've heard the Father is only spirit," said the stranger at Mark's right.

Joseph answered, "That, brethren, is a sectarian doctrine. It is completely false. Both the Father and the Son have bodies like ours. The idea that they dwell in a man's heart is false."

"Where does God dwell?"

"On a planet which is like crystal. There's a sea of glass before His throne." Joseph grinned and added, "You brethren are going to be smarter than me in another minute. But that's all right. Knowledge is power. The man who seeks knowledge will have power."

Then he added, "The earth, when it is purified, will become the same type of crystal. It will be a Urim and Thummim by which all things in regards to an inferior kingdom will be made manifest to those dwelling there. At the same time, this earth will be with Christ. Brethren, I could go on and on, but it behooves us to get to services."

He paused to add, "The principle of intelligence we garner in this life will rise with us in the resurrection. If a person gains knowledge here through diligence and obedience, so much better for him in the next world." Mark watched Joseph and his followers walk rapidly up the hill to the temple grove.

When Mark finally reached Jenny's side, the morning sermon was well underway. John Mark was sleeping with one pink fist curled like a rose bud. Examining the little face, Mark could not find a single feature resembling anyone he knew. He touched his finger against the tiny button of a nose, and gratitude welled up in him. That nose did not in the slightest resemble the beak of the Prophet.

Mark turned his attention to the sermon just as the Prophet said, "I want you to understand, the Holy Ghost is a personage, just as the Father and Son are personages. A man can receive all the gifts the Holy Ghost has to offer, and in addition, the Holy Ghost may descend upon a man, but will not tarry with him."

As the people around Mark and Jenny got to their feet, Jenny said, "Sally's invited us to go home with them."

"It may take all afternoon to get there," Mark said with a grin. "I've never seen such a crowd. And I think you've shown this baby to them all."

"For that, you carry him." She deposited the blue bundle in his lap and stood to her feet. "Oh, what a beautiful day! But in another month it will be hot. Mark, why have they taken so many of the trees out of the grove?"

"They need more room. Look at the mass of people."

"The Saints will be a multitude soon," Jenny murmured as she walked beside Mark with her hand tucked through his arm. "Seems the prophecies are being fulfilled. We will become a multitude."

"Sister, don't forget the rest," the wizened man beside her grinned. "It has been given that we shall take over the state, the whole country and finally the whole world. You mark my words, this young'un will be marching triumphantly around the world for the Lord."

Jenny watched the man limp away and said slowly, "All the war talk hits home with a different meaning when there's a baby." She looked at Mark, and her eyes were troubled.

CHAPTER 27

"Mark, you can't be serious!" Jenny exclaimed. "Take a three-month-old baby on a boat?"

"My dear, this isn't just a boat. It's Joseph's *Maid of Iowa.* Joseph, Clayton, and I need to make a trip to Quincy. The fastest way to go is by boat. Joseph suggested we make a party of it. Seems everyone except you is in favor of it."

"He won't get sunburned?" She looked anxiously at the baby in the cradle.

"Jenny, there are cabins and a big pavilion on the main deck. Joseph has invited a large group of the Saints. We're to leave early in the morning. We should arrive at Quincy with plenty of time to take care of business and allow you women to shop."

Jenny's excitement was rising. "Oh, Mark, it does sound fun!"

The following morning when the steamboat pulled away from John D. Lee's wharf, the sun was just topping the forested hills to the east of Nauvoo.

Jenny found that the pavilion was enclosed with glass and lined with benches. The festive air was immediately apparent. Children in Sabbath best romped about the deck. Women dressed in pastel calico and printed lawn scattered like blossoms around the room. From the galley came the fragrance of spicy cider and popping corn. The freed slave, Abel, now Joseph Smith's adoring, self-appointed slave, sat on the bulkhead watching the activities.

One young matron with a bulging middle and youngsters clinging to her skirts groaned, "Popcorn this early? My young'uns will be sick before they can get sunburned."

Several young girls began organizing games for the smaller children, and the women settled on the benches as their husbands disappeared below deck.

Mrs. Kimball grimaced. "Heber calls it work, but I saw the

liquor and apple-jack they were loading. Oh, well, I suppose they'll work it off by nighttime."

Jenny allowed herself to be pushed into one of the few comfortable deck chairs. The boat was picking up speed now. Wide-eyed youngsters clung to the rail and Jenny caught her breath as the vessel trembled and groaned. Giving a sharp three-note toot, the craft slipped into the main current of the river, and a cooling breeze filled the pavilion. With a sigh of relief, Jenny snuggled John Mark close and curled his hair around her fingers as he began to nurse.

The women were settling into cozy groups. Some sat with their heads together, and their giggles punctuated the trip. Others pulled out satchels of handwork. When Jenny lifted the sleeping baby to her shoulder, Emma Smith caught her eye.

The older woman moved close and touched John Mark's soft curls. The dreamy expression on her face caused Jenny to bite her lip. "Don't look so," Emma said. "There will be more. I shall never give up that hope. Is there anything more comforting than the blessed weight of those soft little bodies in your arms?"

"I've waited a long time for this one," Jenny said softly. "Yes, you are right."

All too soon, it seemed, the boat was cutting speed. After a final bend in the river, the town of Quincy lay before them. While the women and children flocked to the rail, Jenny carried John Mark into the shelter of a cabin to change his diapers.

Mark came to the door. "The men are heading for the courthouse. Will you go with the women?"

"Yes, but tell them I'll come later. John Mark must be fed again before I join them."

The last of the children's shouts had faded away, leaving only the gentle slap of water against the hull. As Jenny went to lay the sleeping baby on the bunk, the sharp scent of alcohol reached her. Turning quickly she found Joseph filling the doorway.

"Jenny, my beautiful one," he murmured, and she realized it was his breath laden with alcohol. He came into the room and shut the door. "My wife."

Anger surged through Jenny, but she determined to remain calm as she turned away from him to button her frock. She fought for composure and finally turned to him. "Joseph, I refuse to even discuss this matter with you. Please leave now and say no more—ever."

He dropped heavily into the chair and said, "Move the baby to the top bunk." She folded her arms and stared at him. "Jenny, my dear, I earnestly desire con—connubial bliss." His tongue stumbled over the words.

"At one time, Joseph, had you snapped your fingers I would have come running. That was before you had a wife. Now I consider this tasteless seduction."

"The grand lady. You are my grand lady. Remember the ceremony witnessed by Brigham Young, Kimball, and Hyde? Remember the book? Jennifer, the book of the law of the Lord is His will written out for you timid females to see. Will you risk the wrath of the Lord by being coy?"

She could see he was fast losing his befuddled air, and she found herself fearing this cold-eyed man. Taking a deep breath, Jenny searched for words to answer him. Suddenly her world righted itself.

"Why, Joseph, I'm not afraid of the Lord near as much as you think. But tell me, what's there to fear?"

"The loss of your salvation. As your husband I will be god to you. I will take you to the heavenlies with me to reign as queen forever. Without me, you'll never have salvation."

Jenny was eyeing the door. The baby stirred and her heart sank. It was impossible to reach both John Mark and the door before Joseph would stop her.

He was speaking. "I must remind you that no marriage is valid until consummated."

"And I will remind you that this is adultery."

"The Lord has shown me it's all right to have fun; it isn't adultery unless we talk about it to others."

His words made Jenny pause, and curiosity picked at her. "Where did you get that idea? Of course it's adultery."

"The Lord has shown me that something can be wrong in one case, but not in another."

"If that is so, then how's a person ever to know what's right and what's wrong?"

"Jenny, you can take my word for it or you can try the spirits. Just pray for a sign. The Lord will pour out on you such a blessing as you've never had before. I will pray for you, but you must also earnestly ask the Lord for this manifestation."

Jenny was silent for a long time, then slowly she turned and paced the room, thinking hard. His words had pulled up deeply buried ideas and impressions, and she must study them out. *Manifestation*. Adela.

She studied him keenly, sensing now what had escaped her attention before. "Joseph, you should know better than to reveal your plan to me. Remember, I was there at the diggings. I know about spirits, too."

"Jennifer, you'll go to hell if you continue to act in this manner."

"Like Mr. Thompson? I've only heard gossip, but I wonder. What kind of temptation did Thompson give in to? Why did he have to die, and how? Is it possible to control the spirits to that extent?"

"Aren't you fearful?" he asked curiously.

She shook her head, saying, "I intend to talk. The first one I'll tell will be Emma." She saw him cringe. "Joseph, I am beginning to think I'm not the only woman in Nauvoo who has had to listen to this from you. If I ever find out anything to support that hunch, I'll make trouble. Remember, I saw you with Eliza Snow."

For a long time Joseph sat slumped in the chair. When he finally sighed and sat up, he said, "Jennifer, I honestly do love you and want you desperately; but more than that, I'm thinking of our future, the eternities, worlds without end. More than losing you here, I don't want to spend eternity without you. That's something, isn't it? I can have any woman I want just by snapping my fingers. Doesn't it matter to you that I *choose* you?"

"No."

She heard the sound of footsteps and Clayton's muffled, timid voice. "Joseph, you'll have to come before the probate judge." His voice was apologetic. "I've had to make out new papers, and you'll need to sign them."

Jenny couldn't understand the word he muttered, but Joseph pulled himself to his feet and left the room. As soon as the door closed, Jenny dropped into the chair. When her trembling ceased, she sat up and smoothed her hair.

By the time John Mark stirred, Jenny was smiling. "Joseph, I'll never be afraid of you again." She paused to wonder at the change in her response toward the Prophet. Finally she whispered, "Either getting rid of the talisman or reading the books has put a peck of religion into me. But somehow I know I need so much more." She shivered, remembering that mirrored image.

Tom found the late June day only pleasantly warm. He nudged his mount, urging the mare to keep up with the carriage moving smartly along the road to Dixon. As he flicked the reins, he glanced at the occupants. Joseph and Emma were visiting her sister in Dixon, Illinois, and from the Prophet's expression, Tom guessed he'd had enough of woman-talk. Emma's sister bobbed her head to emphasize each word.

Joseph caught Tom's eye and he mouthed, "Horse." Tom nodded. As the carriage turned up the lane, he noticed the mounted rider waiting and touched the gun on his hip.

"Hold it, Joseph," he warned, spurring his horse. Tom didn't recognize the man, but when he saw him eye the carriage and slip from his horse, Tom relaxed.

The man's voice was soft, "Judge Adams sent me. Governor Ford let it slip secret-like that he'd signed a writ from Missouri. They're coming after Joseph Smith."

Joseph was standing beside them as the fellow finished and touched his hat. "I'm to offer no advice, and to leave promptly." He touched his hat and turned.

Tom saw the pinched look on Emma's face as she asked, "What will you do? You can't continue to run from them."

Joseph studied her face and said slowly, "That's just what I was thinking. Emma, if you can stand it, I think now's the time to test the Nauvoo Charter." She paled and he turned to Tom. "I'm not inclined to leave just now. Go into town and nose around, see what you can find out and then get back here."

Two hours later Tom arrived back at the house to find two men with the Prophet. There was a sardonic smile on Joseph's face as he said, "These fellas are sheriffs from Missouri—Wilson and Reynolds. They suggest I come into Dixon with them."

"That's a good idea." Tom kept his voice level and relief brightened Joseph's eyes.

By the time Tom located Cyrus Walker and returned to the tavern, Joseph had an audience.

The top story of the tavern served as the jail. Now Tom saw that the upstairs window was open; Joseph was leaning out, thundering at the crowd gathered in the street below.

As the cheers and laughter swept through the crowd, Tom tightened the reins and paused to listen.

In his best Sabbath-morning voice, Joseph was delivering a discourse on marriage. As the fellow beside him roared, Tom said, "What's goin' on?"

"Aw, they shut him up and he's been leaning out the window scorching our ears with Missouri talk. Old Jake found out who he was and asked for a sermon. Funny, he is."

Joseph caught sight of Tom and the man behind him. Hastily he concluded his sermon and withdrew his head.

Walker was in good humor as he followed Tom up the back

stairs. After introductions he said, "Timmons says you're looking for counsel."

"I want the best there is. Are you that man?"

"I'm campaigning for Congress. I don't have time to take on a criminal case now."

Joseph winced. "What's your price?"

"That you make it worth my time to give up campaigning. Ten thousand and the promise of your vote in the election. You gave it to the Democrats last election; the Whigs need it now."

Joseph nodded and Cryus got to his feet. "First I'll file suit for assault and false imprisonment against the Missouri fellas downstairs; then we'll head for Quincy. Judge Stephen A. Douglas is holding court there. It's going to be interesting. We'll have to trail out of here with the sheriffs from Missouri holding you while they're being held by a Dixon sheriff." He was chuckling as he left the room.

"Wouldn't be so funny if it was *his* ten thousand," Tom muttered.

Joseph grasped his arm and Tom saw the fear on the Prophet's face. "Tom, head outta here right this minute. I want you in Nauvoo to round up the Legion." Tom saw the beads of perspiration on Joseph's face as he paced the room.

"These fellas are going to do their best to slip me over the river to Missouri. I feel it in my bones. The only hope is to cut them off. First, get Wight and a few others to take the *Maid of Iowa* to Grafton. They're to head off any boats coming down the Illinois River. I know they're not in this alone. I'm too big a fish for just two men. I want the Legion to meet us at Monmouth."

"Joseph, that's nigh impossible!" Tom gasped.

"My life is at stake," Joseph said softly. "I feel it by the spirit."

Tom sprinted down the stairs. "Old girl, I hate to do this to you," he muttered as he jumped on the horse and dug in his heels.

The Legion had just crossed the Fox River when they caught up with the carriage carrying Joseph, Walker, and the two sheriffs. The bewildered sheriff from Dixon was still holding his gun and looking around when Tom reached the carriage.

He heard the Prophet's half-sob as he exclaimed, "These are my boys. We're not heading for Missouri!"

Tom tried to cover his embarrassment, saying, "There's more, but they ruined their horses gettin' here."

Within an hour Joseph had talked Walker into holding court in Nauvoo, while the Legion relaxed in the shade. "We need a rest tonight or we'll never make it," Taylor said when he heard the verdict, and Tom agreed.

It was two days before Joseph's caravan reached the outskirts of Nauvoo, but the Legion band and all the townfolk were there to meet them.

When Mark arrived home that afternoon, Jenny met him at the door. "Mark, I've been hearing guns. What's happened?"

"Nothing except the Prophet has come home, complete with Cyrus Walker, attorney and candidate for Congress, two sheriffs from Missouri and one from Dixon, as well as an escort of a hundred and fifty troops from Nauvoo."

"The guns?"

"Just celebration. The people and the band marched through town and the Legion popped off a few rounds. A little exuberance. The Prophet's to address the folks in the temple grove this afternoon. Put on your party clothes and dress up the little one. I'll take you in."

By the time Mark and Jenny arrived at the temple grove, people were moving in from all directions. "Mark, there are so many—will there be room for all?"

"Looks like thousands," Mark admitted. "It's good they cut those trees out of the grove. It'll be standing room only."

As they worked their way through the crowd, Jenny murmured, "It's hot already. Oh, look, there's Eliza Snow and Sarah Pratt. I see Sally and Andy on the other side of the Laws."

The crowd began to roar. Standing on her tiptoes, Jenny saw Joseph and several strangers moving toward the platform.

Joseph took his place and the crowd began to quiet. Jenny shifted the baby on her shoulder as she thought of the last time she had seen him. She found herself wondering, *Would he be wearing that happy, confident grin if I were to tell the truth about him?*

She shuddered. The speeches had begun, but Jenny was busy visualizing the horror on people's faces if she were to make her accusations. She glanced at her husband. Even Mark. Never would he believe that horrible story. She shifted uneasily and Mark took the baby from her.

Joseph was telling of his arrest. She listened. "The state of Illinois has given Nauvoo her charter. We have rights no one can take away. If our enemies will fight to suppress us or oppress us, they will fight against our rights. If the authorities of state and nation will not defend us, then we'll claim defense from higher powers."

A murmur swept through the crowd as he continued. "The

persecution which I have suffered is not condoned by heaven. Before it happens again, I promise you I'll shed every drop of blood in my veins and, in the end, I'll see my enemies in hell."

"Mark," Jenny whispered, outraged, "he doesn't have enemies."

There was a hiss and they turned again to listen. Joseph was saying, "To bear the oppression of the enemy any longer is a sin. Shall we put up with sin?" The grove trembled and shook under the *No!* and Jenny was filled with the memories of Missouri. The Saints and the sad-faced people of Missouri all lined up to march across Jenny's imagination, and with the memory she felt a cold chill sweep through her.

She whispered, and Mark bent close to hear, "Will it come again, the fighting?"

Joseph's words swept across the crowd, "If Missouri refuses to hold back the hand of revenge, I will restrain you no longer."

The chanting was sweeping through the crowd as he said, "In the name of Jesus Christ, with my authority under the holy priesthood, I turn the key! No longer shall the heavens restrain your hands. I will lead you to battle if you are not afraid to die for our cause, or to shed blood. I ask you to pledge your lives and your energy for the cause of freedom. If you will help me, then lift high your hand for the cause." Bewildered, Jenny looked around at the sea of hands.

She glanced at Mark's ashen face and cried, "Oh, Mark, let's leave! This is Missouri all over again."

As she turned to make her way through the crowd, Jenny heard Joseph say, "It does my heart good to see your love and support. It is an honor to lead forth people so virtuous and honest."

The next day, July 1, Joseph appeared before the Municipal Court of Nauvoo. When Mark came home that evening, he sank into the rocking chair with a tired sigh. Shaking his head, he said, "Well, unless the courts find a way to challenge it, the matter's settled."

"The trial? What happened?"

"The sheriff from Missouri, Reynolds, did a lot of protesting, but the court, under the jurisdiction of Chief Justice William Marks, tried Joseph and discharged him.

"Under the Nauvoo Charter the Missouri charge of treason was dismissed. Testimony—all by Mormons—showed that Joseph suffered at the hands of the Missourians, rather than being, as they claimed, the aggressor."

"Mark, will that decision stand?" Jenny whispered.

He looked up. "Depends. There's too much of politics in it right now. This is an election year. If the past is any indicator, Joseph's church voting power will play a role in the outcome of the election. Right now he's committed to a Whig vote because of the trial."

CHAPTER 28

With a sigh Mark pulled himself out of bed and went to the window. Dawn was a promise, but as he stood there, feeling as if all the wakeful hours of the past six weeks were pressing upon him, Mark didn't relish the promise.

He had heard the baby's whimper and had known when Jenny slipped out of bed, but that was just one more reminder of the problem heavy upon his mind.

Bracing his elbow against the window frame, Mark let his memories of that June day capture him again and pull him back into the problem. On the day he rushed into the office with the papers in his hands, Joseph, his brow furrowed with effort, was dictating to Clayton.

When Mark apologized and began to back out of the room, Joseph waved him to a chair, saying, "Stay. I'm nearly finished and I want you to hear this."

It was the revelation on marriage—the everlasting covenant of marriage. The words still knocked around in Mark's head, challenging him to deal with the issue. In the quiet of the night, with the press of Jenny's body close to him, he found the words a mockery.

He moved restlessly. He didn't believe in the revelations, or even in the Prophet's calling—but Jenny did, and that was the problem. He found himself whispering, "Lord Jesus, a long time ago You helped me realize the only honest way for me to deal with Jenny's need of You is to keep my mouth shut, never to force my deep desire for her salvation upon her. Lord, it's been difficult, and it's getting worse. I know pushing the truth on her makes me no different than Joseph, even when I *know* my truth is the Bible truth and his is not. Please help."

He waited in silence while the words from that revelation welled up in his mind: *I the Lord justified my servants Abraham, Isaac, Jacob . . . of their having many wives. . . . All those who have this law revealed to them must obey the same. . . . If ye abide not that covenant, then are ye damned; for no one can reject this covenant and be permitted to enter into my glory.*

Mark muttered, "And under the covenant, all these men will be gods, with power and angels in submission. And it's by doing the works of Abraham; in other words—as you are so fond of saying, Joseph—it's plural marriage that saves a man. And any good Mormon who won't go along with this is to be destroyed." Mark turned away from the window, once again affirming his commitment. "Lord, I must trust You to work this all out. You know, don't You? I wake up in a cold sweat thinking of the fearful *what ifs*."

In the kitchen Jenny saw the dawn touching the windows with light. The summer heat was only a misty warmth seeping through the open window.

She sat in the rocking chair holding John Mark against her breast. Deeply conscious of his warm weight, she pressed her lips to his fist and touched the tear on his cheek.

In the quiet she heard the beginning rustle of woodland creatures, the call of birds. From the pasture came the plaintive cry of the lambs. Jenny sighed deeply and snuggled the infant against her. "God's in His heaven and all's right—" she murmured, even then thinking of the imprint these early morning hours were making upon her.

" 'Tis impossible not to feel it," she added, looking out the window. "The beauty, the peace. The deeps. It's like it's being branded into me, all the goodness of God." She sat musing on a new fact. These early morning hours seemed to freshen her memory, and the words stored there surfaced.

"I didn't realize I was remembering the words while I was reading the Bible. Now if I could only find out the *whys* of it all."

"What why?" Mark was beside her, uttering the question as quietly as if the silence of morning rested in his soul, too. He sat on the woodbox at her feet, and their eyes were on the same level.

By the dawning light, she was seeing the curious flecks of blue-green in his eyes. Dreamily she thought to make mention that she had noticed John Mark's eyes changing to the same curious color, but it wasn't the time. Slowly she pressed out words, designed to fit the morning. "God, wrath, beauty. Jesus speaks of peace. Joseph preaches wrath. Jesus says, "Believe"; Joseph says, "Fear." Mark, my head whirls trying to remember the *do's*. Why does the Bible tell us that if righteousness comes by law, then Christ died for nothing?"

His eyes were changing, and for a moment she was caught up in the tenderness, wondering. Then he whispered, "Grace, Jenny. Jesus gives salvation as a gracious gift. Here we only glimpse the perfection of God, but we have hints. It's hinted through the love. He knows there's no way we can be holy, so He gives it."

"It doesn't seem right—to be ugly with all the sin we do, and then just get it." Her voice was brooding. "Seems more right to do something for God."

"There's no way we can *do* enough to be holy. It's like a coat. Through Jesus Christ's atonement, we have righteousness thrown about us. Only it isn't ours until we reach out and accept it."

In a moment she sighed and the words welled up: " 'To appoint unto them that mourn in Zion, to give unto them beauty for ashes, the oil of joy for mourning, the garment of praise for the spirit of heaviness; that they might be called trees of righteousness, the planting of the Lord, that he might be glorified.' " A moment later she quoted, " 'Who shall ascend into the hill of the Lord? or who shall stand in his holy place? He that hath clean hands, and a pure heart . . .' "

He gently prodded, "Why, Jenny?" She could only shake her head, whispering, "I don't know. Sometimes I get so weary for something." Then she whispered, "I love the phrase, 'Who is this king of glory?' It's a mystery, isn't it?" She got to her feet and carried the sleeping baby to his cradle. Now the sun was bright and she sighed with regret.

Mark rode to Nauvoo with sadness as heavy as cold iron resting upon his heart. Just before he left the house Jenny had whispered, " 'Lift up your heads, O ye gates; . . . and the king of glory shall come in.' " Her eyes had been dark pools of yearning.

He had said *Jenny* with gladness on his soul, and then he looked at the sleeping boy. With his vow of silence and forgiveness, how could he say *Jenny, not until . . .*? With every mile he rode, Mark felt as if his heart was breaking with the desire to urge her confession.

He straightened in the saddle; once again he must face Joseph and the necessity of forgiving that man.

July was slipping away, but Joseph still basked in the glory of the Independence Day celebration. To Mark it seemed that nearly every day the Prophet found occasion to mention the crowds of strangers who had poured into Nauvoo to see the marvels and listen to the man who had bested the Missourians and escaped untainted from their grasp.

The newspaper articles that issued out of Springfield did little to dampen Joseph's joy, even though he recognized the heavy hand of Dr. John C. Bennett in them.

The sheriff from Missouri became the joke of Nauvoo when it was learned he had stomped his way to Springfield, demanding that Governor Ford furnish troops in order that he might march on Nauvoo and drag the Prophet out.

Today, when Mark reached the office, both Joseph and William Clayton were laughing with glee. Joseph waved the paper under Mark's nose and said, "See this? The gist of it is that if we vote Democrat, we've nothing more to fear from Governor Ford. We're home free as far as Missouri is concerned."

"It's to Ford's advantage to cooperate with the Lord," Joseph added. As for Washington, in the name of the Lord, I deliver unto you the prophecy that within a few years' time, this government will be overthrown and wasted away. This is judgment from the Lord for their wickedness in supporting the cause of Missouri. We are still an oppressed people, and our rights have not been upheld."

Joseph returned to his desk and began sorting through the papers there. As Clayton prepared to leave the room, Joseph said, "By the way, William, did you take care of the deeds?"

"I did. In June. They've been duly filed. Emma's share is sixty city lots."

"Joseph—" Mark paused and tried to control his anger. "I advised you a year ago that this wasn't to be done. The provisions of the bankruptcy law will not allow you to transfer any property. You're heading for trouble."

"I'll cross that bridge when I get to it!" Joseph snapped. "I'm not concerned. There are too many other things of first importance.

"Must I remind you again that it has been prophesied concerning the war which will soon break out? The Lord has given me to understand that the first outbreak with the shedding of blood will take place at South Caroline. Fear not, Mark, only be faithful to the will of the Lord revealed to you."

Jenny sighed and folded the scraps of calico spread across the kitchen table. "Sweet little John Mark; how about going for a ride with Mama?"

Jenny bent over the cradle. John Mark's arms and legs pounded out his enthusiasm while he crowed with delight.

Jenny scooped him up, saying, "Oh, wet! We're going to visit that nice Sarah Pratt as soon as I make you presentable. I don't have a pattern for these quilt blocks."

Sarah answered Jenny's knock. "Oh," Jenny said in dismay as she looked at the woman's red eyes and blotched face. "I shouldn't have come. Are you ill?"

"No," Sarah sighed and stepped back to allow Jenny to enter the house. "I'm just feeling sorry for myself today."

"Is there anything I can do to help?" Jenny asked timidly.

Sarah started to shake her head, and the tears began. "I don't want to dump my troubles on you. Besides, what I'm going through is nothing more or less than what you'll all be called upon to endure sooner or later if the Prophet calls for the sacrifice."

"What do you mean?" Jenny asked.

"Then Mark hasn't been tapped to obey the priesthood?" she asked bitterly. "Well, just wait; it'll be soon." She glanced sharply at Jenny adding, "You act as if you don't know. Plural marriage, celestial marriage, the everlasting covenant of marriage which no man is allowed to refuse once it is given to him. To refuse is to be damned, and I assure you, my husband is not going to be damned."

Feeling as if she were being backed into a corner, Jenny reminded Sarah, "You know as well as I do that the Prophet's been preaching against the doctrine. There's the pamphlet he's come out against. From the pulpit he's denied the accusations."

"Out of one side of the mouth while he's promoting it with the other."

Jenny remembered that day over a year ago when she had met Dr. Bennett right here in this room. Questions nagged at her, and she had to know. Slowly she said, "Dr. Bennett, that time I met him here, was talking about abortion like it was something happening right here in Nauvoo. Is that true? Was he referring to Saints getting rid of their babies?"

"Yes, Jenny. Remember? He said he did this to prevent *exposure* of the parties involved. He meant Saints."

"I can't imagine anyone getting rid of a baby," Jenny said, cuddling John Mark. "Was it to keep people from knowing about polygamy? If that's so, how can the teaching be from God?"

"It isn't," she said bitterly. "Jenny, use your head. Is it even logical to think the Lord would advocate plural marriage as a means to holiness when the result is a tearing apart of the sweet union of husband and wife?"

For a moment Jenny teetered on the edge of understanding, but even then she knew this step would force her to face something within herself.

Sarah was speaking again. "Joseph sent my husband to England on a mission, with the promise that he would see I was provided with food and fuel for the winter. Shortly after he left, Joseph paid me a visit. He advised me that the Lord had given me to him as a *spiritual wife.* I didn't understand what he meant until he pulled himself up to the top of his dignity and in a stuffy voice said he desired *connubial bliss* with me and hoped I wouldn't deny him. Of course, by then I realized it was nothing except a ruse to get me to go to bed with him.

"I informed him I wouldn't disgrace the institution of marriage by calling his proposal *that.* Jenny, I dearly love my husband. Never could I be willing to sacrifice that sweet relationship. I didn't count on Joseph's insistence, though."

"Oh, no!" Jenny moaned.

Sarah frowned, paused, and then continued. "Joseph threatened to ruin my reputation if I told anyone. Well, you know the rest—how the story leaked out, how Dr. Bennett was accused by the Prophet of doing what he desired himself. You also remember what it did to my husband; when William Law, poor unsuspecting man, got up in the meeting and asked the Saints to lift their hands attesting to the righteousness of the Prophet, my Orson was the only one who voted against him."

"I know it was rumored about that he'd tried to do himself in." Jenny replied in a low voice. "But he's better now, isn't he?"

"Yes." Sarah's bitter voice cracked. In a moment she added, "Yes, Orson's better—and he's become an ardent follower of the Prophet. Seems he can't marry fast enough nowadays." She lifted her face, and finally Jenny understood the black despair in her eyes.

Jenny took a copy of Sarah's quilt pattern and climbed back in her buggy with John Mark. All the way home, while John Mark crowed his delight and waved his hands, Jenny thought about all Sarah had said. She measured Sarah's experience against her own, then compared her Mark with Sarah's Orson and shivered.

As she took the buggy to the barn and unhitched the horse, she said to herself, "One thing is certain in my mind. I must never tell Mark what has happened to me. I couldn't stand to have him become another Orson."

CHAPTER 29

"I can't imagine anyone moving in August, at least this August!" Jenny exclaimed, fanning herself vigorously. "Even John Mark fusses when I hold him because it's so hot."

Mark threw her a quick glance. "Perhaps I shouldn't have brought you into town today. It'll be hotter there."

"Ah, but the picnic with Andy, Sally, and Tamara makes it worth the trip in the heat." Jenny tilted the parasol to shade the baby lying on his bed of blankets on the seat of the buggy. "If you will find a shady spot to leave the buggy, John Mark and I will have a pleasant wait while you take the papers up to Clayton."

She fanned herself again, saying, "And if you manage to drive past the Nauvoo House, I'll enjoy gawking at the men carrying in all the Prophet's belongings."

"I won't take the time to pass," he answered, smiling down at her, "but I shall leave the buggy close enough for you to watch the whole event."

Nauvoo House had been built west of the city on a point of land overlooking the wharf. Although it was not finished, the apartment for the Prophet had been readied, and Jenny knew today was moving day.

The three-story, L-shaped building was of red brick. The length and breadth of it started on Main Street and extended down Water Street.

From where Mark had parked the buggy, Jenny could feel the cooling breeze from the river and see the building. Beyond it were the stables and the wharf. She also saw the last load of furniture being taken in the front door.

Disappointed at having missed the excitement, Jenny studied the windows already draped with red velvet and opened to the cooling breezes. "Oh, John Mark, I do so want to see inside! If only Emma would stick her head out, I'd be tempted to go beg a look. I sure don't want to wait for months until the grand opening."

John Mark waved his fists and screwed up his face to cry. "It was early when you nursed," Jenny moaned in dismay, conscious of the lorries and workmen passing the buggy.

Looking around she frowned, saying, " 'Tis only a couple of blocks to the Mansion House. Could be Emma is there. If not, we could walk across the way to the old farmhouse and sit among the trees."

But before they reached Mansion House, John Mark balled up his little fists and complained heartily. Patting his sweaty little shoulders, Jenny sighed, "You win, tyke; we'll cut through the field and save some time."

Back in the trees, just beyond the old farmhouse, Jenny gratefully settled among the ferns and cuddled John Mark to her.

Here the cool woods formed an encircling arm around the old farmhouse and the stretch of Nauvoo beyond. Even the clamor of workmen and the shouts from the wharf were muffled. The house with its patchwork architecture—originally log, with a new addition of white frame—was nearly lost in the tangle of lilac bushes. As she idly studied the house, Jenny recalled that the original building was part of the old town of Commerce.

Jenny's eyes were nearly closed when a movement near the house made them start open.

A woman dressed in pale summer colors was striding through the meadow toward the house. With scarcely a pause, she approached the door and slipped through. Jenny frowned, then said, "That's Emily Partridge, Emma's girl. I suppose she's been sent after something. If you hurry, babe, we'll go visit with her."

Only a few minutes later Jenny was laying John Mark down on his blanket when another figure approached. She recognized the tall, thin figure in the dark dress. "Well," Jenny said as she watched her enter the house, "seems we'll have our visit with Emma after all."

Jenny was nearly to the door of the house when she heard the angry cry. As she hesitated, Emma rushed through the door and started up the hill.

Jenny called, "Emma!" But the woman didn't stop until she reached the roadway. Her face was stony when Jenny reached her.

"Oh, you," she said in a lifeless voice, turning away. But Jenny had seen her face.

"Emma, you've hurt yourself!" She could scarcely believe

her own words as she blurted out, “Why, someone hit you!”

Emma nodded and dabbed at her swelling eye. Jenny circled her shoulders with one arm and said, “You need a balm on that. The store’s just down the street; come.” As they started down the road, Jenny said, “I never would have expected Emily Partridge to behave like that.”

“It wasn’t Emily.” She paused and then added, “You saw her. I suppose you saw Joseph, too.”

“Joseph?” Jenny asked, then gasped. She was beginning to understand.

“It wasn’t Emily. It was Joseph who struck me.” They had reached the store. Jenny opened the door and together they went to find the ointment. By the time they had made their choice, the door banged open and Joseph rushed in. He paused to look around, and seeing Emma he came to her.

Seizing Emma in his arms, he kissed her. “I’m sorry,” he said. “But, Emma, you know better than to follow me.”

Speechless, Jenny stared after the two as they left the store, arm in arm.

Later that afternoon, Mark and Jenny met Andy and Sally in the temple grove. After their picnic supper the men and Tamara wandered away.

Sally was slowly repacking the hamper as she said, “Jenny, you’ve been terribly quiet today. Is there something wrong?”

Bemused, Jenny raised her head, “Oh, I’m sorry. Lost in thought, I guess.”

“Has something happened between you and Mark?”

“Oh, no, Sally.” Jenny bit her lip and then said, “I saw something today that I just can’t understand. What would you think was happening if you saw a woman go into the old farmhouse, and in a few minutes be followed by Emma, who shortly comes out with a bruised eye, saying that Joseph did it?”

Sally looked startled. “I’d think she was lying.”

“Even when Joseph came into the store later and apologized to her, saying she should know better than to follow?”

“I guess she wasn’t lying.”

Now Jenny saw the troubled look on Sally’s face and said, “Yes, I too have a hard time believing Joseph is like that. Sally, I’ve heard rumors. Sarah Pratt admitted the Prophet’s urging men to take other wives. When I think of Mark being pulled into that situation, I nearly become ill.”

Sally burst into tears. Jenny turned on the blanket and put her arms around her friend. “Oh, Sally, I didn’t dream Andy was involved. Please forgive me for hurting you. But I just can't understand—"

Her voice was very low. "It isn't Andy." More sobs muffled her words, and Jenny could only wait, beginning to fear her next words. Finally she straightened and mopped her eyes on Jenny's handkerchief.

"Do you mind if I tell you all about it? Jenny, I am going out of my mind soon if I don't confide in someone."

Reluctantly Jenny nodded. She glanced at the sleeping baby stretched on his blanket and listened to the laughing voices of their men punctuated by Tamara's shrill voice.

Looking into Sally's face, she nodded again, whispering, "If it will help. Sally, you know how I feel about you and Andy both, I—"

Sally bent forward and buried her face against her knees. "Oh, Jenny, don't say it. You'll hate me when I finish, but that's the chance I must take. See, I'm one of Joseph's wives."

Jenny gulped and took a deep breath. "Explain that."

"Since Kirtland. He began teaching me the doctrine of spiritual wives just after you and Mark were married in '36. That next year we took our endowments. I wanted to wait, but it was starting to look as if we'd be leaving for Missouri soon, and Joseph said the Lord had commanded the marriage to be sealed."

Her brave voice dropped to a whisper as she continued, "I didn't want to do it. But after he got through teaching the doctrine and bade me pray for direction, I dared not disobey the Lord."

"You had a *sign*?"

"Yes." For a moment Sally's face brightened. "I'd prayed and fasted, just like he told me to. One night late I awakened and went downstairs to pray. There I had the most wonderful vision, and I knew I had confirmation."

"What was it?"

She hesitated and fumbled for words. "A—sensation of brightness and a tremendous peace swept over me."

Jenny settled back on her heels and thought. "Well, Sally, I guess I can't quarrel with that. The Prophet's taught us to seek signs and wisdom. I've followed that course myself seeking for power and wisdom. I must confess, though, at times I don't like what I find, and the confusion that ends up inside of me nearly makes me sick. But, according to the teaching, that's Satan fighting against what is being given to us."

"I thought it was just the opposite. Once you said—"

"That they were saying the right way is within us, and that we follow it naturally." She stopped and stared at Sally. "I am getting so confused I don't know what I think. One thing is certain. All you're telling me leaves me churning around inside. Why is the way of salvation so difficult?"

"Shall I tell you more? I think I might be able to get rid of this terrible guilt if you would listen."

Jenny nodded and Sally continued. "That medicine. I think you guessed I'd tried to get rid of the baby. Jenny, I wasn't trying to cause an abortion. I wanted to die; that's why I took the medicine."

Now her sobs were soundless. Jenny watched the agony expressed in the trembling curve of her body. Her own arms felt leaden as she lifted them and pulled Sally close. One more rush of words from Sally explained it all. "I think it was Joseph's baby."

It was dusk. From down the hill came the mingled sounds of laughter from Mark and Andy. Jenny could control her bitterness no longer. "How could you do that to Andy?"

The silence lasted for a long time. Jenny could no longer see Sally's face.

Sally finally moved, sighed, and in the voice of an old, wise woman, she said, "Do you think I have not suffered over it? There hasn't been a day since the sealing that I haven't agonized over it. But I must bow to the wishes of the Prophet, pretending and deceiving my husband, when each deception is nearly the death of me." She was silent, and then as if she guessed Jenny's unspoken question, she added, "If I dared attempt death again, I would."

"Isn't there something you can do? Why don't you ask Andy to leave Nauvoo?"

Sally leaned over Jenny. Her fingers were digging into Jenny's arm shaking it. "Don't you understand? I dare not. My salvation is at stake. I would go to hell most surely. You know, Jenny, not a one of us will make it unless Joseph is there to admit us to heaven."

The men's voices were growing louder as they laughed and romped up the hill with Tamara. Seeing one last agonized glance from Sally, Jenny leaned forward and kissed her cheek. "Trust me; somehow I'll find a way to get you out of this mess."

CHAPTER 30

Jenny left the Relief Society meeting and headed for Joseph's store, carrying a lunch of cold meat and vegetables to Mark.

With John Mark clutched tightly in one arm and the other hand holding the food pail, Jenny slowly made her way up the stairs, kicking her long skirt out of the way as she went.

Halfway up the stairs, she heard a door bang against the wall and Joseph's voice rose above the clatter. "Law, you'll be damned if you don't!"

The angry voice retorted, "And I'll be damned if I do! What a doctrine!"

Feet thundered on the stairs and William exclaimed, "Oh, Mrs. Cartwright! I nearly swept you down the stairs. Here, let me help you." He took the pail and surveyed John Mark, whose face was beginning to pucker.

"Oh, he's shy," Jenny explained, pressing the baby's head against her shoulder. "I'm just bringing lunch to Mark."

"I think he's out. Here, I'll put the pail on his desk, and you can wait."

Clayton was at his desk, hunched over the notebook. Busily dipping his pen, he said, "Morning, ma'am. Mark'll be back in a minute." He wiped his pen and came to pat the baby and beam at him. "Little blessing. 'Tis for all of us if we only mind the Lord and keep His commandments. Now, that William is sure bucking counsel." He sighed gustily, with a wistful look in his eyes. Jenny recalled the Relief Society gossip of some trouble at home.

He continued, "My heart's desire is to fulfill the requirements of the gospel. I pray the great Elohim to bless us all with His will." He paused for a moment, searching Jenny's face, then said, "You know, we don't live to please ourselves. All of this is only to keep the covenants of our God and to earn the right to the eternities He's prepared for us." Clayton picked up his hat and with a smile headed for the door.

Mark arrived as Jenny was still pondering the veiled meaning of Clayton's remarks. They shared the lunch and Jenny left the office, saying, "I'm going to shop and then go home."

By the time Jenny was back in the buggy, she was brooding over the old problem. Halfway home, suddenly the obvious solution occurred to Jenny.

John Mark was asleep and she allowed the mare to amble along at her own pace. There was a touch of coolness in the breeze, and Jenny lifted her face to it. "Of course," she beamed, "how simple! Why didn't I think of it before?"

It was the solution to all the problems—Sarah's, Emma's, Sally's. "It's that talisman. You admitted yourself that it was the power in the talisman causing the problem with you. Is it too ridiculous to believe it's causing *their* problems, too? Granted, they don't have a talisman to pitch, like you did, but he does."

She recalled Sally's ravaged face and her heart squeezed tight. But how would she get Joseph's talisman? "One thing," she told herself, "you're going to have to see a lot more of the Prophet."

"Jenny!" Mark exclaimed, "you've been walking around this house all day looking as if you reside on a different planet. You've studied that potato as if you've never seen one before."

Jenny raised her head. "Oh, Mark, that isn't funny."

"Meaning?"

"I'm having a difficult time trying to understand all the Prophet says, and here you are picking at his sermons."

He frowned and then grinned. "Planet. That was a pun. Why don't you just read the Bible? You know he says he believes in it, too." He came to lean over her shoulder, to peer at the vegetables.

"But only as far as it is correctly translated." She hastily added, "I know, you're going to talk about having Bible sections in the *Book of Mormon*. You're going to say we don't know what *not* to believe."

"No, I'm going to kiss your neck and suggest you forget about the whole subject right now."

She saw his eyes as he bent to kiss her. The frown indicated that Mark wasn't as lighthearted as he seemed. For a moment she wished desperately that she could tell him all. But even with that wish, her soul withered in fear.

The next morning, while she was reading the book of John,

she murmured, "Jesus, I still don't understand, but I wish I knew what I could believe about this Book.

"What does it mean when it says You've come to give life, and that if I follow You, I won't walk in darkness? Why am I condemned already if I don't believe? What does *believe* mean? I believe Mark will come home tonight; I believe the sun will rise tomorrow."

As Jenny stared at the Book, the thought occurred to her that she should believe it all. She shook her head, "Joseph—" The thought seemed suddenly illuminated. *Why believe Joseph?* She caught her breath and examined the question. So many problems would disappear if she *didn't* believe Joseph: that certificate in Joseph's office, salvation through the church. Now another thought came into her mind. It was so vivid that for a moment she felt as if she had literally heard the statement. *The power of the deed will be broken if you tell Mark.*

Aghast, she considered his reaction—the horror on his face, the disappointment, and finally the rejection. With regret she shook her head.

To be done with the guilt, even the possibility of being forced to honor that contract, was a temptation she dared not consider. As attractive as the thought was, she could not risk losing Mark. Taking a deep breath, she whispered, "Joseph has not one hold on me. He knows I would tell Emma. I am no longer afraid of him."

When Jenny heard Mark's horse late that afternoon, she knew he was angry. Standing in the doorway she watched Mark slide from the horse and yank off the saddle and bridle. He impatiently pulled open the gate and slapped the mare across the rump.

As he came up the steps she said, "What's wrong?"

"Speech in the temple grove. You know election is coming up next week. Joseph promised his vote to Cyrus Walker when he was arrested. Well, Hyrum had a revelation. He said he'd asked God how the people should vote. The answer was that God wanted the people to vote for Hoge, on the Democratic ticket. Quite a sensation, this abrupt reversal of what we'd been led to expect. Especially considering Hyrum had previously promised the Democrats the Mormon vote if they would promise him a seat in the state legislature next year."

Jenny paused to think for a moment; then with a sigh and shake of her head, she said, "Well, come have a cool drink and tell me more about it."

He pulled the buttermilk from the well where it had been

chilling. She began preparing dinner as he talked.

"When Cyrus Walker took Joseph's case against the Missouri charge, it was done with Joseph's promise of support in the upcoming election. Well, Walker's the Whig candidate for Congress. Remember the rumor floating down from Springfield?"

Slowly Jenny said, "You mean the trip J. B. Backenstos made to confer with Ford? About the promise in exchange for the Mormons' vote on the Democratic ticket? Didn't they say Joseph would have nothing to fear from the governor? Mark, are you saying there's a possibility Joseph will be voting for the Democrats to keep from being arrested?"

"You know how strong the people lean on revelations." He went to pick up John Mark. "William Law was irate. He got to his feet and chewed out Hyrum, reminding everyone that only Joseph was entitled to have revelations. Then he reminded them Joseph had pledged Walker the Mormon support."

"So what did Joseph say?"

"Only that he was pledged to support Walker, and unless he had a revelation to the contrary, they should support him too.

"Oh, my," Jenny murmured. "Sabbath-day sermon should be interesting."

At the end of the sermon the following day, Mark leaned toward Jenny and said, "You were right, my dear."

She nodded, her eyes riveted on the pulpit. Joseph was saying, "I've no intention of telling you how to vote. I don't have a revelation concerning the election. Matter of fact, I don't believe in troubling the Lord about politics. I gave my word to Walker when I hired him to handle my case against Reynolds, but I didn't pledge him the votes of all the Saints. Now Hyrum advises us that he has a revelation from the Lord instructing that the Saints should vote for Hoge." He paused for a moment and then slowly said, "I must admit, I've never known Hyrum to have a revelation that failed."

William Law was standing beside Mark, and as the congregation began to move toward their wagons and carriages, William fell into step with Mark. Jenny saw his shoulders droop in discouragement as he said, "I wonder if he believes he can get away with this? I'm afraid Joseph's just garnered himself a pack of enemies." At Mark's quick glance he said, "Oh, I still believe in him. I just think he's making a terrible mistake right now."

Sarah and Orson Pratt caught up with them. Orson said, "Law, I heard what you said. Seems we ought to be discussing the situation. Maybe we could get together this afternoon?"

"If you've carried your dinner, bring it and come," Sarah invited. "We've plenty of trees for shade and the breeze off the river hits us just fine."

While the men stood in the shade of the trees on the Pratt farm, the women spread their food across the table.

Looking at the dishes, Sarah said slowly, "When I remember the time we had in Missouri, just getting wheat milled and enough to eat, I'd be grateful for just a speck of this."

Jenny looked at the table. There was snowy bread, creamy butter, ham, fried chicken, a joint of venison, garden vegetables baked into a thick custard, cucumbers floating in vinegar and spices, applesauce, and fried pumpkin chips. The pies looked like apple and peach. Jenny's spice cake, heavy with raisins, released a fragrance of molasses and cinnamon.

Jenny looked from Sarah to Jane. Addressing Jane, she said, "Except for what you've heard from the pulpit, you don't know what it was like."

"I've been fed a constant dose of the stories of the persecutions ever since we've arrived," she said; then she raised her head and added in a rush, "Seems Joseph is bound to not let it die. It cuts a picture of a man not big enough to let by-gones be. Will he hold a grudge forever? I was raised to believe in the importance of forgiving those who sin against us. Even though we're Latter-day Saints, seems there's still a few Christian virtues that need to be retained."

The men came to the table and the conversation turned lighthearted until the table had been cleared.

When William Law leaned back in his chair he addressed Pratt. "Orson, do you believe Joseph's statements today will have an effect on the election?"

"I should hope so," Orson replied. Jenny glanced at Mark. When he sighed heavily, she knew he had an objection, but she also guessed he would save his irritation for her ears. Pratt continued, "We've a responsibility toward these people. They need instruction until they've accepted all that will be given to them to achieve the knowledge necessary for salvation."

"You think knowledge gives salvation?" Mark asked, looking surprised.

"Of course. The Prophet gave that to us."

Mark was asking, "What about the truth concerning God as revealed in the Holy Bible?"

Orson moved impatiently. "In the Bible there's not a thing you can believe in with surety except what is contained in the original. What we have nowadays is a corrupted translation, given out by uninspired men without the authority to translate. I tell you, there's no part that we can accept with certainty as the Word of God. I declare to you that what we have is only the words of men, not the true Word. It is only the skeleton—the mutilated, the changed, the corrupted."

William Law was leaning forward; there was a perplexed frown on his face. "Then what do you trust?"

"The Prophet. He has been given the keys to the kingdom. Through the direct revelation of God himself, we know Joseph is to be trusted."

"But, Pratt, we have only Joseph's word for it," Mark said.

"That's true," Pratt admitted. "But he's also told us to ask God to give us a testimony of the rightness of all this. There's not a man in the church who's asked, who hasn't received."

Law's frown remained. Slowly he said, "One of the things that's really nagged at me has been the willingness of the people to rely on emotion. I've heard things like, 'I *feel* this is right. I know by the spirit, I've been caught up in the spirit. I saw a great light when I prayed. I felt a burning in the bosom.' I'm a practical man; I don't like to go by hunches. I want facts. Why can't we rely on the Word?"

"What word?" Mark asked. "If you're talking about the *Book of Mormon*, then please tell me what I should depend upon. I've been listening to Joseph long enough to realize little of his beliefs come from his holy book, the *Book of Mormon*."

"Well, you can't rely upon the Bible. The *Book of Mormon* clearly sets forth that the Christian church, referred to as the 'abominable church' has taken from the Bible the most plain and precious parts of the gospel," William said.

"God deliver us from ever calling ourselves Christian," muttered Orson.

"I suppose there would be some merit in living by the doctrine of the *Book of Mormon*," Mark added. "I saw in the second book of Nephi the thirteenth verse where old Nephi urges relying completely upon the merits of Jesus Christ for salvation, urging the people to feast upon the word of Christ. It doesn't say a church will save us."

In the silence Mark continued, "But there's more. This hits right at the priesthood. Chapter one of the book of Jacob calls it a wicked practice, this having many wives."

Orson's voice was brittle. "Anything else, Brother Cartwright?"

"I've noticed the book refers to Christ as God, the Father of all things. That isn't consistent with Joseph's saying Christ is our elder brother. I kinda like it where it says God came down and took upon himself flesh and blood and that He shall redeem His people. Sure beats any salvation I can earn for myself through the church."

William and Orson were on their feet when Mark added, "Have you noticed? The book of Alma says that Mary, the mother of Jesus, conceived by the power of the Holy Ghost."

Mark and Jenny were in the buggy headed for home before Jenny dared say, "Mark, you worry me. If Joseph were to hear about this—"

"I'd be labeled apostate." He turned to smile at her, saying, "But the strange thing is, although this goes against his teaching, I'm only giving his words back to him."

In a moment he added, "If I were to ask if—" The smile disappeared and he turned to flick the reins along the mare's back.

"Jenny, I believe there's a move on among the people to break out of the bondage Joseph has placed upon them. There're some intelligent men in the camp who are beginning to think for themselves. One of these days they are going to demand that Joseph give way and take stock of the teaching which he claims comes from God.

"Have you noticed? Back in Kirtland days there was a new revelation just about every time Joseph took a breath. Now it's seldom we get one. Nowadays it's just a matter of Joseph saying jump and the people jump. One of these days they won't."

CHAPTER 31

"The end of August is as hot as July. Here in the temple grove this Sabbath, there's not a whisper of a breeze," Jenny murmured as she settled on the bench in front of the pulpit and tried to fan the squirming John Mark.

"You might as well forget that," Mark said. "He's generating more wind with his bouncing around. I don't think he's minding the heat as much as his mother."

"I nearly wish I'd stayed home with him. He's getting so strong, and I think he's going to have a tooth soon."

Jenny continued to struggle with the squirming baby as the Sabbath service began. She had nearly lost the thread of the message when John Mark went to sleep. While Mark adjusted the blanket across their legs and eased the baby onto his lap, Jenny became aware of the Prophet's words.

Briefly he referred to the death of the Higbee child, and then said, "The time of the endowments in the temple is drawing nigh. The sad death this past week shows the importance of this ordinance. When the parents of a child have been sealed in the temple, their posterity is secured. For all eternity this child is theirs, saved through the virtue of the covenant of the father."

Jenny was still mulling over that information when the Prophet moved on, proclaiming, "I received information which indicates that Sidney Rigdon has given oath to Governor Carlin of Missouri to bind over my life to the Missourians. At this time, I desire to withdraw the hand of fellowship from Sidney Rigdon, and I put this up to the vote of the people."

A rustle of indignation spread through the audience. Catcalls accompanied the lifting of hands. Joseph acknowledged their remarks with a smile and continued, "We've voted unanimously to remove his name, and we will revoke his license. I will advise you that, regardless of the schemer's plans, all the powers of hell or earth together cannot put down this old boy.

I have promises from the eternal God."

John Mark awakened when the shouting began. Jenny was juggling him into quietness when Joseph began talking about the Melchizedek priesthood. "The sectarians have never professed to have the priesthood. In consequence, it is impossible for them to save anyone. They'll all be damned together. Only the priesthood gives power for endless lives."

He paused, and bending forward, said, "I will remind you of the power of the priesthood. You know the sacrifice of Abraham. These everlasting covenants cannot be broken! When God gives knowledge or blessing to a man and he refuses to accept, he shall be damned."

Service was over. Jenny got to her feet, stumbling as she followed Mark. Those words filled her mind. John Mark didn't have a chance to even begin to earn his position in the eternities unless his daddy would accept Joseph's way.

"Jenny, what are you thinking?"

"Oh . . ." Jenny blinked against the sunshine and looked up at Mark. The Sabbath day was nearly over. John Mark was still napping while the two of them leaned over the pasture fence.

"That the world is beautiful and that I love our farm." How conscious she was of evading the real thoughts, even as she turned to glance up at him!

She was aware of his eyes, with those curious flecks of color, watching her. Watching them, aware of their candor, she realized how often in these past weeks Mark had gently probed, urging her to talk. She began to giggle.

"What's that about?"

"I was thinking back to some of the silly talking we've been doing in the past weeks."

"About the girls who are trying to entrap Tom?"

"And the new fall fashions and whether poke bonnets should be allowed in the temple."

Mark's grin faded, "Like the unimportant."

The breeze swept a yellow leaf past Jenny and she whispered, "What, Mark? What is it you want—a piece of my soul?"

"Is that too much?"

"It is until I understand it myself."

"You've changed, you know. I find myself wondering."

She searched his face, not daring to ask: *for good or bad?* She simply said, "All of life is changing. It's nearly autumn. The tourists have gone. Joseph's church is still fumbling and restless. The Saints will soon be worshiping in the temple.

There will be new teachings, the endowments." She was still watching him as he turned away.

Softly now she said, "Do you realize, Mark, even between us there's so much that *can't* be said? We had new teaching today. Joseph said that if we're to be having little John Mark for eternity, if he's even to have a chance at eternity, you must fulfill the requirements of the gospel. There must be endowment."

He turned away, "I'm sorry, Jenny. When a person doesn't believe, he can't live a lie—even for the dearest person on earth."

Jenny contemplated the pasture, the brilliance of the day. All too soon the bronze, copper and gold of autumn would be here, and then the snow. Where were their lives together leading them? She couldn't face that answer.

The peeled log railing of the fence had whitened with age. She ran her hand over the smooth surface, wondering how long it would be until the smoothness turned to slivers.

"So?"

"See, so smooth now. You peel back the bark and it's vulnerable, Mark, like us. How long before it all turns to splinters?" Watching she realized, in the darkening of his eyes, there was pain in the unprobed depths of her husband. Deeply she felt the answer from her own heart even as she bit her lips and turned away.

He held out his arms, and in them she was conscious of passion drowned in a desire for union deeper than physical. It must be the call for endowment. Her sigh was as heavy as she felt. When he finally dropped his arms, she heard his sigh of regret. "We'd better see if the tyke is awake."

That evening, when Mark stepped into the circle of her lamplight, he asked, "What are you reading?"

She brought her thoughts back and lifted her face. "The Bible. Mark, what is God's love?"

He came into the light and sat down. "I suppose what we see of God and understand as love. Salvation instead of what we deserve. Even just holding the world together. If He were to take away His hand, we'd disappear. Certainly considering sin and disobedience, we don't deserve more than that. But He handles us very gently. This should bring us running into His love. I guess God's love is a place where we are to dwell."

In a moment he quoted, " 'But God commendeth his love toward us, in that, while we were yet sinners, Christ died for us. Much more then, being now justified by his blood, we shall be saved from wrath through him.' Jenny, this chapter in Romans says we're justified by faith, not works like Joseph says. It tells us this is a free gift."

She knew he saw her trembling hands. As she shook her head he stopped abruptly. "Mark, it sounds so nice, but I am afraid. Now there's another one to fear for. The fear sends me running; I'll be faithful to my church to the best of my ability. I'll also work to bring some of these teachings of the Bible into our church. We need the best of both. But, please don't ask me to give up the security of this. I've already given up so much."

She saw the curiosity in his eyes and braced herself to answer the words which she had unintentionally let slip.

"Do you regret it?"

Jenny caught her breath. It wasn't what she had expected. He meant unsaid things they had never talked about. The craft. For a moment she looked at Mark, seeing clearly how much he had comprehended even while he held his silence. She whispered, "No, never. I've traded ugliness for God's church." Mark turned away and Jenny returned to the Book.

She bent her head over it. "It says here in John that a man who doesn't love Jesus doesn't obey His teaching." Looking out the window, she asked, "Do you suppose Joseph doesn't know about that verse?"

"Why do you ask?"

"Because I sense so much of fear and fighting in him. Seems it's in him more than the rest of us."

He sat down beside her, and she felt his excitement. "You've caught that? What else have you seen?"

"I'm thinking of a verse, a question. 'Are you foolish? After beginning with the spirit, are you made perfect by works?' Then it goes on to say it was faith that saved Abraham, not doing, and that no man is justified by the law—yet this very day, Joseph talked about the *sacrifice* of Abraham."

She studied her hands for a moment, then said, "There's more. It says if you're led by the spirit, you're not under law. Mark, does it possibly mean even the type of law in the church—all the doing and . . ."

She couldn't finish. Mark took her hands and pulled her close. "Jen—" He stopped. She saw the joyful expression on his face fade. Then caution swept over his features as he carefully said, "Even Joseph couldn't object to the reading and learning you are doing. One of these days he'll have to allow us to do some thinking on our own."

Now she was brave enough to try the verse. "Mark, there's

something else. I think it's a verse even you don't know about."

"What does it say?"

"That in Jesus there isn't such as Jew or Greek, even men and women—we're all the same."

"I know about it."

"Then you see what it means. Oh, Mark, I can hardly believe it!"

"That Jesus Christ doesn't see you as less than me?"

She frowned and regarded him thoughtfully for a moment before slipping away from her original intention into the other thought the verse held. Slowly she said, "No, Mark, I was thinking of the baptism. Joseph teaches that baptism changes all of us who aren't the literal descendants of the children of Israel, so that we have their Jewish blood in our veins."

When Jenny slowly followed Mark up the stairs to their bedroom, she was wistfully thinking of the verse, wondering why she couldn't push aside that amazing thought. *All are alike in Jesus' eyes. All have the same rights—to enjoy eternity, without having a man take them there.*

What would Mark think of that? And what about having a man look at her with respect in his eyes, as if what she had to say was important?

As Jenny slipped into bed beside Mark, she saw the expression in his eyes and paused. Sometimes she felt as if Mark might feel that way. But what would he say right now if she were to pound her pillow and demand he say what he was thinking?

CHAPTER 32

"What is the mystery of God, of Christ?" Jenny pondered as she slowly turned the pages in her Bible. "In here there's talk about the hidden wisdom which God set up before He created the world. Oh, what does this mean? 'Which none of the princes of this world knew: for had they known it, they would not have crucified the Lord of glory.' Why? There's something here so big, and I can't understand it!"

She sat staring at the Book. "The Lord of glory, that's Jesus Christ." As she read further, the puzzle became more complex. When she put aside the Book and started her morning tasks, she mulled over the words which had dropped into her mind. "Eyes haven't seen and ears haven't heard. God has prepared great things for us who love Him! That means even Joseph doesn't know—or does he?"

Those who love God. Did she love God? What did that mean? Joseph didn't talk about *doing* because of love. He talked about earning eternal life by the righteousness of deeds.

Later as Jenny bathed John Mark and dressed him, a verse jumped into her mind whole, impossible to forget. At the most unexpected moments it bounded into her thoughts. " 'Now we have received, not the spirit of the world,' " she murmured, " 'but the spirit which is of God; that we might know the things that are freely given to us of God.' " As she sat down to feed the baby, she considered the words that followed: " 'So the natural man does not receive the things of the Spirit because they are foolish to him. Spiritually discerned.' That's why Joseph is so far above us."

It was afternoon when Jenny carried the sleeping infant to the buggy. Feeling the sweet weight of him brought tears to her eyes. She squeezed him tight and he flung a tiny arm against her. When she bent to kiss the hand, her tears dampened it.

When Jenny reached Joseph's office, Clayton was just leaving. He closed the door carefully and said, "Mark isn't here right now. He's made a trip to Carthage today."

"I know. It's Joseph I want to see." The man looked uneasy and Jenny explained, "It's religious counsel." He reddened.

Joseph opened the door. "Come in, Jenny." His eyes brightened, and for just one moment Jenny remembered the last time she had been alone with him.

"I need instruction," she said loudly as she entered. She heard the shuffle of feet as Clayton went back to his office. Joseph closed the door and motioned for Jenny to be seated.

"Your sermon. About sealing for posterity's sake."

"Yes, what about it?"

She bit her lip. "Mark won't. He says he doesn't believe in it. What shall I do?"

"Jenny, you don't understand the teachings. You've already been sealed to me. When there's a sealing for eternity, the offspring of the wife is automatically credited to the spiritual mate. Your baby belongs to me for all eternity."

The facts lined up in Jenny's mind as she looked at Joseph. John Mark was safe for all eternity. He would have an opportunity for eternal progression, under Joseph. John Mark no longer belonged to Mark; in the sight of God he was Joseph's baby.

She could only stare at Joseph as he leaned back in his chair and made a tent of his fingers. His face was pulled down into a troubled frown. "However, Jenny, I must remind you. Our marriage, with all the rights attested to it, still awaits validation. Until it is consummated, your little one is no better off than an infidel."

John Mark pulled her finger into his mouth and began to suck on it. As she stared down at him, he grinned and waved a pudgy fist. Her heart sank. "Joseph, I must think some more."

She rose to leave. He was still watching and she thought of all she had been saving to ask him. Slowly Jenny said, "I've had so many questions. You are our contact with God. The spirit tells you, and the rest of us only wonder."

"Perhaps you'd understand better if you were to obey the light you have. Jenny, you are not obedient to the gospel."

"The Bible says the blood of Jesus frees us from things the law couldn't. What?"

"The crucifixion purchases resurrection from the dead. This is for all people."

"Is that all?"

"Yes. It is only through obedience to the true church that we have the right to the highest heaven and all that implies:

kingdoms, godhood, eternal progress. It makes the troubles we endure down here seem insignificant, doesn't it?"

"Then, Joseph, what is the mystery of Christ?"

Jenny felt as if her head whirled with knowledge. But her heart was even heavier than it had been when she had first entered the office.

She shifted John Mark to her other arm and hesitated. Joseph waited. "You tell us the Bible isn't translated correctly," Jenny said. "You give us so much wisdom and knowledge, spirit direction. But, Joseph, I don't understand it all.

"Why is it that when I read the Bible, the words sing through me? I can't forget some of them. God so loved us that He gave, that whosoever might have eternal life just by believing in Jesus. Aren't we 'whosoever'? Joseph, who was Jesus? Why does He say we must be born again?"

Clayton was at the door waiting to come in. Apologetically he said, "I don't mean to bother, if you need more time." Jenny shook her head, but her eyes were studying the books and the large charts he held. He shuffled through them and lifted one. " 'Tis of the heavens. The Prophet and I have been seeking the ancient knowledge of the heavens. My, what amazing things we've discovered."

"About the universe?" Jenny questioned.

"No, about the influence of energy and the stars. Of their magnetic force released on the people of the earth. Did you know we are under these influences?"

Feeling even more confused, Jenny shook her head and left the office. As she got into the buggy she murmured, "I still don't understand the mystery of Christ. Why wouldn't the princes have crucified Him?"

"Being a mama is harder on a lady than I thought."

Jenny looked up. Tom was standing beside the buggy, grinning at her and reaching for his nephew. "Hey, big fella. When we goin' huntin' together?" John Mark drooled and reached for Tom's beard.

"I'm sorry; I just didn't see you. Where are you headed? Do you want a ride?"

"Going up to Nauvoo House. Emma's all set to take off on the steamboat, bound for St. Louis to buy some fancies for the place."

Jenny exclaimed, "Oh, the luck! I wish I were going, too. New clothes and new furniture, oh, my! But where do you fit in?"

"Joseph just wants me to settle the lady in. So I'll go up and drive her in the carriage to the wharf."

"Come out for supper with Mark."

He shook his head. "Lee's outta town. Joseph's tapped me for duty at the house tonight. I do want to see Mark; you might let the word drop. I got a lot on my mind, and I want his advice."

"Love or finances?" Jenny teased. Tom glared, and she laughed. "Well, come when you can. It's been a month since you've been out."

"Yeah." He paused. "I heard Mark ruffled Pratt's feathers a couple of weeks ago."

"It's been around," Jenny mused. "Seems Mark's having a harder time keeping quiet lately. Tom, I'm worried for him. He won't sign up for the endowments. You heard the sermon. What does that mean to John Mark?"

"Maybe nothing at all."

Tom stood watching his sister drive out of sight. Her slender figure in the dark calico seemed especially vulnerable, fragile; he wondered at his uneasiness.

Walking back to the stables behind Nauvoo House, Tom was pondering the effect of the summer's assignment on his feelings. "A body can't help being influenced by it all." He muttered, thinking of what he had seen and heard during the past months.

"One thing's for sure. I'll be very happy to chuck this job and go back to tending horses. They don't give me no surprises."

But later, as Tom settled himself on the cot in the back hall of Nauvoo House, he advised himself, "Can't complain about this assignment." Joseph had been finished with his calls early. The two of them had been back at Nauvoo House before ten o'clock. After a quick nightcap, Joseph had gone upstairs, leaving Tom to the devices of the kitchen maids.

New ones, they were, and he missed the friendly Partridge girls. He was still chuckling over the two as he settled himself to sleep close to the foot of the stairs.

The creak of the stairs awakened Tom. Dawn touched the windows with a rosy glow. As he sat up on the cot, Tom saw the heels of Brother Rushton, the steward, disappearing up the stairs. Realizing the man was going after the keys, Tom started up the stairs after him.

By the time Tom reached Joseph's door, Rushton had already tapped and pushed open the door. Tom was behind Rushton as the startled young woman sat up in bed. "Oh!" She pulled the sheet higher and smiled at the two. "My, you startled me nearly as much as I startled you!" She turned and reached for the keys. "Well, for this week, you'll just have to pretend I'm sister Emma."

Tom saw the bedcovers heave, and another head appeared. Joseph sat up. Tom's fascinated gaze froze on the brilliant red nightshirt the Prophet was wearing. After several silent seconds, the Prophet added, "You heard the lady—now be off."

He was still glaring at Tom as Brother Rushton closed the door behind them. "Tom," Brother Rushton said, "I have an idea the General would rather we didn't mention seeing him under these circumstances. Particularly since we'll have to put up with sister Emma being gone all week." Tom watched him go slowly down the stairs, shaking his head.

When Tom reached the farm the next evening, Mark was in the barn milking. He said, "For a young fella without the burden of land and family, you sure do look down in the mouth."

"Might say I am. Might be 'cause I'm fearing what you've indicated."

"Aw, it isn't so bad, dear brother-in-law," Mark was laughing until he lifted his head from the cow's flank. Then his face sobered and he said, "It is? Better pull up a log and tell me about it."

"It's this priesthood thing. I suppose you've heard the rumors, even if you haven't been tapped for it yet."

"I'm on the council. I'm guessing. It's the everlasting covenant of marriage, isn't it."

Tom nodded. "I don't even have one wife, and can't say I'm overanxious for one. Now Joseph is saying I do or be damned. Mark, I've been right happy with the church all along, seemed a jolly way to have religion, even in the rough times."

"Even in Missouri?"

"Aw, that was rough on the women and children. But most of the fellas managed to tough it through."

"Not minding it?"

"How do I say it? When you listen to a fella like Joseph, you manage to swallow the questions and just get on with it." He looked at Mark. "Sure, I know with a family there's fears a body wouldn't have otherwise."

"Tom," Mark said slowly, "do you ever get the idea we might be heading the same direction now?"

"As Missouri? I hate having you put it out in words."

"Maybe it's time for all of us to get our heads out of the sand." Mark had finished the milking and fed the pigs before he asked, "What's on your mind?"

Tom looked astonished, "I thought I said."

"I had the feeling it was something more."

"Aw, I busted in on Joseph and the wife of one of the elders." Mark said nothing, and so Tom added, "At six in the morning they weren't discussing the doctrine of the church."

"I understand there's quite a bit of that thing going on." Mark's voice was muffled as he pitched straw into the corner of the barn.

"You don't act too concerned."

"Let's say there's little one fellow can do. If you want to join a committee for reform, you just might find a bunch of husbands around who are willing."

Tom shook his head. "I have the feeling Joseph will be converting the husbands faster than we can."

"Meanwhile, there's your problem," Mark said soberly. "You want to make it in the hereafter, but on your own terms—which differ somewhat from the Prophet's."

"Aw," Tom grinned sheepishly, "you don't make me sound so good. Matter-of-fact, I guess my big problem is I'm starting to have some questions about the whole deal. I guess I'll just have to find somewhere to sit tight until I get a few answers. I'd hate to decide I'd made a big mistake about Joseph, the church, and his new ideas about the kingdom of God, and wake up to find I have four wives and sixteen kids."

"Matter-of-fact, Tom, that's about the wisest thing I've ever heard you say." He slapped Tom on the shoulder. "Let's go have some supper."

CHAPTER 33

Jenny was peering out the window when Mark came into the kitchen. "Last night's storm blew the rest of the leaves off the trees," she said, "and now it looks like it's going to snow."

"I'm not too crazy about you and tyke out on the road, especially just for Relief Society meeting."

"I hate to miss. Not just the quilting for Nauvoo House, but the gossip. I never imagined this fall and winter would be shoving up such things to talk about."

"Like?"

"Orson Pratt and another fellow are headed for Washington, carrying a petition to Congress. Sarah told me a little about it. She says it's pushing our plea to be made into an independent federal territory. Joseph's also asked that the Nauvoo Legion be incorporated into the United States Army and that the mayor of the Nauvoo be given authority to call out the United States troops whenever necessary." She stopped suddenly and Mark looked up. "You know all this; why are you getting me to talk?"

"Maybe I wanted to hear what was going around in Relief Society."

"Do you think we're getting things differently?"

"Yes. In fact, I have a feeling you ladies are adoring slaves of the Prophet, and that he can convince you to say anything."

Speechless, Jenny looked at Mark. Finally she said, "It's a good thing your eyes are twinkling, otherwise—"

"What?" Now she saw his eyes were very serious.

"Mark!" She rushed to him, and he caught her tight against him. "Oh, Mark, what's happening to us? It isn't just to us two, it's everyone."

"You tell me." His voice was flat, and she leaned back to look at him. Slowly she raised herself on tiptoe and put her arms around his neck. He met her lips, but she saw the shadows in his eyes. He was first to turn away. "Maybe this early storm has more significance than we guessed. Could be a barometer of Nauvoo."

"A gathering storm in Nauvoo?" She paused, then insisted, "But—loyalty to the church. Mark, you just don't give up on a thing because the going is rough."

"Jenny, are you trying to convince yourself?"

She whispered, "Let's have a happy Christmas. Last year was wonderful because of the excitement of a baby coming. This year let's celebrate and celebrate. Let's invite everyone we can think of."

"Jenny," he chided with a smile, "this isn't Nauvoo House. There are limits to the number of people who'll fit into this house."

Jenny made her Christmas plans. But life in Nauvoo continued to change. Before Christmas Joseph Smith's petition to Congress had been rejected.

Mark had been there with the other members of the council when Joseph had received the news and then got to his feet to speak. "I prophesy," he roared, "through virtue of the office of the priesthood, in the name of the Lord, that if Congress chooses to deny our petition, they shall suffer destruction! They will be broken up as a government—God will damn them. There shall be nothing left of them, not even a spot of grease!"

Later Mark explained it to Jenny as he sampled the Christmas cookies. "It was like an explosion of gunpowder. Nearly blew us all off our seats. I guess some of us had our hopes higher than we thought. But I expect by the beginning of the year, something new will be brewing in the fertile mind of the Prophet."

He was thoughtful as he studied the disappointed droop to Jenny's lips, deciding he couldn't admit to her just how little he knew about the unrest in Nauvoo right now. But he admitted to himself that not knowing was downright frightening. One thing was certain. The words *apostate* and *dissenter* were becoming common words in Nauvoo.

Mark had other things on his mind. As he watched Jenny cutting Christmas cookies, he found himself thinking he would like to be a mouse in the corner of Relief Society meeting.

Last summer he had first become aware of the cloak of secrecy being thrown up around the society. But last summer, Mark admitted, the whole town writhed under the weight of submerged feelings. The Prophet had started it when he had introduced the revelation on everlasting marriage to some of the elders.

Then in August Joseph Smith had begun mentioning *emigration*. In September Tom had been one of a group of men who suddenly disappeared. Only Mark, the Prophet, and a sprinkling of others knew the men had been sent on an expedition by the Prophet.

Mark had been in council meeting the day the Prophet had faced the men. His usual jovial air was only slightly dampened as he spread the map on the table and began pointing out territories. "This here is Texas; right now it doesn't belong to the United States. It's land for grabs. I want Lucian Woodworth to go see what it'll take to get a big hunk of land."

With his finger he sketched out an area from the big river in Texas to the gulf of Mexico, from the Rio Grande River to the territorial boundary of the United States.

"But we're not going to lap up the first offer. We want to investigate every alternative. Fellas—" he paused to fix a commanding gaze on them all, one by one, "Things are getting tight."

In a moment he continued, "This here is Oregon. And this area around the Rocky Mountains is barren—worthless, but empty.

"There are high mountains, according to a fella I've been talking to. Good places for a people to hide out and live their lives without the kind of oppression that's been our lot." His voice had been brooding as he said, "Never will we as a people escape persecution. It's a fact that the holier a people are, the more they're bound to suffer for their religion."

And as the men prepared to go, the Prophet ordered them to check out all the locations he had earmarked. Before they left the room Joseph had fastened them with a stern eye and commanded their vow of silence. "We don't know what the next few years will hold for us. I'm not saying we're leaving, but I want all options checked out. Be a Joshua and Caleb, but don't put your heads too high in the clouds.

"We want a reasonable solution for the Saints. We want a decent place to live out our lives where we never again will be persecuted and hounded to death because we choose to follow God."

But Mark couldn't tell Jenny, he decided, as he continued to eat cookies. There was a dark shadow in her eyes these days.

Jenny's attention was on a different country. She was thinking of her interview with Joseph. She continued to make cookies, while her heart was heavy with his words. Little John Mark didn't have a place with her in the eternities until she obeyed the Prophet.

This year Mark made certain the Christmas tree stand was sturdy. The tree stood straight and brave under its burden of popcorn, candy canes and shiny tin stars. Tom came carrying a wooden horse and cow for John Mark.

The Morgans came with Andy's sister, Helene. A determined gleam lit Helene's eyes as she smiled at Tom. The Orson Pratts came, with Orson full of his disappointment with the Washington trip.

Late in the afternoon they all returned to town for a reception at Nauvoo House. It was nearly dusk when they reached the red brick edifice.

"It's like a painting!" Jenny exclaimed to Mark as she hugged John Mark to her. The snow was falling gently in large fluffy flakes. "Just look!" she said, pointing to the sleighs with their graceful lines and bright bells. "Even the Saints are bright in their new Christmas mufflers and mittens." Every window on the lower floor of the hotel glowed with light, completing the Christmas picture.

Inside, Jenny discovered Emma's fat china lamps sporting new red glass shades. Wreaths of holly and garlands of evergreen festooned the polished banister of the staircase, and the red carpeting of the lobby beckoned toward the fireplace and blazing fire.

Sally stopped beside Jenny and whispered, "Look at the chandelier; it glitters like diamonds." In awe they stared up at the prisms, made alive with every fresh gust of wintry air. "It's grand, isn't it?" Sally stroked the marble-topped table and studied the shiny horsehair and red velvet upholstery. "Doesn't Emma look elegant in brocade? My, we Saints are going to be something special yet."

Together Mark and Jenny made their way through the rooms, greeting the guests. There were the twelve, Brigham Young and his wife, Lyman Wight, both of the Pratt brothers, Hiram Kimball, and his wife. Later they found William Phelps and Joseph's younger brother, William Smith.

Jenny lost the thread of conversation moving around them. She was busy thinking about this powerful, tall brother of Joseph's. Tipping her head to investigate his face, she noted the sullen lines. His insolent eyes met hers. Without a doubt he had a caustic tongue, she recalled, thinking of recent issues of the *Wasp*, the newspaper he edited.

As she followed Mark across the room, she murmured, "And now he's our state legislator." Jenny studied the three tallest men in Mormondom. They were spaced throughout the hotel, as if proximity could not be tolerated.

Recent gossip had William Law as a man in disfavor, bordering on apostasy. She looked from him to William Smith, and then to Joseph the Prophet. These men's minds were as forceful as their size. As she watched them, Jenny became convinced that trouble was brewing.

Later, Emma guided Jenny into a small room away from the lobby. Together they settled down to talk while Jenny nursed John Mark.

A gentle smile crept over Emma's face as she played with the baby's curls, and Jenny was emboldened to ask the question on her mind. "I haven't seen Eliza Snow for so long. Has she left Nauvoo?"

The smile faded from Emma's face. For a moment her frosty eyes held Jenny, then she said, "I believe you've asked in innocence. Since you were there when she fell, I'll tell you. Eliza is still in Nauvoo. I don't know where she lives and I've no desire to renew acquaintance. She was a serpent. I trusted her as I've trusted no other woman. She was my confidant, my friend."

Emma paused, and in an icy voice that denied additional questions, she added, "Eliza was pregnant. I understand she's lost her baby."

Later, after Emma left the room and John Mark was asleep, Jenny wrapped him in a heavy quilt and placed him on the floor.

As she got to her feet, she felt a hand on her arm. Glancing down, she recognized the massive gold ring. "Joseph," she said with a tired sigh.

"Have you decided?" he asked. When she didn't answer, he gently urged, "Remember, I've pledged to be god to you. There's no way a woman will make it on her own; she's got to have a husband to take her into the celestial kingdom."

As she hesitated, Jenny recalled that verse and turned. "Joseph, I've read a verse in the Bible that encourages me; I want to believe and accept it. It says that in Christ there's not this division. Neither Jew nor Gentile, slave nor free, male nor female, but that we're all one in Christ Jesus."

He paused and his hand tightened on her arm, "Must I remind you again that to reject the gospel is damnation?"

She looked up, feeling the despair that was coming through her voice. "Maybe I'd rather choose damnation than deny my marriage vows."

He sighed, "Jenny, I've held back on saying this, because I've not wanted to hurt you. But in the eyes of our Lord, your marriage vow doesn't exist. You are living in adultery with Mark Cartwright."

Closing her eyes, Jenny took a step backward and was immediately surrounded by perfume and the cool touch of yellow roses. She felt that Presence and knew the promise.

She opened her eyes and stared up at Joseph. "I've been doing a lot of thinking and studying lately. I've decided the craft is all wrong. I don't want to have that kind of power. See, I have this need inside of me to know God. I guess you might say I've just promised the Lord I'd be a good Mormon and live up to my religion. Joseph, you make it impossible for me to keep that promise if—if what you're saying must be."

There was the creak of the door behind Jenny and Mark was asking, "Jenny, are you ready to go home?"

Jenny was still staring at Joseph as she replied, "Yes, my husband, I am ready."

CHAPTER 34

The January snow was piling up. In the pasture the cattle and horses huddled with their backs to the wind while Jenny stood at the window watching snow inch relentlessly toward the top of the fence.

John Mark had crept across the floor. Seizing her skirt, he tried to pull himself to his feet. "Big boy," Jenny encouraged, smiling down at the bright-haired child. She picked him up and said, "Oh, I wonder if your papa has noticed how your eyes are changing. I'm glad. I want you to have blue-green just like his.

"Now, tyke, let's get that pan of bread into the oven beside the squash and then go for fresh diapers." With another quick glance out the window she sighed and added, "I hope he comes before dark. The snow is blowing."

When the baby was settled on his blanket and the aroma of fresh bread began drifting through the house, Jenny sat down close to the window and picked up her Bible. She hesitated and reached for Mark's Bible, feeling slightly guilty as she did so.

"Such interesting things he writes!" she murmured. A piece of paper marked Isaiah 8, but the paper was blank. Disappointed, she started to close the Bible when words caught her attention and she began to read. She straightened in her chair and caught her breath. It was as if the astounding words were speaking to her. Finally she sat back to think and then read again.

John Mark had been playing with a spoon, and now with spoon still clenched in his chubby hand, he had collapsed into sleep. She wanted desperately to kiss the smile on his face, even as she heard the scripture echo through her mind, underlining the fears. She dropped to her knees beside the baby and whispered the words from Isaiah, ". . . Neither fear ye their fear, nor be afraid. Sanctify the Lord. . . . Let him be our fear, . . . He shall be . . . a sanctuary; . . . I will wait upon the Lord, . . . I will look for him."

The door banged and Jenny was caught with Mark's Bible on her lap. She looked up at him as he stood by the back door. "Mark! What is it?" she gasped, scrambling to her feet.

She stared into his white face, seeing the deep breath he took before saying, "Jenny, nothing." He was covered with snow, except for one coat sleeve. She touched it, seeing the hole.

"Who did it? And why?"

"Could have been anyone. I couldn't see. In this snow he could have been shooting at a bear."

"Mark, not a bear; not even a deer."

"Look, Jenny. I was shot at. I'm not blaming anyone. Not the Missourians, not the bunch from Warsaw or the Destroying Angels. Let's just forget it. He didn't hit me, and I don't think the miss was an accident. He was pretty close."

She helped him remove the coat. "I can't believe such a hole without touching your arm. Not even your shirt. She flung the coat away and threw her arms around him. "Mark, I—I'm afraid. Did you say 'Destroying Angels'?"

Mark tried to laugh it off. No matter how she pressed, he would say no more, but she saw the anxiety in his eyes.

The following morning when Mark reached Joseph's office, the place was buzzing with activity. Clayton was trying to write a letter. Two strangers were waiting to see Joseph; John D. Lee was perched on a barrel in the hallway discoursing on Mormonism to them, while Hiram Kimball paced the outer room and William Law pounded on Joseph's desk.

When Mark walked in, Joseph's attention diverted from Law to Mark. "Will you find the information on the last land deal and show William the bills of lading on the lumber?"

Law was still snorting in disgust as he followed Mark. "I've never seen such a slipshod office. He's got every worker in town over at the Nauvoo House, and I've begged for weeks to get fellows to work for me. Mark, there's still folks out there waiting for housing. I'm about to take things into my hands and hire out of St. Louis."

Mark was removing his coat. William stopped abruptly and fingered the patch Jenny had stitched over the bullet hole. "What happened?"

Briefly Mark explained. He saw Law's frown, the slanted glance. William dropped his voice. "Think it was the Angels?"

"I try to refrain from thinking so."

"That's not wise." He paced the room, closed the door. When he returned he dropped his voice. "Six months ago, one of the brethren came to me in secrecy to tell me the Destroying Angels had been commissioned to get me. I didn't take him too seriously for a time." He paused. "As Joseph says, a word to the wise is sufficient. Watch the Whittlers next time you walk through town."

They heard the creak of floorboard and Joseph came through the door. He dropped a sheaf of papers on Mark's desk. "Read this report. I need advice. Briefly, President Tyler, in his address to Congress the first of the month, advised setting up military posts along the route of the Oregon Trail to provide security to emigrants and travelers. I propose petitioning Congress to allow us to be that army. I'm asking to be appointed an officer with power to take volunteers and patrol the western borders of the country for the purposes of law and justice."

He left the room and William Law checked the invoices and left. Mark had just begun to read when the explosion of voices from Joseph's office had him running for the outer door. It wasn't the first time visitors had been protected from Joseph's temper.

But it was the first time it had boiled over into the outer office. Joseph Smith came stalking after Hiram Kimball. Mark caught the word *steamboat*. Knowing Kimball owned a number of wharves along the river, he paused to listen to the exchange. Joseph bellowed, "I don't care if you own the water, too! You are stealing the city's right to wharfage. You'll settle the affair and turn the money over to the city or I'll blow up every steamboat in dock!"

John D. Lee came into the outer office and said, "Well that's about as slick a way of getting rid of the froth and troublemakers as I've seen."

Joseph turned and snapped, "What?"

"Those fellas out there. Just time-wasters, wanting to see Joseph for themselves. Asking how many wives you've got. But you started yelling and they decided they had business down the street."

Joseph was still frowning as he took his hat and coat and headed for the door.

John followed Mark into his office. "How's that pretty little wife of yours? Did I hear right about you havin' a young'un?"

Mark sat down to answer Lee's questions and listen to his rambling talk. After a few moments of lighthearted chatter, Lee turned to a serious subject. "Cartwright, how's this spiritual wife doctrine settin'?"

"With me?" He paused. "I know little about it. The Prophet gave us initial teaching on it. He hasn't pushed to make me add to my family. So all this means is that I'm safe so far. Lee, I think you know me well enough to know I'll buck it all the way."

Lee scrutinized Mark. "You'll be your own man," he said slowly, looking down at his hands. He slanted a glance at Mark. "I advise you to walk more careful. Joseph's touchy right now. Seems he's very impatient with slow learners."

"Are you warning me, John?" The man looked surprised, and Mark continued. "Last night, on my way home, someone took a shot at me."

John squinted at Mark. "Given the climate around here right now, I'm not surprised. Just remember Joseph's getting very touchy and impatient. He's mighty fearful about people who talk too much, especially about the celestial kingdom."

"Seems to me Joseph's gone to meddling when it involves marriage."

"He has the keys and the revelations. The pamphlet put out by Jacobs shows people aren't ready for deep teaching. You weren't at council meeting when Joseph said, pointing to William Marks and Parley Pratt, that if he were to reveal the will of God concerning them at that moment, they'd feel called upon to shed his blood. 'Course, he went on to say they should be surrendering themselves to God.

"From the looks on the faces and the consequential action some of the brethren took," Lee continued, "I'd say he managed to give them a mind sensitive to the fear of the Lord. I'm glad to see some of them went marching right up to find out the will of God for them.

"He's not proclaiming it in public now, but there's no need. Having the book of the law of the Lord and just following what the Lord instructs is keeping the Prophet and the Saints pretty busy. But then the Prophet made it pretty clear our obligation. There's just no way, without plural marriage, that man can attain to the fullness of the gospel. Joseph's made it clear that we've got to learn to be gods ourselves, especially in order to be equal with our Savior."

Lee paused a moment and then added, "Personally, I think some of those who were not living up to their religion took it pretty hard when Joseph advised their spouses that their marriage relations weren't valid on account of not having an authority to hear their vows. He did give them liberty to go if they wanted. This living together and having children when there's alienation between the two is just plain sin. The pamphlet made that clear."

John Lee got to his feet to leave and then turned to Mark. "How do you feel about all this talk of Joseph running for president of the United States?"

"I guess I haven't heard enough to give it much thought," Mark said slowly.

Joseph came stomping into the office, shaking snow from his clothes. "Well, the High Council's just started pressuring me to throw my hat into the ring. I couldn't take them seriously for a time. Seems now I'll have to, just to keep peace among the brethren." He chuckled and threw himself into Mark's chair.

"First off, there's a need to get feelers out. I intend to send out letters to every candidate and see just how they'll stand on the Mormon question. Mark, that's where I'll need your help. I need a little touch of culture to the whole affair. If it doesn't go any further than raising a little dust, at least by the time it's all over, Congress will see we're a force that merits respect and recognition."

"Joseph," Mark argued mildly, "you can't raise enough votes to do anything except make a fool of yourself."

"I intend to claim two hundred thousand. With the converts we're adding to the church, I'm certain of this number." He jumped to his feet and headed out of the room.

"There's less than twelve thousand people living right in Nauvoo," Mark objected.

He looked at John D. Lee's long face as he started to leave Mark's office. "Here I go again," he muttered. "I can see me stomping. It's hard enough to preach the gospel out there without a cent to keep me going, not to mention the ridicule I get. But to go out there and build up Joseph for president of the United States with the kind of reputation he has . . ." He was still shaking his head when he closed the door behind himself.

Mark was still sitting at his desk, staring at Joseph's papers and thinking, when the Prophet returned to his office. "By the way, Mark, gird up your loins. Within the next month or so the organization of the Council of Fifty will get off the ground. I want you in it, and I won't take no for an answer."

Mark looked up at him. "I was just sitting here wondering what other mountain you'll climb. President of the United States . . ." He paused to shake his head and then held up his fingers. "At this time you are mayor of Nauvoo, judge of the municipal court, merchant of the biggest store in town, hotelkeeper, head of the temple building committee, real estate agent, contractor; you handle the recording of deeds in town; you own a steamboat; you are the sole trustee for the financial affairs of the church, lieutenant-general of the Nauvoo Legion, spiritual advisor, and head of the church."

"You can't guess what will be next?" Joseph chuckled, "Stay close, Mark, you'll see. You know the Lord has willed this church to be spread around the world. I aim to see that happen."

"You're an ambitious man, Joseph."

"I have my failings. But I'm also a tried man. There's a constant warfare between the two natures of man."

"Do you believe the Lord wants that?" Mark asked. "The Bible says we are to live above sin, to not be entangled in the things that hold us slaves to sin."

"Every man has equal chance at salvation. It is true, however, that some men have a greater capacity of improving their minds and controlling their passions through denying unrighteousness and cultivating the principles of purity. We all have our free agency. It lies with the power of mankind to rise above and claim eternal life—if only man will be faithful to God's will and obey the priesthood in these last days."

That evening when Mark reached home, Jenny was at the door to meet him. She brushed snow from him and anxiously searched his face. "Did . . . did—how was your day?"

"Fine. Uneventful, unless you consider it exciting to hear the Prophet threaten to blow up the steamboats in the harbor and admit he's considering running for the office of president of the United States."

Jenny stared at him for a moment and then slowly said, "I knew you would be tired; I milked the cows."

CHAPTER 35

It was a bright February day. The clouds were scooting across the sky like kites and the air was filled with the smells of spring. Jenny spent the day airing bedding and washing linens. A new lamb wobbled in the pasture and she carried John Mark out to see the little creature.

Loath to return to her kitchen tasks, she lingered at the pasture fence, balancing the baby and letting the wind rip through her hair. What a sense of freedom the blithe wind gave!

Watching the air billow her skirt and apron, she closed her eyes and pretended she was a kite. John Mark drooled on her neck and she laughed at him. "You will remind me that I'm only your dinner ticket! But that's all right." She fell to musing over the contrasts in her life.

The thoughts made Jenny shiver. Less than two years ago she had been Jenny the witch. Closing her eyes she contemplated the darkness of that time, measuring it by thinking her way back into the pattern of that life, with its promises and desires.

She considered the charms, even the talisman. "Is it possible?" she gasped. "Was I really like that?" For a moment she clung to the thought of the talisman. She had told Tom she regretted getting rid of it, for one reason—Mark. As she thought of their early love, she began to yearn for the power the talisman had given. "Face it, Jenny," she whispered. "Without that talisman, Mark would have never married you."

For a long time Jenny stared out across the pasture, scarcely aware of the pattern of bright green and yellow. When, with a sigh, she turned toward the house, she was caught up short. The weather-beaten house seemed tiny and dismal, but instead of the peeling gray paint she saw sharp views of the life it had sheltered for nearly three years now.

"Then there were two, now there are three. Then there was Jenny the witch, now—" Abruptly she recalled Mark's face. Did the light in his eyes, the tender smile, tell her something about herself that she had failed to see?"

With her eyes closed she considered herself now—the questions, the Bible. Now her eyes popped open, recalling: "The Lord is my shepherd; . . . I lie down in green pastures: I am come that they might have life, more abundantly. Except a man be born again, he cannot see the kingdom of God. For God so loved that he gave his Son. For by grace are ye saved through faith, the gift of God." John Mark pressed his head against her and she opened her eyes and smiled down at him. And then in a moment the sweet peace of the words moved away from her.

"Beautiful words," she whispered, "but I don't understand them. God, are You there listening? Please—"

With a troubled sigh she turned and walked to the house. The thoughts contained in that Book were bigger than life and beyond her understanding. But even worse than not being able to understand were all the fearful things Joseph had threatened.

In the pasture the mare whinnied and she looked toward the road. A buggy was coming, moving rapidly down the lane toward her. She waited, fearful and uneasy, then her eyes widened. It was William and Jane Law. As they got out of the buggy, William appeared troubled. "Come in," she said slowly.

"Is Mark at home?"

"No, but he will be soon. I'll fix some tea for us."

As soon as Jenny placed John Mark on the floor, he began to cry. Jane Law picked him up and carried him into the parlor.

The teakettle was throwing steam into the air and Jenny was placing cups and saucers beside the plate of cookies when Mark walked in. She heard the surprise in his voice as he welcomed the Laws.

Just as she carried the tea tray into the parlor, William offered Mark a newspaper, saying, "Have you seen this?"

"No, I haven't."

William read aloud: " 'You and your followers have considered yourselves a separate nation just as much as any foreign nation. Because of this, and because your tribe indicates a desire to cast off all ties relative to the government, while at the same time you take it upon yourself to create a new one more to your liking, we consider this action treason.' This is the *Warsaw Signal*, February 15, 1844." While the men were still looking at each other, William spoke again. "You know Joseph has supported his own ideas by saying any people trying to govern themselves under laws of their own making are in direct rebellion against the kingdom of God."

Slowly Mark said, "We find ourselves, by following the Nauvoo Charter, being regarded as guilty of treason."

William Law added the next thought. "Yet to fail to do so puts us in jeopardy of our souls."

Mark continued, "If, in fact, the Nauvoo Charter is God's will."

William Law took a deep breath and said, "Nearly a year ago I approached Joseph and accused him of engaging in practices which the Christian church has always regarded as iniquity. I challenged him to reform himself and the doctrine he is pushing on the church. I tried to force him into confessing his sins and cleaning up the church, with the threat that I would reveal his acts to the world if he failed to do so. He refused."

Mark said heavily, "We'd all guessed you and the Prophet were having troubles, particularly when he referred to you as the Judas. What are you going to do about this?"

"I don't know, Mark. It deeply troubles me."

"Have you considered leaving the church?"

Jenny saw the way both of the Laws reacted to the question. William said, "Mark, I blame most of these troubles on Dr. John Bennett. Joseph isn't a false prophet. I believe he's fallen from grace and I'll do anything in my power to help him and restore truth and integrity to the church. But leave? I can't, for the sake of my soul."

Mark leaned forward. "I wish I could persuade you otherwise. From reading the Bible, seeing the promise of salvation through Jesus Christ, I believe Joseph is deluded, walking completely away from the biblical foundation of truth and righteousness in Jesus Christ. With all my heart I would like to see you, and others who feel the same, leave."

"What about you?"

"Someday, but not now."

"Mark!" The exclamation burst from Jenny and he turned to look at her. His eyes were pleading but she felt only the sensation of being wind-tossed away from a sure foundation.

William admitted, "There are others like us—a group who have reason to be unhappy and uneasy under Joseph's changing role. Mark, we want you to meet with us and let's attempt to find a solution to the problem. It isn't to be a gripe session, although one purpose will be candor with each other. None of us realizes the depths to which the other has suffered under the controls Joseph has put upon us. Will you come next week to the meeting at Higbee's store? Bring your wife and son."

When the Laws stood to leave, William said, "You realize, don't you, that these problems won't be resolved immediately? We may be months hearing grievances and trying to come to a solution."

Slowly Mark said, "I honestly wonder if we will have that much time." He tapped the newspaper William held.

It was Relief Society day. The mild February weather encouraged Jenny to make the trip into town. "Three months since we've been to meeting," Jenny informed the laughing John Mark as she bundled him and tied him to the seat beside her. He crowed with delight as the mare smartly clipped off the miles into town.

At meeting, Jenny had just settled down with her quilt block when Sally came into the room. Jenny waved at her friend and made room for her on the bench. "You're looking poorly; you've lost weight," she whispered with a worried frown. Sally nodded without answering. Jenny watched her slowly assemble her quilt block and began to stitch.

Jenny leaned forward to whisper, "You caught?"

Sally's eyebrows lifted but she shook her head. "Just feeling poorly. Like I can hardly drag."

"Why don't you come home with me? I'll fix supper for us all and you can rest."

Sally shook her head. "Tamara. She'll be out of school before Andy's home. You come to us."

Sally continued to answer in monosyllables. Feeling more compelled than curious, Jenny followed Sally home.

When she saw the disarray of Sally's house, Jenny turned to Sally with a worried frown. "I think you are very ill, or there's something desperately wrong somewhere. Will you please talk to me?"

Jenny saw the tears in Sally's eyes and put her arms around her. "Oh, Jenny, it's really nothing I can put my finger on. It's just life is so—" She paused to rub at her eyes and then tried to smile. "Jen, I've everything a woman could possibly want, yet . . . I'm in the true church, and we're both living up to our religion. I have a beautiful daughter, a nice home . . ." Her voice trailed away and she moved away from Jenny.

"You tried suicide last year and now you're scarcely living. I suppose I shouldn't pry, but thinking of last year, I'm afraid to not insist you talk." Sally's hands trembled as she mopped at her eyes.

Jenny took charge. "Go sit in that rocking chair. Here, rock

John Mark. He's nursed and ready for sleep. I'm going to make things a little brighter around here."

She nudged Sally toward the chair and turned to shove the teakettle to the front of the stove. "I'm going to boil some eggs for you. Where's the bread?"

After Sally had eaten, she allowed Jenny to lead her upstairs. "Now you stay there until you sleep. I'm going to sweep the floor and wash the dishes."

While Jenny had her hands in the dishwater, washing the piles of dirty dishes stacked around the kitchen, she began to think.

Sally was living up to her religion. Jenny recalled how she'd always admired and envied the composed, elegant Sally—the woman who looked as if she'd never sinned in her life.

But at the picnic last August Sally had confessed her problem to Jenny. Jenny's hands moved slowly in the water.

With a sigh she said, "Seems if the Lord were in this marrying, Sally should feel like the most holy woman in town. Seems, too, I should feel differently about Joseph's proposal to me." Sally had the witness of the rightness of the marriage. Knowing should have taken care of the guilt.

Jenny addressed the ceiling. "Seems, God, You ought to have been able to take care of her guilt. She's feeling so bad about the situation. If she's got guilt, I sure don't want this to happen to me. But what about John Mark? Seems, God, I'm getting to the place where I don't want to have anything to do with being holy. I just can't forget the promises Mark and I made. When it comes right down to it, I just guess I don't want to be a queen of heaven."

She was scrubbing the pot, crusty with burned-on food, when she looked ceilingward again. "If there's another way on earth to settle my eternity without displeasing You, I'd jump in a minute. Right now the biggest problem I have on my mind is how to make certain my little baby isn't left out."

Jenny found a chunk of meat and some vegetables. By the time she had the meat browned and the vegetables peeled and snugged around the roast, she had managed to shove aside her own needs. Sally's were critical.

When John Mark began to cry and Sally came into the kitchen with him, Jenny had found the Bible. She took the baby and sat in the rocker. Sally sat at the table and touched the Bible.

"Is that your solution to it all?"

Jenny chewed her lip, wondering how much she could force

herself to say. "Sally, religion isn't working for either one of us. You know Mark's against endowment. You know what Joseph had to say about sealing our posterity. Well, in a way I'm just as troubled about my religion as you are. Seems you are living up to it as well as a body possibly could, and it's not doing a thing for you except making you desperately unhappy. I sure wouldn't settle for what you're having. So, it seems we both need to look for a better way.

"Months ago Joseph told me I ought to be studying the Scriptures. I started out reading the *Book of Mormon* and then the Bible. Well, I've ended up reading just the Bible. Mostly because I'm discovering it's teaching me things, like the fact that God loves us and He's trying to help us along the way.

"Sally, I fear for you. Unless you pull yourself up short and begin to make some progress with the Lord, I don't think you're going to—"

"Keep living?" Sally sighed.

"Why don't you begin by reading in the book of John?"

"I've read it before."

"Did you believe what you read? Jesus came to give us life. If we believe in Him we'll spend eternity with Him." Jenny chewed her lip. "Come to think of it, if we can spend eternity with Him, just by accepting the idea He's died for our sins so we don't have to—well then, where will Joseph be? If he is there, well then, I think we've found an easier way to get to the same place."

"Oh, Jenny, you're making my head whirl!"

Jenny looked at Sally in dismay. "I'm sorry. I want so badly to help you, but I just don't know how. I'm not happy with my religion and you're not happy with yours. According to what Joseph's been teaching, you've progressed a lot further than I have. Just looking at your sad face and seeing the mess of things, I can't say I envy you one bit."

Sally cradled her head on the book and began to cry. In desperation Jenny looked down at John Mark, "Young'un, hurry with your dinner."

To Sally she said, "While we're waiting on John Mark, turn to the eighth chapter of John and start reading. About verse thirty-one, I think. I don't understand it all, so maybe you can help me, too."

Wearily Sally pushed herself up and began thumbing through the Bible. She found the section, then slowly said, "This is to the Jews."

"Well, didn't Joseph talk about our blood being changed into children-of-Israel blood when we got baptized? So I'm thinking it must apply to us."

She looked down at the words and said, "Well, he's telling the Jews if they *continue* in His word, they are His disciples." She paused to read silently and when she lifted her head there was a wondering excitement in her voice. "It says here that they'd know the truth and the truth would make them free. Jenny, is Jesus *promising* that if we read this Word, it's going to make us free?"

"It sounds like it, doesn't it? Almost makes me think I dare not read! But go on—there's more, and it's so big I can hardly get my mind around it."

Sally frowned, but dutifully she bent over the Book. She murmured the words: "The Jews tell Jesus they're not in bondage—like us, huh? We have the promises. But Jesus tells them that if they sin, they're a servant of sin." She shifted impatiently and lifted her head. "Jenny, this isn't helping at all. I just don't understand—"

Jenny urged, "Go ahead, read some more. It's the next part that won't leave me alone."

" 'If the Son therefore shall make you free, ye shall be free indeed.' "

Jenny was speaking softly. "There's more, in another place He says He's the way, the truth and the life and that no man comes to the Father except through Him. And He says that if we keep His word, He'll love us and *manifest* himself to us. I think it's meaning we'll get to know Him."

It was getting late. Regretfully Jenny got to her feet. "Sally, I've got to go home. Mark will be there. I've put supper on to cook for you." She reached out to touch her friend. "Please read more, and *hope* in what you read."

She lingered a moment longer. The shadows were back in Sally's eyes and Jenny felt her sadness as she turned to leave.

CHAPTER 36

"Oh, Mark, he isn't a baby anymore!" Jenny wailed, but she couldn't help beaming down at John Mark. The toddler, standing on sturdy legs, teetered slightly as he tilted his head to look up.

Mark crouched down, carefully patted the crown of bright curls and surveyed the little blue and white suit. "Looks like a little sailor in that outfit. Wanna go fishing with Pa?" John Mark crowed and launched himself toward his father.

"Well, it's to Sabbath meeting right now," Jenny said, turning to watch the baby stagger across the floor.

"He's as efficient as a toy boat in a mud puddle," Mark chuckled as John Mark steered clear of the kitchen stove, bounced off the wall, and headed back.

"Andy and Sally are bringing Helene to dinner after meeting. If we see Tom, let's bring him home too."

"I don't expect to see him," Mark stated, getting to his feet. He looked at Jenny. "Tom's one of the strugglers right now."

"What do you mean by that?" Jenny put the lid on the roaster and shoved it into the oven. "With another piece of wood in there now, we'll have dinner as soon as we get home."

"I'll wait a few minutes," Mark said. He was still studying her face and Jenny looked up. "Tom is beginning to wonder if he wants to push on with Joseph's teachings. You know he's been asked to join in the Council of Fifty."

"What's that?"

Mark shrugged. "I can tell you little, my dear, except that right now Joseph is causing a flurry among some of the men, the ones to whom he's revealed the kingdom of God secrets."

"Not you? Not his prize attorney?"

"That's correct. And there's good reason for that. From what I've gathered just by observing, the men come out of those meetings feeling one of two ways."

"I don't understand."

"They're either elated—walking on air, or they're scared, angry, and depressed."

She studied him for a moment before saying slowly, "Mark, at Relief Society there's been some of the women acting the same way. The whispers about spiritual wives are growing into more than the usual snickers and teasing.

"I'm seeing troubled women. Embarrassed ones. Some are whispering that their husbands are angry, threatening to leave the church. They mentioned the fact that the *Book of Mormon* teaches against polygamy, calling it a whoredom.

"Others are outraged, like the Laws. They want a change. I know for a fact that some of the families have invested a great deal of money in the church to build the temple and buy property."

She turned to pick up John Mark's sweater and her shawl. Mark hesitated and then said, "Jenny, I have a feeling that trouble's brewing out there. We may be called upon to make some big decisions, and in a hurry."

She saw his eyes, but her fearful thoughts were running ahead. *The church, the endowments, John Mark.*

After Sabbath meeting, while Mark and Jenny were walking back to their buggy, they listened to the couple in front of them. The woman was saying, "Why does Joseph keep talking about polygamy? Nearly every week he seems to feel called to deny a new charge."

Her husband replied, "I'd like to know why Joseph keeps bringing up the Missouri issue. I'm sick of being reminded of those bad days. If he'd just let sleeping dogs lie, we'd all be better off. The good Book tells us to forgive, and I think that's pretty good advice."

When they reached the buggy, Mark said, "Well, what are *you* thinking?"

She looked surprised. "I was thinking about what Brother Kimball said a couple of weeks ago, comparing it to the *Book of Mormon*. Mark, the *Book of Mormon* says there's no chance for a person after death. I take that to mean there's not one thing a person can do to change where he'll spend eternity once he dies."

Mark nodded. "That's right, and the Bible agrees."

"But," she continued, "Brother Kimball indicates these sinners will go to hell, have the corruption burned out of them and then end up in heaven as servants. Then the sermon today talked about the unredeemed being angels forever."

"I heard it too," he said looking at her with a quizzical frown.

"And there's no chance for an angel to be a god?"

"Well, not according to the church doctrine. Jenny, what is troubling you?"

"Well, then, I can't understand how an angel named Michael can become Adam who was God. That's the creation story."

Tom was waiting for them when they reached home. But his happy grin disappeared when the Morgans' buggy wheeled in behind them. "Oh," Mark groaned. "Poor Tom; he'll have to put up with Helene."

After dinner Tom and Helene, with Tamara in tow, disappeared down the lane while Mark and Andy wandered out to the barn. Jenny settled John Mark for his nap and began the dishes. "Sally, why don't you just sit in the rocking chair and talk to me?"

She was shaking her head as Jenny spoke. Seeing the dark shadows in her eyes and her restless pacing, Jenny handed her a dish towel. They worked in silence until Jenny said, "How are you feeling now?"

Sally shook her head. After another long silence, she said, "The worst part is deceiving Andy. It's getting to the place where I can't pretend any longer, and he thinks it's his fault."

"Why don't you just ask him to take you away from here?"

"That wouldn't solve the past; besides, remember, I'm earning my right to the eternities."

Jenny finished scrubbing the roaster and turned to Sally. "Have you been reading in the Bible?" She shook her head and Jenny stood watching her helplessly. Finally she said, "The only person I can think of who'd be able to help you is Mark. He knows so much about the Bible—"

Sally turned and looked at Jenny with a puzzled frown, and Jenny realized the separation between them. "Sally, I should have told you. I believe the Bible is God speaking to me, telling me how to live, what to think about Him. He tells me about sin and forgiveness. The words in the Book give hope when it seems impossible." She paused and searched Sally's face. "Do you understand?"

"I understand that you have changed. You used to use the charms and the secret things. They frightened me, mostly because of the way you looked when you used them. But they were mysterious and exciting, too. Now—you're talking about the Bible, and Joseph says it isn't translated correctly. He says corrupt men have done this. Jenny, I'm too fearful to trust when you say *trust* and he says *don't.*"

The look on Sally's face told Jenny that she had closed the door.

In the late afternoon the Morgans left for home. Mark stood beside Jenny as the buggy rambled down the lane. He saw the hopeless expression on Jenny's face as she turned away.

Tom was saying, "Come on, Mark, let's go try that new fishing pole of yours."

"In the river?" Jenny asked slowly. "Well, go along. I don't want to hike down that steep bank. Maybe I'll bake a gingercake."

Mark led the way across the pasture and into the woods. "There's a pretty good path right through here, and I've managed to trample it down. I'd like to get a good-sized bass. Think this pole is strong enough?" He peered at Tom. "Something wrong?"

"Naw, not much. Just talk again. There's a rumor floatin' around that the Lodge is in trouble. Seems the Grand Worshipful Master from Springfield is a mite upset. They're claiming we're corrupting the Masonic ritual. They've ordered Joseph to send the records into Springfield, and he's takin' his time about doin' it. I 'spect we'll lose out yet. Mostly I don't like them charging us with bein' clandestine, whatever that's supposed to mean."

They scrambled down the last slope and made their way out on the rocks. Tom continued, "Seems to me that the Lodge was the best thing that's happened to the church in a long time. Seemed to give us new direction."

In silence Mark threaded the line and Tom baited the hook. Then he handed the pole to Tom. "Here, you use it first."

Tom cast out and flashed an approving grin. "That's smooth!" They settled down on the rocks and watched the line drift.

Mark shifted his weight on the rock and heard the clink of metal. As he turned toward the sound he saw the disk catch the sun as it dropped from the rock to the sandy shore. "I wonder—might be a coin," he murmured, jumping off the rock.

"Got a bite," Tom said. "Aw, lost the bait." He pulled in the line and reached for the worms as Mark crawled up on the rock. "Well, what did you find?"

Mark pulled the disk out of his pocket. "Thought it was a dollar, but it seems to be some kind of medallion."

Tom dropped his line into the water and turned to take the medal. "Looks like lead. Hey, there's writing and numbers on it. I bet that's Jenny's. She mentioned having a talisman and was wishing she had it back."

"Did she lose it?" Mark asked, studying the curious disk.

"I can't rightly remember. All I know is she was wishing for it. Seems it means a great deal to her—more'n a good luck charm." Tom turned quickly, "There!"

Mark watched him pulling in a big bass. Tom grinned up at him. "Might be, if she doesn't want it, you ought to be using it for fishing. Sure works."

When they walked into the kitchen, Tom held out the fish and sniffed hungrily. "Well, here's supper. I'll trade for some of that cake."

He put the fish on the table. "Jen, is this your talisman? Mark found it down on the rocks."

Mark saw the color leave Jenny's face as she took a hesitant step toward Tom and slowly reached for the disk. For a moment, before her hand closed around it, Mark thought she was going to refuse it.

He watched her close her fingers around it and tuck it into her pocket. Then he remembered why the little disk seemed familiar. This was the talisman he had seen lying beside her mittens on the mantel of their cabin in Missouri.

CHAPTER 37

The first Monday in March, on the way into Nauvoo, Mark met Orson Pratt and they completed the ride together.

Orson said, "March is in like a lamb; does this foreshadow life roaring like a lion in Nauvoo this spring?"

Mark looked at him. "Not unless you know more about life than I do. As of last week I was thinking life had tamed down a bit."

"Well, I know Joseph's been touching men for the honor of being on the Council of Fifty. He's calling them princes and saying this will be the highest court on earth."

As Mark continued to listen to Pratt, pricks of apprehension began to make him uneasy. Orson interrupted himself to ask, "You've been asked, haven't you?"

Slowly Mark said, "Yes, but I'm beginning to wonder what I'm getting into." Pratt's eyes were sparkling. Mark said, "I suppose it's just a juvenile fear of the unknown. But I hope Joseph's kept the rest of you men better informed than he has me."

When Mark walked up the stairs to the office, he found Tom waiting for him. "Well, Brother Tom, I didn't expect to see you this early in the morning. Clayton, yes, Joseph, maybe, but Tom, no." Now he noticed Tom's grin was uneasy.

He glanced at Joseph's door and Tom said, "He ain't here yet, that's how come I am."

"Spill it; he'll be here shortly."

"You been tapped for the Council of Fifty?" Mark nodded. "Planning on joining?"

"Do I have a choice?"

"On account of Jenny? Maybe not. I come a-beggin' you to do it." Mark let his eyebrows express his feelings. "I know," Tom added. "But there's some weird things a-movin' into town. We're goin' to need some normality to the proceedings."

"Thanks, Brother," Mark said. Tom let his chair crash down

on all four legs as he headed for the door.

Tom's eyes under the thatch of straw-colored hair were as bright as marbles. "She still got the talisman?"

Mark shrugged. "I suppose so." Tom left the room and clattered down the stairs.

John Mark was sitting in the middle of the kitchen floor pounding his wooden spoon on a tin pie pan.

Balancing the talisman on her fingertips, Jenny stood beside the stove. In the two weeks since the charm had been returned to her, Jenny had pondered the significance behind its return. Night and day, the thoughts had nagged her.

Jenny sighed and carried her brooding thoughts into the parlor away from John Mark's clatter. She sat in the chair beside the table and looked at her Bible. Strange, she mused, it was starting to look like Mark's, with the edges curling out in that inviting manner, suggesting all sorts of interesting things inside.

She murmured the verse she had discovered yesterday: "And Elijah came unto all the people, and said, How long halt ye between two opinions? if the Lord be God, follow him: but if Baal, then follow him. And the people answered him not a word."

She closed her eyes and let the thought drift through her, to carry where it would. "Mark," she whispered, and her fingers tightened around the talisman. When she felt the tears on her face, she knew that she had decided.

She addressed the Presence. "I won him by unfair means with the talisman. I deserve to lose him. But more than that, the Book is telling me that I can't claim anything of God. The knowing, the gentle love of Jesus, the promise that's leading me along—none of this is mine unless I do just as those people in the book of Acts did when they burned the charms and books."

With a sigh, Jenny got out of the chair and then paused. For only a moment did she hesitate; then quickly, while she dared, she ran up the stairs and pulled out of the trunk a paper-wrapped parcel.

Back in the kitchen Jenny lifted the stove lid and shoved the green book and the talisman in. John Mark abandoned his pie pan and came to stand beside her. He looked up at her with the solemn blue-green eyes of his father.

The book caught fire and the talisman slipped down through the ashes. Jenny replaced the lid and knelt to take John Mark in her arms. "Da?" he questioned, and she buried her tears in his blue sailor suit.

After Jenny fed John Mark and carried him up the stairs, she found it impossible to leave him. Together they snuggled under the quilt. She watched as his eyes closed, and kissed the damp hand he flung at her.

She slept, and she dreamed. Rising out of sleep she was conscious of the spiraling, the flash of the silver chalice, and the wash of purple wine. The words were on her lips, "I baptize thee in the name of Jesus Christ." Jenny took a deep breath and was conscious of relaxing, sinking into the softness of sleep.

Mark and Orson rode home together, each silent and heavy with thoughts of that first council meeting. Mark wondered if Orson was signifying by his silence that he, too, was feeling the slash of words, the violation.

Just before they reached the Pratt farm turnoff, Orson tilted his head and looked at the full moon. "Guess it takes a man who is called of God, one who's communed with the Almighty, to put forth a vision no mortal would dare dream."

Mark's heart sank; he couldn't think of a reply. Orson continued, "I nearly need to pinch myself. Imagine what this world's going to be like in another few years! Somehow I can see Joseph striding along, king of the whole world, but I just can't see a humble man like me." He turned, "I suppose the biggest fear is trying to imagine handling the people like a monarch is supposed to."

He looked curiously at Mark. "You're his attorney; did you have any idea that he was going to be made king of the kingdom of God?"

Jenny and Mark were at the breakfast table when Tom came. John Mark had porridge running down his chin and he was crowing his delight at the world. "Birthday boy," Jenny said; she was kissing his curls when the door opened.

Seeing his face, she whispered, "Tom." He crossed the kitchen and dropped heavily into a chair at the table.

Fingering the knife and fork lying there, he said, "I couldn't take having you find out when you drove into Nauvoo. And I knew you'd want to go to the funeral."

They waited, and finally he lifted his head. "Sally." After another pause, "Andy's takin' it pretty hard. She'd taken something."

Jenny was rubbing her numb lips, saying, "Less than three weeks ago—oh, Mark, I could see—I tried to tell her about reading the Bible. I felt so helpless, but I honestly didn't think this would happen. It's my fault, isn't it?"

"How could you possibly think that?" She shook her head and pressed her lips together.

The events only became real to Jenny as she stood in the shady grove, seeing the long wooden box, the somber faces, the dark coats. Andy was holding Tamara in his arms.

While the tears began streaming down Jenny's face, she caught a glimpse of Andy, and a burning anger began to move through Jenny.

Jenny and some of the other women went home with Andy and Tamara to help out. They stuck spring flowers in a water glass and positioned them in the middle of Sally's table. They made the house neat, but it was chilled, and quiet. There was nothing more to do for the silent man surrounded by the hedge of Saints. Jenny took her shawl and left.

On the steps she paused. Surprisingly the sun was shining, and it was spring. John Mark's birthday month; life was still moving on. She took a deep breath and felt the dredges of her anger surfacing.

Mark had taken John Mark, freeing her to set order to Sally's empty house. Walking slowly down the street, she turned toward Mark's office, caring little that her black skirt was dragging in the dust. *If Joseph is right, then Sally's secure in the eternities, holding forever the position as Joseph's queen.*

And if he was wrong? She lifted her head and began slowly walking up the stairs to the office. Somehow she knew he was.

A solitary person occupied the office—Joseph, not Mark. He turned and she briefly saw his troubled face until it lightened into a smile. "You've come to see me?"

"No, I was looking for Mark. He has the baby."

"I know. Nice looking tot. He's headed for home with him. Said something about diapers."

Looking at him, for a moment, Jenny burned with anger. Trying to calm herself, she shuffled ideas—that talisman belonging to Joseph, the surging unrest moving throughout the Mormon kingdom, the whispers and fears. Her own secret, which she had not dared reveal to Sally.

For a moment she was caught wondering. If she had told Sally of her own secret shame, would Sally still be alive? She shivered, nearly sick with the thought.

"You've lost your friend." Joseph was speaking with a brooding air. "I'm sorry. I'm also guessing that the loss has made you aware of your precarious position." She studied the stuffy words and watched as he turned from the window.

He straightened his shoulders under the funeral black of his silk coat. One hand, the one wearing the heavy gold ring, moved to smooth his hair.

"Queen of heaven?" She moved restlessly. "Joseph, are you aware of *how* she died?"

He nodded and the sadness touched his face, leaving it colorless. The blue of his eyes, intensified by his pallor, possessed her attention momentarily. In that second, nothing else existed.

She moved and turned away. "Do you see your part in this?"

"My dear, obviously Sally was weak, unable to handle the pressures of life. I must say it takes a strong, magnificent woman to live up to the promises of heaven extended through the priesthood. Don't blame me for her death. I've only acknowledged the pressure of the mighty hand of God upon my life. I dared not live otherwise."

"I know Sally wanted more than anything to escape hell and please God. Andy is a good Mormon; why couldn't she have been sealed to him instead of you?"

"Because the Lord gave her to me, just as he gave you to me. Are you going to tempt the Lord until you become another Sally—unable to face life?"

Busy with her thoughts, she didn't answer, and he said, "Jenny, come here."

She turned and he was holding out his arms, smiling. "And if I refuse?"

"You won't. You're just as fearful of failing to live up to your religion as Sally was—only my dear, I've more confidence in your strength. Also, remember that little boy."

Jenny trembled, but at the same moment she felt an unexpected strength slipping into her. She remembered the dream of the chalice. Strange how that wine seemed to flow over her when she needed it most! Wine. Blood. The blood of Jesus. The atoning sacrifice. No more sins, nothing to be escaped. She considered.

"Joseph, why is it so much easier for people to do something for their own salvation rather than just believe in an unseen gift?" She didn't wait for his answer.

"Remember? I told you to leave me alone or I would tell Emma."

"Go right ahead. She won't believe you. Emma chooses to see only what she wishes to see. She will deny the spiritual wife doctrine."

He was still waiting and smiling, confident now.

Jenny turned and walked toward the door. "Joseph, I want

you to hear this. I renounce the church, your revelations, your gold book. I renounce the doctrine of spiritual wives. Just as God tenderly led me to the place where I shed the fear of the spirits and was able to renounce witchcraft, now I am being led to renounce you and all you stand for.

"I tremble with fear—you've put that into me. But I also cling to Jesus Christ. In reading God's Word, I can't see that He wants anything of me except my belief, and that seems such a little thing to do for Him. But I have to trust in the *littleness* of my doing, and believe if there's more He wants of me, He'll tell me."

"You've nothing to go on," Joseph said, his face glowing as he lifted it. "I've the personal revelation of the Lord."

"I had the personal revelation of a beautiful woman who disappeared when I clung to the name of Jesus Christ." She paused and thoughtfully said, "I know that when I started reading the Holy Bible and reaching out toward Jesus, I found out about the One who was God, the Savior who died for my sins—all of them—so that I didn't need to die—"

Joseph turned away. He shoved his hands into his pockets. "Apostate. Totally and completely apostate. Jenny, I'll give you until the middle of June to repent, and I will not come to you begging. When you repent, let me know."

CHAPTER 38

Jenny was nearly home before the brooding heaviness settled down over her spirit. She had sailed out of Joseph's office with the sure knowledge that she had taken a firm step in the right direction. But as she rode homeward the troubles swept over her. Sally was gone. Andy was stunned, alone. Dark, fearful undercurrents swept through Joseph's kingdom, and she had just told him she wanted no part of it.

But she had a part. A document still existed with her name beside Joseph's. He had issued his warning.

What possible action could he take against her? The spiritual wife doctrine was being denied right and left. For a fact she knew there were few in Nauvoo who had been instructed in the celestial marriage doctrine. He dared not reprimand her publicly.

She dismissed the question and went back to the other worries. A barrier stood between her and Mark. She closed her eyes, trying to avoid thinking of what she had surrendered when she burned the talisman.

He came out to the buggy to meet her. "I was worried," he said as he cradled John Mark in his arms. "Did you have trouble?"

"No. I went to the office to find you and stayed to talk to Joseph." Shadows came into his eyes, full of unasked questions. At the same moment, she sensed that nudge she was beginning to recognize. *Tell Mark.*

She shook her head and sighed. He held her arm as she stepped out of the buggy. "Take the baby. I'll handle the rig."

At the end of the week Mark carried home the news that Andy was leaving Nauvoo. She asked, "You mean leaving the church?"

He took a deep breath. "I went to see him. He's one angry man. Blames everyone except himself for Sally's death. I'd been worried about her for some time, but I'd guessed there was trouble between the two of them. How do you step into a situation like that?"

Keeping her silence, Jenny shook her head. He added, "He didn't say he was leaving the church, but I wouldn't be surprised. You know there's been a goodly number who've left."

Jenny wanted to question Mark about that, but she didn't dare. He picked up the milk pail and added, "Tomorrow there's to be a meeting over Higbee's store. William Law told me it's important and suggested you come."

"Higbee? Is he in on the rumbling? I thought he was one of Joseph's attorneys."

"He is, and he also has much to be disturbed about." Jenny looked at Mark as he headed for the door.

As the door closed behind him, Jenny said, "Something tells me, husband, that there's a lot going on that you keep to yourself."

John Mark began to bang his wooden spoon on the oven door and Jenny scooped him up. "Diapers, ugh!" As she headed for the stairs, she picked up Mark's jacket. A newspaper tumbled out. She kicked it out of the way and continued up the stairs.

Jenny forgot about the paper as she hurried to prepare their evening meal. When Mark came in, she asked. "Do you mind feeding him these mashed carrots?"

He grinned and kissed her cheek. "Tell you what. Let me go out and chase Indians out of the pasture while *you* feed him carrots." He picked up John Mark and said, "One spray and you get them raw."

At dinner he said, "My coat. Did you see a paper in it?" She nodded and carried it to the table.

"There's two here. Joseph said they weren't his, so I brought them home to read."

"Why don't we subscribe?"

"These are the *Warsaw Message.* After reading a couple, I decided I didn't like the tenor of them. Now I'm not so tender-skinned."

"What do you mean by that?"

"You've heard enough about and from Warsaw to guess the type of coverage they give the Saints."

"Well, I know they've done enough complaining about us; there's a constant stream of tales about Saints taking their cows and everything else."

Later, while Jenny washed dishes, Mark read the papers and commented. "This January 17 paper is really ranting. Says some in their area are talking about exterminating the Mormons. Sounds like Missouri. They're saying that thousands of women and children must be driven out. 'Scattered like leaves before the storm' is his phrase. I get the feeling he's quoting some ruffians with the express purpose of frightening us."

Jenny had hung the dish towel when he added, "The other article isn't quite so benign. He's quit dodging with nice talk, saying, 'Your career of infamy cannot continue but a little longer! Your days are numbered!' No wonder."

"What?"

"Oh, I was thinking it's no wonder Joseph is getting serious about emigrating westward." Jenny lifted her hands in dismay and hastily Mark said, "Don't fret. There's nothing substantial to the talk yet. You know Tom was in on the looking around last fall. Above all, don't be guilty of starting rumors. That's the last thing this community needs right now."

"Mark, you tell me so little. But I get the feeling there's much rumbling going on."

"You'll find out at the meeting. Unfortunately I've been so busy myself I haven't been able to pass the time of day with the grumblers. Might be that's an advantage. Joseph's getting sharp with the troublemakers."

Late the next afternoon, on the way to Higbee's store for the meeting, Mark and Jenny rode past the Morgan house.

Already there were signs of neglect. Jenny winced and Mark reached for her hand, tugging her close to him. Feeling as if her heart would break with weight of unspoken feelings, she looked at him. Strangely, the white line around his lips made her heart lift. Perhaps Mark wasn't totally indifferent to their problems.

The sun was setting as they walked up the stairs at the back of the shop. There were several people in the room. Jenny was conscious of the wary glances the men exchanged while the women continued to sit apart.

When the stairs creaked again they all turned. Jane Law was unwinding the heavy black veil as she followed her husband into the room. Soon another veiled woman entered and Law got to his feet.

"There's no need to advertise our presence with loud talk. Please pull your chairs together." When the rustle had subsided, he continued, "I've talked with a number of you. There have been enough problems and ugly situations arise that several of us decided it was time to take matters into our own hands, to bring together some of the Saints who've expressed a desire to see reformation in Nauvoo before matters are completely out of control."

He paused and then added, "I want you to understand, I'm not trying to destroy the church. I only want to see it brought back to its original purity. I continue to believe that Joseph Smith is a prophet sent from God. However, I believe he's a prophet fallen from grace.

"As a brother, I believe it is my duty to warn him and to go about instigating reformation in the church. If you are in agreement, please lift your hands."

Again he continued, "There are a number of things we need to discuss. We've made plans to assemble for just this purpose. I realize it's an act which will be considered treason by Joseph if it comes to his ears. But if we are united in body and purpose, he will be forced to listen to us."

"Brother," came a voice from the back of the room. "I've been praying for this since Kirtland days. Now we are fighting for our lives as a church body. Reformation or nothing."

A babble of voices rose, and in dismay, Jenny listened to the catalog of wrongs being named. There were labor disputes mentioned and William Law growled out his protests against the edict the Prophet had issued to excommunicate any wealthy man buying land without his permission. Dr. Foster protested the wholesale hording of building materials for the construction of the temple and the Nauvoo House. "We've people living in tents because we can't buy lumber!" His voice was rising and William rumbled out a warning.

And in the end, there was abrupt silence. Slowly William got to his feet, reluctantly he said, "It seems we've still the main point to cover, one which burdens our hearts, and in some way has touched us all.

"I tried my best to handle this problem just between the Prophet and me. He would not listen to me, nor would he seek counsel from elders in the community. In a stormy session I suggested to him that we must have reformation. As deeply as it was needed in Martin Luther's time, we need it in this new church now, before it is too late.

"I pointed this out to Joseph. I remonstrated, even threatening to go before the High Council myself if he didn't do it voluntarily. I insisted he confess his sins and promise repentance or I would expose his monstrous seductions to the world. He told me that he would be damned before he would do so, since that would cause the overthrow of the church.

"Sadly, I believe he has no recourse. The matter must be resolved in a godly manner. It is utterly impossible to think of any other course of action."

Suddenly Dr. Robert Foster jumped to his feet. At the sound of his wavering voice, Jenny turned and saw the shocked face of his wife one second before she buried it in her handkerchief. He was saying, "Brother, you force me to tell you the problems we've had. Unexpectedly one day last winter I arrived home to find my wife and Joseph enjoying a fine meal together. It was the Prophet's bold friendliness and my wife's obvious dismay that alerted me.

"After the Prophet left I insisted my wife tell me what was going on. Of course, in an effort to protect the Prophet, she refused. It was only after a great deal of painful argument and even threats"—he paused to clear his throat before continuing—"that I was able to get the story out of her. It seems the Prophet had been endeavoring to talk her into unlawful intercourse with him by saying the Lord had commanded it. He called it the spiritual wife doctrine."

In the silence, Higbee got to his feet. "You are all aware of the smear of adultery the Prophet falsely spread around my name. I know of others who have been dealt the same blow in an effort to hide the Prophet's sins. My brother is one. William Law's wife has been subjected to pressure and insult. Kimball's wife Sarah has been likewise insulted."

Chauncey Higbee stood. "My brother is right. Let me add that I know for a fact that some of the leading elders have up to ten or twelve wives apiece. These righteous men, flaunting their holiness, are leading a secret life of sin, and at the same time denying it.

"Let me tell you about the *Book of the Law of the Lord*. This book is kept nice and handy at the home of Hyrum Smith, ready to be revealed to unsuspecting women, who are told that it was the Lord himself who instructed that the names hidden under those seals be placed there. Many a young woman has discovered her own name there when she has opened it in the presence of the Prophet."

With an angry shout, Jackson got to his feet. "I must inform you that there's good evidence of a conspiracy in Nauvoo which could well cost Smith his life. If it is not too late, reformation could help, otherwise . . ."

It was late that night, while Jenny was stuffing the sleepy baby into his nightgown, when Mark gently asked, "Jenny, you are about to cry. Do you need to talk?"

She shoved John Mark into his arms and ran from the room.

Mark kissed the boy and tenderly tucked him into his bed. Although he could hear Jenny's sobs, he lingered until he knew the child was asleep.

Jenny was in the rocking chair. Mark picked her up and sat down, cradling her as gently as if she were John Mark.

When the crying ended, he mopped her eyes and cuddled her face against his shoulder. "You wouldn't do that if you knew!" She cried again.

Finally she could stand the tension no longer. "Oh, Mark, I was one of those women opening the book!"

His heart sank, but he held her close as she sobbed. "I know," he said.

And then out of a long silence, she asked, "You do?"

He spoke quickly, "Jenny, look. I have forgiven you. That's all I have to say. I can't control your life, but I can forgive, and only that is necessary. I won't ask anything, and I'd rather not know."

His arms were tight and warm, reassuring, Jenny decided. She sat up to look at him and in the glow of moonlight she could see the forced smile, the shadowed eyes. "Mark, now I see it as a terrible injustice to you, regardless. I do ask your forgiveness. I've hated it all."

He pulled her head back to his shoulder and they continued to sit in the chair in silence. With a sigh Jenny sat up. "Would it help if I were to tell you that the day Sally was buried, I told Joseph I renounced it all—the church, him, the books, the revelations. All. I just don't accept it as being from God." She spoke gently, "Mark, go up to bed. You're exhausted. I . . . I need to stay here for a time."

Jenny wrapped the shawl about herself and, as Mark went up the stairs, she got back into the rocking chair.

She contemplated the quiet emptiness inside herself. With shame she said, "Oh, Lord Jesus. You told me to tell him; I would have saved us both so much grief if only I had said this weeks ago."

She continued to sit in the chair. Drained emotionally, her thoughts drifted—not toward the disclosures of the evening but instead toward the spiraling change in her life. Mormonism had seemed a step upward from the craft. First she had renounced the craft, and now Joseph's church.

But there was emptiness. She contemplated the flatness of her disappointment. The Bible had promised joy, peace. She felt only emptiness.

Then came the familiar nudge. Now words welled up, and this time she listened as Jesus said, "Verily, verily, I say unto thee, Except a man be born again, he cannot see the kingdom of God." And then in a moment she was murmuring the words,

"If thou shalt confess with thy mouth the Lord Jesus, and shalt believe in thine heart that God hath raised him from the dead, thou shalt be saved."

She sat up straight. "Jesus Christ, You are God and You came to this earth to die for my sins. I believe that I don't have to do anything but accept Your gift to me."

Jenny began to cry, but when she could, she ran upstairs. "Mark!" She shook him, burrowing in with him and putting her arms around him. "Mark! Why didn't you tell me about how I'd feel?"

He came up out of the pillows and blinked at her. Seeing the joy in her eyes, he pulled her into his arms and said, "Thank you, Lord Jesus." Then he grinned down at Jenny. "Why, I suppose I thought the Lord ought to have that privilege."

CHAPTER 39

Joseph marched into the office the next morning. Dropping the stack of papers on Mark's desk, he said, "Here it is. The petition to Congress, just like I promised you. Look it over, and let's get it off. I'm asking them to make me an officer in the Army. I'm going to need power to raise a hundred thousand volunteers—and that's what it'll take in order to do a decent job of guarding the western borders of the United States. With what I've promised them, I don't see how they can possibly refuse."

He paced the office, cracking his knuckles as he enumerated, "I'm going to hold out hope of deliverance to Texas, as well as protect Oregon. They're being threatened by England and France. In short, my stand is for deliverance from tyranny and oppression for all the people."

"It's a pretty ambitious petition," Mark stated, picking up the paper.

"Not out of line. Hyde said Stephen A. Douglas gave him the word that if he were in my shoes, he'd resign from Congress and be on his way to California in a month's time."

Joseph headed for the door and then turned, "Mark, there's a Council meeting tonight—the Fifties. Be there. It's important."

After supper that evening Mark rode into town with Orson. When their horses met at the roadway, Mark said, "If we keep getting these meetings, I guess we'll have to encourage our wives to spend more time together. John Mark keeps Jenny busy, and I know she doesn't like him up late, but still—I don't like to leave her alone."

"Haven't seen that brother-in-law of yours lately."

"Joseph's sent him back to Texas with Woodworth. I guess things are looking pretty good there." He slanted a glance at Orson who gave him a twisted grin.

"Naw, I don't think there's a danger of our being pushed out. I don't think the Prophet does, either. Things have simmered down. Bennett seems to have quit his dirty work. Time will tell. If there're as many people flocking into Nauvoo this year as there were last, I'd say that's a barometer of goodwill toward him."

The meeting got underway promptly at eight. Joseph was chuckling when he came into the room, and Mark relaxed.

Shaking his head, Joseph said, "Trust Rockwell to come up with that idea. Wonder if his pigtail was responsible."

Kimball said, "It's your problem if you don't like it. You made such a to-do about it, he decided to keep it. Where's he tonight?"

"Outside," Joseph remarked tersely. Briefly there was a shadow in his eyes. "He seems to think there's a need for real caution. That's why the frocks."

There was an exclamation from the back of the room and Pratt said, "I'd heard someone saw Rockwell sneaking around town all dressed up like a lady. General, Port's too big to pass as any kind of a lady."

The smile faded from Joseph's face as he said, "My life is in danger. It isn't the forces outside Nauvoo I fear. Some little dough-headed fool in this city causes me more anxiety than all the forces of Satan out there. It's the traitors within the circle who keep me awake nights. I've said before, I say again, we've a Judas within our group."

Joseph shook his shoulders as if freeing them from a specter, and he passed on to other business. Catching Mark's eye, he told about the petition, adding, "I fully expect them to grant our request; so fellas, start planning your lives around this."

When Joseph braced his feet and shoved his hands into his pockets, Mark moved uneasily. Joseph said, "Nauvoo's growing. It's no longer a peaceful little town. There's unrest, contention. I've asked Wight and Rockwell to expand the Angels. I'm feeling the tide moving against me and I intend to be prepared. There's rumors," he paused and his restless eyes swept over the men.

"I've had some reliable sources advise me of a type of unrest we can't abide. Rattlers in the woodpile.

"So far I haven't been able to get enough money together to print the revised Bible. This is contrary to the wishes of the Lord. However, until that is done, I'll take upon myself to teach you on the subjects the Lord wants revealed at this time.

"In the revelation concerning celestial, or in other words, everlasting marriage, there is an item mentioned which we need to pursue. The Lord has revealed in this section the subject of destruction in the flesh in order to save the soul. If a man or woman under the shield of the new and everlasting marriage, commits a sin or transgression against the marriage, that person shall be destroyed in the flesh.

"Likewise, under the shield of this marriage, a wife caught with a man other than her husband shall be destroyed in the flesh. The purpose of this command is to show the sacredness of this everlasting union.

"In conjunction with this revelation, I wish to show another command which shall point out the seriousness of our standing before the Lord. In the book of Mark, chapter 9 and verses 43 through 48, we find the admonition, given in the new translation, in regard to cutting off the hand. That hand is your brother. Therefore, if your brother offend you, it is better for you that he be cut off than for the both of you to enter hell. Every man is to stand or fall by himself. So you see, what the Lord is telling us is that it is better to kill the offending brother than to let him pull you down into hell.

"Now, brethren, I must remind you again, you have been given the blessings of the priesthood. Go out and do the works of Abraham."

"General," came a timid voice from the back of the room. "Are you meaning to tell us we're *obligated*? One of the fellas the other day reminded us that the laws of Illinois are against plural marriage."

"I have reminded you before that the laws of the state are an abomination. We shall not keep them when they go against the laws of God."

Mark could no longer hold his tongue. "I just read the *Doctrine and Covenants*, section 58, verse 21, where we are advised against breaking the laws of the country. There is the promise given that by keeping the law of God, we have no reason to break the law of the country."

The meeting ended and Mark headed for the door. He felt a hand on his arm and turned. It was John D. Lee and he was wearing a perplexed frown on his face. "A word, Mark." When they were outside the building, Lee continued, "You know this group is the council of the gods. You don't seem to realize the seriousness of your attitude. Mark, don't you yet accept the teaching that without plural marriage a man can never attain the fullness of the holy priesthood and thereby be made equal with the Savior?"

When they parted company at the end of the street, Lee was still shaking his head.

Jenny was sitting in the rocking chair with her Bible in her lap. She looked up and smiled when he came in. Squatting on the floor close to her he said, "Before I left this evening I noticed you had something on your mind. What is it?"

"Oh, Mark, I suppose these last few weeks have given me the jitters. It's probably nothing. But after I left Relief Society meeting this morning, I headed down the street intending to shop. I saw one of the Whittlers out. He was sitting on a stump at the watering trough.

"When I passed he got up and walked along behind me. If I hadn't known about such men, I probably would have thought nothing of it."

She paused to gulp and added, "It was all I could do to keep from running. I really don't think he intended to harm me, but he followed down the street, whistling that terrible flat tune and all the time whittling on that stick. I turned once and he was looking at me."

"Jenny, the Whittlers are for the purpose of chasing the enemies or apostates out of town. There's no reason to fear, particularly since you are a harmless woman—not a threat to anyone."

Mark continued to examine her face for a moment more, then uttered that request he had been holding back for over a year. "Jenny, shall we leave?" He watched the hope flare to life in her eyes.

She looked around the room. "Mark, this place has been such a big part of our lives; but yes, I'm ready to leave."

He got to his feet and his thoughts turned back to the evening. "Jenny, will you trust me to get us out of here at just the right time? Also, please don't mention to anyone that we are planning to leave."

When she stretched for his kiss, she hesitated, and he saw the fear in her eyes.

"What is it?" he whispered against her face.

She leaned back. Her eyes were searching his face. "Mark, now you trust me. There's still something I need to confront Joseph with."

He hesitated, then said reluctantly, "All right. The Lord's brought us thus far."

Her face lighted. "Ebenezer! Mark, I read it! Thus far—He'll still be there, won't He?" The wistful look was a question, and he caught her close.

In the morning when Mark reached the office, Clayton was there to meet him. Mark was surprised by the expression of genuine concern in the man's eyes. Leading the way into their office, Clayton faced him with a worried frown.

"Mark, I like you. You're nearly apostate, but there's something of value in you. I'm sure the Lord will use you in the kingdom if you will only listen to counsel."

"Clayton," Mark said mildly, "I have no intention of living differently than the Lord wishes me to. Now, what is the problem?"

"Your contrary speech last night. Anything the Prophet says is just as binding upon us as if God himself said it. Even if he gives advice opposed to previous advice, do it."

Clayton took a deep breath. "Those of us close to the Prophet will be asked to carry a heavy load in the next year. Much will be demanded, but it will be the chance we've been waiting for." He leaned confidentially closer. "It's been in our minds for some months. Now we're certain. Joseph will be running for president of the United States."

The man paused to pace the floor in quick steps. "Phelps and I have been working on a platform. So far I believe we are doing very well. Now, when it gets down to writing campaign speeches, I don't believe I'll have the spunk that Phelps does."

He looked at Mark, but despite his friendly grin, a shadow darkened his eyes. As Mark picked up his papers, he was very aware of the warning.

When Mark walked into the house that evening, he gave Jenny a quick kiss and said, "Just saw William Law. He's pretty worried. Seems to think word's leaked back to Joseph about our meeting. There's to be another meeting this evening, so let's head back to town as soon as possible."

The warm April day was dissolving into dusk as Mark and Jenny reached the outskirts of Nauvoo. They were riding briskly down the street, headed for Higbee's store, when they both saw the dark-coated man disappearing up the stairs to Joseph's office.

Mark explained, "That's Clayton. I didn't tell you, but a conversation I had with him this morning gave me the distinct impression that he's caught wind of the meetings. Jenny, will you do something? Go upstairs and talk to Clayton for half an hour.

"I don't want him seeing the bunch of people heading up Higbee's back stairs. Would you, please?" He grinned. "Of all men in town, I trust you with Clayton. I'll take John Mark with me, and I'll leave the buggy at the stable." Jenny nodded and Mark added, "The longer you keep him the better for us."

As Jenny reached the top of the stairs, Clayton's alarmed face peered around the doorjamb. "Mrs. Cartwright, you gave me a start! Is something the matter?"

"No, Mark has business in town this evening. I want to look for a book to read."

"Mighty dry reading you'll find here."

"What do you have? That book is thick enough to look interesting."

"It's charts and horoscopes. Joseph and I have been studying the stars. We spend quite a bit of time searching the heavens for a sign. There's much of ancient knowledge to be learned in this manner."

"That sounds interesting; astronomy?"

"No, astrology. Remember, I showed the book to you some time ago. This is the divination of the influences of stars on human endeavors. By studying out their positions and consulting these charts, we can get an idea of what's going to happen in the future. We also begin to comprehend the outcome of these forces on the people around us." He paused, studied her, then said, "You look like you're pretty interested in the science. Seeing it's you, if you want to come with me, I'll let you have a look through the telescope."

Cautiously, remembering her mission, she asked, "Where is it?"

"Just down the street. Joseph has it all set up on top of Mansion House."

"Why, I think I would like that."

Outside dusk had given way to darkness. Clayton took her arm, saying, "Look at those stars. This will be a good night to view them. Now, watch your step. We don't keep a light in Mansion House. No sense advertising our business. Just hang on to my coattail and I'll get us across the hall and into the secret staircase."

"Oh," Jenny murmured. "I'd heard Joseph had built in a hidden staircase—but why?"

"To escape his enemies. It leads to the roof. More'n once he's gone up these stairs in a hurry and dropped down through the trees."

The door creaked, and the dark figure holding the telescope straightened. Jenny stepped out onto the rooftop. By moonlight she saw him blink. "Hello Joseph. Clayton has been telling me about the studies and volunteered to bring me along to see the telescope."

"Jenny!" Surprise and excitement in his voice assured

Jenny of her welcome. She approached the table and he said, "Come here. I'll point out the stars we'll study tonight and then Clayton can tell you the significance behind their positions. Would you like us to do your horoscope?"

Without answering, Jenny took her place and stared into the telescope. "Oh, my! Even the moon is fascinating. What planet is this?"

Jenny took her eyes away from the telescope and turned. Clayton was bending over the charts, shading a candle from the breeze. "Windy up here. Come here, I'll show you this chart. What's your birth date?"

"Clayton, I've read enough to know astrology and horoscopes are related to witchcraft. I don't want my horoscope plotted."

She turned to Joseph. "You've come down hard on the Saints for even having a taint of the craft around, the charms and the witching rods—why are you seeking signs in the stars?"

He was chuckling, "Jenny, my dear, how righteous you are! But we need all the help we can get; besides, the study of stars is interesting. I'm fascinated by the movement of the earth forces. I intend to discover the mysteries of the universe."

"I remember, from reading the *Book of Abraham*, how the stars were explained. That Kolob is the one close to God, and governing the others." She hesitated and then said, "Tell me, Joseph, about something that's worried me for some time. In the *Book of Abraham* it says the gods organized the world, meaning more than one god and yet in the Book of Moses, He says, *I created*—just one God. Why the difference?"

"Come here and look at the shooting stars and quit worrying about something that's beyond a woman."

She continued, "Moses, the sixth chapter, refers to Adam, Man of Holiness, and then goes on to call Jesus Christ his only begotten. Joseph, I'm confused. The Bible doesn't call God Adam."

Impatiently he turned, "Jenny, I refuse to quarrel with a woman. I've told you the Bible hasn't been correctly translated. You've no right to question the very writings of God." Facing Clayton, he added, "Why don't you go back to the office and get some books for our sister to read. Take your time."

"Clayton," Jenny said, carefully watching Joseph, "if you leave, I'll scream my head off. Out here in the open air, the sound will carry quite a ways. Just stay here; there's not one thing Joseph and I will be discussing that isn't fit for your ears." Clayton shifted uneasily and Jenny added, "I mean it, and I shall begin right now."

Clayton sat down, and Jenny stepped closer to Joseph. "I've been wanting to talk to you for some time. Joseph, I've been listening to some of the women—both the things they've said and the hints they've dropped. I don't think what's going on in Nauvoo is of the Lord, simply because if it were these women wouldn't be so desperately unhappy.

"Sally told me before she killed herself that she couldn't handle the guilt of deceiving her husband by allowing you to love her. There are many other women just as desperate.

"Joseph, you've preyed on our fear of God and a deep desire to be holy; but more than that, I am aware of the strange attraction you hold for women, because I've felt it myself.

"Once away from you, I've suffered guilt and wondered why I was so attracted. Joseph, it might be just you—but I don't think so.

"You know I had a talisman. Until I made up my mind to get rid of it, I felt an almost irresistible attraction in your presence. Joseph, you know I was involved in the craft for years. But what you don't know is how it corrupted my life, twisting me with fear. I tried to escape that fear by being a good Mormon, but that didn't help.

"I soon discovered you and your church held me with bonds of fear. You've taught it is wrong to question and that we must give total submission to you and the church. You used the spiritual wife doctrine as a whip. And I know I wasn't the only one. I'm certain you've used the same whip on other women, and with more success."

Jenny stopped to take a deep breath. "Joseph, I've come to ask you some questions. Because you see, I still don't know the heart of you. Can you honestly say you are called of God? If the welfare of your church and your people are of the utmost importance to you, if you really love us, will you please get rid of the talisman?"

For a moment he stared at her in astonishment. "I am certain," she said, "that it is the link of Satan in your life, destroying us all with a doctrine that is from the evil one." His face was beginning to soften into a grin.

Reaching into his pocket he pulled out the talisman and held it up, balancing it on his fingertips.

For a moment Jenny teetered on her toes, tempted to snatch it and fling it over the rooftop and into the inky night. Then she relaxed. The decision must come from him.

He kissed the medal and slipped it back into his pocket. "No, my dear. I can't live without the protection of the talisman."

Even in the darkness she could see the change on his face. His eyes were shadowed; the lines on his face and the timber of his voice spelled fear.

Slowly and thoughtfully, he spoke as if he had forgotten her presence. "At times it seems I've collected more enemies than friends during my life. I fear they'll never be satisfied until they have my blood. Could it be my days are numbered? No, it shall not be. The Lord has work for me to do. He'll not call me home before my time."

He stirred, and the old arrogant grin returned. "Meanwhile, my dear, I intend to make the most of my time." He reached for her.

Jenny sidestepped. "I still have lungs," she warned. "Joseph, that isn't all I have to say. You told me to read my Bible as well as the *Book of Mormon* and the rest of the writings. I did. It wasn't long until I found the Bible holding my complete attention.

"Joseph, it was God speaking to me! I heard the love, I saw Jesus living, loving, teaching repentance, begging people just to reach out and accept the gift of himself. I wanted to be friends with that Man and I discovered that touching Him was touching God.

"Joseph, I found it was utter arrogance to think I could earn my way to heaven. God says He owns the cattle on a thousand hills and He doesn't want our sacrifices. He wants our love."

Jenny stopped. She could see her words were wasted. "The talisman?"

"I intend to keep it. I need all the protection and help it has to offer."

When Jenny reached Higbee's store the meeting was over. She stood blinking in the lamplight while Mark dumped the warm, sleepy child into her arms.

CHAPTER 40

"Young man, if you don't hold still I'll never get you dressed, and your father will take you to Sabbath service wearing only a diaper." Jenny paused to kiss John Mark's upturned face. "There." She set him on the floor.

Mark was chuckling. "Remember last year? He was only a mite. Can hardly believe a year could do that to a baby."

Jenny straightened Mark's collar and said, "It's time to be thinking about another. She frowned at his expression. "You don't like the idea?"

"I think if we're wanting to hear the sermons, we'd better get going."

"Church conference," Jenny murmured. "Joseph won't lose his opportunity to state what's on his mind. Today the crowd will be the largest in months. Has Willian Law told you who the spies were at Higbee's?"

Mark shook his head. "Could come out in the sermon. Are you ready to leave?"

When they reached Nauvoo, Jenny stated, "It's fortunate the weather's clear and warm today. Look at the size of the crowd."

Mark's voice was only a rumble and she leaned close to listen. "It's a good time for strangers to mingle in with the Saints to get a feel of things." He gave her a quick look and explained, "There's enough to whet the curiosity of any number of people."

"Politics?"

He nodded. "There're thoughts floating around. John D. Lee's been calling Joseph the salvation of the nation. The newspapers are rumbling about it, at least those who are seriously considering Joseph's talk about running for president. They're dropping phrases like 'the monstrous union of church and state' under Joseph."

"Is that good?"

"Terrible—unless you want someone telling you which church to belong to." Mark found a spot under the trees, helped Jenny out of the buggy, and picked up John Mark.

Joseph and the elders marched to the pulpit. After a brief reference to Elder King Follett, who had been killed in an accident the week before, Joseph began his sermon. "There are few in the world who understand God. In order to help you along the way, we must go back to creation. We see the great Elohim sitting yonder as He did at the creation. Some call me a false prophet. I will prove them wrong by helping them know about God. If I can bring you to a knowledge of God, persecution against me should stop.

"For now, I will go to the beginning. God himself was once as we are now. He is an exalted man, seated on His throne in the heavenlies. In addition, God the Father dwelt on earth, just as His Son Jesus did. As the Father had power to lay down His life, so also did the Son. As He had the power to take up life again, so did the Son. I tell you, my brethren, you have got to learn to be gods yourself.

"The Father worked for His kingdom with fear and trembling; we must do likewise. Jesus treads in the footsteps of His Father, inheriting what God the Father did before Him. We shall all do likewise."

Joseph paused before adding, "I've been reading the Bible in Hebrew, Latin, Greek, and German. I find the German nearest to the translation the Lord gave to me. Now, I want you to hear me. It doesn't say God created the spirit of man. It expressly says He put Adam's spirit into man.

"The mind or intelligence of man is coequal with God himself. God never had the power to create man's spirit. That would be like God creating himself. Remember, intelligence is eternal." As Joseph paused, his brooding eyes swept the people listening with upturned faces. "Some of you will reject this word. If I were a false teacher no man would seek my life. If a man thinks he is authorized to take away my life, let me say by the same token we are justified in taking away the life of every false teacher.

"Knowledge saves a man. In the greater world to which the spirits go, a man can be exalted only by knowledge. I address you apostates; when a man turns against the work, he seeks to kill me. I warn you, such persons cannot be saved."

As Jenny and Mark turned to join the crowd making its way out of the temple grove, Jenny said, "Mark, there's Tom!" She waved frantically, and they pressed toward each other through the tide of people. Jenny embraced Tom, saying, "You shall come home with us! We didn't even know you were back."

They had nearly finished dinner when Mark asked, "Tom, what's the Texas situation?"

"Pretty hopeful, if Joseph's serious about pulling up stakes. I can't believe it, though. There's been too much invested here."

"Might be necessary," Mark added, reaching for more chicken.

Tom squinted up at him. "That bad, huh?"

"Yes, he's worried. Nearly every time he speaks it comes out that he's worried by the opposition. I think he reads every newspaper in the country."

Mark saw Tom's quick look and said, "Yes, he's confided in me, but I don't think the Saints for the most part know how deeply concerned he is."

Jenny glanced at Mark and Tom said, "What's going on?"

"As close as you are to Joseph, I expected you to know."

"Don't forget I've been out of town for over a month."

Jenny interrupted. "Let's talk of something else. Tom, I've finally come to the point where I had to reject Joseph's church."

"That comes as a shock right now. Any good reason?"

"I've been reading the Bible and I've come to see either I go Jesus Christ's way or Joseph's. I can't have both, because they are completely opposite each other."

He studied her face, reached for the plate of bread, and said, "I guess I'm not surprised, come to think of it. Mark's a pretty strong talker."

She lifted her chin. "Mark didn't influence me. I simply—" She stared at Mark, then looked at her brother. "Tom, after the fascination of everything else wore off, I just came back to where I belonged. I was going to say I chose, but I didn't. It was more like the Lord had my hand and just pulled me back to where I belonged.

"Once I decided, there was no alternative. I felt like I was home." She leaned across the table to look at Tom. "Do you know the feeling?" When he shook his head, she said, "Well, I didn't, either. I didn't realize all the things I didn't like inside of me would be the very things God would take away. Sin."

Tom said slowly, "You said 'fascination.' What do you mean?"

She faced him without flinching. "Witchcraft, Mormonism. They were fascinating, you know. An obsession."

Mark followed Tom out to the barn and watched him saddle his horse. As Tom swung himself onto the mare, he said, "So

Jen's got religion. Did she ever tell you about jumping into the river?"

"No," Mark said slowly, "and after what happened to Sally, I'd never ask."

Mark was thinking, as Tom rode down the lane, that his brother-in-law looked as if there was another question he wanted to ask. Jenny and John Mark came out of the house, and Mark watched as the sun caught the baby's bright hair and turned it into a halo.

Mark struggled with thoughts he couldn't allow. At times just knowing about the plural marriage seemed to make it more difficult. If she hadn't told him, could he have put the whole thing out of his mind? He sighed and walked slowly toward his family.

Tuesday evening when Mark rode into the yard, Jenny was sitting on the back steps while John Mark charged about the yard carrying his wooden spoon. She fluttered her fingers at him and he went on to the barn.

When he carried the pail of milk into the kitchen, he said, "I thought you intended coming to the office after Relief Society meeting."

She looked startled. "Oh, I did. Just forgot. I hope I didn't delay you." Mark shook his head, wondering but not daring to question. As he put the milk in the kitchen, he added another question to the list in his mind.

That night of the meeting at Higbee's store, nearly frantic with worry, he had questioned her about the delay. She had been short when she answered his question. Briefly, she stated she had been on the roof with Joseph and Clayton.

They were still sitting at the table after dinner when Jenny met his eyes and slowly said, "Today Emma passed around a statement which she had prepared and submitted to the *Nauvoo Neighbor*. Have you seen it?"

He shook his head and waited. Jenny sighed deeply. "In essence it rails against Dr. John C. Bennett's spiritual wife system. Mark, that wasn't his idea!"

"He's accused of it, whether or not he's to blame."

She continued, "Other than placing the blame on him, it was really a nothing statement. She mentioned polygamy, bigamy, adultery, and so on. One of the women whispered to me that she'd heard Dr. Bennett claim that all the Relief Society women were to be the Prophet's wives." Lifting her face, she said, "Mark, this is so terrible! There are so *many* women in the group."

As Mark blew out the lamp and they started up the stairs, he was miserably aware of the questions rising up in his heart. Why did she care how many there were? He watched as Jenny pulled the blanket over John Mark. Would he ever be totally free of the taint Joseph had left on his marriage? He needed that freedom in his life. Strange that it had to be dealt with every day.

He paused in the doorway. "Jenny, I think I'll go down and read for a while." He turned away from the hurt question in her eyes.

At the end of the week, as Mark rode into Nauvoo, William Law met him with newspaper in hand. "Well, friend," he said heavily, "the guesses were right. There's a neat little article here in the *Nauvoo Neighbor* detailing nearly everything we discussed at that first meeting at Higbee's.

"There's even a fairly accurate account of Joseph's attempted seduction of Mrs. Foster. No comment by Joseph in the article, just the sublime implication that he is being persecuted." He shoved the paper into his satchel. "Brother, I think our hand is being forced."

"What is the next step?" Mark asked slowly.

"Depends," Law said. "You haven't been suspected yet. So far as Joseph knows you're untainted. That's good, since you're his attorney. I'd like to suggest you keep it that way for the sake of the free flow of information, which we'll need badly."

"Sooner or later the Angels will be able to link us."

"Probably, but let's play for time. There's to be a meeting tonight at Higbee's. Stay home, I'll bring you up-to-date later. If need be, I'll ride out to your place."

He started to turn away and then said, "By the way, Mark, I still believe in the Prophet. I intend with every power of persuasion at my disposal to call Joseph to genuine repentance."

"It's a waste without confession—at least to the brethren, if not to the whole church. He's in too deep to profess change without it."

"That could be nasty. What about the presidential election?"

"It would ruin any hopes," Mark added.

"Nevertheless, it must be done."

"You've been threatened before."

"You're referring to the Destroying Angels?" Mark nodded. "Then let me tell you what I intend. Since Joseph won't take my call for reformation seriously, I intend to set up a church of my own. I feel this will force his hand. I've also ordered a printing press. Joseph and I'll be trading tit for tat before June rolls around.

"Also, if there isn't immediate action on Joseph's part, I intend to sue, charging him with adultery."

Slowly Mark said, "William, you are a very brave man. I'll help you as much as I can. Are you certain I'll be most valuable by keeping my mouth shut?"

He nodded. "By the way, Higbee's suing Joseph for five thousand dollars, charging him with slander."

CHAPTER 41

When Mark entered the livery stable that blustery April afternoon, Tom was at the forge and William Law was with him. "Heading for home?" Law asked. Mark nodded as he threw the saddle on his mare, and Law added, "Well, I'd ride with you, but I've an errand that will detain me about fifteen minutes." His eyes held Mark's.

"I'll see you some other time," Mark said, leading his horse out. He looked at Tom. "If you're out our way tomorrow, stop for supper." Tom nodded and reached for a nail.

Mark lingered on the trail until William caught up with him. "Why the secrecy? Tom can keep his mouth shut."

"Can't risk the information I have. Foster's been gathering a bunch of witnesses to use against Joseph in this trial called against him. Seems Joseph got wind of it and set up a secret council meeting. The outcome? Foster, Wilson, Jane, and I were all excommunicated. Without a hearing," he added. Mark watched him silently as he slowly shook his head.

"It was really a blow," Law continued, "but not a one of our group is willing to back down now."

Slowly Mark said, "By rights I should have been on that council; Joseph didn't say a word to me."

"The first meeting of our new church will be this next Sabbath," Law said. "I just wanted you to know, but don't put in an appearance. We still need you where you are."

By the time Mark reached home, he had decided to say nothing to Jenny for the time being. He kissed her and said, "There's a big parade and speeches in Nauvoo tomorrow. If it isn't too blustery, would you like to go?"

Her face lighted, "Oh, Mark, how nice! What are we celebrating?"

"Nothing that I know of. I think it's just a show of force. You know the Prophet is getting ready to announce his candidacy for the presidency. A parade will raise everyone's spirits."

The following day was warm and sparkling from the nighttime shower. As they joined the wagons and buggies streaming into Nauvoo, Jenny said, "This parade must be more important than you thought. Look at the people."

"Finding a place to leave a buggy is getting to be a problem," Mark said. "I'll let you and John Mark off here in front of the Nauvoo Mansion. Walk toward the business section, and I'll meet you."

Carrying John Mark, Jenny hurried across the street. A flurry of activity at the front door of the hotel caught her eye, and she paused to watch. Emma, followed by her children, was being helped into a handsome new carriage.

"The grand lady is going to be in the parade too," the wizened, gray-haired lady at her elbow said. "Do you know when the Prophet's mother will return to Nauvoo? I knew her back in Palmyra days. I'd surely like to visit with her."

Jenny shook her head. "Nauvoo is getting so big I can't keep up on any of the news. I haven't visited with Lucy Smith for years. Doubt she'd even remember me. So you're from Palmyra. I lived at Manchester for a time." Jenny searched the woman's face, trying to place her. They continued down the street toward the speaker's stand draped with bunting.

The woman was saying, "My, who would've guessed Palmyra would produce a prophet? I rise up and call myself blessed for knowing him in the beginning years."

Jenny saw Mark and waved. With a smile she walked away from the woman. Mark said, "Let's stand here, close to the platform. Joseph's on old Charlie; Emma and the carriage as well as the Legion are ready to start. I expect we'll hear the band in another minute."

He was right. By the time the band passed in front of the platform, the crowd was in a frenzy. Mark, with his lips close to Jenny's ear, said, "This is very military. Hear the drums? They know how to beat life into anything that moves."

The band was beyond them now and Joseph's horse Charlie appeared. Carefully curried until he resembled black satin, the prancing horse magnified the glory of the Prophet. From the helmet topped with a plume of ostrich feathers, to the glory of his blue coat decorated with heavy gold braid, he was the epitome of the office of lieutenant-general of the Nauvoo Legion.

As he passed, a murmur of appreciation swept the crowd. Looking at the people around her, Jenny smiled, seeing the blind adoration on their faces. But suddenly she frowned. For the first time she perceived Joseph in a new light—the contrast between his grandeur and the threadbare black coats and dingy calico of his adoring subjects.

Long before the last of the Legion had passed, Joseph had taken his place on the platform. The elders were with him. Jenny moved impatiently and shifted John Mark. With a grin Mark took the child, whispering, "Aren't you glad they didn't all march today? It's reported there's four thousand of them now."

And when the street was once again quiet, hushed and waiting, Joseph stood before them. "What do you all say about today's glory?"

The roar was deafening and a chanting swept the street. "Joseph! Joseph!" came the cry. For a moment Jenny felt separated from it all. A cold chill touched her as she studied the faces of his followers.

Silence descended abruptly, and Joseph lifted his face skyward. "In the scheme of human events, I calculate to be an instrument. By the word of the Lord I shall set up the kingdom of Daniel. Through this act there will be a foundation laid which shall revolutionize the world. But I assure you, my dear brethren, it shall not be by the sword nor gun that I shall possess in the name of this kingdom. No, my friends, in these latter days the power of truth shall press so heavily upon all nations to such an extent that they shall under necessity humble themselves to obey the gospel." He paused momentarily and then said, "All America, from north to south, from coast to coast, is Zion. It is our inheritance! I am a smooth polished shaft in the quiver of the Almighty. He shall give me dominion over all."

The chant rose again. Jenny concentrated on the words, *There ain't gonna be no war no more, there ain't gonna be no war.* Mark bent over her, whispering, "Little do they know that the Prophet is planning to have an arsenal and to manufacture powder. At the same time his army shall continue to grow."

During the week Nauvoo subsided back into the usual workaday world. Only those closest to Joseph knew the decisions being made.

Mark walked into his office one morning and discovered it had been turned into a convention hall. During that morning, the puzzle pieces fell abruptly into place.

When he stepped into the assembly of black-coated men, Joseph was standing before them with a handful of papers. Mark noted that Joseph had dressed in black in honor of the occasion.

Nodding at Mark, Joseph said, "I have in my hands copies

of the numerous letters written to Congress in an attempt to win attention, support, even recognition of our rights as a beleaguered people. We have had no reply promising satisfaction. Until we are a political force, we shall not win the attention of this country.

"I am convinced we'll be robbed of our constitutional rights until we stamp our feet hard enough to win respect." He paced the room, saying, "I've contacted every candidate for office, asking their views on our plight and have received no satisfaction from that quarter. Therefore, I shall declare myself candidate for president of the United States of America."

There was a muffled roar of approval as Hyrum Smith got to his feet. "We want a president—for the people, not for a party!"

Throughout the day the men huddled over the table. A platform was written out, while ideas shot around the room: "Reduce Congress!" "Establish a theodemocracy, where God and the people hold power to conduct affairs in righteousness!" "Bring Texas into the union!" "Abolish slavery!"

Then in a quiet moment, George Miller's voice rose, "If the election's successful, Joseph and the Council of Fifty will at once establish dominion. Fellas, that's us. You ready to take over?"

Before the day had finished, Rigdon had been reluctantly acknowledged as Joseph's running mate. Joseph stood to his feet. "I want every man in the city who can lisp a clear sentence to hit the campaign trail. Advocate the Mormon religion, purity of election. Call upon the people to be on the side of law and order. Campaign. Put our name before the people!"

"Hear ye, hear ye!" Wight shouted, jumping to his feet, "I make a motion that on July 13, we assemble in New York for the purpose of holding a national *Joseph Smith for President* convention."

Later, as the men rushed out of the room, Mark chewed his lip and contemplated the shambles of paper and debris left behind in his office. He studied his desk and wondered about carrying home the work he had intended finishing.

Joseph approached. "Mark, you look down in the mouth about it all."

Mark looked up in surprise. "Well, not about the day's events. I was thinking of what I didn't do today. But since you ask—Joseph, you don't have any expectations about winning this election. But have you considered what this interlude means in the lives of these men? Some of these men are going out simply because they feel forced into it. That's bad—for them and for the image they'll project."

"Since when have you been concerned about my image?"

"It isn't *yours*," Mark frowned. "It's the image of the people; the mindlessness of your absolute control. From the council on down, everything in Mormon country smacks of subservience. You may control the people now, but it's going to backfire. Either they'll break free or some firebrand will do the breaking for them. Your platform holds high a happy view of freedom, but it's only to allow you to do as you please. I can't believe you really have the best interests of the people at heart."

Mark's heart was heavy as he started for home. As he reviewed the day and thought of the direction Joseph was leading, he shook his head. "Poor old John D. Lee. I hope someday that his faithful sacrifice will merit him more than the crumbs at Caesar's table."

Law caught up with him. "I hear you. I get the idea you're against faithfulness."

Mark slanted him a glance. "Faithfulness, of the kind John D. Lee has, belongs to God. Given to man or cause instead of God, it leads to slavery."

William's eyes were bright and questioning for a moment; then he asked, "Was Joseph served the summons?"

"Yes," Mark shook his head. "I'm not too confident. He laughed it off, saying he had a complete record of his actions and even the most mundane of daily activities to support his righteous life. If the court accepts his records, it could be bad."

"Well, brace yourself, Attorney Cartwright. I've filed suit against the Prophet charging adultery and polygamy. Considering Joseph's second favorite lawyer is now suing him for slander, I hate to think where that leaves you."

When Mark walked into the house, Jenny was in the kitchen. John Mark clung to her skirts. With his face tilted upward and the tears coursing down, he cried.

Mark looked at Jenny's tired face, watched her rub at the perspiration on her brow. "Oh, Marky, be a good baby," she moaned.

"What's the trouble?" Mark asked, astonished even then that he could look beyond his own problem.

"Laundry, fussy baby, late daddy, and burned potatoes."

"I'm sorry." He kissed her cheek and picked up John Mark. Jenny was blinking tears out of her eyes. He said, "Why don't you sit down and rock the tyke. I'll do something with dinner."

The tears fell. "Don't you ever want to hold him?"

"Jenny, I love holding him," he explained patiently, "but you're exhausted. In a minute I'll put both of you to bed." He pulled her against his chest, wondering how he could convince her of his plan and how he could let them go.

She pulled away. "I'm fine. We'll have bread and gravy, unless you want eggs."

John Mark was tucked into bed early and Mark went down to help with the dishes. Jenny was still sagging listlessly over the dishpan. She tried to straighten and smile when he picked up the dish towel. Studying her tired face, he decided he had found a reason.

Speaking lightly he said, "First thing tomorrow I am going to make arrangements for you and John Mark to take the stage to Cleveland to visit Mother. She's been begging for a visit since the baby was born. I can't get free, but there's no reason you can't go."

Jenny was staring at him. Slowly she lifted one soapy hand and touched her face. "Mark!" she whispered. "Oh, Mark, please don't make me go!"

"I thought you liked Mother."

"I do, but Mark, not now."

"Yes, now." She moistened her lips and the expression in her eyes brought him a step closer. "Jenny, don't look like it's the end of the world. I'm doing this for your own good."

"What's happened?"

He sighed and said, "Come sit down." She hesitated and he eased her into the rocking chair. For a moment he studied her face, trying to understand the sadness he perceived there. He took a deep breath and decided the truth would be the only thing she would accept.

"I saw William Law this afternoon. He's filed suit against Joseph Smith, charging him with adultery and polygamy. At the same time there's Foster's suit and now Higbee's suit. It looks like, unless Joseph chooses a defense attorney from out of Springfield, I'll be handling his case."

"I realize you'll be busy for the next several months. But Tom could stay here if you'll be out of town."

"That isn't the point. Jenny, I'm trying to say it gently, but I don't know how. There's going to be a very unsavory trial. I know William well enough to realize he's not going to back down from exposing the facts even if he treads on our toes." He could see she still didn't comprehend. "Jenny, I love you and I've forgiven you for what—" He took a deep breath.

"Let's put it this way. I refuse to allow your name to be

dragged in the dirt. The only way that can be avoided is by your leaving until this whole affair can be settled."

She was silent for a moment before she asked, "What about the other women? We heard some of them at the meeting. Won't they be pulled into witnessing?"

"I'm afraid so. Right now, knowing how Joseph will fight, I guess every woman who has ever been involved with Joseph will be forced to testify. That's why it is absolutely necessary for you to leave."

"I don't like it," Jenny said slowly. "But if they will have to talk about their troubles with Joseph, it seems only fair that I do the same thing." She lifted her face. "Mark, don't you think that's what Jesus would want me to do?"

"No!" He jumped to his feet and paced the room. "I refuse to allow my wife to be shamed in that manner." When she began to sob, hiding her face in her hands, Mark knew himself defenseless. "Look, I've got to take care of things outside. There's no point in discussing this further."

Jenny lifted her face. He tightened his jaw and waited. She wiped her eyes and slowly got to her feet. Stepping close she looked at him intently. He watched despair creep over her face. As she turned away, she said flatly, "Very well. I'll be prepared to leave day after tomorrow."

CHAPTER 42

"Jen! Are you home?"

Jenny walked slowly down the stairs and set John Mark on his feet. "Hello, Tom. I'm surprised to see you."

Tom blinked, "You all right?" She nodded and he said, "Mark invited me out for supper."

"He did?" She frowned and looked around the room. "That's strange."

Tom looked down at the trunk. "You going someplace?"

"Yes, Mark's sending me to his mother's place until things are resolved."

His glance was sharp. "You mean the suits? The newspapers are full of the wildest stories. I sure didn't have any idea there was—aw, yes, I did; but still—"

They heard Mark's horse and Jenny headed for the kitchen. She sighed and reached for her apron. "Fortunate for you I've planned a good meal." She glanced at him. "John Mark and I are leaving on the stage in the morning."

"It's going to be rough on Mark, facing that mess without having you around."

"Tom!" Mark opened the door as she cried, "this isn't my idea. I'm not deserting Mark—he's *sending* me away. I want desperately to stay."

"Jenny!" She saw Mark's face was white as he reached for her arm. "Little love, this is going to be more difficult for me than—but I simply can't allow you to undergo the kind of treatment Joseph's promising." Jenny shook his hand off, sank her teeth into her lip and turned to the table.

Her voice was flat as she said, "Well, come to supper. There's pot roast." She began lifting the meat and vegetables to the serving platter.

Mark picked up the baby and said, "Come on, fella, let's find that bib."

"You mean a baby that size is eating real food?" Tom marveled. "I—Jen!" He started after her as she dashed out the backdoor.

When Jenny returned to the kitchen, Mark and Tom stared at her. Mark said, "Jenny, you're ill!"

"It's just the smell of meat. Mark, feed the baby, I'm going to lie down."

"Jenny—" Mark's voice was commanding and cold.

She faced him and lifted her chin. "I'm pregnant." There was a moment of silence, a moment of waiting, and Jenny headed for the stairs.

"Jenny!" She turned around and saw the agony on his face. "No matter. I'll accept this one as mine and love him as much as I love little John Mark." For a moment she was motionless.

"Mark!" She rushed at him, pounding his chest with her fists. "What are you saying? I can't believe I'm hearing you!" She turned to run and he grabbed her arms.

"Jenny, face it. You'll never be happy until you're willing to confess this to God. I've told you I forgive you. Please!"

Flinging off his grasp, Jenny turned and ran across the room. She snatched up John Mark and ran back to Mark. Shoving the toddler into his arms she said, "Look at that child's eyes and tell me they aren't yours!"

John Mark was crying and Mark cuddled him close. Staring at Jenny, he said, "You can't be certain; besides, it's not necessary to prove anything."

Suddenly limp and shaking, Jenny sat down in the rocking chair and whispered, "Mark, you're saying you believe I was unfaithful to you. Never, never, Mark! I would *never* do that to you."

She could see he didn't believe her. "And you expect me to believe you could be Joseph's wife and not submit to him?" he asked. "There are the facts. It's common knowledge that Mark Cartwright's wife tried to commit suicide while he was gone."

"Suicide!" Jenny's voice trembled with horror. For a moment she stared at Mark and then at Tom. "Tom, tell him—"

"Jenny, Joseph told me about it."

"Joseph!" For a moment Jenny was frozen motionless and then she began to laugh.

Mark had her in his arms. "Jenny, stop or I'll shake you; you're going to be—"

She shoved his arms away and rubbed her eyes. "Oh—but then you'll never believe it."

Slowly Mark said, "Maybe you'd better tell me about it. You know there are questions you never answered about that time, and questions I didn't dare ask."

"That marriage; it's so stupid! I don't know why—but there was this book. It all seemed so high and holy and far away. For eternity. I never dreamed there was anything else involved. He tried to tell me there was, and that the marriage was invalid until—" Suddenly she grinned up at Mark. "Can you possibly believe I always managed to outtalk him?"

For a moment she sobered and then shuddered. "Except for that sermon about posterity. I went to him. I intended to ask how I could help John Mark since you wouldn't take endowments. He said that because of the spiritual wife doctrine, all my posterity belonged to him. But then he said there would be no hope for John Mark to be with me in the eternities unless I validated the marriage. He confused me, but I never yielded. Mark, if you could only know how horrible it was!"

She got to her feet, coming close to look into his eyes. "Do you remember our marriage? That was the first time I ever *felt* God. But I didn't know it was Him. I just thought it was love; and because of it, I knew that our vows were so important I couldn't ever break them. Mark!"

Jenny saw the relief and joy in Mark's face and she held out her arms.

Behind her Tom was saying, "Well, tyke, let's go feed the cows."

On Monday morning, just before Mark was ready to leave for Nauvoo, Jenny was able to say. "Now that you really believe in my innocence, may I testify? I'm still ashamed of myself, and of the ugliness of the whole affair, but, please! If nothing else, maybe I'll be able to convince some other Sally—" Her voice broke, but in a minute she hurried on. "I know it'll be painful for you, but I feel it's necessary."

From the shelter of his arms she sighed with contentment. "Mark, these past few days have almost made me hope again."

"About what?"

"Our marriage. We had such a wonderful marriage and then suddenly it all seemed to fall apart. It happened when I was pregnant with John Mark—"

"Because I was certain he was not my baby. I'm sorry." He felt her tears and asked, "What is it?"

"I thought it was because I threw the talisman away. See, I had the talisman when I asked you to marry me. Always I thought the talisman made you love me. But if you do now and I don't have the talisman—well?"

He saw the changing expression in her eyes and said, "Why are you crying now?"

"When I didn't have it, you loved me enough to accept me and the child, even when you thought it was Joseph's!"

He kissed her fingers. "John Mark does have eyes like mine—funny I never noticed. I just kept looking for him to develop that terrible nose."

"Oh, Mark!" She gulped and dabbed at her eyes. "You'd better go. John Mark is banging on the oven door with his spoon, and my morning sickness is threatening."

Before Mark left the house, he swooped John Mark up in his arms, tossed him, and said, "Son!"

When Mark rode into the livery stable, Tom was leaning against the door looking very serious. Mark tilted his hat back and waited.

Tom headed for the harness room and Mark followed. Picking up a harness with a loose buckle, Tom examined it carefully, avoiding Mark's eyes. "Mind telling me how I get the kind of religion you and Jenny have?"

When Mark finally reached the office, Joseph was pacing the floor and frowning. After glaring at Mark he said, "Seen the newspaper?"

"No, I can't say that I have. I carried one home last weekend but forgot to look at it."

"I hear your wife is leaving town."

"Naw, she's changed her mind. Feeling poorly with a young'un. She said to give you a message." Joseph waited. "She said tear up the paper—you'd know which one. She said since it hasn't been validated, it isn't doing you a bit of good." Mark grinned and added, "Well, I guess I'd better go see what I can work up in the way of a defense."

Mark's grin vanished when he saw the stack of newspapers on his desk. He sat down and began reading. When he finished, Joseph was waiting, leaning back in his chair with hands behind his head.

"So the *Times and Seasons* considers your accusations against Higbee too indelicate to print. Joseph, rather than helping your cause, every story that comes out is an indirect reflection upon you. Soon people will begin to wonder why you've let these affairs continue."

Finally Mark finished the last paper and, folding them together, dropped them in the trash. "They are worthless to our defense. I'm not certain these stories will help the others either, but one thing I'm very certain about is that they will focus the eyes of the nation on Nauvoo."

Joseph shuddered and got to his feet. "One thing is clear; I need all the help I can get. I'm going to ride into Carthage and see if I can round up some more legal help. Wonder if I can talk Stephen A. Douglas into giving me a hand?"

Before the month of May drew to a close, a grand jury in Hancock returned indictments against the Prophet, charging him with adultery and perjury. Joseph succeeded in getting indictments voted against Dr. Foster and Francis Higbee with the charge of false arrest and slander.

"One thing I can say for certain," Tom remarked, after the first trial, "the trial of Foster and Higbee drew nearly as big a crowd as the Legion parades do on a good day." He paused to reflect before adding, " 'Course, the trials had all that sensational mud-slinging to advertise them. Guess they lived up to promise."

Mark had to agree with Tom. "One good feature; maybe by the time the court gets around to hearing Joseph's case, things will have calmed down a bit. It's been continued until next term of court."

The last Sabbath day in May, as Jenny and Mark prepared to go into Nauvoo for the service in the temple grove, Jenny asked, "Have you heard anything about the church William Law started?"

Mark shook his head. "I do know several of the men have been working night and day setting up the new press. They've even started writing, so it shouldn't be long now before they're producing a newspaper."

"I'm excited and frightened for them," Jenny murmured. "They are very brave men. I'm just grateful they've insisted you keep your distance."

This Sabbath Mark was able to find a shady spot close to the platform, so after greeting friends, they settled down to listen to the sermon.

Jenny whispered to Mark, "You think the walls don't have ears in Nauvoo? I've talked to three women this morning who asked me why I didn't go to Cleveland. Fortunately, I have a wonderful reason for not going." She beamed at him.

Within minutes after Joseph began to talk, the audience shifted uneasily and exchanged glances. He was saying, "Considering it all, the Lord has fortunately given me the ability to glory in persecution. Oppression can madden a wise man and a fool. As for this beardless boy—give me a chance to whip the world.

"I'll stand astride the mountains and crow. Always I'll be the victor. And in the end, innocence and truth will prevail. Ye prosecutor and ye false witnesses, come at me! All hell, boil! I shall come out on top of you all."

Joseph paused to lean forward to catch the eyes of all who would look, saying, "I've every reason to boast. No man has done a greater work than I." His hand swept the congregation. "See this multitude? I hold them all together. Even Jesus had trouble keeping a crowd following Him. Jesus' followers ran away from Him, but you don't see mine running away, yet. Since the days of Adam, I am the only man standing who alone can hold a church together. No other man has done such a task."

Sobering now, he said, "Only God knows the charges brought to bear against me are false. What a thing—this ugly charge of adultery! My brethren, I am the same man I was fourteen years ago when the church was born. I am innocent of the charges, and I shall prove my accusers wrong."

CHAPTER 43

The morning of June 7 dawned clear and warm. The thunderclouds which had clustered on the horizon were gone. As Mark headed toward Nauvoo, he looked at the sky and brooded, "Would that it were as clear in our city!" As he said it, he realized how often he had been saying the same thing.

He was still mulling over the comparison as he rode on. Mark had nearly reached the outskirts of Nauvoo when the dark figure on horseback came out of the trees. Frowning, he pulled on the reins and quickly scanned the trees. If the man were an Angel, there would be more behind him.

The man rode quickly and confidently toward him. Mark gave a sigh of relief as he recognized William Law.

Mark stopped in the shade of a tree. "You had my heart in my throat," he muttered as Law pulled his horse close.

"Better be cautious." William's terse statement was underscored by his tired, white face. He pulled a newspaper out from under his coat and handed it to Mark. "Thought I'd better give this to you now. Might not get a chance later; besides, it'll be wise for you to be forewarned. It's the first issue of the *Nauvoo Expositor.* We tried to say it all, in case there's not another opportunity."

Mark glanced sharply at the man. "I trust your fears are only a reflection of fatigue."

William shook his head. "Let's say I don't expect Joseph to accept this in a good-hearted way. We've taken precautions. Don't go to the pressroom; we've a couple of thick-skinned Missourians standing guard just in case."

"You really are concerned," Mark said slowly, glancing down at the paper. "I take it you've resigned yourself to a fight."

"We're standing by, expecting the worst. And the minute it happens, we're heading for Carthage." William touched his hat and guided his horse out to the road.

For a moment Mark watched as man and beast disappeared

through the trees. He sighed and opened the newspaper and began quickly skimming the articles. "Emmons, huh? Looks like he's done a thorough job. Fair, pointed, but not cheap."

He read, "We most solemnly and sincerely declare . . . God being witness." His eyes picked up the words—"A doctrine taught secretly, denied openly. . . . We set forth for all to see the principles of Joseph Smith. . . . whoredoms, not in accord with the principles of Jesus Christ."

Quickly now, with rising excitement, Mark glanced through the articles. One revealed the seductions of immigrant women, done under the promise of holiness. Mark recognized the story of Martha Brotherton, the young woman he had escorted home from Joseph's office. How he remembered her anger!

"Our hearts have mourned . . . bled at the wretched conditions of females in this place. . . . Impossible to describe without wounding . . . but truth shall come to the world." Mark found Jane Law's story and Mrs. Foster's.

Finally, with a sigh he slowly folded the paper and tucked it into his saddlebag. "Well," he muttered, "these next few days are going to be interesting." He flicked the reins and nudged the mare with his heels.

Mark had just reached the office when two members of the Legion thundered up the stairs. Throwing him a sharp glance they went into Joseph's office. Mark followed.

Joseph was at his desk. With a clenched fist he pounded the newspaper spread across its surface. "I want every issue of this paper picked up, even if you must beat on doors to get them. Lies, filth! Burn them all! You fellas are supposed to be my eyes and ears around Nauvoo. Why didn't you tell me Law had a press and that he was ready to print?"

The men left as hurriedly as they arrived and Joseph headed for the door. He paused. "Mark, I'll be at the city council offices. I don't know what I'm going to do, but if I need you, I'll send for you." For a moment his eyes were questioning, suspicious.

"If you've information, I want it. If you haven't read the paper, which I doubt heartily, there it is. Filter the crowd who'll rush in, and calm the fears."

Mark shrugged and picked up Joseph's copy of the paper and carried it into his office. Clayton was preparing for a hurried departure. "I'll be with Joseph, recording the meeting and writing letters. Now's no time to slack off on the record-keeping. It'll be the record-keeping that'll save him in the suits. You heard him last Sabbath."

Spreading the paper on his desk, Mark sat down to read.

Polygamy was only one of the issues. Now Mark mentally applauded William. He was clearly pointing out the Prophet's desire to bring the country under control of the church. He read, "We do not believe that God ever raised up a Prophet to Christianize a world by political schemes and intrigue. It is not the way God captivates the heart . . ."

The paper went on to catalog the misuse of the Nauvoo Charter, the financial maneuverings of the Prophet and his constant denunciation of Missouri. Now the article called for a limiting of Joseph's power, both in the church and in the city. It charged Joseph with his responsibility of obedience to the revelations, while at the same time censoring him for his *moral imperfections*.

Mark snorted and dropped the paper. "Law, you were very nearly too sweet. But knowing the Prophet, there's going to be a tornado sweep through the streets of Nauvoo."

The city council was still secluded that evening when Mark headed for home. Again William drifted out of the trees. "Lot of good I'm doing you," Mark addressed him. "I don't know anything except fellas were instructed to pick up the papers and burn them."

Law nodded and said, "Nevertheless, you could be pulled into the meeting yet. They'll need legal advice."

"Might be Joseph's too hot to think of that."

At home Mark kissed Jenny and swung John Mark up in his arms. "The *Nauvoo Expositor* published its first issue."

Jenny turned quickly from the stove. "Oh, let me see!"

"Aw, don't I get my supper first?" She hugged him and gave him a gentle push toward the table. As he sat down, he said, "I've a feeling the Prophet knows he's facing the biggest crisis yet. There have been rumbles in the church all along, but this is the worst."

Jenny handed him the potatoes and said, "Looking back and comparing it with now, I'm seeing more coming out for discussion. In the past it seemed Joseph was on top of a problem, stomping it into the ground before it could be worked over."

After supper Mark handed the paper to Jenny and said, "Go ahead and read it now. I'll wash dishes. Maybe by the time I finish chores, you'll have finished it."

When he carried the milk into the house, Jenny was thoughtfully staring at the wall. She looked toward Mark as he set the pail down. "I've a feeling Joseph's missed his chance. Couldn't he have saved himself if he'd pushed his revelation on marriage out in the open? Perhaps if we'd all had it served up at once, there'd have been no room to question—or would there?"

"Depends. You questioned. The Laws and Fosters and Higbees have. I suppose the deciding factor is, and always will be, a desire to get to know God personally and find out what *He* thinks."

"Mark, how many people realize God *is*? Are they aware of God to such an extent that they *know* He's seeing everything, participating in every thought, caring about us?"

On June 10, Joseph was back in his office. Mark blinked in surprise when he walked up the stairs and faced the open door. The Prophet had his feet propped on the desk and his hands linked behind his head. His grin was easy and friendly. "Come on in, Mark," he called.

"I take it all the problems have been resolved," Mark said. "Well, if that's the case, I have a few papers here for you to look over."

When he returned from his office, Joseph's feet were on the floor and he looked prepared for action. There were two folded sheets of paper under his elbow and his smile was confident as he said, "The council is in meeting. I expect to hear their decision shortly."

"You as mayor are letting them handle it?" He merely nodded.

It was nearly noon when George Harris breezed into the office with a jovial grin. "Well, General, the matter's settled. We need you back at the chambers to sign a couple of papers." Joseph got to his feet and picked up his papers. As he headed for the door, Harris addressed Mark.

"Might as well know the council has denounced the paper as a nuisance. We've had a lengthy hearing, and that's the conclusion we've reached."

"What will happen now?" Mark asked.

"It'll be removed."

Anger swept through Mark, leaving him feeling powerless. He got to his feet, saying, "So much for democracy and freedom of speech. It was nice while it lasted. But I suppose that was to be expected." Mark saw the dark expression in Harris's eyes, and as he headed for his office, he wondered if just perhaps the man was uncomfortable with the decision of the council.

When Mark reached the livery stable, there was a cluster of men hanging around. He met Tom's eyes, saw his questioning eyebrow, and waited.

"Mark, know what's going to happen?" He shook his head.

"If the Prophet's innocent, he'll smooth the matter out."

"Maybe he will if he's guilty."

"No doubt. Either way, we won't know."

One of the men shuffled his feet. When Mark looked at him, the man's anger erupted. "It's a shame we can't know what's going on around here. It's also a shame a fella can't express himself or uncover dirt without being fired upon."

"You'd better keep *your* mouth shut, Simpson, or the roof'll come down on your head," another man warned.

The next morning Mark knew his first moment of uneasiness when he passed the tree where William Law had been meeting him. He had pulled the mare down to a walk, hoping Law would catch up with him.

The rumble of the Daniels' wagon approaching caught his attention. He turned to salute old Daniels. "It's been a long time since I've seen you folks."

Daniels nodded and licked his lips. "Got rid of my cows. The boy's taken off to go west, and I couldn't handle them myself. Now I'm going into town to see what new exitement is poppin'." Remembering Daniels was a Gentile, Mark studied his face, noting the sparkle there.

"Excitement?" he repeated slowly.

"Yeah, old Smith tore up the new *Expositor* press and punched out a few lights—that is, poked a few adversaries." He paused to study Mark's face and added, "I hear Missouri's promised to send a bunch over here to help out Warsaw and Carthage when the fightin' starts."

"You think there'll be a fight?"

"Think Joe's not going to start a ruckus?"

Mark hastily bid farewell and dug his heels in the mare's sides.

When Mark dashed into Joseph's office, for a moment he felt as if he'd been dropped back into yesterday. Joseph's feet were on his desk, his hands behind his head; he was grinning broadly.

Mark folded his arms. "What's been happening?"

"Well," Joseph drawled, "there's this little newspaper trying to start up. Seems nobody around here liked it much. You might say it's closed, outta business."

"What happened to freedom of speech?"

His eyes widened. "*We* still have it."

"Joseph, you know what I mean. I read that sheet. The charges brought against you were true. And they were brought by a man deeply burdened for truth, honesty, justice and—righteousness."

Joseph's chair hit the floor, and his grin vanished. "Mark, you're my employee. I bode no insurrection."

"Or unfettered thought." Mark paced the room, thinking. When he returned to Joseph's desk he said, "What is your next step?"

"Just to hang in here and fight all the brush fires."

"How much longer do you think you can manage? Joseph, that paper used the term *despotism*. Are you aware of the number of responsible, thinking people in Nauvoo who see you that way?

"I've a copy of the *Warsaw Signal* which some brother shoved in my hand as I started up the stairs. It contains an article by Foster. I've only scanned it briefly, but here's one damning statement which will not escape the public's notice. Foster accuses you of hiring Porter Rockwell to shoot Boggs.

"How long do you think it will be before Governor Ford gets wind of this? Have you anticipated your defense for destroying a newspaper in a land which holds great stock in freedom of speech?"

Mark paced the room again, took a deep breath, and headed back to Joseph. "As your attorney I suggest you start mending fences now. First, before those fellows sue you again—which would ruin you—go offer to settle out of court by financial reimbursement and a promise to allow their newspaper to publish within the city. Then," he paused and took a deep breath, "give them what they want. Your repentance and confession."

Joseph's face settled into lines of suffering. "Mark, will you be a Judas, too? You are asking me to deny my Lord by refusing to acknowledge the priesthood and honor the revelation."

"Hogwash!" Mark exploded. He paused long enough to control his temper, then said, "Joseph, I resign as your attorney, as of this minute. I've stayed here much longer than I should have. But it was always with the hopes of giving you the real help you need. I see now that's impossible."

"I agree with your decision," Joseph said stiffly. "You have been around much too long. You realize I hired you only because of Jenny." He acknowledged Mark's astonishment with a grin. "I'd had my eye on her for years. I just didn't dare make her my spiritual wife until I could do so without fear of disclosure. I no longer want her."

Mark carried his box of legal books down to the livery stable. Dropping his load just inside the tack room, he addressed Tom. "I've left Joseph's office. Until I come in with the buggy, may I leave my books here?"

Tom's astonishment changed into a grin. "Man, am I ever glad to hear that! The way things are going around here, I was beginning to fear for you." He shot Mark a look.

"There's rumbles about blood atonement. You know that's doctrine. At meeting Joseph referred to his translation of the New Testament in Matthew and Mark where he said the arm and so forth really means a brother, that it's better to do away with a brother than to let him pull you into hell."

When Mark turned toward the door, Tom added, "By the way, I just got word that when Joseph and his bunch moved in on the newspaper office last night, the Laws, Fosters, Higbees, and a few others headed for Carthage."

Mark sighed with relief. "So that's where they are. Law told me they might go."

Tom added. "I heard this morning they've sworn out warrants for Joseph, charging him with riot and arson."

The door banged. Simpson came into the tack room. "Did ya hear? Sheriff from Carthage tried to serve Joseph and the others with a writ. They're all over at city hall right now."

"What's going on?" Mark asked.

"Well, the sheriff wanted to take the bunch into Carthage, but Joseph pointed out the writ didn't specify which justice of the peace, so the fella had to give in. They're meeting with the Nauvoo justice right now."

Mark sighed. "Well, that settles that. Under the Nauvoo Charter the case will be dismissed. Those fellows had better hightail out of town or Joseph'll shove them in jail for coming after him."

CHAPTER 44

At first Jenny reacted with shock to Mark's news, and then she exclaimed, "Then we can leave Nauvoo right away! Oh, Mark, I'll be so glad to go. Something dark and brooding hangs over the whole city."

"I'll go into Nauvoo tomorrow to see about selling the livestock and placing the farm for sale. Do you want to go?"

Jenny replied, "Yes, I'm curious." But she said it with a shiver as she searched Mark's face for reassurance.

On the trip into Nauvoo the next day, they met Francis Higbee. He pulled his horse to a stop and said, "I hear you quit Joseph flat. Made any plans?" As Mark explained, Higbee held out his newspaper. "See this editorial in the *Warsaw Signal*? Might be a good idea to get out of here. You're between Warsaw and Nauvoo. That won't be good if there's problems." As he turned to go, he said, "You might be interested in the parade going on day after tomorrow. Joseph's rallying the Legion."

Jenny leaned over Mark's shoulder to look at the paper. "Oh, Mark, it says 'war and extermination.' We must go! There's John Mark to think about. Look at these words—this is a challenge to action. The editor's calling the Saints infernal devils and advocating powder and balls to settle the matter."

She leaned back to look at him. "Jenny, don't look so frightened. This is Illinois, not Missouri." But he added thoughtfully, "Joseph's ability to arouse so much opposition everywhere he goes is frightening."

Mark and Jenny had completed their errands by noon. Mark was shaking his head in disappointment as they carried their picnic basket into a heavily wooded area between the stream and the temple. "Taylor didn't offer me much encouragement about selling the place. Seemed harassed and impatient. I know he had more important things on his mind. The talk going around is gloomy."

They ate their lunch in silence while they listened to the distant clamor of Nauvoo.

John Mark went to sleep and Jenny's eyes were heavy when Mark whispered, "I'm going back into town. I need to stop at the stable for my box of books. Why don't you nap, too?" Jenny nodded and curled up beside the baby.

Voices awakened Jenny. Her first thought was of the baby, but he was sleeping soundly. Cautiously she sat up. The note of anxiety in the hidden speaker caught her attention. As the voice rose, she recognized it. It was Joseph.

Quietly she shifted her position and listened. A heavy, sober voice answered him, and Joseph returned bitterly, "We are ruined people."

The heavy voice questioned, "I don't understand; why do you say that?"

"It's this spiritual wife doctrine. It will prove to be the downfall of us."

"I know." For a moment the older voice caught, nearly sobbing, then asking, "Joseph, Joseph, what can be done?"

Joseph continued, the bitterness twisting through his voice. "I'm convinced this path leads to destruction. Do you see? I have been deceived. It doesn't promote glory—instead it's a curse. Unless this can be stamped out of the church immediately, we'll be forced to leave the United States, fleeing for our lives."

Jenny didn't hear the older man's reply, but Joseph's voice rose again. "You haven't accepted the doctrine. You go to the high priesthood and threaten to excommunicate anyone practicing plural marriage. Only this route will rid the church of the damnable heresy."

Jenny heard the buggy, and the voices stopped. She watched as Joseph and his companion got up and moved out of the trees. She saw them pause to greet Mark before leaving.

When he came to her with the question in his eyes, she pulled him close, relating the conversation.

Mark and Jenny were there in the early morning when Joseph stood on the reviewing stand outside Nauvoo House and faced the troops. The sun glinted off his sword and brightened the gold braid adorning his blue jacket. As he waited motionless, Jenny saw the breeze pick at the ostrich plume on his helmet, giving life to a scene which suddenly seemed unbelievable.

Then Joseph moved and the crowd below him stirred. The unreality was gone, and life moved on. Jenny slowly turned to see the cluster of men in uniform, fanning out across the city street. Beyond them clustered the entire populace of Nauvoo.

As Joseph began to speak, Jenny sensed the rapt attention of his audience.

He referred to the *Warsaw Signal* article, which Mark and Jenny had seen, saying, "We are American citizens. The liberties our fathers won shall be cherished by us." His voice deepened, "But again and again it seems we shall be forced to stand for right. My men, you must be prepared to defend your lives, homes, even our godly heritage.

"Some think the enemy will be satisfied with my blood, but I assure you they will thirst for the blood of every man whose heart contains a spark of the spirit of the fullness of the gospel. The enemy will destroy everyone—man and woman alike—who dares trust and believe in all God has inspired me to teach. But I tell you, Israel, there must be freedom for all! Freedom to live and worship. Will you stand by me to the death? Will you promise—" The shouts of *Hosanna!* drowned the voice of the Prophet.

Jenny watched his smile and waited. In the silence he said, "It is well that you have promised. Otherwise I would have gone there," he pointed westward, "and raised up a mightier people." Unsheathing his sword, Joseph shouted, "I call God to witness. Freedom and justice for the people, protection from the mob, or my blood shall be spilled in the effort of freedom."

The Sabbath day came upon the heels of Joseph's address to the Legion. On that morning Mark looked at Jenny and said, "Do you want to hear Joseph today?"

With a sigh she studied his face. "It's hot and the oppression lies heavy upon me, but yes. Like you, I'm anxious, too curious to stay away. I wonder, what will he say next?"

As Mark and Jenny rode into Nauvoo, they were very conscious of the line of frosty-eyed men guarding the roads. Jenny whispered, "Mark, what is going on?"

"It's obvious. Joseph is not going to let one stranger into Nauvoo. He's established martial law. You might say in the midst of freedom, we are a fortified city."

When Joseph began his sermon, Jenny sighed with disappointment. He was talking about consecration.

Raising his arm, Joseph cried, "My people, I want you to prove your loyalty in time of need. Consecrate—yes, come forward and give us all your property that the manifold blessings shall rest upon you. Place your all at the feet of the apostles. There must be a speedy completion of the temple if the wishes of the Lord are to be fulfilled."

Abruptly he turned to face the line of elders and high priests behind him. His voice was deep and accusing as he charged, "There are those among you who will betray me. You have delivered me up to the enemy to be slain."

After service Tom joined Mark and Jenny. He shook his head at their offer, saying, "Joseph has put me on to guard him. Sending so many of the men outta town to campaign for him has left us short-handed. Fortunately, it won't last for long. He's dispatched letters to them all, telling them to hightail for Nauvoo."

"Then he's getting worried, isn't he?" Mark asked. Tom nodded, saying, "Much as I am uneasy about this whole affair, I'm trapped. I'll be dogging his heels until some of the fellas are back in town."

"It could take a long time to round them up," Mark cautioned with a worried frown.

Tom was shaking his head. "Naw, maybe not." After a moment he added. "Don't worry about me. I did some thinking about it all. Seems I've ended up feeling sorry fer Joseph. I see him a-pullin' his house in on his head. Right now I'd just like to stick close."

He was silent for a moment and then added, "Just a few minutes ago, Joseph was getting set for an inspection tour of the defenses around the city when a guard came up to him with a note from Governor Ford. Seems he's had wind of the *Expositor* burning, and he's asked Joseph to send some of his men to Carthage to confer with him. Taylor and Bernheisel have gone. They're pretty levelheaded."

"Tom!" Mark exclaimed, "I don't like the sounds of that at all. It's what we've all been fearing, though. Does Joseph have counsel to represent him?"

"I don't have any information. Look, Mark, I'll keep you informed. You folks lay low out at that farm."

Tom was at Nauvoo House late Monday night when the two men returned to Nauvoo. It was Taylor who said, "Joseph, Ford insists you go to Carthage for trial. He's saying it will help everyone to see you're interested in obeying the laws of the state. I didn't like the sight of so many of your enemies hanging around Carthage, and told Ford so. I think he's a tad uneasy too, but he said to come without a Legion guard for the sake of peace. He'll see you're protected."

Without answering, Joseph paced back and forth before the cold pit of the fireplace. The tension in the room rose; Richards mopped his brow while Bernheisel shifted uneasily on his chair. There was a sound of scratching at the door and Joseph whirled.

"Just that mongrel dog of yours," muttered the guard, shifting his rifle.

"Let's go in the dining room!" Joseph snapped. "Tom stay outside the door. Are you armed?"

It was dawn when the door to the dining room flew open and Joseph came through. "Tom, I'm convinced the mob's after just Hyrum and me. Get into town and see that everyone settles down to business. You know, life as usual, just as if there's not a fear afoot. When the militia comes in, let 'em search.

"Hyrum and I'll cross the river tonight as soon as it's dark." He turned to the guard at the door. "Get a replacement in here. Now, here's a list of things we'll need. I'm taking Rockwell, Tom, and a couple of others. We'll be headed west before Ford knows what's happening."

The next night, across the river in Montrose, Tom, with Joseph and Hyrum, worked in the shed behind the home of the Saint who had taken them in. "Nearly finished," Joseph grunted, yanking on the ropes securing the load on the wagon. "Wish Rockwell would get over here with the rest of the goods. I'd like to be out of here while it's still dark. A hard day of riding will put us into the trees in Iowa, then we'll be running free."

Tom was grateful for the darkness hiding the dismay on his face. When the board snapped outside, Joseph swung his gun and crouched. Porter's heavy voice said, "Joseph?"

When he came into the light, Joseph slowly put his gun away, saying, "What's the problem?"

Rockwell sat down and scratched his head. "The feeling's bad in Nauvoo. Everyone's seein' this as you skipping out on them instead of helping. They're callin' you a coward. Emma's sent you a letter."

Joseph moved close to the lantern and, after reading, said slowly, "She's begging me to come back and face trial. I can't believe she'd ask this." His voice was stunned.

The silence had become almost intolerable when Joseph sighed and looked at Rockwell. "What do you think I should do?"

Rockwell's jaw dropped. He looked uneasily around. "Joseph, how come you're askin' me?" He shrugged helplessly and Joseph turned to Hyrum.

"Before we left you voted to face the music. What do you think we should do now?"

Hyrum's face brightened. "If we return they'll be convinced of the divine call behind our mission."

There was silence for a long time, and finally Joseph nodded. Rockwell said, "The boat's waiting at the dock."

Early the next morning Joseph dispatched a message to Ford, advising him that he would surrender. Then he sent messengers to round up the city council, officers of the Legion, and trusted members of the priesthood.

It was past noon when Joseph came out of Nauvoo House and mounted Charlie. Facing Tom he said, "I want you to come with me. For your information, I've instructed the men to gather up the personal arms in the city and stack them. We don't want to be caught short like we were in Missouri. I'm certain Ford will be in here to gather up the state's arms. If he happens to think that's all there are, well, fine."

Just outside of Nauvoo, the little band met Captain Dunn with a company of militia. Dunn reined in. "Sir, we've been commissioned to procure the state's arms."

Joseph nodded and said, "Come. I prefer escorting you to avoid any problems. I've some men who are more loyal than thoughtful."

The gathering of arms took up most of the afternoon. The shadows were long and the sky full of pastel clouds when the group turned their horses toward Carthage. Just outside of Nauvoo the Saints lined the road, watching their Prophet, Hyrum, some of the elders, and members of the city council as they passed on their way to Carthage.

Joseph raised his hand in answer to their salute. "Israel, take care. Like a lamb to the slaughter, I go. My conscience is clear. Toward God and man there is no taint of offense."

CHAPTER 45

It was late when the party reached Carthage. As they rode down the city streets, Tom was seized with apprehension. Every mile of the way was lined with troops.

By the time the group reached Hamilton House, the troops pressed close on their heels. Now Tom could spot a new group sprinkled throughout the troops.

Shabby in their dress, faces set, unmoving as stone, they watched the Saints. Porter muttered, "Them's from Warsaw and Quincy. I recognize 'em."

As the militia parted, allowing Joseph and his party to enter the hotel, the rumble of sound erupted into jeers and cat-calls.

Through the open door the group from Nauvoo could see the crowd pressing close. As the tempo of the shouting grew, just as abruptly there was silence. From overhead came a crash and a thin reedy voice shouted, "Go back to your homes! You want to see Joseph the Prophet? Tomorrow will be soon enough. Go!"

"Governor Ford," muttered the desk clerk. He nodded at Joseph. "May want to confer with you. Dan'l here will take you up to your rooms."

Assembled in Joseph's room, they listened as he gave terse orders. Tom watched the play of expression across the Prophet's face and felt his own heart squeeze with fear.

"Rockwell," Joseph said, "I don't know what's going to happen. I mistrust these hoodlums. Stay as close as possible tomorrow. If it looks like trouble, head for Nauvoo. The Legion will have enough munitions to rescue me."

The next day Tom still sensed the restless, heavy mood of the town. When they had breakfasted and followed the governor out into town, they discovered the troops were again lining the street.

Governor Ford gave his instructions in a low voice, and Joseph turned to his men with a sardonic smile. "We're on exhibition."

As instructed, the men grouped and fell in behind Governor Ford and General Deming. Tom watched the dapper young governor stride toward the first line of troops. With a slight bow he said, "Gentlemen, I present to you the Prophet, General Joseph Smith and his brother, General Hyrum Smith."

So they proceeded down the line until they reached the Carthage Grays. As Governor Ford started to deliver his introductions, a ripple of unrest swept through the troops—a sneer, a shout, then cat-calls were thrown at the men. Under the blast of sound, Tom heard the Governor's mild rebuke, but General Deming wheeled and approached the men.

"Men, you have shown conduct unworthy of the uniform you wear. I hereby place you under arrest!" he barked.

As Joseph, followed by Hyrum, Porter, and Tom, returned to the hotel, the Prophet used the cover of noise to say, "I've retained two Iowa attorneys to represent me. They should be here by the time we appear before the Justice of the Peace. Tom, you keep your eyes on the street. I want Porter inside."

Just before noon, Porter appeared, his face long. "Nearly made it home scot-free for now. The case got set up for next court, and Joseph and the other city council fellows were released on bonds. But lo and behold that fella Bettisworth, the one turned loose on Joseph by the apostates, well, he slapped Joseph with a warrant charging him with treason and rebellion against the state of Illinois.

"They were sayin' the charge was for calling out the Legion to make war on the citizens around the county and then for puttin' Nauvoo under martial law."

Late that evening Constable Bettisworth appeared again, this time with an order to transfer Joseph and Hyrum to jail.

"No good talking," Porter grumbled to Tom who was again posted in the hallway. "Governor Ford agrees it's outta line, but he's saying they'll all be safer in jail overnight. Joseph's wrung a promise outta Ford, so it looks like Ford's going to take Joe into Nauvoo tomorrow."

Porter paused, looked at Tom, and added, "Seems the governor's been getting reports of counterfeiting and other crimes going on in Nauvoo, so he's taking men and going to investigate." He paused and said, "Don't bring up a fuss if you don't see me no more. Hang in with the Prophet unless it looks like you need to go for help."

That night, on mattresses spread on the floor of the jail, the men restlessly tossed and talked in low voices until one by one they drifted into sleep.

Even Tom's eyes were growing heavy when he heard the Prophet turn. "Tom—" In the darkness Joseph's voice seemed thin, without its usual vigor. "Tom, are you afraid to die?"

Slowly Tom said, "Joseph, do you really think the time has come?" There was silence and Tom thought about all Mark had said to him about being saved by grace. He thought about his own decision to trust in God through Jesus Christ. He thought, too, of the peace that had come to dwell in his heart. Peace—was it peace? More than peace, it seemed like a happy confidence telling him that he'd taken the only possible course.

"Joseph, seems a body ought to be at peace inside even if he's going to die. I read in the Bible that the Apostle Paul said he'd rather go be with Jesus Christ than to just keep on living. I'm not certain right now that I *wouldn't* rather go on living, but I'm not scared. A bullet can take a man mighty fast."

In the morning, Joseph told Tom about his dream. "There was mud, rising up to my ankles, clinging, like chains, holding me fast." Tom saw the sweat beaded on the Prophet's face.

"Joseph, seems from reading the Bible that I get the idea, no matter how bad a body is, God will forgive him if he's just willing to go it Jesus' way."

Joseph was silent a moment and then he turned. "Here's what I want you to do. Get out on the streets, listen. Find out what's going on. If there's a plot, I want it uncovered."

As Tom started down the stairs, the guard followed him. Coming close to Tom he murmured, "You look like a nice lad; why don't you just take off? There's going to be trouble. Too much has been wasted to let old Joe escape now."

For a few minutes Tom hesitated as he stood in front of the jail. Finally he turned and loped down the road toward the center of town.

He found Governor Ford in his office. As Tom related the whispers of the guard, the governor's frown deepened. "Nonsense!" he snorted. "There's no possibility of any such thing happening. The troops from Warsaw are being sent home. Don't worry; your Prophet will live to stand trial. Go home to your people—there's nothing you can do here."

Tom wandered through the town, trying to listen to the fragments of conversation coming his direction, all the time looking for one familiar face.

In the late afternoon, a chance conversation slipped the news to him that Governor Ford had left for Nauvoo, and the Prophet wasn't with him.

Tom started for the jail at a fast walk. Suddenly he stopped.

Porter had seeded his mind with an idea. Joseph needed his men to defend him. Last night one of Joseph's visitors had slipped both Joseph and Hyrum pistols, but that wasn't enough.

Tom turned and headed for the stables. Getting his horse, he rode casually beyond the outskirts of Carthage and then he dug his heels into the mare's sides. Tom was an hour out of Carthage when he saw the cloud of dust billowing above the trees. With instinct born of fear, he pulled his horse aside into the woods and waited.

The group of horsemen swept silently past him. They were moving rapidly, but Tom had time to see their faces. For precious minutes Tom sat in the saddle and puzzled over the spectacle he had seen. All of the men were wrapped in rags, their faces painted in grotesque patterns of red and yellow. Some were crudely painted, smeared with black.

Their hard, swift passage clamored for Tom's attention. Suddenly he whipped around and headed back to Carthage. As he rode he was filled with the sense of the futility of his mission. But he also knew there was no alternative.

Long before he reached the jail, Tom heard the shouts, the gunfire. As he pulled up in front of the jail, Tom threw himself from the horse and ran. Abruptly there was a lull in the firing. For a moment, while all action was suspended, Tom's feet slowed and he looked up.

He saw the Prophet outlined in the window, watched his hand come up in a familiar Masonic gesture, and heard the cry, "Is there no help for the widow's son?" Overlapping the cry was the blast of gunfire, and Joseph pitched forward through the window.

Tom had seen dead men before; he turned away and climbed back on his horse.

"Listen!" Jenny straightened in her chair and cocked her head. Beside her Mark stood, caught, listening with one hand outstretched. Jenny crossed her hands and pressed them to her throat. The thunder of the cannons seemed to come from all directions, and the concussion struck her heart, filling her with terror.

Wildly she looked around, "Mark, it's everywhere!"

"Warsaw, Quincy, Carthage, Montrose," he named them as the explosions continued.

She saw his face and threw herself into his arms. "My husband, is it war?"

He shook his head and held her close. They stood together,

holding their breath and listening. Suddenly a new sound burst upon their ears. Distant, dim, then picking up new voices, the bells tolled.

She searched his face, not knowing the question to ask. In wonder he said, "Those aren't sad bells; they're rejoicing!"

"But Nauvoo hasn't a bell," Jenny protested. His answer came slowly.

"I don't think Nauvoo has a reason to rejoice."

In the morning Tom came. His face was ashen as he dropped into the rocking chair and told his story. Finally he sat at the table and ate the breakfast Jenny prepared for him, saying, "If you want to pay homage, we best start soon. I came during the night to carry the news and alert the Legion. They will be bringing the coffins to Nauvoo House soon."

"He was a friend—of course we will go," Mark said, and Jenny listening nodded her approval. Their eyes met. Many things still lay unsaid between them. But she understood the expression, and felt the same deep emotion as their hands stretched toward each other.

Long before they reached Nauvoo there was the sound of muffled drums, the clink of horse's hooves on stone. And then they heard the weeping Saints and the shuffle of the Legion's feet.

On the street leading to Nauvoo House, Jenny and Mark, holding the baby, stood close together, watching as the wagon carrying its burden of black-draped coffins slowly creaked past.

While dust powdered upward behind the horses, Mark turned to see the masses pressing in waves of black toward Nauvoo House. "Jenny, I would like to express my condolences to Emma, but let's slip around the back way."

By the time Jenny and Mark had walked through the trees and approached the Nauvoo House through the back trails, the queue of Saints extended through the streets, beyond the mill, the newspaper office, Joseph's store, and beyond the stables into the temple grove.

Mark took Jenny's hand as they started down the steps toward the coffins. As they neared, a woman in black rushed forward. Jenny watched her convulsive weeping as she made her way to the coffin.

When she extended one trembling hand to touch Joseph's coffin, Mark said slowly, "That's Lucinda Morgan Harris." Strange that she seems so very—"

"Yes, I know," Jenny murmured. Her attention was caught by the man approaching Emma Smith.

She watched him bend over Emma's hand, press something into her palm, and then move away. When Jenny and Mark reached Emma, her reddened eyes were staring at the circle of metal in her palm.

Hesitantly Jenny moved forward, wondering whether to kiss that icy woman or merely shake her hand. But the sight of the disk stopped her.

Shuddering but fascinated, Jenny stepped close to Emma and looked down at the talisman. "Oh, Emma," she whispered. "Please, please throw it away!"

The bowed woman in black straightened and looked at Jenny. "I shall not; it belonged to my dear husband." Slowly she added, "Dr. Richards recovered it for me. It was in his pocket."

Clasping the medal to her bosom, she said softly, "Little I have to remember his greatness, but always I shall have this precious token. And it was precious. You see, for as long as I can remember he's carried this medal."

Dread filled Jenny as she clasped the woman's hand. Jenny knew she was shivering. "Believe me," she pleaded, "the powers of darkness work through such items. I would be amiss if I didn't warn you. Don't let the powers reach out and taint you and your children."

Emma pulled her hand away from Jenny, and with a touch of her usual spunk she snapped, "Powers of darkness! My husband was a virtuous man. Don't think to deprive me of the last link I shall ever have."

As Emma turned away the tears stung Jenny's eyes, blurring into one mass of blackness—the woman, the covered coffins, and the line of weeping Saints.

Mark's hand was on her arm. She covered it with her own as they turned to go. Back in the shadows they passed another black-clad woman. As she turned away, Jenny recognized Eliza Snow.

Jenny shivered again, this time for the Jenny who very nearly joined the ranks of these dark-clad wives.

Silently they walked back through the trees again. When they found the path, Jenny stopped and turned. She looked back at the Nauvoo House and the coffins. "Poor Joseph."

Thoughtfully Mark said, "It'll be the legend of Joseph which will live on. At the hands of his people history will be kind to him. Soon even these Saints will forget the pain and bondage he has inflicted upon the seekers of the truth."

"Mark, I'm so grateful."

"Jesus Christ?"

She nodded. "Why did He allow us to be blessed with truth? Why did He allow us to escape? After all the ugliness of my life, why did He care enough to just *give* me a gift so precious? Gladly I would have worked my fingers to the bone for the rest of my days, just to earn it."

"To earn salvation, to earn His love? Jenny, my darling wife, there's no way you could have earned it, even working your fingers to the bone. You received it because you wanted it. Salvation is a free gift, but it isn't cheap. It cost God's life."

Jenny nodded and linked her arm through Mark's. She couldn't speak for the tears that rose in her throat, but Mark understood her silence. He smiled and squeezed her hand, and together they walked toward home.